MW01196070

Friends...
Brothers...
Soldiers All.

Peter B. Davis

Copyright © 2010 by Peter B. Davis

All rights reserved, including the right to reproduce this book or portions thereof in any form whatsoever. For information, address Lulu Publishing, Inc., 3101 Hillsborough Street, Raleigh, NC 27607.

Manufactured in the United States of America

First Edition

10 9 8 7 6 5 4 3 2 1

ISBN: 978-0-557-13527-1

DEDICATION

This book is dedicated to my eldest and youngest brothers:

Captain Jeffrey Davis, Commander, Carrier Air Wing Eight, United States Navy.

Special Agent Christopher Davis, United States Department of Justice, Drug Enforcement Administration.

You guys are my heroes!

And to the entire Davis mob: Mom, Dad, Kiko, Evan, Jenny, Kathy and Paul.

Chris, Jeff, the author, Dad and Mom

I WOULD LIKE TO GIVE A SPECIAL THANKS TO THE FOLLOWING WHOSE NAMES AND CHARACTERS APPEAR IN THE BOOK:

Master Chief Machinist Mate Hershel "MC" Davis (SS, PJ, DV), United States Navy (Retired). A veteran with thirty-four years as a UDT frogman, SEAL and Command Master Chief. There isn't enough good that can be said about this man and being around him was a life-changing experience. The day I met him, after he identified me as a former Naval Officer, he called me a cake-eater and told me he was going to be keeping his eye on me, knowing as he did that we Officers are a lazy lot and do little more than stand around at parties, brown-nose, complain, drink champagne and hit on other guys' wives. Hopefully I changed his mind about at least one cake-eater because I've never liked champagne. Thanks for all the good words Master Chief.

DEA Unit Chief Peter Swicker;

DEA Special Agent Pedro Guzman;

DEA Special Agent / Pilot Colin McNease;

DEA Special Agent / Pilot William "Billy D." Dwyer;

DEA Special Agent / Pilot Jon "Warbaby" Warrington;

DEA Special Agent Christopher B., a.k.a. "The Other Chris";

DEA Special Agent Alister Fraser;

DEA Special Agent Jim "The Punisher" Waddell

Mauricio "Mau" Lacle;

CIA National Clandestine Services Operations Officer "Jack";

Captain Steve Simonis;

GMG2 Steve Weiss, USN;

John Vincent Herrick;

Marc "Gucci" Moreno;

David "Grease" Cerio;

Adam "Adze" Priestley;

Jason "Argo" Arena;

Ron "Benwha" Ball;

Robert "Lemon" Lemon;

"Porno" Peter Rademacher;

Eddie "Warlock" Cathell;

Ejazz "Jazz" Meghji

"R2";

"Kola";

"Guinness".

And my editors Katrina Schmitt, Katy Sokolewicz and Jeff Wooldridge for their dedication to the completion of this mission!

MISTAKES, SINS AND OMISSIONS

Where possible I have used the real names of the people involved. Due to the sensitive nature of the work and on-going or future operations, some would not allow me to fully identify them or their faces, but they will recognize themselves and for them, and me, that will be good enough. As well, in everyone's life story there are a variety of characters who come and go who are important to the story but whose names are forgotten or just never known. In these cases, I happily substituted names of friends who weren't a part of this story but none-the-less are valuable to me, and it is my way of saying thank you for being my friend.

Like the people doing the work, some of the task forces, units, callsigns, sources and methods had to be changed either for security reasons or the personal protection of the people involved. To those men and women who see their organizations or names mislabeled, mis-numbered or simply missing, let me assure you that this was an intentional blurring of the truth. You know who you are, I thank you for the valuable work you're doing and I write about you with pride.

There are lots of photographs in this book, some of which perhaps shouldn't be, but hey, who leaves a non-secure, USB-cable-ready computer lying around in a camp filled with spooks (Rabbit!)? Because it is not my intention in any way to compromise the sources-and-methods I was exposed to, I have cropped, blurred or removed anything that could even remotely identify the collection method, platform or locality within the Area of Operation. Thanks to everyone who took the time to get me what I needed.

On the subject of conversations and events, I have written them as best as I remember. For those where I was not present, I've done the best I could using a bit of novelistic flair and the third-person remembrances of my brothers.

DISCLAIMER

All statements of fact, opinion, or analysis expressed are those of the author and do not reflect the official positions or views of the CIA or any other U.S. Government agency. Nothing in the contents should be construed as asserting or implying U.S. Government authentication of information or Agency endorsement of the author's views. This material has been reviewed by the CIA to prevent the disclosure of classified information.

Central Intelligence Agency
Publications Review Board
IHII IP Building
Washington, D.C. 20505
21 September 2009

CHAPTER ONE

I am lying on my stomach, as I have been since just after the sun went down, aware of every small stone and geographic irregularity under my body. It's a moonless night and as dark and dirty as black tar heroin. There is no hint of dusky light beyond the mountains to the east to portend another blazing day under a cloudless brown sky. In the middle of the day, the temperatures hover around 120 degrees and at night they plunge to a balmy 99.

My right knee is bothering me from remaining still for so long. When I was younger, my big brother pushed me from behind while we were snow skiing, my skis crossed and I went over the knee the wrong way. Every now and then it will pop while I'm walking or ache when there's pressure and I can't move it, like now. Even though no one is around us, movement is one of the principles of concealment we try to control as much as possible (the others being sound, smell, silhouette, shine, shape and shadow).

My elbows, though, are in heaven because I'm wearing thick hockey-style protectors on them. I should be wearing similar ones on my knees but I couldn't find them as I was packing to go. I have a feeling someone else's knees are pretty happy though. Once we get back in the helicopter I'm going to carry out a little impromptu equipment inspection, and if I find the ones with my initials on the inside, someone's gonna have some 'splaining to do.

All in all, except for the general discomfort associated with lying on rocky ground (and my knee), I am feeling pretty good.

I am proned-out in a small depression in the hot, hard dirt with the muzzle of my rifle just clearing the lip and the forend resting on my backpack. Inside the pack are some protein bars, extra magazines for the rifle and my Glock handgun, a first aid kit, spare batteries, a homemade Ghillie blanket I can lay over me for camouflage in the event I'm still here when the sun comes up and a few water bottles. One of the bottles is to pee in and is covered on the outside with duct tape so even if I can't see it I'll *feel* it's different and not take a drink from it by accident. The protein bars were removed from their wrappers and stored in Ziploc bags because the manufacturer's foil packaging makes a hideous racket when being opened. There are some sheets of Saran Wrap, toilet paper and an empty Ziploc I've also wrapped in duct tape because if I have to use *that* bag, its contents could be confused with a protein bar in the dark and that's something I'd rather not think about.

There is little immediately past the end of my rifle but litter and a few stunted palms no more than three or four feet high. The palm fronds are too stiff to be good windage markers; they're superfluous anyway because there isn't a breath of air to stir them. Also, either because I don't remember or because I've never thought about it when skulking around, I'm noticing the ground here isn't really flat. It's wildly ridged and warped, like small dehydrated waves washing onto a trash-strewn, dusty shore.

On top of my rifle is a long scope that turns my night green and also superimposes a tiny laser-generated dot calibrated to my bullet's point of impact. The dot is visible to me but the man in the distance doesn't know it's resting on the center of his chest.

He's standing in the grimy doorway of a mosque and is overly backlit from within. Because of the scatter through my scope, he looks like he's shrouded in an emerald-green fluorescent fog. He's wearing light colored baggy pants and a very long shirt hanging nearly to his ankles. It's a traditional Pakistani outfit except for the AK-47 hanging from his shoulder; even these days an AK-47 rifle isn't *that* traditional. From this distance I can't make out his face, though even if I could it wouldn't matter because he is not the client's Target of Interest (TOI). We call him "Guard One" though for a bodyguard he doesn't really seem too aware of what he's supposed to be doing. He looks around, smokes a cigarette, steps back inside the mosque, comes back out and glances here and there, but he doesn't really *look* at his surroundings or try to define a threat that could be lurking. Like us.

There is a "Guard Two" but he is out of sight inside the mosque with the TOI. Unlike his partner, he's wearing western trousers and a jacket and does not carry a visible weapon.

The mosque itself is as architecturally unexciting as a discarded packing box, square with double doors on the western side facing me and small oblong windows on the other sides that dribble out a dull yellow light so weak it barely reaches the ground. There are minarets on the corners of the roof like stubby ballistic rockets aiming at a heretical heaven. The mosque's rear is to the sharp mountains where, within the hour, the sun will rise and sear down on us like Mohammed's spotlight on the infidels. The building anchors a village stretching north, though calling it a "village" gives it credit it doesn't deserve since it is little more than a collection of white one-story stone and dirt houses strung out in a very narrow valley. It is so dark,

10

desolate and forgotten I idly wonder if the people who spend their lives here have access to (or have ever heard of) the Internet, cellular phones or the war raging around them.

I don't know exactly where the village is. We arrived in a matte brown, noisy, so-past-its-service-life-it's-gotta-be-illegal-to-fly CH47 Chinook helicopter to a set of geographic coordinates I wasn't shown. After landing, we patrolled north about ten kilometers and our exfiltration plan is to turn around and run south back to the helo.

Next to me, on my left, sharing my dirt ditch is a man who introduced himself as Rabbit when he arrived in our camp yesterday. He's a little shorter than me, mid-thirties with shaggy hair and a ratty moustache and beard. He's in decent shape though, trim like a runner, and speaks in that peculiar dialect of southern United States Army or Navy (though never Air Force). He is "Client."

He's looking through a long lens with a camera attached to a photo ring adaptor on its rear; the entire unit is mounted on a low tripod. The camera has a small black rubber antenna on it and is probably transmitting live images. Like the rest of us, he's wearing a Personal Role Radio, or PRR, on his head only his is a dual-frequency unit and most of the time he's whispering to his other team orbiting above us around thirty thousand feet.

Benwha is about ten meters to my right, also keeping "eyes on" the mosque, targets and wandering worshipers. Gucci is targeting the rear of the mosque at a distant right angle to the three of us. Kola is a few hundred yards behind us keeping an eye on our backs because you never know when some farmer, shepherd or little kid might come wandering through. Porno, the last member of the squad, is with the helicopter and the pilots, providing their security. He drew the short straw and got screwed out of having any fun tonight. He had made a big deal about not being able to come with us, but I think he was just doing it for show. Having spent years as an intelligence

11

geek with the South African Merchant Marines in Antarctica, I don't think he's really too keen on this desert weather. In fact, he spends a lot of time relaxing in the freezer unit back at the camp, which also provides him the opportunity to jump and scream, "BOO!" when anyone wanders in to forage for something to cook (it's pretty funny, except he might get smoked some night doing that). Either way, he didn't have to hike in six miles, lay in the dirt all night trying to stay awake then hike six miles back out, so maybe it's a wash for him.

On check-in, Gucci identified the three beat-to-shit pick-up trucks that, according to our briefing, never move. Since then, we've maintained radio discipline; we know where we are, we know where they are, so there really isn't much to talk about. If something happens we'll sort it out, but in the meantime we are quiet.

The rest of the client's team isn't really overhead. Instead, above us is a Predator Unmanned Aerial Vehicle (UAV) relaying his comms from here to wherever. The Predator watches us with its thermal imagers and cameras, every now and then swiveling to check on the helicopter and pilots at the other end of the valley since they're out of radio range. Rabbit occasionally informs us there is no one around us we don't know about.

I watch Guard One come outside again and this time move a little farther away from the building. A few minutes later other men start leaving, walking casually towards their little pieces of personal poverty. No one is moving fast, no one looks overtly fanatical or Islamically militant. It's just another morning after prayers.

"Here we go." Rabbit whispers and I also hear it come over the foam speaker on my left ear. I know from the briefing a laser designator in the nose of the Predator is now beaming on the roof of a house at the other end of town.

We counted the men going in and know all but two have come out. The only people left inside are the TOI and Guard Two. I move my rifle off Guard One and focus on the door. I am here in a defensive role but it never hurts to have someone important under the dot and it settles on the TOI, invisibly predicting his death as he appears in the doorway.

He's dressed like Guard One; that's all the detail I can make out. I slide the sight to Guard Two. He's looking around a lot and seems more switched on than his partner. The three men meander off and I can almost feel Benwha's rifle barrel moving slowly in unison with mine. Death in stereo. The three men walk away from us, away from the mosque, away towards their house. "Package is in the open," Rabbit whispers. "Green light."

Above our heads, the missile will be leaving the wing. As it dives towards the earth, fins on the rear will open to direct it toward the splash, the dispersion of invisible light from the laser designator in the UAV as it beams on its target. In the nose of the missile a camera will be homing in on the splash and feeding images right up until impact.

"Motherfuck!" I hear Rabbit mutter. "Missile malfunction. Launch negative. Stand by," he says over our net. There is more hushed conversation with someone, maybe back at Langley, maybe the embassy in Islamabad.

I'd like to think he knows what he's doing with this malfunction and I'm sure he doesn't want collateral damage, nor do I, especially if collateral damage means us but I'm not going to pin my safety on what I'd *like* to think. I keep my eye on the scope and whisper out of the corner of my mouth that he needs to direct the designator be faced in a neutral direction in case the missile decides to let go unexpectedly, somewhere away from our helicopter, the route back or us. I also tell him he needs to verify that the Master Arm switch at the rear site has been turned off; this will lock the missile to the Predator.

Peripherally I see him turn my way for a second and look as if he's going to say something, then goes back to his camera and starts whispering again. I listen closer than I had been and hear him relay what I had said. He looks back at me and nods and then asks, "Who's tracking the package?" on our frequency.

I go back to the scope. Under my right third finger a small, wireless push-to-talk button is Velcro'd to the handgrip of my rifle. I press it and whisper into the black plastic microphone next to my lips that I have eyes on.

"Benwha has eyes on," I hear in my ear.

"Gucci has eyes on."

More quiet talk from the client to someone else.

"Gucci, can you take Guard One from there?" he asks. Gucci is closest to the mosque and the three men.

Guard One?

"Negative," he whispers back. "I don't have the angle." From his point of view I'm guessing the three men are probably walking abreast, parallel to his bullet's trajectory and Guard One is on the far side of the TOI.

"Roger that. Start your exfil now. Can anyone else make the shot?"

They are walking straight away from me, there is no wind and they're at almost exactly the distance I calibrated the sight at our Known Distance Range. I give him an affirmative, as does Benwha.

I feel a gentle elbow in my ribs to get my attention and then he speaks directly to me not using the radio, his mouth close to my ear. "Change of plan," says Rabbit. "We're turning off the recorders and the cameras are on the helo. You understand? No one is watching us. I want you to wait until I say the words 'green light' before you do anything, understand?"

"Yes." I whisper without moving.

14

"When I say 'green light' I want you to shoot Guard One, the guard carrying the AK. He's wearing a pajama shirt and from our point of view is on the far left of the three men."

"Tally ho." I reply not using my radio or taking my eye from the target scope.

"He's to the immediate left of the TOI."

"Got him."

"Describe your target."

"Left pajama shirt, AK."

"Do not hit the TOI," he says very slowly.

"Don't hit the TOI." I confirm back to him.

"I say again, do not hit the TOI."

Jesus Christ this guy can beat a dead horse. "I got it!" I whisper curtly.

"Okay." He talks a little more on his other net and then over ours says, "We're taking a shot. Everyone remain weapons tight. We are not under fire. Acknowledge."

"Benwha."

"Gucci."

"Kola."

Rabbit confirms Gucci is on the move and then, to me, whispers quietly and firmly, "Green light. Do it now."

For the two weeks prior to Rabbit's arrival both my squad and another were scheduled for daily shooting practice on the Known Distance Range, which was unusual. Normally we'd hit the range a couple times a month and fire at metal and cardboard targets at 200 yards with our issued AR-10s. Suddenly we were shooting at 400 yards with the special rifles normally kept in hard black cases. When we laid-up in the desert tonight, I aimed a laser rangefinder at the mosque and it came back at 350 yards. Obviously someone knew weeks ago I, or someone like me, would be in right about this spot.

Rabbit had briefed us before we took off, though it was fairly sterile. His brief followed our SMEAC format, meaning Situation, Mission, Execution, Admin / Logistics and Communications. The situation portion was pretty much blank and we weren't told anything about the TOI beyond the fact he existed. Rabbit's mission wasn't discussed, only its execution.

Our mission is to protect the client.

During the briefing Rabbit talked about "sources-and-methods," client-speak for anything classified beyond our level of need-to-know, the way they do business, their tradecraft.

We were shown photographs of the mosque and the village taken from overhead and ground level at different angles and distances.

The TOI's day, we were briefed, was to be up and at the morning call to worship, the *fajr*, which occurs before sunrise. He was always the first one in and the last one out and had been following this pattern for some time. We expected him to follow it this morning just as he did. This was source information but we were not told the method used to collect it.

We *were* told the Predator would have a Hellfire missile attached to a hard point on the wing, and when Rabbit passed the word it was going to whack the TOI's house and its occupants.

Since all of us are ex-military, we have at least a passing knowledge of Hellfire capabilities and delivery, but we were re-educated during the briefing. Under normal circumstances the missile launches by its own internal rocket that propels it off the wing up to about nine hundred miles per hour. Then on impact the warhead detonates and that, coupled with the tremendous velocity of the missile and its laser-guided accuracy, is what makes it so effective. However, the client was concerned the missile would be too much

16

for the target structure, neighbors and surrounding area, so they made some modifications to it. They changed the delivery parameters, removed the warhead, deactivated the rocket motor and drained the fuel package. Basically, made it a Hellfire without the Hell. Or the fire. When given the launch signal the Predator would simply let go of the missile as if it were being jettisoned instead of fired. The end result would be a one hundred pound, four foot long, guided steel football moving at terminal velocity slamming into the roof of the house. The impact would still be spectacular and loud, just not explosively so. And when the remains of the missile were recovered and reconstituted, there would be no doubt who had delivered it.

As he says the word "light," I push the safety one click with my thumb and move my index finger from the side of the receiver into the trigger housing. I take a deep breath, let it out slowly and press the trigger backward.

The rifle cracks and jerks. I feel the recoil in my shoulder and ride it into my body, keeping my eyes on the target. I see Guard One bounce forward as if punched from behind and fall face first into the dust; tackled by an invisible linebacker.

The TOI is slowing, looking at his flattening bodyguard, obviously confused because the rifle round moved much faster than the speed of sound and no noise has reached him. A moment later the sonic boom washes over him, echoes off the mountains and rolls back over us. He snaps his head around vaguely in our direction as his other guard grabs him by his shirt collar and shoves him roughly back towards the mosque, the closest place to hide.

Rabbit whispers something on the other channel. I can barely hear him with the ringing in my ears.

Then in my earpiece, "Let's go...back out quietly. RV[1] at Point Alpha and RTB[2]."

"Benwha."

"Kola."

"Gucci."

I am quickly but quietly moving backward on my elbows, trying as best as I can to keep the flat of my knee off the ground. If we aren't gone most-rapidly, we will be visible in the coming daylight. I grab the spent brass cartridge and slip it into my pocket. You don't leave sign if you can avoid it.

The sun is fully up as we fast-patrol back to the helicopter. Sweat has already dampened my shirt though the desert-dry air keeps it from staying long. We are strung out in a line, weapons up, Rabbit in the middle, me at the tail like the silent rattler of a snake. The big scope is back in my pack, replaced with a standard Aimpoint for fast targeting. My area of responsibility is to the rear so I spend most of my time scanning or actually walking backward, carefully placing my feet toe-to-heel so I won't trip, land on my ass and possibly give us away by sound. Even with the Predator above us watching for hotspots we have to assume at any critical moment one of those guys will be off taking a piss, flirting with a woman, getting a pizza or basically doing anything except what he is supposed to be doing, which is watching out for us. We must look out for ourselves, or we might wind up in the shit and we'll have no one to blame but ourselves.

There has been no pursuit from the village yet and we're staying as close to the hills as possible. There's a track in the dirt which could be a road, but it is well west of us.

I'm focused on my field-of-fire and not thinking much about the man lying back in the dirt but as I patrol, looking down my barrel with both eyes

---

[1] Rendezvous
[2] Return to Base

open, I'm looking down the barrel of another rifle some thirty years in my past. It's as if the part of me in the here-and-now is on autopilot. I am threat-aware, my rifle is moving, and my concentration is where it's supposed to be, but at the same time the 110+ degree morning is overlaid with a bone-chilling night when I stood under a tree, surrounded by people I didn't know, a .22 caliber bolt-action in my hands.

It was a freezing night in upper Michigan, and we were sitting at our kitchen table when a friend of my dad's showed up with his buddies and a young girl. They were going raccoon hunting. I was just a kid but the pretty girl with her gold, wire-framed glasses standing with her dad had pulled my attention and when the big man asked if anyone wanted to go I said yes without even thinking about it.

We sat in the front seat of an old pick-up truck for the ride to the hunting ground. There was no heat, no radio, and my leg was against hers. There were dogs and other trucks when we arrived in a big cornfield, hard-packed in the November cold, the ground like ridged concrete under my tennis shoes. Away from town the sky was black and clear and full of stars.

Dogs howled and everyone gathered under a huge tree. Each person, including the daughter, took a shot at the 'coon that had scampered up there to hide.

Someone gave me the gun, a thing I had never held before, and said it was my turn. I pointed the gun straight up and in the top branches saw nothing except the reflection of flashlights mirrored in the eye of a terrified animal that had been chased by frenzied dogs. The sight on the gun was a simple, low-tech metal blade. I pointed at the glinting eye I saw above my head and pulled the trigger.

Because it was a .22, there was no recoil, just a bright flash of light as the bullet banged out. Moments later, a heavy weight fell from the top of the tree, ricocheting wildly like an incongruously furry pinball bouncing between irregularly spaced flippers.   Off the branches it came, landed with a meaty thud and lay in an unmoving, lifeless heap. Everyone laughed and patted my shoulder and the girl gave me a kiss on my cheek as I looked down at the animal sprawled at my feet, a smoking hole where its eye had been. Pride swelled in me for finding a new skill that had won me the heart of a pretty girl but at the same time I felt an awful, sickening guilt for killing something that meant me no harm.

In fact, it is exactly the way I feel right now walking out of the desert.

Photograph "borrowed" from Rabbit's Briefing Packet.

Heading to the operation.

Predator UAV. Hellfire missiles are attached to
hard points on the wings.

AGM-114 Hellfire missile.

CHAPTER TWO

A cup of hot tea sat on the gray metal railing, the label of the teabag beating a silent staccato against the colorful emblem of a golden eagle above the number 8 on a background of the American flag. Below the 8, in gold letters, were the words "FACTORY TWO", his personal callsign. Someone had crossed out the word "TWO" with a black marker and written "ONE" underneath it.

The night was not quite over nor was the day quite started and the pink glow to the east lent just enough light to define the horizon and indirectly brighten the sky though the sun wouldn't be visible for some minutes yet. Captain Jeff "JD" Davis, the man holding the cup knew, having spent so many years at sea, this was Beginning Morning Nautical Twilight. It was his favorite time of day. It hadn't always been, but after twenty-three years in the Navy and three young children stateside, the opportunity to sleep through it had long since passed, so he made the best of it and called it his favorite.

Up on deck the breeze was quite fierce. The speed of the giant aircraft carrier through the calm sea was generating a near-gale force wind in excess of thirty miles per hour down the flight deck. The wind wiped away all other sound as the USS Theodore Roosevelt (CVN 71) steamed north, surrounded by the smaller ships in the Strike Group.

He tugged the collar of his summer-weight green nylon flight jacket up, more against the wind than the temperature as it was already approaching one hundred degrees. Soon, though, he'd be down in his air-conditioned deep-freeze of an office wading into the never-ending stream of e-messages, reports and requisitions. Without the jacket *there*, he'd be a popsicle.

Once flight operations got underway he'd take his place in "the big chair" on the bridge with the Admiral and the ship's captain. With any luck he might get back outside to watch the sun set. Not likely though.

He glanced down at his "there I was" Rolex, the watch ubiquitous to all aviators. The Air Plan showed the first launch in just minutes. It was an H-60 Seahawk helicopter from HS-3 that would loiter as Plane Guard in the ship's starboard Delta holding pattern for search and rescue duty in case one of the launching fighters wound up in the ocean instead of the sky.

He heard the electronic snap of speakers coming to life all around him, speakers that would put any concert venue to shame because these had to be heard over the noise of launching and recovering fighter jets, propeller transports, helicopters and "yellow gear" tractors. The snap was followed by the booming voice of the Air Boss, the man responsible for all movements of aircraft (and their attendant personnel) on the "ground" and airborne within five miles.

"On the flight deck...now launch the Alert 15 CSAR[1] helo. All personnel will be in the proper flight deck equipment, helmets on and buckled, visors down, sleeves rolled down, float coats on. Check all pockets and pouches for FOD[2]. All those not in the proper flight deck uniform leave the flight deck at this time. Start the Alert 15 helo...start 'em up!"

Looking down, JD could see men moving around on the dark gray deck, slinging here and there like brightly colored M&Ms in purple, green, yellow, white and red. Their reflective-colored jerseys and cranials (helmets) designated their jobs, and after years of living on carriers, he instinctively knew where each man was walking or running, what he was preparing to do, and what would be happening next.

He took a sip of his tea then turned and stepped into the passageway instinctively lifting his leg high over the "knee knocker," the metal combing that forms the frames for watertight hatches. It took only one good shin-bang to forever remember the end product of bone against steel. Walking through the ship to his office, he nodded at an occasional familiar face and anyone who addressed him as "CAG."

His office door sported the same emblem as his coffee cup. Compared to the majority of rooms, or "spaces", onboard the ship, JD's was considered as luxurious as a suite at The Plaza Hotel in New York City with its large desk, couch, two brown leather chairs, a forty inch plasma screen TV on the wall, and thick carpet covering the gray steel floor. Through the adjoining door he had his own bedroom with a large double bed, though the

---

[1] Combat Search and Rescue on fifteen minute alert.
[2] Foreign Object Debris or Foreign Object Damage, depending on the context.

mattress was as institutional and uncomfortable as those found in maximum-security prisons.

Strangely enough, this wasn't supposed to be his for another year. Just weeks ago, he was invited to the Admiral's quarters where the Admiral, the CAG and the ship's Commanding Officer explained to him that CAG's presence was required for an indefinite period "on the beach," with no further details offered. The three of them laughed at the imbecilic look on Jeff's face as he was told of his premature promotion, though they were quite solemn when the Admiral presented him his new orders as Commander, Carrier Air Wing (CAG) Eight.

At his desk JD began plowing through endless traffic on the classified email system. He mechanically absorbed pertinent information across a range of subjects: serious repeat maintenance "gripes" about aircraft in the individual squadrons of the Air Wing; personnel problems; training and readiness issues. As he addressed each one, he made and discarded mental notes, frequently forwarding messages to his subordinate squadron's Commanding Officers, electronically adding his own signature where needed.

Among the messages was a brief notification in terse teletype-speak regarding the crash of a civilian aircraft in Pakistan with an unknown number of US Government personnel aboard.

CHAPTER THREE

The Miami Field Division consists of two white, three story buildings on the west side of the city between Miami International Airport and the edge of the Everglades. The Division is incognito in its corporate blandness, just two of many similar buildings surrounded by a tall hedge and a small guard shack in the middle of the Doral Office Park.

Christopher Davis was sitting at his desk, his face still hot and red from his pre-work run through the Doral golf course. Even at 7 AM the early August weather was hot and humid enough that the sweat couldn't evaporate leaving him cooking and a bit dizzy even after he showered and walked across the street to the office.

He was leaning back in his chair, his foot hooked into one of the lower drawers, looking through a three-year-old fugitive file that wasn't his, that he knew nothing about and held as much interest to him as would reading the chemical ingredients of aspirin. Fugitive case files were routinely and randomly assigned to agents in the Division when a Case Agent transferred to another division or retired. Under normal circumstances, once a case was opened it could only be closed after an arrest was made and the target acquitted or adjudicated guilty. If the target failed for any reason except death to stand before the court, the file stayed open. There were open cases stretching back twenty years.

In the folder he was dripping sweat into, he read how the target of the investigation had posted a bond and taken the first plane home to the Dominican Republic where he remained, in federal law-enforcement vernacular, "fugitating." As neither local law enforcement in the DR nor the US Marshal Service knew his whereabouts, the case would remain open, be reviewed once a year and a DEA-6 Report of Investigation filed for administrative purposes.

Fugitive case management sucked.

It was dull work, but this morning the mindlessness of it served Chris perfectly as he reflected on last night's conversation that culminated with his now *ex*-girlfriend Nora telling him it was time for her to move on to someone more ready to commit, someone who could join her in taking a relationship to the next level. Someone like, well yes, the dentist she was interning for.

"Chris Davis!" called the Group Supervisor from the only private office within the bullpen. The cube farm itself was very clean, very white and as sterile as Chris' current emotional state. The only color came from a totally uninspiring shade of gray wall-to-wall carpet and several man-high, felt-covered partitions placed between desks to give everyone a perception of privacy. With the exception of some posters of Martin Luther King over one of the other desks, the walls were as blank as Chris' concentration.

He got up from his desk, walked around the divider past Chantelle, the group secretary who was sitting quietly, wearing a bright summer dress, one ebony hand curled around her ear as if she was listening to the calming waves of the ocean through a beach shell. She was absolutely motionless, as if hypnotized by what she was hearing.

"What's up?" asked Chris quietly, stepping in to the office but watching the secretary, mesmerized by her stillness.

The GS's name was Ricardo House and emphatically preferred to be called Ricardo. He was a very tall, very thin black man who dressed exceptionally well, better than anyone else in the Division, always in three piece suits, tie firmly knotted at his throat, vest buttoned, and jacket on even when sitting, as he was now, at his faux-wood veneer desk, both his in/out trays as empty as his secretary's gaze. "Some guys from Phoenix, part of Operation Emerald Clipper, are at the Airport Marriott on 836; they're the guys that seize planes. They're debriefing a CS[1] and we need to send someone 'cause we're their sister group. What're you doing now?"

Being fascinated by the secretary. "Nothing. Fugitive files."

House nodded. "It's you then." He passed over a piece of paper with some names on it and a telephone number. "Give these guys a call and help 'em out with whatever they need. Where's your brother?" he asked glancing at his watch.

"Down in tech."

"Take him too."

Chris' "brother" in this case wasn't one of his four familial brothers but rather his partner, "But like totally in a non-gay way," he would always add. He once mentioned "his partner" to the guy cutting his hair who got all bubbly to the extent Chris was worried the dude was going to blow some gel into his hair that doesn't come from a bottle; it was a valuable lesson in semantics.

---

[1] Cooperating Source, an informant

Like Chris, his partner stood just over six foot one, just over two hundred pounds and had the same shade of dirty blond hair. Like Chris, he routinely wore blue jeans, t-shirts and tennis shoes to the office. Like Chris, he didn't mind working out in the gym across the street before work or taking an easy run on the golf course footpath. And like Chris, he was also named Chris. Since Chris Davis had checked-in one day prior to his partner, his partner forever became known as "The Other Chris." When they were together, they were called "The Chrises," like some 1980's Swedish pop band.

Christopher Davis and The Other Chris graduated from the same class at the Justice Training Center in Quantico, Virginia, and were both assigned to HIDTA[1] Group 31 in Miami. Group 31 was new and understaffed. There were rumors more senior agents were going to be assigned as they rotated in from foreign embassy assignments, but right now there was a big office, lots of empty desks and dividers, and a couple of windows looking out at the Doral.

Manpower-wise, in addition to Ricardo and The Chrises, there was a large black agent named Harold (hanger of the aforementioned MLK posters); a kind of dopey guy named Brent who wound up being the butt of the wave of practical jokes launched by Jim 'The Punisher' Waddell (self-named for "The Punisher" bobble-head statuette on his desk and the black T-shirts with the white skull he was always wearing); and Alister Fraser, a nearly humorless, glass-half-empty ex-policeman who, as a former Washington DC patrolman, motorcycle officer and pilot, was by far the most experienced law enforcement veteran in the group.

It was rare only new agents would be assigned to a group but House had also just graduated from the GS training class, and as there were no groups lacking supervisors, a new one had been formed and was being staffed

---

[1] High Intensity Drug Trafficking Area

with whomever was available. In this case it was brand spanking new, fresh shiny-faced agents.

And Chantelle. Not lazy, nor enthusiastic, just there. A victim of a GS-5 paygrade with no potential for promotion, entrenched in US Government service, and untouchable as an associate member of the National Association of Black Narcotics Agents (NABNA). She spent most of her time not doing much of anything to the extent The Chrises typed their own reports and maintained their own case files just to get them done. Brent and Harold would have typed their own as well but said they couldn't type and consequently stayed peripheral to everything so they wouldn't *have* to type anything. The Punisher handed his in to her in longhand and waited patiently, sometimes up to thirty days, until they came back his way for review, often so massively mistyped the errors would flow off the paper and land in tiny clumps at his feet. Al simply refused to write reports or open cases, frequently voicing his mantra, "Big cases, big problems; small cases, small problems; no cases, no problems."

To Chris Davis, the meeting at the old Marriott next to the expressway was as dull as the décor, though the older agents from Emerald Clipper seemed excited. Davis and The Other Chris just sat talking quietly on the two double beds while the Emerald Clipper guys and the dark skinned CS sat at a small round table next to the window with the curtains closed.

"Anything from your woman?" asked The Other Chris quietly so as not to disturb the debriefing. He was sipping from a can of Coke the visiting agents had thoughtfully brought.

"Last night. Dumped me. I think she's got something going on with the guy she works with, but who knows. Said she didn't want to wait anymore. Said I'm afraid to commit."

"Are you?"

Davis laughed softly. "Duh!"

The Other Chris, who was married and happily henpecked said, "Got to grow up sometime dude. Be unhappy. Join the rest of us. Come to the dark side."

Chris nodded. "Yes, that's just what I need."

"Well, if there's anything I can do..."

"Um..." he suggested softly quickly segueing into what he thought was a clever change of subject that could work to his benefit, "You can take my fugitive cases. Give me a little more time to mourn Nora's leaving me. Besides, I didn't see any on *your* desk. It's not fair. I got three from Group One. Al got two. You got nothing."

"Wrong, *mi amigo*. There were *five* waiting for me this morning. Fucking five?" He paused, "I don't think Ricky likes me."

"Probably because you call him Ricky."

After a while of joking around, they grew bored with the dark room and listened in as the guys from Phoenix debriefed their CS about an airplane, a Golden Eagle 421 twin-engine turbo-prop he said had been used in a drug deal in the Bahamas. The plane was parked at the Signature Aviation FBO[1] ramp on the north side of Miami International Airport. The CS answered questions from the two Phoenix agents for almost two hours before they were satisfied they had all the information they needed. They said they were going to go to the airport and take a look at the airplane, take some pictures, ask some questions at the FBO, then do whatever it was they did to secure a warrant on the aircraft that would be the first step in securing its seizure. When asked if they wanted a ride over there, they replied they had a rental and knew their way. This sure wasn't the first time they had been to Miami.

They left, and The Chrises were getting ready to go when the CS, a Latino, whose name neither of them knew or in all honesty cared to know,

---

[1] Fixed Base Operator; a general-aviation terminal.

asked, "You guys interested in shipping some coke up from Colombia? I got a friend who's a pilot and he knows a guy in Kendall that says he's got a big load he wants flown in."

And just like that, The Chrises first case was born.

They stood in House's office and relayed what they had been told by the CS. House started asking them questions to which they did not have all the answers. The questions weren't so difficult, but The Chrises just weren't seasoned enough yet to know what to ask a CS at a first meeting, how deep to delve or what else to really do to get a case going. Their training at the Academy had been thorough, to be sure, but had been focused on shooting, physical training, raids, driving and lots of classes on law, undercover operations, forms and report writing. The finer points of investigative interviewing techniques were expected to be learned on the job by watching and listening to senior agents assigned to a group.

"You get his telephone number?" asked House knowing the two guys standing in front of him were doing the best they could.

They both nodded.

"Okay, call him up and have him come here to the office, and we'll all sit down and have a talk with him, see what he really can do. Where's he from?"

The Other Chris answered, stabbing his finger at House, proud he had at least one good answer so far. "Cuba!" he said energetically. "He was a Mariel baby." He was referring to the group of refugees who had sailed their rickety boats from Cuba to the US in 1980 and were now making South Florida their home. The Other Chris had carried out most of the interview because his wife was Cuban and he had worked at Miami International Airport as a baggage handler before becoming a Special Agent for the Drug

Enforcement Administration and so he had some things in common to keep the CS comfortable and chatty.

"And how does he know the pilot?"

Davis answered, "He's a pilot too.   He says his buddy flies commercial."

"How does the guy he knows know the guy in Kendall?"

This time both men shrugged.

"Does he know where the stuff's coming from?"

"He just said Colombia," answered The Other Chris.

House raised his eyebrows. Clearly he was considering how realistic what he had just heard was, how much his agents had gotten right, and further considering that since the group's activation, they had no cases - nothing House could contribute to at the weekly ASAC[1] meetings, no arrests, no "powder on the table."

Every group on a monthly rotating basis stands "duty group." When assigned "the duty," any general calls coming into the switchboard and any walk-ins who have information that could be useful are routed to the duty group, and within the duty group, given to the day's duty agent. Oftentimes those calls end in someone becoming an informant, and most cases come from informants, of which the agents in Group 31 had none yet. Unfortunately, since the group was new, and in an attempt to get some cases going, House had volunteered the group for "duty" two months in a row, but nothing had yet panned out. Perhaps this would be their first.

"Could be something, and it's not like you two are burning down the house (ha ha) with anything more important right now.   If nothing else, it could be good practice learning to interview a CS. So call him up and get him in here today or tomorrow and we'll listen to his story. Have you run him in

---

[1] Assistant Special Agent in Charge

34

NADDIS[1]?" Both men shook their heads. "Okay, call the Emerald Clipper guys back and see what they have to say about him, if they've dealt with him before today, and if so, how good was his info and how much have they paid him. If they have his CS number, go down and talk to Milo and take a look at his CS file. When you call him to set up the meeting, get his driver's license number, DOB, address, phone number, whatever. Make sure Milo's file is up-to-date and then run all of it in NADDIS and NCIC[2] and let's try to have something on him when he shows up. And ask him for his buddy's name and anything else he knows about him too. In fact, when you call him see if his buddy's around. Have him bring him along and let's get it from the horse's mouth."

The meeting ended and The Chrises left, feeling for the first time they weren't just stealing oxygen, getting lots of free time to work out, and collecting a paycheck.

The next morning, The Chrises, GS House, the CS and his friend all met in an interview room on the first floor of Building One.

The interview room, one of two, primarily served as secure cells where prisoners could be held awaiting transport to the Federal Detention Center downtown, but they were also used to isolate CSs, to prevent them from learning who other DEA agents in the building were. Entry to the area was via a code set within a recessed box, the buttons shielded so prisoners couldn't see and activate the doors. Outside were several wall-mounted boxes where agents could store their guns before going in. They weren't being used today as this was a friendly meeting and the agents had left their guns back in their desks.

---

[1] Narcotics and Dangerous Drugs Information System, DEA's propriety intelligence database
[2] National Crime Information Computer, a similar system belonging to the FBI

35

Before the meeting, The Chrises supplied their boss with the following: Emerald Clipper had originally signed up the Cooperating Source two years ago. He had provided intelligence that led to the seizure of a Cessna 310 in Tampa and, in addition to what he had given the Emerald Clipper agents the day before, was providing information on a Lear 60 currently undergoing maintenance at the Signature FBO at the Fort Lauderdale International Airport. (Although several of the aircraft were located at Signature FBOs, there was no evidence Signature was in any way involved). The CS, whose first name was Carlos, had never been arrested, had no entries in NADDIS beyond those documenting his assistance on the aircraft seizures and no entries in NCIC. He had a commercial pilot's license and was a US citizen.

His friend Francisco was an airline pilot, a Colombian, unmarried and living in Kendall, a neighborhood to the south and west of Miami. NADDIS and NCIC returned negative results. Francisco was a young man, 26 years old, thin and very friendly, not at all nervous about being in the DEA jail answering questions on the spot from three strangers, his presence there probably due to of an off-hand remark he had made to a friend, like gossip.

The story Francisco told was interesting but not earth shattering because at this point it was nothing more than one person's tale. Until the information he gave could be checked out thoroughly, it was un-actionable. His neighbor, a Mr. Enrique Serrano, approached him last month because he knew his neighbor was both a pilot and a Colombian: a pilot because Francisco regularly wore his First Officer's uniform to and from home, and a Colombian because of the Colombian flag on the rear windshield of his car. According to Francisco, Serrano walked to Francisco's driveway and introduced himself while Francisco was washing his car. Both men had seen each other across yards for a year so it wasn't too bizarre for one neighbor to introduce himself to another. Serrano talked with Francisco about cars and weather, and though both were from Colombia and had similar backgrounds, they had no friends or acquaintances in common, Serrano originally from Cali and Francisco from Medellein.

In the course of the driveway conversation, Serrano asked Francisco if he knew any pilots in Colombia with an airplane, anyone who would be willing to fly something "big" to the US, someone Francisco trusted.

Francisco replied he had lots of pilot friends but none with their own planes. He told Serrano, with no other motive than being a good neighbor, he would ask around and if he heard anything, he'd let Serrano know. That was the extent of the first and only meeting between the neighbors. Francisco had related the conversation to Carlos during a casual dinner one night, not knowing Carlos was a paid informant for the DEA.

When asked by House why Carlos had not mentioned this story to the Emerald Clipper agents when he was being debriefed, he replied he thought the agents from Phoenix only seized planes and wouldn't be interested in anything else. House and The Chrises later discussed that and found it to be plausible. As a courtesy to the Emerald Clipper agents, House offered the case to them because it was their CS supplying the information, but their GS demurred and said since Miami had started with it, they could have it.

On the following morning, Davis wrote a DEA-6 Case Initiation Report on the interview detailing what Francisco, identified in the report as an "undocumented Source of Information," had to say, adding the address of Enrique Serrano and a request that a NADDIS number be generated for Serrano. House told him not to submit it just yet, to wait until they had something a little more concrete before actually opening the case.

The Other Chris said after lunch he would write a CS packet for the division CS Coordinator's office, giving Francisco's personal information and requesting a CS number. From this point onward Francisco's name would never be used in any written reports, only his CS number. In the event of a trial, when all reports would have to be given to defense attorneys during the discovery process, his identity could be protected.

The next step was to learn as much about Serrano as possible. The Chrises divided up the work. Davis walked downstairs to Technical Services and checked out a digital SLR camera and then drove thirty minutes to Kendall in his unmarked government car, his "G-ride." He located Serrano's small pink house in the quiet residential community and did a drive-by, taking pictures through the windshield. His one-time pass also netted him photos of the cars parked on the grass and the license plates of a brown Volvo and a maroon mini-van of indeterminate make. (Being a single man, Chris' knowledge of "soccer-mom" cars was less-than-that of, say, his married and fathered partner.)

While Davis was in Kendall, The Other Chris typed up an Administrative Subpoena to the telephone company asking for any numbers registered to Serrano's home address. He also asked for any other numbers registered to Enrique Serrano. This request would have to be hand delivered to the BellSouth Security Office, which happened to be located, coincidentally, near the Olive Garden Restaurant off the Palmetto Expressway at the Mall of the Americas. The Chrises pre-planned lunch with The Other Chris driving the rest of the guys from the group. Lunch was always an important part of any investigative day.

As the investigation started to take shape, The Chrises began to develop a picture of Enrique Serrano. There was a mortgage on Serrano's house from Bank Atlantic. Serrano was making minimum payments and had little equity; the house, if indicted, would probably be returned to the bank. He owned both vehicles outright, which made them subject to seizure in the event they could be tied to any future crime. Davis had pulled up a copy of Serrano's driver's license on the computer, so they now had a picture of him as well as his wife and son who were also living at the house. Serrano was average height for a Colombian, which was to say five feet seven inches tall, with a wide plain face, ebony black hair combed back straight from his forehead, and wide-set dark eyes that stared criminally into the camera lens.

A database search, also supplied by BellSouth, listed several telephone calls both to and from Serrano's house to a number in Cali, Colombia.

At the GS's direction, The Other Chris sent a teletype to the DEA office at the US Embassy in Bogotá, Colombia, requesting they contact the local telephone company and identify the address and owner of the telephone number.

There was one more piece of information The Chrises needed and that was Serrano's cellular phone number. In a morning meeting with the entire group when new case information was discussed with everyone present, GS House recommended it was time to send Francisco in to Serrano, to let him know he had found someone with an airplane who might be willing to make the trip from the US to Colombia and back. At the same time, Francisco could get Serrano's cellular number so the two men could stay in touch. Once The Chrises had the number, they would determine which cell company provided the service and subpoena them for records. Cellular telephones were everything.

On the day Francisco was going to meet Serrano, he came to the DEA office to be briefed by the agents; again, everyone met in the interview room. Rudy, an agent assigned to the Technical Services Division, had also been invited and brought a variety of listening devices. It was the intention that every meeting Serrano attended would be taped and hopefully videotaped or photographed. Francisco had been asked to wear his pilot's uniform, and in his left hand pocket below his pilot's wings was a large ballpoint pen. Rudy asked for it, took a good look, reached for one of his black plastic suitcases, opened it, took out a similar sized pen and held it up for everyone's inspection. "Anyone have a problem with this?" No one did. Rudy unscrewed the pen, slid in two AAAA-sized batteries, put the pen back together and handed it to Francisco who put it in his shirt pocket. Rudy took another case and stepped out of the room into the adjacent cell. After a minute of silence, he yelled out, "Say something!"

House stood up and stepped to the far side of the room, as far as possible from Francisco and the pen. "Can you hear me?" he asked at a conversational volume.

"Loud and clear," called Rudy. He re-entered the room, placed the receiver case on the table and opened it again. He pointed out a cord that plugged into a cigarette lighter and informed them the receiver would run on internal batteries for about an hour in the event they had to turn off the car or couldn't get power to the lighter for any reason. He also explained the machine would make a recording on a mini CD, of which there were two in the case. He had one of The Chrises sign for the pen and the receiver case; upon the completion of the operation today, the equipment would have to be returned and inventoried. He turned towards Francisco, "The pen also works if you need to write something. It's got a small ink cartridge, good for a couple of quick notes but not much more."

"So, Francisco," began House. "Let's run through this meeting that you're going to have, yeah?" Francisco nodded. "Today's meeting has several points. Firstly is to let him know that you've thought about what he was asking and might have someone who'd be interested. Secondly it's to swap cell phone numbers. It's okay to give him yours and it would be great if he gives you his. Okay?" Again, Francisco nodded.

"Do you want me to ask him about Colombia?" asked Francisco looking at everyone across the table from him.

House shook his head. "No, I don't think that's a good idea just yet. If he wants to talk, by all means let him but I'd rather you didn't ask him any questions. Eventually the plan is to have you introduce him to one of our agents who will take care of that, and it removes you from the game so that if this ever goes to trial, it'll be our agent on the stand and not you.

"Now, if he asks about the guy you're going to introduce to him, I'd rather you don't give him any information at this point because we don't know who the undercover is going to be, and if you say he's Colombian and the only guy we have available is Mexican or Cuban or whatever, then it won't work out and we might have to waste a lot of time trying to find someone to fit the bill, so just tell him you're going to have your buddy call him directly and they can do the deal. That work for you?"

"Yes, sir."

"Good. Now, when you go in, we're going to have a couple of agents on the street near you. These two guys," he motioned at The Chrises, "and me and another agent. We'll all be in our cars and parked somewhere in the neighborhood. When you get out of your car, don't look for us and when you come back out of his house, don't look for us. You're in uniform now. Did you come here directly from your house?" Francisco nodded. "So if you show back up at home and he saw you leave this morning to come here, then he'd know you didn't just get in from a flight. So, why would you leave home and return so shortly afterwards? Could your flight have cancelled?"

"Yes, sir. It happens all the time for maintenance."

"So that's what happened, yeah? You went for a flight to...?" he asked waiting for Francisco to fill in the blanks.

"No, I didn't fly. I came here for the meeting."

House nodded and rolled his hands. "Yes, I know that, but if he asks you where you were supposed to fly today when the flight cancelled for maintenance, where would you tell him you were supposed to be going?"

41

"Oh," said Francisco. "Um…I could just say I was going to talk to my Chief Pilot."

"Yeah, that's even better, in case he decided to check the flight schedule on-line or something. Okay, you went to your meeting, yeah? Now, when you get home, just park your car in your driveway and walk over to his house, knock on the door, and if he invites you in, just go in. Meet with him; talk with him a little. If you can get his cell number so your buddy can call him, great. When you feel comfortable, head back to your house, change your clothes but keep the pen with you because we'll need that back, and then meet us at the Hooters on the other side of the turnpike. It's far enough from your house no one will see you and it's a pain in the ass to come all the way back here. You know where I'm talking about?"

"Yes, sir."

"Good. Well then, let's go and have some fun!"

The two Chrises drove together and Ricardo and Harold went in Harold's gold Lincoln Continental, which had previously been seized by another enforcement group and placed into service. Francisco was driving his own white Honda. Ricardo, Harold and Francisco would wait at a McDonalds close to Francisco's house until all the surveillance and monitoring equipment were in place, and then send Francisco in. Too many unknown cars, all with darkly tinted windows, could be suspicious to any third parties on the street or to Serrano if he happened to be looking outside.

"Hey, did you know that Harold and Chantelle are related?" asked Davis as he drove along the turnpike faster than the speed limit but not so fast as to get pulled over and delay the operation.

He could feel The Other Chris looking at him. "What the fuck is you talking about, man?"

"Yeah, no shit. I heard it from Rita in Group Three. She was saying that they're cousins. That Harold's mom and Chantelle's mom are sisters."

The Other Chris was silent for a minute, deep in thought. "Let me see if I can get this straight," he said tapping his upper lip. "Harold's driving a brand new Lincoln. You and I are senior to Harold, and I'm driving a Cutlass and you're driving this piece of shit. Jim and Al are senior to Harold and they're sharing a ride, and Brent doesn't even have a car. And again, we're all senior to Harold. Harold's related to Chantelle. And Ricardo makes the vehicle assignments. Chantelle and Ricardo...?" continued Chris quietly, almost to himself, looking off in the distance as if the answer were hanging there in the bright blue Florida sky.

He picked up the microphone under the dash and looked at the LED numbers on the front to make sure they were on the right channel. The switchboard assigned them channel 3, a car-to-car frequency on the encrypted UHF DEA network that wouldn't hit any of the local repeaters and broadcast all the way into Ft. Lauderdale eighty miles to the north. "3104 from 3102."

"What!" snarled Al Fraser who was already parked down the street from Serrano's house keeping "the eyeball" on the house and cars. Al wasn't angry. It was just his way of being funny. He never really was, but he amused himself.

"Any change?"

"Negative. I'm parked four houses east on the opposite side of the street. I'm in a driveway but there's no other place to park. Both cars are there and no one's come in or out."

"10-4. I've got Chris with me, and 3101 and 3107 are together in 3107's car. When the CS goes in, we're gonna park on the street north of the house to listen to the wire. Can you keep the eyeball from there on both houses?"

"10-4"

43

"Cool. Stand by."

Davis drove onto the street behind Serrano's and stopped approximately halfway down the block, about where he thought Serrano's house would be on the other side even though he couldn't see it because of the worn, wood slat fences separating the yards.

"3101 from 3102."

Harold answered even though the call had been for Ricardo. "Go for 3101."

"3102 and -04 are in position."

There was a pause as The Chrises assumed Ricardo was telling Harold what to say. "The CS is heading in."

"Roger." Both men sat quietly, the receiver in the back seat of the car, a portable antenna snaking out the rear window and attached to the roof by a powerful magnet. The Other Chris turned in his seat and pressed the record button on the minidisk. A green light went on under the switch indicating the digital recorder was working. Another cable was strung between the two front seats and plugged into the cigarette lighter. About a minute later, the speaker next to the recorder crackled, cut out, crackled again.

"I've got an eyeball on the CS." reported Al.

The speaker was alive now. The Chrises listened to salsa music coming over the wire from the pen in Francisco's pocket.

"This is 3103," said The Other Chris on the radio. "We've got a good signal from the wire."

"3101 copies," said Harold.

They listened as the car came down the street two houses away and could tell when Francisco was parking in his driveway. The engine stopped, the car door opened and they heard a bell warning the key was still in the ignition. The bell silenced. Francisco's footsteps on the concrete and then nothing as he crossed the grass.

"CS is out of his car and walking to the target house." Al was narrating what he could see so everyone would know what was happening.

"Good signal on the wire," repeated The Other Chris.

"3101 copies."

A knock on the door of Serrano's house. A pause. Another knock. The door opening. *"Hola, Francisco!"* said Serrano. *"Como te ha ido! Venga, venga!"* The Other Chris translated to Chris, "He just invited him in."

"CS is entering the target house."

"3101 copies."

The Other Chris tried to translate but the Cuban-Spanish he knew was different than Colombian-Spanish, plus, the speed at which he spoke and translated with his wife was on a much slower level than the two native speakers. He was able to pick out a few words here and there and pass them on but was unable to keep up with the high-speed conversation between the two men filtering into the recorders. "He's giving him numbers now." They listened to the men moving around through the house, each occasionally closing his eyes trying to form a mental picture from what they were hearing. Then they heard a doorknob turning and a door swinging open.

"CS is exiting the target house." Al reported.

"Gracias, amigo. Hasta." "He just said thanks and later."

"CS is walking back to his house. CS is entering his house." Everyone waited in position for about five minutes, until Francisco came back out and got in his car. "CS is in his car, heading west. 3104 will remain in position for five mikes[1]." He didn't want to leave immediately after Francisco just in case Serrano, or another third party, were watching as it might look like he was following the other car.

---

[1] minutes

"3101 copies. Nice job everyone. See you at the meet spot." Harold was still speaking for Ricardo. The compliment coming from his mouth was less impressive than if Ricardo had given it himself.

Following Francisco's debriefing in the parking lot of the Hooter's restaurant, the group reconvened back at the Division. As with every investigative operation, there were reports to be done. Anyone who had taken notes would be required to keep them for trial discovery. A surveillance report would have to be done as well as a report of the meeting between Serrano and the CS.

The entire group was sitting around the office, some on chairs with their feet up, some on desks. It was very relaxed. "Okay," said Ricardo, "tell me the plan."

Davis started. "Chris and I have decided this case has gone on long enough and Serrano's wasting our time, so we're going to his house and shoot him. We're drawing straws to see who gets to pull the trigger."

Ricardo nodded. "Good. What's next then?"

"Well," Davis continued, "barring that, we really don't know if we're actually talking about drugs here. The Bogotá office hasn't gotten back to us so as far as we *know*, the telephone numbers are to his family back there. We need to have someone talk to him and find out if we're just spinning our wheels or if there's really something dirty here."

The Other Chris took up the briefing. "We talked to Mauricio in Group Two. He said he'd be willing to go UC[1] for us as the owner of the plane and meet with Serrano. He says he can be vague about what kind of plane he's got, just play it off to not knowing who Serrano is and not wanting to give up too much information. After this face-to-face, Mau says he can

---

[1]Undercover

46

talk to the guy by telephone whenever we need. He's got a couple of cases going right now but says he's not going out of town anytime soon so that won't be a problem.

"As the owner of the plane, Mau's going to need details like where the plane's going to go, how much it's bringing back to negotiate payment, and he says he thinks it'll probably take a couple of meetings before Serrano's going to be comfortable enough to tell him everything he needs to know, but if nothing else, we'll know with this meeting if we're talking about drugs or emeralds or hookers."

Ricardo nodded. "Anyone have anything to add?"

Al chirped up. "If it's hookers, can we still do the deal?"

Mauricio 'Mau' Lacle was a senior agent within the Miami Field Division, in his late-thirties, bull-like, tough and strong, always laughing with junior agents and ready to teach them something if they would listen. Originally from Curacao, he grew up speaking Spanish and Papamiento, a curious mix of Dutch, Portuguese and Creole. He had lived in Miami for ten years and was more than happy to play the part of a wealthy aircraft owner. He figured he knew the right questions to ask, the right things to say and most importantly, the right time to be quiet and listen to a bad guy loop a noose to hang himself.

The group decided they should allow Serrano to buy Mau lunch, an idea Mau liked as well. He suggested a Nicaraguan steak house at the Bayside Mall near the Port of Miami, one of his favorites. All the agents in the group knew where the restaurant was located though few had ever eaten there as 1) it was outside most of their budgets and 2) it wasn't a Hooters. There was a parking lot just beside the restaurant where the surveillance car with the recorder could be parked. When asked what type of "wire", or listening device, he wanted to carry he suggested another cell phone and said he'd feel comfortable carrying two; many people were doing that.

"You want me to call him now and set up lunch?" Mau asked The Chrises. Even though he was the most senior agent in the room, he was here today assisting and therefore, subordinate to the case agents. Both nodded.

Mau took out his phone and Davis handed him a piece of paper with Serrano's number on it. He sat down on the corner of a desk and just before hitting "send," loudly announced, "UC call going out!" to alert everyone to be quiet.

Almost immediately he started talking rapid-fire Spanish. The conversation was brief and at one point while he was talking, he looked down at himself. He looked to the agents after ending the call. "No problem. Two o'clock at Los Ranchos Bayside. I told him what I'm wearing so he could ID me. I'm going to go down and get a wire. You got a 284[1] filled out?"

Davis gave the Tech copy to Mau who would need it to sign out the phone. He had already put a copy into the new Serrano case file that was being kept in a combination-protected file cabinet and would send a copy to headquarters in DC.

"You want to leave here around one? Give us plenty of time to get set up?" The Chrises agreed. At this point no one thought there would be a need to follow Serrano away from the meeting but they would need someone inside the restaurant providing security for the UC, and since The Chrises would be monitoring the surveillance recorders from the parking lot and Harold and Ricardo were the best dressed, Ricardo decided *they* should be inside.

The Chrises pulled up outside the restaurant and took a parking spot close to the restaurant but not within view of the restaurant windows. The

---

[1] DEA Form 284, Request for Consensual Monitoring (Non-Telephonic)

magnetic antenna was not yet attached to the outside of the car and wouldn't be until Serrano was inside the restaurant. It wouldn't do to have the car all "antenna'd-up" with two guys sitting in the front seat and have the target pull into the parking spot next to them; if the bad guy were in any way switched on, he'd recognize the surveillance instantly. Mau had already parked and was standing inside a gift shop across from the front door of the restaurant, waiting comfortably. The undercover never entered before the bad guy just in case the bad guy showed up with trouble. Ricardo and Harold were settling at a table; the restaurant was only about half full.

Just after two, Enrique Serrano walked into the restaurant, spoke to the hostess and was shown to a table. Ricardo picked up his phone and called The Chrises in the car and told them Serrano had arrived and to turn on the recorder. They did, then slipped the antenna onto the hood and reported they were getting a great signal from Mau's phone. Ricardo signed off and immediately called Mau, told him where Serrano was sitting and hung up; he and Harold prepared themselves for one of the few real perks of the job besides shooting someone: expensive food paid for by the government. Serrano sat quietly, his eyes on the door, and when Mau walked in a few minutes later, he stood with a big smile and motioned towards him. They sat comfortably. The Chrises monitored the meeting, slightly depressed they weren't getting in on the nice free lunch.

Back at the Division everyone sat around the office, Harold belching happily in the corner next to Ricardo. Mau was quite happy with the way the meeting had gone and filled everyone in on what had been discussed: Serrano had been pretty straightforward, his only attempt at cleverness being he referred to the product he wanted flown in as shirts. "So, he said he's got five hundred shirts in Colombia and wants them brought here. I asked him if we were talking about shirts that weigh about two point two pounds each because

I would have to do fuel figuring based on the weight we were carrying. He understood immediately that we were talking about kilos and said yes, so while he hasn't said the word cocaine yet, he's admitted on tape that we're talking about a load of shirts weighing exactly five hundred kilos. That's probably going to be good enough for any jury to make the connection when they hear the tape and read the transcript."

"He wasn't suspicious at all?" asked the GS.

Mau shook his head. "Not a bit! Is like we're *hermanos*. The impression I got is this man is not the drugs. Maybe he's the money, though when I told him I would charge him three thousand per shirt transportation fee, he said he'd have to get back to me on that. Plus, when I asked him what kind of time frame we were talking about, he said he'd have to talk to the owner of the shirts to make sure they're where they're supposed to be at the right time. I didn't get the feeling he was in any great hurry. It was very relaxed which also makes me think he might just be a go-between between the drugs and the money and not really have any info of his own. He'll probably have to run everything by everyone else, so that'll be a good chance if you're working his phones to ID the other players."

The GS nodded at The Chrises who nodded back. He was genuinely pleased.

"I took him flying!" said Francisco, bubbling with excitement. The Other Chris had called Francisco a few weeks after the meeting with Serrano just to touch base, keep him informed on any developments with the case, which were few, and to keep him interested.

"You did what?" said The Other Chris motioning to Davis to pick up the phone and listen in.

"Yeah, man," continued Francisco. "I called him up and told him I had rented a plane and was going to go up to see some horses and asked if he wanted to go. I thought it would look good to him, you know, that I had some money."

"Dude, what the hell are you talking about? Do you have horses?"

"No, man, look, Chris. A friend of mine owns a stable and some horses up in Palm Beach, so I called *mi amigo* and told him to tell his people to act like I was a player guy and to call me Don Francisco, like they saw me up there all the time, you know…be very friendly like I own the place or something important like that."

Both Chrises were looking at each other wide-eyed, shaking their heads, The Other Chris trying to stay calm. "Did you talk to him about the deal we're working on?"

"Of course!" he replied like Chris was an idiot for even asking. "We were walking around the stables, and he was really impressed and everyone was walking around saying, "Good morning, Don Francisco," and how good it was to see me again, and he was just really impressed, man. This did good for the case!"

"But *what* did you guys talk about the case?"

"Well, after he sees all this, he's really happy with me being his pilot and says that he wants me to fly for him for this, and he's been talking to his people and says the flowers… he calls them flowers. I don't think he remembers he told you they were shirts the last time… but that the flowers will be at an army base and that the ATC will be paid off so the plane can fly in without having to stop for Customs and can go right to the base and land. Pretty good, right?"

Davis mocked banging his head up and down on the desk, the phone still held to his ear.

"I don't suppose you got any of this on tape?" he asked brightly.

"No, man, I don't have a tape recorder. But I could have! He didn't search me or anything. He was really impressed!" Clearly Francisco was happy with what he had done and wasn't feeling the love coming back from the agent at the other end of the phone.

"Yes, but Francisco," said The Other Chris calmly, as if he were talking to one of his children, "all that information would be really useful to us on tape when he goes to court. Right now, we've just got the conversation from the meeting at Los Ranchos. If we had a tape where he was talking about flowers and Colombian military bases and paying off ATC that would make the case against him really strong. See what I mean? You can't be meeting with this guy without telling us or even talking to him without us knowing so we can monitor the meetings. Not just for information but for your safety."

"Well, okay, Chris, but everything he told me I could tell in court then, right?" he asked sounding a bit deflated at what he had thought was a good deed to help the case.

"No because that's hearsay. That's why we record everything. You can't tell a jury what someone else said. And the whole reason we brought in Mau was so that if there's a trial, you won't have to testify because Mau's testimony as an agent will be more credible to the jury. And as long as we're taping everything, there's no chance that Enrique can say we entrapped him somehow. If you meet with him without us, he could try to say that you were talking him into doing something he didn't want to do and that could ruin the case."

There was silence on the other end.

Chris continued. "It's okay, man, but please, *please* don't do something like that again, okay?"

"Okay." The voice was quite subdued.

The two men listened while Francisco repeated the whole story. Writing the details down on paper, they thought about how this report was going to look when it crossed their supervisor's desk demonstrating the two novice agents couldn't control their informant. Shit.

Chris Davis pointed at himself and motioned to the receiver in the hands of The Other Chris who nodded and held his hands together in a praying motion. Davis took the opportunity to try to salvage some of Francisco's enthusiasm. "Well, it's all water under the bridge now, right? But since you've brought it up, you know if this thing goes forward, at some point we are going to be needing a pilot to fly to Colombia. Since you brought Serrano to us and now he's so in love with you, are you interested?"

There was a long pause. "How come you don't use your own pilots?" asked Francisco, his voice still sounding glum from the spanking The Other Chris gave him.

Chris explained to him DEA's Special Agent / Pilots were not allowed to fly in undercover capacity outside the United States. That being the case, DEA was going to have to contract the undercover services to people who would eventually be signed up as Confidential Sources.

"Do you know any other guys that do work for us that have a plane?"

"*Si*, I do know a pilot. He told me he had made a lot of money once working for you guys. I haven't talked to him since then, but he had his own Turbo Commander."

"That's a kind of airplane?"

"It's a twin engine turbo prop."

"Are you trained to fly it?"

"I can fly it, yes, but only as a copilot. My friend would have to be the pilot in command."

"If he still has it, can it get from Miami to Colombia and back?

Francisco laughed, sounding better. "No, my friend. Colombia is a long way from Miami. We'd probably have to stop in Jamaica or Haiti then

53

in Colombia, but Colombia is a big country so depending on where we had to go, we would need more fuel there."

"Okay. We'll worry about this later if the time comes. But in the meantime, see if your buddy is still around and if he has his plane and if he wants some work."

There was a pause. "How much will we get paid for this?"

"Dude, I have no idea. We're just starting out. I'll have to talk to my boss, and I'm sure a lot would have to do with how much we're getting flown in, if we make any arrests, seizures, you know. But for now, let's just see if he's still around, okay?"

The next time Francisco spoke to the agents was to inform them he had found the pilot he had been introduced to, the guy still had the same plane, and it was parked at Ft. Lauderdale Executive Airport. The agents decided to make it a short day, leave Miami and head north to Ft. Lauderdale to visit with the pilot, and head home from there. In other words, they were taking a "Federal Friday," sort of a tradition of ducking out to get an early start on the weekend. Other versions of Federal Friday included "checking out addresses" or "meeting with some local cops about a case." Usually these meetings, if they occurred at all, did so at, or near, a Hooters.

The Colombian pilot Francisco introduced them to was tall and chatty, always moving around, touching his plane, pointing at buildings or the sky, just glad to be alive and a part of the airport around him. He was also more than happy to talk to the agents about flying to his home country. He told them he had done a similar mission with DEA years ago and was well acquainted with the procedures he would have to follow. Additionally, he was already a Confidential Source and had a number, which would make processing him quicker and easier.

The only problem, as he saw it, was the plane did not have the range necessary to make the journey to and from Colombia; to make this flight would require the installation of internal fuel tanks.

"Is there a problem installing them?" asked Chris Davis.

"You mean, besides the fact that they're expensive?" he replied with a smile. "And illegal? And expensive?"

Neither agent was aware it is, indeed, illegal to modify an aircraft with internal fuel tanks without FAA approval and an STC, or Supplemental Type Certificate, being issued. Such a process, the pilot explained further, was "government red-tape long," detailed, and potentially costly.

Putting that problem aside the agents asked if he knew someone who could do the work. The pilot said the work itself was not so difficult, the supplies were readily and commercially available, and if the agents could figure away around the STC, then he was willing to have the work done on the plane.

On Monday morning, after a brainstorming session with Ricardo and a conference call with the Group Supervisor at the DEA Air Wing in Ft. Lauderdale, a decision was made whereby the agents would type up a letter stating the work illegally being done on the aircraft was directed by the DEA and said letter would be kept by the pilot. Additionally, the agents would "seize" the aircraft registration and airworthiness certificates to prevent the pilot from using the plane without the agents being aware of it. In reality, the pilot *could* fly the plane without the certificates, but if he were given even the most cursory "ramp check" by an FAA inspector or local law enforcement officer and didn't have the required paperwork, the aircraft would be immediately impounded and subject to seizure, a financial risk no plane owner would ever be willing to take.

The agents delivered the signed letter back to the pilot in Ft. Lauderdale with his assurance the work would begin immediately.

In an amusing testament to the effectiveness of the "war-on-drugs" in South Florida, two days later Chris Davis answered his phone and found himself talking to an agent from the Ft. Lauderdale DEA office who was standing in a closed hangar at the Ft. Lauderdale Executive Airport where work was being done to have internal tanks installed on a twin-engine Turbo Commander. The agent had received a call from an informant of *his* who had been painting the outside of the hangar, looked in through a crack in the window, saw what was going on and called the agent who handled him. The agent was reading the letter the pilot had given him and wanted to know if it was on the level.

While the work was proceeding on the plane, The Chrises walked to an adjacent office in the Division and were introduced to an Air Force 2nd Lieutenant in civilian clothes who was the official liaison for Operation Yankee Flyer, a joint DEA-military program that coordinated airborne operations like the one The Chrises were starting up. The two men were given a list of things Yankee Flyer would need including date and time of the flight, tail number and type of aircraft, pilot's name, departure point, destination if known, verification the plane was equipped with an operable HF[1] radio, and on and on.

"What's going to happen," the Lieutenant explained, "is that on the day of your op, we're going to send a message to all the military aircraft and ships between Miami and Colombia. There's going to be a special transponder installed in your plane that only the military can track and isn't visible to civilian ATC radar. We'll also give you an HF frequency that your

---

[1] High Frequency. Radios capable of transmitting and receiving over exceptionally long distances. Depending on atmospheric conditions their range can extend thousands of miles.

pilots can monitor and that all of the military units will be monitoring if your guys run into trouble."

"Holy shit!" said The Other Chris, "Are you kidding me?"

"Not at all," laughed the Lieutenant. "And in the event there's an AWACS[1] on station, they'll track your airplane as far into Colombia as they can. We'll also contact the MILGRU[2] at the embassy in Bogotá because it's possible your plane could trigger an "End Game." You guys know what that is?"

Both men shook their heads.

"End Game" is the term for a military response which is usually terminal for the target aircraft, if you know what I mean. We've got to let them know that your plane isn't a credible target and they can relay that to the Colombians in the event that they launch for a shoot-down. The AWACS will also be watching the air base in Barranquilla, and if they see jets lifting off on an intercept profile, they can get on the radio to the Colombians and stand them down.

"Also, the plane carrying the coke can't come anywhere unescorted near the US border because… well…because it's going to be carrying coke on board and if the pilot decides at the last minute that whatever you're paying him isn't worth nearly as much as the drugs, he might decide to detour somewhere and have a sale. So what usually happens is we have the plane land at Guantanamo Bay, Cuba, where the coke's offloaded and secured by you guys because you'll have to maintain chain of custody on it from that point on. Then either DEA or military aircraft'll fly it back to the US. I have a go-by for the form you'll need to get the coke into CONUS[3]. If that all works for you, we'll also message Gitmo and get a PPR."

"A what?"

---

[1] Airborne Early Warning and Control System aircraft
[2] Military Group
[3] Continental United States

"PPR." He explained. "Prior Permission Required. Landing a civilian airplane at a military installation requires a PPR. We'll take care of that for you."

As The Chrises walked back to their office, they were stunned at the amount of preparation going into their operation.

Following the meeting with Yankee Flyer, Mau was asked to contact Enrique Serrano to see if he had any further details about where the plane was supposed to go and how, exactly, it was supposed to cross into Colombian airspace without clearing customs and when headed outbound, how not to get shot down by the Colombian Air Force. This information would hopefully lead to more indictments if the agents could get specifics on who was helping Serrano move the drugs out of the country. Mau said he'd make some calls and get back to them.

After a week their pilot called informing them the tanks were in, he had done an engine run-up and the fuel was feeding, so as far as he was concerned, he was ready to fly. He was going to submit a bill for the installation of the tanks and told them, following his weight-and-balance calculations, with the plane fully loaded with the fuel he'd need coming out of Colombia, he could carry exactly 880 pounds of payload, and that didn't include an average-sized copilot. He also wanted to know how much he was going to get paid for this mission. The Chrises said they'd get back to him on that last part.

Armed with that information, The Chrises had another meeting with the 2nd Lieutenant from Yankee Flyer to keep him updated on the status of the plane. He told them he'd arrange to have the transponder installed. As they were talking about weights of the plane and the pilots, he mentioned he thought it was not a good idea to have Serrano's neighbor Francisco go in the plane.

When The Chrises asked why not, he explained. "Here's the thing. If you send this guy Francisco down as copilot, the bad guys could decide to keep him down there as a guarantee that their drugs get delivered up here. If something happens and someone winds up getting arrested up here or the drugs disappear, he could wind up dead. I don't want to tell you how to run your operation, but I've watched a lot of these things go and I'd suggest that you send just the one pilot down. That way there's no hostages and nothing the bad guys can really do except load the plane and keep their fingers crossed."

The Chrises passed the recommendation along to Ricardo who, after thinking about it, agreed as well. They discussed the length of the trip in terms of flight time on one pilot, but if Francisco went along and was left behind, the pilot would be making the trip alone anyway. It also made sense from a financial standpoint because if they were only paying one pilot to make the trip instead of two, upper management would be more likely to approve a bigger payment for the pilot.

Davis mentioned they'd told Francisco he'd be getting paid to go there as well and might be pissed off they were reneging on their agreement. Ricardo told him they'd still be paying Francisco something, just less than the pilot making the trip. When asked about an amount, Ricardo told them he'd let them know later in the day after he spoke to the Assistant Special Agent in Charge.

Mau came into the office and related he'd talked to Enrique Serrano. Serrano said the load was ready and he was glad his friend Francisco was going along to watch out to make sure everything went according to plan. This led to a discussion of how they were going to pull Francisco out of the picture without making Serrano suspicious.

"I could shoot him in the leg," suggested The Other Chris.

"We could say he fell off one of his horses," said Davis.

Ricardo was smiling vaguely. "You know, you could take him down to Jackson Memorial Hospital and have a cast put on his leg and do just that."

"I get to shoot him? Awesome!"

Mau was also laughing. "That's not a bad idea, with the horses. It's creative, it totally makes him un-flyable, it's not suspicious, and no one's going to want to wait around until his leg heals."

"We're not kidding here, right?" asked one of The Chrises.

"Nope," said Ricardo. "Take him down and put a cast on him. Well, maybe not a cast but a leg brace or something, and get him some crutches, just something he can use as an excuse not to fly. The ASAC said if we get the coke in a reasonable amount and make some seizures, then Francisco's earned ten thousand dollars for setting up the deal. We're going to give Carlos five thousand for the initial introduction, and we're going to pay your pilot twenty-five thousand, which ain't bad for two day's work."

Mau related when he talked to Serrano, he pushed for more information on how the plane was going to transit Colombian airspace without the clearances, but all Serrano would tell him was ATC and the military had been paid off, and upon getting the tail number of the plane and a date of travel, he'd get that information where it needed to go and then get the coordinates of the landing zone to Mau. For obvious security reasons, Serrano, while trusting, didn't want to give away too much on the off chance something wasn't right with the whole deal.

The next morning, Francisco met the agents at the Field Division. Together they went to Jackson Memorial Hospital and, after identifying themselves to the emergency room staff, got Francisco outfitted with a leg splint and a nice, new, shiny metal crutch. Back at the office, Ricardo inspected the work, gave it a thumbs-up, and after a short meeting with

Yankee Flyer, decided the plane would fly on the following Wednesday morning. That information was also passed to Mau to pass to Serrano and the pilot was put on stand-by. When Francisco left, he said he'd call if there were any problems with Serrano accepting the story that he fell off a horse.

On Wednesday morning, the day of the flight, The Chrises, Al, Harold and Ricardo all drove up to Ft. Lauderdale to see the pilot off as well as to introduce Al and Harold, who would be meeting the pilot in Guantanamo Bay on the return trip and relieving him of his burden.

They took a look at the plane, the full, white fuel tanks, and fuel lines in the back. The pilot told them how some military guy put the transponder behind the bulkhead in the tail and done a nice job with the work; it was all but invisible. He had checked the HF radio and had the right frequency inserted. He showed them his charts and they all confirmed the coordinates given to Mau were, in fact, directly over a Colombian military airfield. Davis retrieved the DEA letter authorizing the installation of the tanks, returned the airworthiness certificate and registration, and showed him the US Government check for the amount of the installation of the tanks stating it would be waiting for him when he returned. Letting him take it with him would be criminally stupid in case he were searched. With handshakes all around, the pilot started the engines and departed to the east.

On the way back to the Miami office, Al and Harold were dropped off at the Jet Center in the Ft. Lauderdale International Airport where the DEA Airwing was located, hidden in plain site as just one of many small aviation businesses under the terribly innocuous name of "Jackson Aviation." The only difference between this office and the rest on the same floor were the two closed circuit cameras in the hallway aimed at the door so anyone wanting to enter could be seen from the inside before the door was buzzed open.

The DEA Airwing was providing transportation to the U.S. Navy base at Guantanamo Bay in one of their King Air twin-engine turbo prop aircraft. Al and Harold had to be in position when the drugs arrived from Colombia to initiate the chain of custody of the evidence that would follow it from that point until the eventual trial.

The Airwing had been requested not only to provide transportation for the agents, but also to transport the drugs from Cuba to Miami where it would be weighed, tested and then stored at the DEA's heavily guarded warehouse until it was needed for either operational reasons or for court. Unfortunately, due to logistical requirements, the King Air was going to drop off the agents in Cuba and then continue south to Bogotá where the plane was based.

Yankee Flyer contacted the U.S. Coast Guard and was told they had a Casa airplane available and sitting in Guantanamo and would be more than happy to fly the evidence as far as Key West where it would be transferred to a helicopter and from there, flown to Miami with the caveat that the DEA agents would travel with and maintain custody of the evidence.

At about 9 PM, after finishing takeout dinner at their desks in the quiet empty office, The Other Chris picked up the phone and called the number supplied to them by the Yankee Flyer 2nd Lieutenant. The phone was answered at the other end by a very sexy, breathy, climb-between-the-silk-sheets-with-me female voice with its origins in the Orient. "SOUTHCOM Air Operations Duty Office, Sergeant Kulbuppha speaking. This is a non-secure line. May I help you?"

"Hi, Sergeant Klub…Koopa…I'm sorry, what was it?"

"Kulbuppha, sir," she replied with a smile in her voice. "Please call me Thiwan."

"Okay, Thiwan. My name's Chris B████, from DEA. We have a plane in the air with Yankee Clipper - "

He was interrupted. "Stand by, sir." There was a click, and the line went totally silent like she had hung up on him. After another click, Sergeant Kulbuppha returned to the line. "Sorry about that, sir. Do you have the unclassified operations teletype supplied to you through your liaison?" He did, and said so. "Very well, sir. Can you please tell me the identifier word that is on page one, line twenty-three of the message?" She waited while he scanned down the paper.

"Mmm...the word is 'pianoplayer.'"

"Very good, sir. Please stand by." A click again, and he waited patiently, hearing no background noise while on hold. The line came alive. "Thank you for waiting, sir. This is unclassified information I'm passing to you: Your target went feet-dry at nineteen forty-three Z^1. Do you have a secure line, sir?"

"We can get to one in our other building. What's the problem?"

"No problem, sir, but if you can call me on a secure line I can give you more details on your target as well as the platform information that's monitoring."

The Other Chris shrugged. "Oh." He looked at Davis who was listening in on the other phone, and both men grinned and nodded at each other. "Sure, do I just call this same number?"

"Yes, sir. Once you go secure, we can give you any other information you need. Also, sir, I'm looking at the operations message and have two telephone numbers," she read off the numbers. "Are these valid?" The Other Chris told her they were. "If you like, sir, I can call you when we

---

[1] Zulu time / Universal Time, Coordinated / Greenwich Mean Time.

get a track on your target, and if you'll call back on the secure line, I'll fill you in."

"Cool! Thank you Sergeant."

Davis said, "Wow…do you think she's as hot as her voice?"

"Man, I hope so!"

Around midnight, The Other Chris' cellular phone started ringing. "This is Sergeant Kulbuppha, sir, SOUTHCOM. Can you please call me on a secure line?"

The two agents walked out of the building, across a small courtyard and into the Administration Building where, on the second floor, the Miami Field Division Communications room was located. A grumpy old woman who was rumored to have been there since DEA and Customs were merged in the '70's manned it, an unlit cigarette hanging perpetually from her mouth. She ignored the agents as they went into a small office where a Secure Telephone Unit was sitting on a desk.

"SOUTHCOM, Sergeant Kulbuppha. Are you ready to go secure?" Davis, who was manning the STU, said he was. "Going secure." On the side of the STU was a key connected to the telephone with a flex-tie, the kind the agents used in lieu of handcuffs. As long as the key was inserted and turned correctly, the phone could function as both a regular telephone or as a secure line for conversations up to Top Secret; both agents had received a brief course of instruction on this equipment while at the Academy. Davis pushed the button labeled "Secure" and watched as the LCD readout on the face of the phone went from "Non-Secure" to "SOUTHCOM / SECRET."

"This is Sergeant Kulbuppha, how do you read?" The voice sounded the same, a little more distant but no less babe-ish.

"Loud and clear." asked Davis.

"I also have you five by five, sir. Here's what we have. An E-3 AWACS, callsign 4 Delta 965, is tracking your target's mode two. The platform picked up the mode two one seven minutes ago, headed north, at that time eight zero miles south of Santa Marta, Colombia. 4 Delta 965 also has a co-located mode three transponder showing an altitude of twenty-five thousand feet. 4 Delta 965 reports no intercept aircraft airborne from Barranquilla. Stand by, sir, let me update that report." There were more clicks and she returned to the line. "That is correct, sir. 4 Delta 965 shows no intercept aircraft airborne from Barranquilla. Additionally, at this time a Navy Destroyer, callsign 2 Zulu 358, is holding a valid mode two track on your target; your target is feet-wet and has joined the airway proceeding northbound. Neither platform has a copy of the target's IFR flight plan but based on current course and speed, compute ETA Gitmo at zero six four five Zulu. Per the op plan, Gitmo has been notified of the ETA and there's a U.S. Customs Falcon, callsign Omaha One Seven, with a tasking order in place to launch and intercept your target at the Cuba FIR[1] Boundary and trail it into Gitmo. Is there any other information I can provide you, sir?"

"Wow…no Sergeant, that's awesome! Thanks very much."

"Not a problem, sir. SOUTHCOM clear."

"Is it possible to be in love with a voice?" asked Davis hanging up. "Because if it is, I'm all there."

The Other Chris laughed. "You are one lonely motherfucker."

"Yeah, you better not introduce me to yours."

"My what?"

"Mother."

"You need to get laid."

---

[1] Flight Information Region

"True 'dat. But putting *that* aside for a second, I don't mind telling you that while all that military crap sounded really cool, I didn't understand ninety percent of the shit coming out of her mouth!"

His partner laughed. "She's a woman. Why would you?"

Al Fraser called the next morning and reported the plane had arrived, followed five minutes later by a Customs Falcon jet. The packages had been downloaded from the plane and weighed on a portable scale the base operations staff used to weigh baggage and came to one thousand thirty four pounds, or four hundred seventy kilos. Al had made a small cut on a randomly selected package for testing, and it tested positive for cocaine.

He had also debriefed the pilot who had indeed landed at a Colombian military base. The bigger news was the cocaine was loaded into his plane by *uniformed soldiers*!

High fives went all around the office and the Yankee Flyer group, and the rumor went that high fives were traded as far up as the office of the Special Agent in Charge of the Miami Field Division.

Late that same afternoon, the Coast Guard delivered the cocaine to the Opa Locka Airport in north Miami.

Opa Locka is an old, general aviation airfield right in the heart of North Miami that started its life as a pre-World War II Navy training base and also served as the launch point for Amelia Earhart's infamous flight. Now it is a sad resting place for dozens of discarded planes, from small Cessnas to vintage warbirds to commercial airliners, all waiting to be cannibalized or demolished. At one time there was a huge blimp hangar on the perimeter of the field that was spectacularly detonated into a huge fireball for the filming of the movie *Bad Boys*. Also on the field are the US Customs Air Wing, with its collection of heavy attack helicopters and executive jets, and the US Coast Guard Air Station.

66

Since Chris was going to be unloading almost a ton of dirty packages and was going to be doing it on a military base, he showed up wearing the camouflage BDUs he normally wore to the range. Joining him were three vehicles filled with heavily armed agents who helped get the packages into the trunks of the cars to drive them to the warehouse where, the next morning, analysts from the DEA's drug laboratory would precisely weigh and catalog each package for evidentiary purposes. Until the operation was completed, however, none of the packages would be further tested because there was a good possibility someone would be inspecting them, and the packages had to be pristine.

On the way to the warehouse the cars detoured into the Field Division where the packages were unloaded and placed on a table, and photographs were taken with the agents of the group, Ricardo and the SAC for public relations purposes when and if the opportunity arose.

At the same time, Mau joined them and a photo was taken against a blank white wall with him holding one of the packages. The outside of each package had a small red sticker of an eagle in flight the producers in Colombia had added so someone could identify it at a glance. When the photo of Mau was taken, the red eagle was clearly identifiable. The picture would be given to Enrique Serrano in the next day or so to verify his "shirts" had arrived safely and were available for pickup at the agreed-upon price of three thousand dollars per kilo, or $1,410,000.

Many more high fives were given around. For any agent, this was a huge case that could be parlayed into fast-track promotions but the fact it had been pulled off by two youngsters fresh out of the Academy was pretty stunning and lots of senior agents wanted to give their congratulations.

First thing the next morning Mau called Serrano and another meeting was set up at Los Ranchos Bayside. This time, however, Davis and his

67

partner got to sit inside as a small reward. Ricardo told them to order anything they wanted, except booze, and to have a good time.

The meeting went calmly and The Chrises were pleased to see Serrano's face blossom into a smile when he looked at the photo Mau gave him. On the back, Mau had written the total weight of the packages. Hopefully, somewhere down the line Serrano would be arrested, and the photograph, with his fingerprints on it, would be located; one more link in the chain to be used to convict him.

After lunch, Ricardo called The Chrises into his office and told them it was time to get started working on an affidavit that would be presented to an Assistant United States Attorney (AUSA) who would edit and then send it up to the Department of Justice attorneys in Washington D.C. who would meet with the Attorney General to request a Title III Wiretap Authorization.

There was already a pen register and trap-and-trace on both Serrano's cell phone and home hard-line, and the data was being analyzed by the Intelligence Group. These devices did not provide the content of conversations but did give a real-time record of the numbers he was calling as well as the numbers of those calling him.

The SAC had, after a long meeting with Ricardo and the Country Attaché (CA) in Bogotá via phone, mandated the case be expanded to more closely include the embassy whose agents would liaise with their vetted units of the Colombian Police in an attempt to locate, track and arrest the violators in Colombia.

A large part of the expansion had to include wiretaps on Serrano. The vetted units in Colombia, having been supplied with the telephone numbers, had identified a suspected cocaine trafficker named Pablo Herrera. Since Herrera was not a US citizen, the DEA there was requesting assistance from the CIA and its own intelligence resources for electronic eavesdropping on

68

Herrera. Having the wiretap authorization approved on the US end would close the circle on everyone being monitored.

"We may have a problem," said Mau, ambling into the Group office after greeting everyone with a happy *Hola!* "I just got off the phone with Serrano." He didn't have to say he would be recording these conversations, as it was standard procedure. "He said the guys in Colombia don't want to pay for the coke up front because they don't have the money. They want us to give 'em some, and they'll sell it and then pay us with the proceeds of the sale, and then we'll give 'em the rest of it."

"Fuck that!" said The Chrises in unison. "They want us to front the dope? We can't do that. We'll never get the money."

Ricardo had joined the conversation from his office and was standing quietly, his arms crossed, a frown on his face.

Mau was giving The Chrises a "calm-down" gesture with his hand. "I know, my friend. I agree, and I didn't tell him anything. I just put him off and told him I'd call him back. I don't like it so much either, but it's *possible* that Herrera doesn't have access to that kind of money. These guys, they make their money, they spend their money. They don't plan for the future." He wagged his finger at The Chrises. "Let this be a lesson to you. Always save some money for a rainy day. Don't be like a drug dealer."

The Chrises sat there shaking their heads. Davis opened his mouth to speak, "So -"

"And it's not exactly like we're fronting the dope because it's *their* dope!" interrupted Mau. He looked at Ricardo.

"Well," began Ricardo, rubbing his face, "I'd really like to get our hands on the money. Powder on the table and money in the bank." He looked at The Chrises. "Do you guys have any suggestions?"

The Chrises shook their heads and sulked.

Mau gave a sideways nod. "How about this, how about I call Serrano and tell him I'm on my way out of town for a few days and when I get back, we'll talk. That'll give us a little time to do some planning, and maybe it'll put a little pressure on him to talk to Herrera to kick loose some money for Ricardo's bank account. I'm sure Herrera isn't going to love the idea of that much coke sitting around somewhere in Miami. The longer he doesn't have control over it, the more likely the cops could find out about it. If the coke isn't all his and he's sponsoring the deal with other guys and something were to happen to it, he's going to be held responsible and that's never a good thing. His idea has to be to get the deal done as fast as possible and get the coke back into the hands of someone he knows and trusts."

The Other Chris asked, "Do you think the AUSA would allow us to front any sizeable amount of dope on the hope of making a bigger arrest later?"

Both senior agents shook their heads.

Ricardo decided they would wait a few days and see what happened.

Chris Davis was sitting at home watching TV when his cell phone started ringing. He looked at the number and saw it was The Other Chris. "What up, man?"

"Dude, we've got all sorts of shit happening! Francisco just called and said Enrique showed up at his house with two other guys and one of them had a gun. Enrique was screaming that he wanted his stuff."

"Oh fuck!" said Chris getting off his couch and walking in a circle around the coffee table.

"Yeah. Anyway, he told Enrique to fuck off or he was going to call the cops and slammed the door; he said they weren't threatening him with the gun or anything, just that he saw one. He said Enrique and his buddies left and then he called me. I called the Metro-Dade guys, and they're on their way to meet him at Hooters and get him into a hotel for a few days."

"Jesus Christ," said Davis.

"I called Ricardo too just to let him know. He said we'd get it worked out in the morning. The Metro-Dade guys are supposed to call when they pick him up."

"Fuck. Are you going down?"

"No, man, can't. I'm watching the kids." He paused. "You gonna go?" he asked, sounding guilty for saying no and hoping his partner would follow his lead.

He took a deep breath, calming himself down. "Yeah, I better. He's our guy. And," he continued, his voice brightening, "it'll give me a good excuse to use the lights and siren. Sweet!"

Everyone sat around the office the next morning drinking coffee, discussing what had happened. Francisco had driven in as well and was waiting in the interview room in the other building.

"So what do we do now?" was asked all around. The other agents in the group were also invited to throw out ideas. Al, in typical Al fashion, took the hardcore Al approach and said, "Fuck 'em. Tell 'em the price just went up, and we're getting it in advance or we sell it ourselves."

Everyone laughed a little. Mau, the most experienced of all, smiled but shook his head. "That's not a bad idea, but unfortunately I don't think it'll work."

Ricardo agreed with him. "I'm guessing he's getting a lot of pressure from the guys in Colombia."

"Yes," continued Mau, "You know, if we really *were* dealers, we probably would front part of the load. But we're not. We're the good guys and at the end of the day, we're not here to get money; we're here to arrest people and get powder on the table. Since we already got the powder, it's my suggestion that it's getting about arresting time."

The supervisor was nodding. "Yeah, like it or not, I think it's time we shut Enrique down. We've still got the guys in Bogotá working on that end and if we can get Enrique in handcuffs, he may be willing to make some phone calls to the bad guys and help us wrap them up." He looked at The Chrises. "It's still a great case and has a lot of potential for getting more guys on the conspiracy indictment, but Mau's right.

"Francisco's in some danger right now because obviously Enrique is trying everything to get his drugs back and may want to use Francisco to get to Mau, and we can't keep him on ice forever. Mau, I'd like it if you could call Enrique and read him the riot act. Let him know that *you've* got his shit, not Francisco, and that Francisco's an innocent party in all this, that he just introduced you, and that he scared the shit out of him, and you want him left alone because he's making waves and doing stupid shit that could get cops involved."

"Okay."

"And Chris, set up a meeting today, this morning, with the AUSA and tell him everything that's happened in the last twenty four hours and get his take on it as well."

"Okay."

Davis' face was grim as he listened to John Herrick tell him what was going to be required, in his opinion as Assistant United States Attorney, not only to get a conviction, but also to increase the chances Serrano would plead guilty at the initial appearance, saving both the AUSA the time prepping the case and the government the expense of the trial.

Herrick said the actual evidence against Mr. Serrano was circumstantially good, but in terms of something that could be presented to a jury was weak. Today's juries are used to movies, videos, and taped recordings documenting a person's guilt, and The Chrises had little of that, just some conversations.

"What about charging him with conspiracy?"

"That's actually pretty weak too. You can prove he's made some calls to Colombia because you've got his phone records, but the phone records don't prove that Serrano was actually talking to Herrera, who by the way, has never been convicted for drugs. He could have been talking to anyone at Herrera's number: the guy's wife, butler, whatever. And Serrano gave you the coordinates of the runway in Colombia, but can you *prove* someone else gave them to him or that he *knew* it was cocaine he wanted brought back? I mean, yes we know he knew, but can you *prove* he knew? And to show conspiracy, you have to prove he actually conspired *with* someone and we don't have that. We have a lot of assumptions but assumptions are not proof, and his attorney will ping us to death on that." Chris was happy the AUSA kept saying "we" as opposed to "you", like he was part of the team, not the lawyer just instructing the client.

"So you're saying we have to prove he knows it's coke. How are we going to do that?"

The AUSA told him, and Chris' face broke into a huge grin. "You're kidding, right?" asked Chris. "You don't think he's going to find that a little weird?"

Herrick, a young, innovative man who Chris liked and respected, answered back immediately, "I think he's going to be too shit-scared right then that he's not really even going to notice it."

Chris pursed his lips, moved his head back and forth, smiling and considering. "And it'll be too late, right? I mean, at that point he's ours anyway."

"Pretty much, yes. About the only thing he could do right then that might prove his innocence at trial, which isn't going to happen because he's not innocent and isn't thinking about being in court, would be to close the trunk, get on his cell phone, call nine-one-one and walk away. He won't do that, and he's going to have to go with it. At that point, yes, he's ours."

"Yeah, okay. I'll pass it by the boss and we'll do it that way. Dude's going to shit, though. I mean, literally, he's going to *shit!*" Then he had another thought and laughed even harder. "We'll stick him in Harold's car."

Mau was sitting in Ricardo's office with The Chrises standing in the doorway. "So here's what I told him," said Mau. "I was really pissed that he went and threatened Francisco, that Francisco doesn't know about our business, and he's liable to screw the whole deal if he keeps acting crazy. He's calmed down now and apologized for going off the deep end. He knows that what he did was stupid, but he really wants to meet to arrange the delivery of the coke. So, I figured we could set up a meet and I'll drive a car with like a hundred keys [kilos] in the trunk. I'll just spring the dope on him, give him the key, and tell him to call me after he's sold it to give me my money. He definitely won't be expecting that, but it'll put him in the trick bag because he can't just leave the car sitting in a parking lot. I figure he'll freak out some more because he's not a dope-guy and isn't going to know what to do with the car, so maybe he'll make some calls, maybe he won't, but either way, he's going to have to do something and then you've got him."

Ricardo was smiling and biting a fingernail. "I like it!" He looked at the clock on the wall. "It's 11:30 now. Let's plan for the meeting this afternoon. One of you Chrises talk to tech and see if they've got a car with a kill switch already installed. The other one of you go to the warehouse and get a trunk-full's worth of kilo packages and bring them back here. We'll load 'em up, Mau'll call Serrano to set up the meeting, and we'll convoy from here. Al!" he shouted.

"What!" Fraser shouted back from his desk then came strolling into the office past Chantelle's empty desk.

"Call the Airwing and see if they have a helicopter they can put in the air, and let them know we're going to have a big load on the street."

Al snapped off an open hand salute and shouted, "Roight!" in a passable imitation of a WW2 British Army officer.

"And I want you in the helicopter too. If they can pick you up here in the parking lot, fine. If not, then Opa Locka or wherever they think's most convenient." He pointed a finger at the door. "Go."

Looking at Davis and his partner, he said, "You guys, one of you get going on an op-plan. The whole group's here and you can use them however you want. The car's going to be immobilized, so him getting away in it with the dope isn't much of a factor, but we've got to be prepared in case someone else shows up. Someone'll have to keep an eyeball on the car and the dope at all times. Mau'll drive the car there and after he leaves, he can sit it out and won't be assisting in the arrest. That leaves you two, me, Harold, Brent and The Masturbator or whatever he calls himself. Six guys should be enough. Questions?"

"For the op-plan," began The Other Chris, "Where are we doing the meeting?"

Mau and Ricardo looked at each other. "How about TGI Friday's at Dolphin Mall," suggested Ricardo. "It's public but away from the mall, plenty of open parking where we can keep an eyeball on the car. You and Enrique can get set up for a late lunch. Once we have the car in the lot, you can call him and tell him where you'll be."

Mau rubbed his chin. "Warrant? For the house? We want that picture of the coke that I gave him."

Ricardo nodded. "Yep, that too." He glanced at his watch again. "I don't think we have time for an affidavit. As soon after the arrest as feasible, we'll try to execute a Consent Search on the house. I'll talk to Group Three and get their agents to do the raid."

Everyone was standing in the Division parking lot. No one was wearing their vests or black raid jackets yet; they'd suit up just before the meeting at the restaurant. Tech had loaned the group a brand new white van. In the back were approximately one hundred square packages, each one a kilogram of cocaine.

"So, just to get this straight," said Mau. "When I park the van in the lot, I'll cut open one of the packages and put the ignition key in it, sticking straight up right on top so he can't miss it. Then when I meet him, I'll give him the door key, tell him where it's parked, and I'm out, right?"

Davis nodded. "Yep, that's what the AUSA wants. He said there's no way Serrano will be able to plead that he didn't know the van was loaded with drugs because he's going to be holding an ignition key covered in coke. Pretty funny, right?"

"Okay," said Ricardo. "Me and Harold will be in the restaurant keeping an eye on the meeting. When Serrano leaves, we'll follow him out and get in our car. Whoever has the eye on the van will call out what's happening but no one moves in until I give the word." He looked at everyone and got nods in return. "Once it goes down, we'll all convoy back here. Questions? Good." He clapped his hands. "Then let's go and fuck this guy's day up."

Everyone got in their cars and checked in on the radios. Davis, standing next to his partner, took out his portable radio. "3102 calling Flint unit."

There was a pause and then a reply, and in the background Chris could hear the thudding of a helicopter. "3102, this is Flint 411." "Flint" is the collective callsign for the DEA Airwing.

"Flint 411, what's your twenty?"

"We're about a mile and a half west of the Division. We can see all of you guys right now in the parking lot. We're going to stay west of you but can't go farther south of the meet spot because it's in the MIA[1] approach corridor."

"10-4."

Davis turned and held out his hand, palm up. "Speed, Surprise and Violence of Action."

The Other Chris slapped it hard. *"That's* what gives us satisfaction!"

The cars pulled out of the lot with the load car in the middle of what is euphemistically called a "federal convoy." The drive to the Dolphin Mall was relatively short, only about ten minutes. Mau, driving the load car, parked in the lot directly in front of the TGI Friday's in a spot under some trees where there were few other cars to block the view so all the agents in the mall lot could see him. "I'm calling the target now." He reported over a portable radio. There was a few minutes pause. "Target's on the way from his house. Say's he'll be here in about twenty minutes. Kill switch done. The van's dead. I'm clear."

The agents watched as Mau exited, walked to the rear of the vehicle and opened the door. He leaned in, opened the package, and placed the ignition key as instructed, then closed it and walked towards the restaurant. As he passed Ricardo's car, he tossed the portable radio through the window. A few minutes later Ricardo and Harold got out and followed him in.

"All units, this is 3102. I'm parked about ten spots away from the load car and have the eyeball." With the primary eyeball set, the other agents

---

[1] Miami International Airport

maneuvered through the lot, parking their cars where they were close enough to move when the bust signal was given but not so close the cars and dark windows would stand out. "Flint, do you have an eyeball on the van?"

Al's voice came back over the radio. "Affirmative. We're just west of the parking lot."

Davis rolled down his window to see if he could hear the rotors cutting up the air; he could, though he couldn't visually locate it. "Can you guys back off a little more? We'll call you in when he enters the lot."

There was a pause while the pilot and Al discussed positioning the helicopter. "That's affirmative. We're going to orbit to the north and climb a little and keep an eyeball. The pilot says he can stay on station for about an hour and a half."

The wait was a very tense time and although it was less than a half an hour, it seemed to drag forever until the radio came alive. "3102, 3105. I've got the target. He just pulled into the parking lot. He's driving the maroon van. Stand by." The radio clicked off. "He's parking nose-in, two rows north of the load car."

"3102 copies. Tally ho."

"He's getting out of the car now. Target is wearing a blue polo shirt and khaki pants."

"3102 copies." Davis was dialing Ricardo's cell phone to pass on the information.

"I didn't see anyone else in the car with him."

"3102 copies."

Davis' phone rang. It was Ricardo, talking quietly. "They're meeting right now at the bar. He looks pretty pissed off…wait…our guy is giving him the trunk key now…our guy is leaving…bad guy is just standing there… wait… wait…he's getting on the phone."

"UC is leaving the restaurant." Reported one of the other units. Then a few minutes later, "Bad guy is out of the restaurant."

"UC is clear, walking to the mall."

"3102 copies."

"Bad guy is standing in the lot. He's just looking around."

The Punisher reported, "3101 is out of the restaurant with 310...um...fuck...with Harold."

"UC is entering the mall. No one's behind him."

"Bad guy is still standing there. He's looking at the load car."

"This is 3101. Meeting went well. I just talked to the UC. He's clean and hanging out in the bookstore. The bad guy was pretty surprised when he gave him the key. I don't have an eyeball on anything."

The Other Chris was on the radio. "Bad guy's in the lot, standing by his car, looking at the load car."

"Bad guy's walking towards the load car. Everyone stand by." In the other cars the agents would be slipping into their Kevlar vests and jackets and giving their weapons a final check to ensure the magazines were firmly seated and rounds were in the chambers. Engines were starting as everyone prepared to pull out, drive to the load car, and block it in on the off chance the kill-switch didn't function and the van actually started.

"Bad guy's walking around the van. Stand by. Stand by. Bad guy's...bad guy's walking away from the van. He's walking back towards his car. Where the fuck...whoops, sorry...is he going? Bad guy's getting in his car."

"This is 3101. Who's got the eyeball on the load car?"

"3102 has the eye."

"3102, pass the eye and stay with the target." Even though the radios were encrypted, the target's name was never passed over the air.

"Roger."

79

"Bad guy's backing up...he's turning for a northbound exit."

"This is Flint...we've got an eyeball on the bad guy's car."

"This is 3102, I'm set up for a northbound takeaway. I've got an eyeball on the bad guy. He's staying in the mall...he's circling to the north. Flint, I'm two cars behind the bad guy."

"10-4, I see you and the bad guy. He's staying in the inside lane. It doesn't look like he's exiting the mall."

Davis kept a few cars between him and Serrano who seemed to be just driving around the mall's parking lot. He kept a running tally going for the other agents who were still mainly parked around the load car. After about five minutes, they were back where they started from, in front of the TGI Fridays. Davis got on the radio. "I think this guy's lost." He was laughing as he said it. "Looks like we're going for lap two." The two cars, with the helicopter in the distance, kept circling the lot. No one was talking much on the radio. There was little to be said by anyone except Chris.

Around and around they went. As they were approaching lap five, Serrano pulled back into the Friday's lot and parked where he had been before.

"Bad guy just got out of his car. He's waving at someone...stand by. We've got another vehicle, looks like the Volvo with two passengers. Stand by. They're stopping next to his vehicle. He's going over to talk to the driver. Stand by. He's pointing at the load car. Stand by. He just reached into the car and handed something to the driver. Bad guy is walking towards the load car. He's at the rear."

"Flint's closing."

"Bad guy is opening the door. Bad guy is reaching in. Door's closed, bad guy is moving to the driver's door. Bad guy is getting in the driver's side."

Ricardo was on the radio, his voice up half an octave and loud. "Go Go GOGOGO! Take 'em down. Somebody block in the Volvo!"

Davis was closest, moving slowly down a lane of parked cars. He slammed the accelerator pedal and drove up directly behind the Volvo, threw his into park, and jumped out taking his .223 automatic rifle. Keeping his body low, he ran to the passenger side of the Volvo and pointed it in at the faces of the men inside, screaming as loud as he could, "Police, hands up, show me your hands," and then in Spanish, "*Manos arriba! Policia!*"

At the same time, The Punisher came running up to the driver's side of the car and, living up to his nickname reached in, grabbed the driver by the hair, and literally *pulled* him through the window and onto the ground. Immediately overhead, the helicopter had pulled into a low hover, pulverizing the air in a maddening, deafening, disorienting dirt storm.

The Other Chris had driven his car in front of the load vehicle and with his machine gun was aiming over the roof of his car and pointing through the load car's front windshield, shouting for Serrano to get his hands up. One of the other agents, The Other Chris wasn't sure who as he was so focused on Serrano, opened the van door, pulled Serrano out and put him face down on the pavement. The Other Chris moved around the back of his car to point his barrel directly at the top of Serrano's head. Someone, he thought it was Ricardo, yelled, "You move, you're dead."

Davis was still dialed-in on the passenger in the Volvo. With his right hand holding the plastic checkered grip of the rifle, he opened the door with his left and screamed, "On the ground!" The passenger, a Latin-looking male of about 40 years, quickly got out of the car and laid down. Chris stepped back so he was standing at the man's head, aimed in on-target and said nothing more. From the corner of his eye he saw Harold step in, kneel down and handcuff him.

Chris looked up and took in the scene around him. The helicopter was now backing off and the air was quieting. Agents were everywhere. The Punisher was again pulling his handcuffed prisoner up by the hair and pushing him towards the load car. Serrano was not to be seen, but The Other Chris was aimed in at the concrete, so Chris assumed that's where Serrano's skull was. He pushed *his* prisoner towards the load car and turned him over to Brent. Then returned to the Volvo, looked inside to make sure no one else was hiding there and did the same to the van. Satisfied everything was under control, he walked to the load car in time to see Ricardo's head pop up and look around, visually checking the status of the vehicles, his agents, and the bystanders who were standing wide-mouthed and pointing.

The Other Chris stood, hauling Serrano to his feet, a shiny pair of cuffs on his wrists!

The Other Chris.

82

Special Agent Alister Fraser.

Enrique Serrano's house and vehicle in Kendall.

Opa Locka Airport.

The "load car."

CHAPTER FOUR

The Geneva Convention defines a mercenary as a person who:

(a) Is specially recruited locally or abroad in order to fight in an armed conflict;

(b) Does, in fact, take a direct part in the hostilities;

(c) Is motivated to take part in the hostilities essentially by the desire for private gain and, in fact, is promised, by or on behalf of a Party to the conflict, material compensation substantially in excess of that promised or paid to combatants of similar ranks and functions in the armed forces of that Party;

(d) Is neither a national of a Party to the conflict nor a resident of territory controlled by a Party to the conflict;

(e) Is not a member of the armed forces of a Party to the conflict; and

(f) Has not been sent by a State that is not a Party to the conflict on official duty as a member of its armed forces.

According to this definition, as I was specially recruited to fight in an armed conflict, paragraph (a), and have taken direct part in the hostilities, paragraph (b), am earning a substantially excess amount of material compensation (US dollars) and am here for private gain as opposed to military duty, paragraph (c), and am not a member of the armed forces, paragraphs (e and f), I am considered a mercenary.

However, as I am a citizen (therefore a national and resident) of the United States, which *could be considered* a Party to the conflict, I do not fall under paragraph (d) and, therefore, am not a mercenary.

But at the end of the day, we are not in an armed conflict *with* Pakistan. So it's a moot point.

Since we're not at war with Pakistan, we (the US) have no right to violate or intrude on their sovereignty in any way, except as they allow us. In fact, no active-duty military personnel are permitted in Pakistan. Period.

Without delving too deeply into the history of the War-on-Terror, let me just say there exist several classified Memorandums of Understanding (MoU) between our two countries. The original purpose of the MoUs was to allow a small group of non-military, embassy-accredited civilians to service a remote listening post with the caveat all intelligence would be immediately made available to their intelligence and military services. And that's where the mission crept.

"Mission creep" is a military concept of expanding a mission beyond its original, intended goal. It's usually undesirable because each new task tends to be a little riskier. If successful, it breeds further, more ambitious attempts, each snowballing to the next, usually only stopping when a final, catastrophic failure occurs. It has been my experience mission creep is the inevitable by-product of the "can-do" spirit that doesn't allow one to say "no" to one's superior (unless the idea of "promotion" doesn't exist to the person saying "no"). It has also been my experience that no matter how comically stupid or wildly off-the-wall the suggestions are, they are accepted by those below with a snappy salute and a "Very well, sir."

I can almost picture the conversations at the OGA[1] when the MoU was put into place and how it crept from that to where we are now:

Q: "What assets do we have in Pakistan?"

A: "A SIGINT[2] relay. Sends info to the embassy; we share the output with ISI[3]. It's in a local Pak army garrison."

Q: "I don't like the idea of sensitive equipment not being watched over by us. Think we could rotate some techs on-site from the embassy, let 'em live with the army for a week at a time, care for the equipment, that kind of thing?"

A: "Not a problem." Primary mission complete, according to the MoU.

Next meeting.

Q: "Our guys out in the boonies say they don't feel comfortable living with the Pak army. It's pretty tough going and they're not really the outdoor types. What about making it a little more livable?"

A: "Well, we could move them out from the army camp and put together a little place for 'em to live. We'd have to make sure they were properly taken care of in terms of basic living needs, food, electricity, etc.... We could probably contract that out to Marriott or KBR. Keep them close to the Pak army for security. Not a problem." Facility expansion.

---

[1] Other Government Agency. Generally refers to intelligence agencies without actually divulging their identities
[2] Signals Intelligence
[3] Pakistan's Inter-Services Intelligence

Next meeting.

Q: "My boss wants to know if we have anyone that could deploy remote, real-time ground sensors in-country. I told him yes. Do we have anyone?"

A: "Well, we have those tech guys that live at the listening post."

Q: "But they're geeks, right? We can't send geeks into Indian Country. We'd need operators for that. But they can't be military; you know what I mean...can you contract some? And you know, if we're going to do that, why not have them take over the security from the Pak army next door. More bang for our buck, so to speak."

A: "Not a problem." This was our entry into the original MoU.

Next meeting.

Q: "My boss says the info we're getting from the ground sensors is useless; too far south from where they need to be. ISI says they've located some passes in the mountains that need to be monitored real-time, and the UAVs aren't always available. Can our operators get up there and take care of it?"

A: "Well, that's too far to go in the trucks they have."

Q: "Any way we can get them more properly deployable over longer range?"

A: "Not a problem." Helicopter.

Next meeting.

Q: "ISI's got locating data about one of their targets. They don't have assets in place and want to know if your guys can recon the meeting, snatch the target and turn him over to them?"

A: "Not a problem." Now we're operational in a clandestine capacity.

Next meeting.

Q: "My boss says it might be a good idea to have someone out there, some of our guys, to manage and coordinate things like that last op. Better communications and whatnot."

A: "Not a problem." C^3 *:Command, Control and Communications.*

Next meeting.

Q: "We've localized a Target of Interest. We've also confirmed through other sources that ISI's known about him the entire time and didn't tell us and won't give him up. Any chance your guys can snatch him?"

A: "Not a problem." And now we're covert.

About once every two weeks, a white C-130 will drop in with generator parts, spare whatevers for the helo, pallets of water, like that. Think every now and then it flies out of here with those packing boxes carrying much more valuable cargo than they arrived with?

We have gone from simple care-taking and security in a high-threat environment to a (quasi-) legal, deniable unit being used in support of *covert* US intelligence operations under the guise of *overt, clandestine* missions on behalf of a foreign nation's intelligence service.

We are "The Engagement."

I had been lying in a hammock in a shaded open-air pavilion, a guitar next to me in the sand on a brilliantly bright beach in Fremantle, Australia, when I received an unexpected call from an old colleague. A retired Navy SEAL who had kept in touch with his contacts in the intelligence community, he wanted to know if I was interested in deploying "downrange," a term that refers to the area beyond the muzzle of a gun where the bullets fly. I didn't know exactly *where* "downrange" was but I was jobless, living on savings, with no employment in my foreseeable future. I said yes immediately.

Based on his recommendation, the OGA he was recruiting for did an extensive background on me, re-validated my Top Secret security clearance, sent me to a training camp to ensure my tactical and shooting skills were up to snuff, backstopped a Diplomatic Passport and gave me a job here in "the camp."

We aren't really called "the camp." I don't know we're called *anything*, though I've heard my boss refer to it as Site Bravo. So Site Bravo it is.

To some very high-ranking officers in the ISI, we're probably referred to by the name of the town several kilometers away, which, like the town where our last op had gone down, is little more than some colorless huts and a mosque. I have no doubt to the small contingent of Pakistani Army who lives in the brick and stone "compound" next to us on the other side of a few rolls of concertina wire, we are just called "The Americans."

Geographically, this part of Pakistan closely resembles the Southwest United States, and in fact occasionally, I have heard some of the guys call this place "Little Yuma." I've never been to Yuma but now have an idea what it must look like: brown, rocks, shale, brown, mountains, dusty and brown; whether it's the ground, sky, dust devils, our clothes or our tents...brown.

In the center of our camp, in the middle of this bleak brown nowhere, plopped down like Dorothy's falling into Oz, is a small square house surrounded by high walls (as if there were anyone around here to keep out). It is the nerve center of Site Bravo, and we call it The Alamo.

The top of the house, accessible by a set of jury-rigged plywood stairs at the rear, is the real reason we call it The Alamo - if the shit ever moves out of the mountains to the north of us and into our fan and we can't boogie out of town, then it's where we, hopefully as John Wayne-like as we can, are going to make our last stand. It is the highest point in Site Bravo and from there we can see well into the hills to the east and west, the security post out by the hangar, and every conceivable avenue of approach.

When we first arrived, the roof of the house was just a roof. We laid plywood flooring and a waist-high railing where we wrote laser-range-determined distances to strategic marks in our threat environment. We stacked AT-4 anti-tank rockets in their dark green containers out of the way but within easy reach along with cases and cases of both 5.56 and 7.62 ammunition and RPG launchers, their grenades in heavy green canvas-flapped bags. Capable of much longer-range shooting are single-barreled .50 caliber machine guns on tripods, their barrels and working parts covered with black garbage bags and canvas wrappers to keep the dirt out. We fortified the entire area with sandbags and built a simple second roof to keep the wicked sun off.

We do not have business *inside* The Alamo. My boss, the Master Chief, can come and go as he pleases but inside is the lair of the real boss of Site Bravo, the client, who introduced himself when he arrived as Big Mike. He's not that big and I'm guessing his name isn't Mike. Why Big Mike? Who knows, but he's got to be called something and Big Mike is as good as anything.

Except for Big Mike, we collectively refer to anyone who isn't one of us as "client" or by their job; no need for us to know their real names or for them to know ours.

On the subject of names and callsigns, mine's Meat. I'd like to say it has to do with my heroically-sized endowment...but like Big Mike's moniker, it has nothing to do with reality. Mine comes from two Venezuelan musicians in Ft. Lauderdale, Florida. When we first met, I introduced myself as Pete, which they repeatedly pronounced it as Pit. No, I said, not Pit like Brad Pitt, but Pete, like meat. Thus was born Pete the Meat, *Senor Carne, Senor* Meat or just Meat.

Big Mike's Table of Organization consists of a physician's assistant to care for our scuffs and bruises and a communications specialist who has a cot in the radio room and is never, *never* outside that room unless either Big Mike or the medic spell him for physiological breaks or a quick exercise walk inside the fence. There are also two ex-US Army pilots to fly the helicopter and a mechanic doing double duty as an armourer. Those three guys have their own little hooch by the hangar. We get an occasional visitor, like Rabbit, but they're usually only here for a day or so and then vanish. (There was a time, however, when a group of US Army Rangers and a few guys with British accents stayed for just over a week. They came in jeans, not uniforms, and brought lots of briefing material. Pakistan has several nuclear weapons storage sites, one not too far from here. We hadn't known that. The visitors wanted us to have some insights and training on what was expected from us in the event the US National Command Authority decided the facilities had to be seized to prevent their contents being compromised. Because of our proximity, there was every chance we'd be the first bodies arriving and would be expected to take and hold the facility until it could be turned over to other units. They put us through our paces and left some nifty training aids that we've incorporated into our own training scenarios.)

Outside the house but inside the castle walls are two large tents. One has a big red cross painted next to the plywood door. The other is the TOC, or Tactical Operations Center. Inside are a couple of laptops for personal emails (10 minutes a day and no surfing the web!), three satellite telephones always kept on chargers, a few bicycles, a filing cabinet, some finely tuned sniper rifles in their hard cases, and a bunch of E and E (Escape and Evasion) packs consisting of more ammunition, RPGs, GPS receivers, food, water, maps, gas cans, radios… all the things we will need if we ever have to blast out of dodge for the long ride through the desert to the shore where hopefully the Marines can extract us. We have no delusions in the event we do have to split, things will have seriously turned to shit and it will be a tough go, but we try to be like the Boy Scouts and BE PREPARED.

Our E and E is based on two separate threat scenarios, one unlikely and one extremely credible. The unlikely scenario is based on a massive assault by Al-Queda or Taliban who have moved south undetected from the tribal regions to attack our base. While not outside the realm of possibility, we discount this for the most part because while we are a pain-in-the-ass to them, we're not *so* bothersome we think they would organize an assault the size necessary to be effective. And if they do, the fleet of UAVs continuously transiting overhead will hopefully pick up that big a troop movement. I'm told the "rear sites" in Islamabad and Langley constantly monitor those UAVs, and we'll be gone long before the bad guys arrive.

The more credible threat is the current leadership of the country may not want us around any more. There are some back home in the US who complain the President of Pakistan isn't doing enough to help fight "the war on terror." In my opinion, those who complain are too politically un-savvy to take into account the situation he has in front of him. He is the leader of a country that is overwhelmingly Muslim. While the majority of those Muslims are not hard-liners or fanatically anti-American, they are first and foremost supporters of their religion and he is caught in the middle of being President to and representing his people on the one hand, and on the other hand trying to support the US in *their* cause, which is not only represented as anti-Muslim, but also involves having a foreign army on their soil. I don't know one American who would stand by a US President allowing the same thing.

Lately the Pakistani government has been taking a tougher stance with the US and a more conciliatory tone with the fundamentalists, as evidenced by the Taliban taking control of the Swat Valley. While *we*

94

haven't been directly addressed, we can't help but think it might be coming, and when it does, we might go from being "The Americans" to "The Enemy." We have to BE PREPARED that at any moment, the 52 soldiers living on the other side of the concertina wire could open up on our camp, or the occasional Pakistani Air Force fighters who do low passes might start dropping bombs on our tents.

In preparation for an attack from our Pakistani Army neighbors, we home-built some Claymores, and using glue, paint and tumbleweeds, cleverly camouflaged them and inserted them between our camp and theirs, facing into the concertina wire. We also fabricated a few mines and buried them in our own no-go-zone. And the big .50 cals. sleep with their barrels pointed casually down at our neighbors. Honor the closest threat first.

We figure if we ever have to go, we'll have about ten minutes notice the shit is inbound to get the perimeter collapsed back to The Alamo, throw the packs in the trucks and start heading out. The helicopter is programmed into the E and E plan, but we have to assume at the critical moment we need it, it won't fly or the pilots will be disabled or dead. If there is a squad outside the fence on an op, they'll be on their own until the military can mount a rescue, or they'll have to make their own way out. On the other hand, if there *is* a squad outside the fence, it's likely they'll have the helicopter with them, so their trip could be a lot faster and more comfortable than whoever is in the trucks.

As to the actual ride, we all know we have to head south but don't know exactly how far because we don't know exactly where *we* are! I've done a bootleg search on the internet using Google Maps and the coordinates I pulled off one of the GPSs, but they don't match: The terrain's different; there's no road where there should be; the house isn't there. From a large selection of topographical and aviation charts of the region, I tried the same thing: no runway, no structures, no town. So either the GPS is being spoofed at ground level or someone at the Agency employing us is "error-izing" the satellite images and maps. Either way, it's kind of spooky the way we've been erased.

Another part of BEING PREPARED is communications security. Inside The Alamo just to the left of the front door, guarded solely but effectively by a handwritten "KEEP OUT" sign, is the comms room. It contains a cot with a sleeping bag, and a long table against the opposite wall. It's jammed with black boxes stacked two and three high, computers, extension sockets, plugs, orange power cords strung everywhere, printers and file cabinets with dial combinations for classified document storage. The electronic equipment generates a lot of heat so we installed a separate air-conditioner unit in the window.

Normally, in a high-threat environment communications and documents are made frangible in some way, either with devices that burn at such high temperatures everything's destroyed, or with small explosive charges embedded within the equipment that can be detonated should the need arise. For whatever reason, the radios and file cabinets inside the Alamo were not so equipped, so when we were setting the place up, we had to innovate. We ran a string of electrical wire from the TOC through the wood floor, out the tent wall and buried it deep under the sand (which we covered with plywood sheeting to prevent its damage by people transiting the area between the tent and the Alamo). We drilled a hole in the comm room outer wall and ran the wire through it. From the hole it went into the documents safe where one of the guys fabricated incendiary grenades with blasting caps as triggers. From the blasting caps we also "daisy-chained" a few short lengths of detcord that we plugged into cone-shaped C-4 packages strung from the ceiling, the wide parts of the cones facing downward like tiny, unlit lampshades. Another string of detcord was threaded through the cooling inlets into the cases of the most sensitive electronics.

In the TOC, where the wire came up through the floor, I had duct-taped it to a table and written on the tabletop very brief, declarative "KISS" sentences in black, indelible magic marker exactly how to pull the wires apart and connect them with the initiator, which in this case is a car battery, its silver contacts covered with red plastic drinking cups held in place with more duct-tape. The instructions have to be kept that way because in an E and E scenario, the person charged with blowing the comms room might not be someone with explosives experience; could be a pilot or the comms guy himself. Whoever it is might be panicked, hurt, deafened or just generally incapable of higher-order thinking at that moment. I was "Keeping It Simple, Stupid" because if the moment ever comes to use that battery, the "stupid" might be me and I'll need to get it right!

Speaking of the comms guy, I have only seen him once or twice. He's a short, bookish man, but I have to give him a lot of credit to be working and living with all that boom wrapped and strung around his room since his equipment gives off enough electromagnetic energy to send static charges into the wires and start a chain reaction that would really give him a message he isn't expecting.

Outside the Alamo walls is where we exist when we're not on an op. It's a comfortable living, comparatively, as we have air-conditioned tents to sleep in, cots we don't have to share, an outdoor gym, a fresh-water shower, and even a washing machine and dryer. We have a Morale, Welfare and Recreation (MWR) and galley tent. In the MWR are some books, a few chess and backgammon sets, their pieces long since lost, a popcorn machine, and a big-screen TV that shows five channels of the worst programming imaginable courtesy of the American Forces Radio and Television Service (AFRTS, which we pronounce A-farts). Back when I was in the military, it was called the *Armed* Forces Radio and Television Service but political correctness made that a no-no; heaven forbid our military should be portrayed as being so aggressive as to actually be *armed*. Luckily, we also have a DVD player so contaminated with sand movies are barely playable.

And the white C-130…sometimes on its way in brings fresh vegetables, frozen pizzas, and believe it or not, lobsters! Barbarians we may be, but we eat quite well.

Right now there are sixteen of *us* in the camp: three squads of five men and a sixty-three year old retired SEAL Master Chief, who has a bald head, a white handlebar moustache and freakish, Andy Rooney eyebrows. He grumps and growls a lot, but he matches it with a booming laugh and the balls to be up every morning at the crack of whenever he feels like it, waking to do at least thirteen pull-ups and a four mile walk / limp around the camp. He's a tough old nut, but I've met few men that command more respect so effortlessly.

Our three squads have rotating duties based on a seven-day workweek. One squad is on security detail, manning several 3' x 3' posts constructed entirely of plywood outfitted with a deck chair, telescope, thermal imager resembling a long camera lens, and night vision goggles for when the sun goes down. Someone is always on top of The Alamo maintaining the overwatch as well as coordinating the security detail, passing messages to the rest of the camp (better radio reception up there), and being prepared to man the big guns.

One squad is operational and is either outside the fence or eating, resting, working out, augmenting the security squad or training.

After we had set up the camp and realized we'd be doing more than just providing protection services, the Master Chief decided we needed a training regimen to keep us from getting bored and sloppy. Kola volunteered to take on "personal trainer" duties as he has a BS in exercise physiology, an MS in occupational health and is a gym machine! As a former defensive tactics instructor, I told MC I'd handle that part of the training. Jazz was tapped for CQB[1] instruction. Since we already have a gym, Kola has everything he needs; the only equipment the guys need for my training classes are their hands, pads and some pistols and knives I cut out of plywood; Jazz requisitioned MP-5s and M84 Stun Grenades (commonly called "flash-bangs") and built a "shoot house" tent away from the main camp so stray rounds wouldn't do any damage.

MC oversees the Known Distance Range where we shoot our long guns and pistols.

A normal training day consists of a run before sunrise followed by a session on the weights. If Big Mike has anything, we'll get an intelligence briefing and threat assessment while we digest breakfast, or "Doc" will give us some medical refreshers: trauma management, drug administration, that kind of thing. Next comes defensive tactics: hand-to-hand combat, grappling, knife fighting and all the other forms of bruising I can come up with. That's followed by a qualification course on the Known Distance Range or live-fire practice and movement drills in the shoot house. It's hot, dirty work, but we take lots of water breaks and while we do, Jazz and his crew rearrange the inner walls, the furniture and the stuffed clothes that substitute for real bodies. We're all used to doing live-fire drills with real people inside playing hostages and bad guys, but MC said we're too short of live bodies if we fuck it up.

Occasionally at night we'll run a "red gun" exercise. Red guns are training aids, exact replicas of real firearms but totally safe. Since we don't have any "real" red guns, we use our own weapons after checking, then double- and triple-checking they are empty. The operation starts with a SMEAC briefing, and whether the target is a single can of tuna snatched from the tent where the pilots live or one of the pilots themselves, we run it just like

---

[1] Close Quarters Combat

we would in the "real world," emphasizing good intelligence, stealth, tactics and teamwork. We did get into a little hot water the first time we snatched a pilot as we used some of Doc's best pharmacology, and when the pilot woke up in the medical tent, he was none-too-pleased at the bruises, raw skin from the flex ties or the fact we had doped him while he slept. MC ran interference for us, explaining to Big Mike that: the pilot was doing nothing, since the helo was going through an inspection cycle and therefore unflyable; we have a spare pilot; we needed the practice; and pilots are whiners anyway. And Big Mike *was* impressed that we were able to steal the pilot while his buddy slept in the next cot over. Still, lesson learned. Next time, we're going to grab the mechanic. Or maybe Big Mike.

The guys who aren't on security or ops duty join in the training and take care of housekeeping for the camp. The Master Chief, with thirty-plus years of living in enough shitholes to know, has painstakingly written the duty roster: chow tent to be swept and mopped after every meal; TOC swept and "dusted" daily; shower tent bleached; vehicles fuelled; dry goods storage tent inspected for rats (we have a pellet rifle for the little critters); generators monitored; water jugs stationed throughout the camp filled; refrigerators restocked with water bottles; sandbags filled; batteries for blowing up the comms center tested; and the least desirable job...servicing the latrine.

The latrine is a one-man plywood room, a wood bench with a hole cut out, and a bucket beneath which the user lines with a garbage bag when he does his business. Then he (he's only - no girls allowed in this campground) takes out the bag, knots it, and puts it in a garbage can. Every morning before sunup, someone from the housekeeping detail puts on heavy cotton gloves, takes the bags out, puts them in a truck, and drives them out to the "south forty" along with the general camp garbage and several five-gallon cans of diesel fuel. He dumps everything into a pit, covers it with the fuel, stirs it up to get the fuel everywhere, tosses in a book of matches, and then steps back because the fire and heavy black smoke smell like…well…burning shit.

I spent my morning at the gym and am now sitting by myself at the pool, avoiding the rest of the guys. Some time ago, we had nailed together a frame out of 2x4s and laid in some heavy-duty plastic sheeting, filled it with water, built some chairs out of more 2x4s, built some low tables out of still more 2x4s and plywood, and thus, our beachside resort with infinity pool was borne. Unfortunately the combination of constantly blowing sand and high temperatures tend to turn the pool into a sludge of hot mud if we don't stay on top of it, but this afternoon the water is crystal clear and cool, having just been refilled by a hose pulled from the shower tent.

"What's up, killer?"

I look up to see Master Chief Hershel Davis limping up into the pool area. He's wearing shorts, a gray t-shirt and flip-flops.

"Don't call me that." I tell him turning back to my book.

"Yeah, I know," he says sitting down next to me. "Sounds like *you* took a suck on the big shit lollipop."

I have no comment except to think *where does he come up with this stuff?*

"When we first opened up shop here," continues MC taking off his flip-flops, "we were given very specific limitations on how we were going to do business, what we could and couldn't do. I know none of this has been explained to you, but that's because it's above your level of need-to-know and I'm not going to get into specifics. I also want you to know I green-lighted the op according to the briefing but having read the after-action reports and, more importantly, getting a higher-classification debrief from Big Mike…while I understand what was done and why, it's a gray area but does

101

lean towards targeted termination, and that's one of the things *my guys* don't do.

"Now, as far as *I'm* concerned, Rabbit giving you a kill order was a bad call, but that's not my decision to make and I understand that sometimes ops call for a certain...*flexibility*. But he did receive real-time approval from the client for what he did and you acted on his instructions."

I don't need him telling me he thinks it was a bad call...I *know* it was a bad call.

"Say something," he says.

I'm not what you would call an introspective person. I don't spend a lot of time (and when I say that, I mean I don't spend *any* time) thinking about subjects I have no answer to: religion, politics and emotions, in my mind, all fall into that category. You either believe or you don't; you either care or you don't; you either feel or you don't. That being said, just because I don't think about those things doesn't mean I don't recognize their concepts, and right now I'm talking about emotions, specifically anger and my relationship with it. I don't come across it very much and actually go way out of my way to avoid situations or people that put me in the position of having to feel it or its derivative: Stress. I know anger is the one emotion that, when you talk about a situation that made you mad, you get just as worked up as you were when it was actually happening. I know when I've been exposed to a situation that has me going, the best thing I can do is be alone for a day or two, avoid conversation and re-hash, let it settle out, and then compartmentalize it and not visit it again. I'm sure Dr. Philgood would tell me that's not a proper or grown-up way to handle it, that I should confront the problem, work towards resolution, hold hands, sing kum-ba-ya or something, but my response would be that's just not *my* way, and *my* way works for me and leave me alone before I direct *my* anger at *you* with a loud bang.

"Nothing."

"Say it."

I know I have to guard against letting my mouth getting me in trouble, as it sometimes does. I'm just so colossally angry and even now, with what little conversation I've had, I feel it closer to the surface where I don't want it to be.

"Master Chief," I say turning to look at him, "I really don't want to talk right now."

"Yeah," he growled, "that's obvious, but you're gonna whether you like it or not because right now I'm not sure where your head is, and you're no use to me until I know."

"Look, Master Chief," I say trying to keep my breathing slow, "it's not anything you can help me with and I really...*really*...don't want to talk about it."

"What is it you're pissed about? That it was a bad call? Or that you're a back shooter?"

Blast off. "Hey, fuck you, Hershel!" My mind goes white, and I am in the one place I hate being. My words are coming fast and hot, and I'm not even *thinking* about what's coming out. "That was a bullshit op. That wasn't protection. That wasn't *de*fense. That wasn't even close to being the op we were briefed. That was an assassination of some nothing dude that wasn't a threat to me, or Rabbit or anyone else. Rabbit shouldn't have put me in that position, and I shouldn't have pulled the trigger. That dude wasn't even the target!"

He shakes his head and absently twirls his moustache. "Nope and nope."

"That wasn't the job I signed up to do. I'm not here because I like to kill people. If you're not sure where my head is...were we having this talk when we snatched that guy and got in a firefight and Simple got killed? No we were *not* because that was righteous and this wasn't! I'm pissed off because I got put into a situation and I don't like the call I made. I'm not afraid to do this job. I don't complain and you know that. And I'm not saying the guy I shot did or didn't need to die. I *am* saying he didn't need to die right then, like that, like…not…not a fucking bullet in the back." I say quietly, deflated. "That was…"

"What?"

I search for the word and then know the word but don't want to say it. I don't even want to *think* it and I cover my mouth with my fist to keep it from coming out.

He takes a deep breath. I think he's going to say something but he doesn't. He slides forward and sits in the deep end of the pool, which is the same depth as the shallow end, about a foot and a half. Just then, one of the other guys, Grease, comes strolling up the platform in a swimsuit. MC looks at him and says, "Go away." Grease glances at us, does a sharp about-face and disappears.

He splashes water on his bald head; his moustache uncurls and droops. "I wish I could tell you something so you wouldn't feel bad, but I can't. I asked Big Mike to give me something about the op that I could tell *you,* but…" he shrugs, then continues, "I can tell you this. When I was in Viet Nam and Somalia and wherever, sometimes I had to do things I didn't like. They were pretty shitty and most guys didn't like doing it. But at some point we all had to trust that what we were doing was right, even if it didn't seem like it at the time. That's what this work is all about."

I just look at him. "And?"

He shakes his head. "And…nothing. Look, when you were in the Navy, you were prepared to drop bombs on people you never saw and maybe kill really, *truly* innocent people, and then swagger your big brass balls over to the O-Club and buy the round because you were an "Aerial Assassin" and probably never give it another thought. Right?"

104

I shrugged.

"All of us," he said more gently than I would have expected from the old bastard, "we do what we do because it's war, and like it or not, no matter what you want to tell yourself right now, I'm telling you that that guy was the enemy. This isn't always combat like you expect it to be like when Simple got dusted, but nor is it some gosh-damn cowboy movie either where doing what you did makes you a bad guy." He leans forward and spears me with a look from under those great bushy eyebrows. "Or a coward."

God, he's a smart fucker.

"So you didn't like it and too fuckin' bad, pardon my French. But sometimes it's what we do, and if you don't like it bad enough, I can have you on a plane next Thursday. But for now, what's done is done. You've mope'd, you've kept your mouth shut, which I respect, but now it's done. Okay?"

I don't say anything.

"*Okay?*"

I nod.

"Say it," he orders.

"Okay. It's done. No more mopeing."

He grins at me and reaches out his hand. I lean forward and help him to his feet. He gets out of the pool and makes his way to the edge of the platform. He steps down into the dirt then stops and turns back to me. "I want to tell you something, by the way, apropos of nothing."

"What's that?"

"You are, by far, the most un-officer-like officer I've ever met. After your tour, if you ever want to re-deploy, you better request to come back to my camp." He turns and walks away, leaving me with my book.

I don't want to say that was the nicest thing anyone has ever said to me, but if it isn't, it sure comes damn close.

Training cadre'.

The medical tent.

The main camp. The TOC is in the foreground.

Our health club.

The pool. The Alamo is in the background.

MWR Tent.

Galley and kitchen tent.

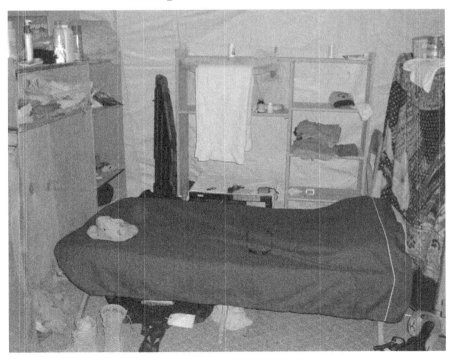

My suite.

A soldier and the author.

A dust devil just outside the concertina wire.

Grease on "chore-evasion" ops.

The white C-130.

Contractor acknowledges that the type and nature of the activity in connection with the Engagement has been thoroughly explained to him and that he fully understands the extreme danger involved in the Engagement as well as danger in the preparation and the training for the Engagement.

Contractor understands and acknowledges that the location of the Engagement is volatile, hostile and extremely dangerous and that the U.S. is conducting continuing military operations in the region. Contractor understands and acknowledges that by voluntarily agreeing to participate in the Engagement, he is voluntarily, expressly and irrevocably assuming any and all known and unknown, anticipated and unanticipated risks which could result in physical or emotional injury, paralysis, death, or damage to himself, to his property, or to third parties, whether or not such injury or death is caused by other independent subcontractors to (██████), known and unknown domestic and foreign citizens or terrorists or U.S. governmental employees.

Contractor understands that such risks simply cannot be eliminated without jeopardizing the objective of the Engagement and expressly agrees and promises to accept and assume all the known and unknown risks existing in providing services to (██████) in connection with this Engagement. The risks include, among other things, the undersigned being shot, permanently maimed and/or killed by a firearm, sniper fire, landmine, artillery fire, rocket propelled grenade, truck or car bomb, civil uprising, terrorist activity, hand to hand combat, disease, poisoning, etc., suffering hearing loss, eye injury or loss; inhalation or contact with biological or chemical contaminants (whether airborne or not) and or flying debris, etc.

P.B.D.
Initials

112

Contractor fully appreciates the dangers and voluntarily assumes these risks as well as any other risks in any way (whether directly or indirectly) connected to the Engagement.

Contractor understands and acknowledges that the Engagement and all Services performed and materials and information generated in connection therewith are a matter of national security and extremely confidential. In connection with the Services, Contractor will be privy to Classified Information (including the identity of the Contracting Party, reconnaissance photos. Contractor shall maintain in secrecy, all information in accordance with the terms of this Agreement, and shall not use the information other than for the purposes specified herein, or disclose the information to any third party without the written consent of the other Party. Such information, whether marked or identified as such or not, may include, but is not limited to, the mere existence of the Engagement or any details thereof, the identity of the Contracting Party, reconnaissance photos, maps and any and all other information in any way related to the Engagement.

Initials

JD sat at his desk in his office, head down, eyes closed, lips pursed as he digested the information in the emails from his wife, who was living back in Washington D.C., and similar emails from his mother, father, sisters and friends - everyone on mom's mailing list - about the crash in Pakistan.

JD looked up, glanced around the office as if to anchor himself back to where he was, and sent an email home with his POTS[1] number in Norfolk, Virginia that would ring right on his desk on the ship. Then he picked up the receiver, glanced at the phone listing sitting under a piece of Lucite that covered the desktop, and punched in the extension.

"Flag Admin, Commander Allison speaking."

"This is CAG. I need to see to the Admiral right now."

"Roger that, CAG. He's here. I'll let him know you're on the way."

---

[1] Plain Old Telephone Service

CHAPTER SIX

The aftermath of the bust at TGI Fridays was anti-climactic.

The helicopter had taken Al down to Kendall where he joined the agents from Group Three in the service of a Consent Search of Serrano's home. The consent was granted by Serrano's wife who was stunned to speechlessness by the appearance of nine heavily-armed agents at her front door. The search focused on Serrano's "office," and among his personal papers was the Polaroid photograph Mau had given him at Los Ranchos.

The driver of the Volvo was Serrano's seventeen-year-old son who had driven the other man, Serrano's neighbor, Ernesto Uribe, also a Colombian, to the lot to pick up Serrano's mini-van and return it to Serrano's home. Even under intense interrogation, neither the son nor Uribe admitted to any knowledge of what Enrique Serrano was doing at the TGI Fridays or what was in the van. Neither had a criminal record or NADDIS number. The AUSA said to kick them loose.

Serrano's own interrogation proved impossible as the first word out of his mouth was, "Lawyer."

A specialist from the lab walked over with a test kit, rubbed chemicals on Serrano's hand, and noted the change in color proving the presence of cocaine. Photographs were taken of his hands and would be included in the case file. Serrano was fingerprinted, photographed and driven down to the Federal Detention Center.

The key was sealed in an evidence envelope after also being tested for cocaine. The kilo package of cocaine that had the key in it was re-sealed and re-weighed to verify none of the coke was missing.

The drugs were returned to the warehouse, the van was returned to tech, and high fives were given all around.

What *was* climactic was the phone call Davis received the following day while sitting at his desk preparing for his grand jury testimony and wading through the paper tidal wave that inevitably washes over an agent following an arrest and seizure: surveillance reports, undercover reports, arrest reports, non-drug evidence forms, receipts for seized items that all had to be catalogued, indexed and put into storage.

"Hi Chris," came a very sweet, cheery, upper-class British voice. "This is Rachel Dalglish at the lab. I'm doing testing on the four hundred seventy kilograms you submitted."

"Hey, what's up?" he replied, rolodexing his memory, trying to come up with a face to match the voice.

"Well, two of your submitted packages tested negative for cocaine hydrochloride."

"Okay, so it's only…" he was doing fast math, "four hundred sixty eight kilos. That's still okay."

"It's okay but the interesting thing is the other two. The outer wrapping is the same, although the inner packaging is quite different. Also, they have the same eagle emblem on them, but the eagle is blue instead of red. It is the same decal, though, just a different color."

Chris was shaking his head. "Okaaay." He said drawing the word out waiting for the specialist to get to the point.

"Right. Well, as I said, they tested negative for cocaine, but they tested positive for diacetylmorphine."

Chris sat up straight. "Heroin?"

Rachel started laughing. "Quite. And very pure. We've done spectrographic analysis, and it is negative for diluents or adulterants, as pure as I've seen outside a laboratory." He smiled at her pronunciation of 'la-bore-a-tree.' "We entered the results in STRIDE[1] and got a correlation. Its signature exactly matches a shipment intercepted coming out of Afghanistan three months ago; definitely from the same manufacturer. I have a case number for you, and I should think you could contact the agent that handled it." She passed the number to Chris who would look it up in NADDIS and

---

[1] DEA's proprietary drug analysis database.

117

definitely contact the agent. Heroin moving through Colombia into the US was highly unusual, though it had been discussed for years.

"Ricardo!" yelled Chris getting up from his desk. "Check this out...."

The discovery of heroin elevated the bust within the Miami Field Division as well as in the press conference the Special Agent in Charge held in the training classroom, the 468 kilos of cocaine and the 2 kilos of heroin placed separately around the SAC for the cameras to capture. Of course, The Chrises' names were not mentioned nor were they present at the conference. As potential undercover agents, their identities need not be made public.

The day after the conference they were present in the SAC's office, along with Ricardo, to discuss the heroin. The information had already been passed to the Country Attaché in Bogotá with the request his agents and the vetted units put a bit more priority into Pablo Herrera.

Davis had spoken to Pedro Guzman, the agent who had seized the heroin in Afghanistan. Apparently Pedro had gotten a tip from an agent in Islamabad who had gotten a tip from an informant that a load of heroin would be coming via mule train into Pakistan for transport south to the coast where it would be placed on a ship. The informant had nothing on the identity of the ship or the exact date the train would cross the border or when the ship would sail.

Based on the informant's information, the agent in Pakistan had talked to a CIA officer, who was attached on a part-time basis as liaison to the DEA, about piggybacking a surveillance mission onto one of the Predators flying round-the-clock along the Afghanistan / Pakistan border. The DEA Country Attaché in Islamabad and the Resident Agent in Charge of the DEA office in Kabul agreed the takedown, should it occur, would have to happen on the Afghanistan side of the border because of the large US presence there, though both offices would share in the credit on the teletype notifications to DEAHQ[1] in Washington.

Within a day the informant had re-contacted the agent in Pakistan and alerted him it was the night the mule train was being fired up for the journey, which would cross the border near the town of Qwost. Phone calls went back and forth between embassies and offices, and almost immediately the Predator's cameras began swiveling to target that section of the border.

In Islamabad, the DEA agent was invited into the highly classified rear site within the embassy to take part, looking over the shoulder of the Predator operators at the black-and-white monitors. On the Afghanistan side of the border, Pedro and two DEA Special Agents / Pilots were sent from the embassy in Kabul to the airport where they and their King Air 350 were put on standby.

Upon receipt of a message to the CIA office at Bagram Air Force Base, a platoon of US Navy SEALs boarded a US Army helicopter and were flown to the forward operating base at Qwost.

At approximately 10 PM, the UAV operators in Islamabad identified the mule train.

The SEALs, who had been sitting in the helicopter with the engines turning, immediately lifted off and flew to a blocking position where they waited for the mules and their handlers to come to them. The Predator clearly recorded a protracted firefight where three of the five Afghanis were killed with no losses to the SEALs.

The surviving Afghanis, wrists and elbows flex-tied behind their backs and heads covered by hoods, along with the bodies of their compatriots, were flown to Bagram. Upon landing, the smugglers were placed in a holding area for later interrogation. The DEA agents flew to Qwost, retrieved the heroin and returned to Kabul.

---

[1] Drug Enforcement Administration Headquarters

Listening to Pedro's story, Chris was impressed with the smoothness of the operation as well as the cooperation that had occurred between the variety of agencies involved, something he also related to Ricardo when he debriefed him on the seizure of the heroin. Unfortunately neither the informant, Pedro, nor the agent in Pakistan had any information on other loads crossing the border, loads that were obviously the source for the heroin transported to Colombia and landing from there into the hands of the DEA agents in Miami.

Assistant United States Attorney John Vincent Herrick was adamant in his opinion that there was nowhere near enough information to indict Pablo Herrera, the Colombian source of the drugs, in US Federal Court. Herrick had contacted Enrique Serrano's attorney to see if Serrano was interested in cooperating with the government in exchange for consideration or a plea bargain but was told Serrano would not be willing to cooperate. Though not a surprise, it served to separate Herrera even further from investigative efforts of the DEA in Miami.

The Other Chris was in a telephone consultation with the DEA office in Bogotá when Chris Davis walked in the next morning. They waved at each other, and Davis started in on paperwork with half an ear on what his partner was talking about. When The Other Chris hung up, he filled Davis in.

"I told them what the AUSA said about arresting Herrera. They said that if we wanted them to, they could ask their vetted unit to get a search warrant and if we wanted to, we could ride along."

"What's a vetted unit?"

The Other Chris shrugged. "Don't know. But if they're willing to do it, I think it's a good idea. Maybe we'll get a trip to Colombia out of it."

In a meeting with Ricardo later in the day, the supervisor agreed with The Other Chris that if the Colombian Police were willing to go after Herrera, then who were they to stand in the way? He asked if either agent wanted to travel to Bogotá, and both Chrises energetically volunteered. Unfortunately, due to budget restrictions, Ricardo would only be able to send one man, so The Chrises flipped a coin and The Other Chris came up the winner. Davis went back to his desk to continue his paperwork while The Other Chris and the GS drafted an email to the Bogotá Country Office letting them know he was on his way.

Three days later Davis got a phone call at his desk. "Dude!" shouted The Other Chris, "We hit paydirt!" Davis laughed and told his partner to give him the details. "Well," said The Other Chris, "first of all they met me at the door of the airplane and escorted me right through immigration and customs, which was pretty cool." He had flown down on American Airlines into the capital city. "Everybody down here has armored SUVs with bulletproof windows for G-rides. And they can use them for personal business; they don't even have to have personal cars!"

"Did you take your gun with you?"

"No, man, I wasn't sure what the rule was, but they gave me one when I got to the office. Anyway, we went to the embassy and they told me that their vetted unit, which are local cops that are polygraphed and trained in the US and then operate down here, had Herrera under surveillance in Cali, so this morning we flew over here in the DEA plane. I'm in the house now. By the time we got here, the cops had already hit it. They were supposed to wait for us before going in, but I guess Herrera was up early and they wanted to do it before he left.

"Dude, this is so different from the way we do stuff. They would ask him questions and if he shrugged or didn't answer up right away, they'd clock him in the head with a phone book or something. I couldn't understand most of the stuff they were yelling at him, but they told me he admitted knowing

Serrano but didn't say anything about the coke or the heroin. He's got a pretty nice house, though, big pool in the back yard and a couple very hot maids.

"And man, they're searching the shit out of the house. It's awesome! They tore holes in the walls, ripped up the carpets, pulled the kitchen cabinets off the walls; I mean they're just whaleing on the house. I think they're getting their aggression out about something for sure." The Other Chris laughed and Davis laughed with him.

"Anyway, get this," continued The Other Chris. "They went through his cell phone and there was a number with a prefix they didn't recognize, so we went on line and Googled it and it came back to…wait for it…" he teased, "Afghanistan!" he said in a sing-song voice.

Davis punched his fist into the air. "Fuck yes!" he shouted to the empty office. "Fuck yes!"

The Other Chris called back with more evidence that the search had turned up. The vetted unit had located a floor safe in the pool's underground filter room and Herrera, seeing the writing on the wall, had given them the combination. Among the contents was a piece of paper with latitude / longitude coordinates. The Other Chris had relayed them to the MILGRU[1] at the embassy where they were plotted on a wall map of Colombia; they landed directly over the military base their informant's plane had flown into where the cocaine had been loaded. The search had also uncovered a pad of stickers depicting red and blue eagles the local cops didn't recognize at all and dismissed. The Other Chris proudly identified them as the same from the cocaine and heroin packages.

Davis sat with Ricardo filling him in on The Other Chris' success in Colombia. Like The Other Chris, Davis saved the Afghanistan connection

---

[1]Military Group

122

until the end. Like Davis, House was exceptionally pleased. The Miami Field Division was used to dealing with huge amounts of cocaine and marijuana, but heroin in multi-kilo amounts was a rare find. The fact there was a link between the heroin and Afghanistan was even better. That novice agents had developed a case linking heroin and Afghanistan and Colombia and a possible violator *in* Afghanistan was the best! House had no doubt the SAC would be passing this on to the Administrator in Washington and, since the far end of this case had its fingers in the war zone, it was possible it might even get mentioned to President Obama in one of his daily briefs. Goddamn!

"What did the Colombian police do with Herrera?" asked House.

"Well, according to Chris, a magistrate showed up at the house, which I guess is pretty standard stuff, and the guy typed out an arrest warrant for him on the spot. I was going to call the AUSA and see if this is enough to indict Herrera here and maybe get him extradited."

House was nodding. "Okay, good." He looked at Chris while his mind changed gears. "How do you guys plan to handle this whole thing? I only ask this because this case is starting to get big and it's just the two of you."

"What do you mean?

"Well, I see three different avenues you're going down right now." He laced his fingers on top of his head. "Serrano and his trial unless he decides to plead out. You said the AUSA wants to seize the house, but I haven't seen any paperwork yet on that, or the cars, plus one of you is going to have to be available for the trial as case agent.

"Secondly, you've got Herrera in Colombia and the possibility of his indictment here, and based on what Chris found, I'd be very surprised if the AUSA doesn't take this before the grand jury, yeah? That means one of you'll be testifying and I've never come across an AUSA who didn't require a bunch of bullshit, time-consuming follow-up work." He held up three fingers.

"If you get an indictment, main Justice is going to be involved with the extradition so you guys can expect a trip to DC as well as going back to Bogotá to escort him up when the time comes. And then there'll be trial prep for *that*."

He paused for a second. "I lied. There's four avenues. I just thought of another one because someone in the Colombian military allowed the use of a base to trans-ship the coke, and you said someone was paid off to allow the flight to come and go without their radar operators making them land for customs inspection on the way in or out, and no one alerted the military, or they did and someone there was covering it up. *That's* going to be a hot potato because of all the money the US pours into Plan Colombia. PR-wise it could be a huge black eye for their military, but that's too far above our pay grades to worry about right now. I'm sure there's some agency within the Colombian government that deals with those issues, but that's going to require some effort on someone's part as well. In fact, when we're through here, I'll put in a call to the CA and see if he can point us in the right direction. He might want to assign one of his agents to the case so don't get your titties all in a twist if he does. If you don't think you can juggle the military part of all this, we might think about passing it to the country office and let them work it. Your call. It could be really interesting but logistically might be too much, especially since neither of you guys speak Spanish and you don't live there.

"Whoops. Five. Now you've got a link with Afghanistan that we don't want to let slide, though I'm not sure what we're going to do with that yet.

"So, you and your brother need to think about all the irons you've got in the fire. Right now the other guys aren't doing too much of anything so if you need some grunt work done, bring it to me and I'll dole it out, but the big things are going to fall to you guys. So just keep thinking ahead, right?"

Chris nodded and, taking a page from Al Fraser's book, snapped up a crisp, British salute. "Roight!"

The Other Chris stepped into the office, walked up to Davis' desk and took a deep bow. "The hero has returned."

Davis applauded him briefly. "Good to have you back, man. It's been busy as shit here." The two had talked constantly while separated, each Chris updating the other on evidence being gathered and the case's progress in Bogotá and Miami.

In a not-so-surprising development, Enrique Serrano had changed his plea to guilty, which meant a huge load of run-around work was suddenly not necessary. During discovery, the government was obliged to turn over all its evidence to the defense to assist them in building an effective rebuttal case. It had been the AUSA's opinion Serrano would eventually change his plea once the process of discovery had begun and he saw the evidence arrayed before him.

John Herrick, the AUSA, had asked the DEA to produce an evidence list. Davis had done so, and at the AUSA's request, had included transcripts of the meetings between Mau and Serrano at the restaurant in Bayside as well as photos of the cocaine in the drop-car and the laboratory analysis of the cocaine residue recovered from Serrano's hand on the day of his arrest. Serrano's defense attorney had received the evidence stoically, according to Herrick.

Initially Herrick had offered Serrano, through his attorney, a lighter sentencing recommendation to the judge if Serrano would plead guilty *and* assist in the investigation of Pablo Herrera in Colombia; an offer that was instantly rejected. Colombians were infamous for not rolling-over on people higher in their organizations, especially if there were family members still living in Colombia.

The plea change had come the day after the AUSA met with Serrano's attorney and informed him of the arrest of Herrera in Colombia. Serrano's attorney had returned, hat-in-hand, and asked if the offer was still on the table for a sentence reduction in exchange for cooperation. Herrick related to The Chrises he actually laughed *out loud* at Serrano's attorney as he told him *that* ship had sailed. Obviously Herrera's arrest was the nail in Serrano's coffin and Serrano knew it.

The sentencing hearing was scheduled in two weeks time. Herrick said he would push for the maximum fifteen years.

From The Other Chris' side, the evidence recovered from Pablo Herrera's house had been copied, cataloged and entered in NADDIS. The actual evidence, sealed in DEA evidence bags, would remain with the Colombian National Police, except for the stickers and the paper with the geographic coordinates, which were in a safe in the DEA office at the embassy. In the event Herrera were extradited to the US, *that* evidence would be couriered up to Miami for the trial, but for the time being it would remain in Colombia for Herrera's trial there.

Herrick had scheduled a grand jury to indict Herrera in one week's time. The Other Chris would be testifying and would present copies of the evidence recovered in Colombia as well as producing one kilo each of cocaine and heroin with the colored stickers attached. Serrano's guilty plea would be entered by the AUSA, and The Other Chris would then detail the links between the two Colombians with phone records from Serrano and Herrera's admission he knew Serrano. The AUSA was positive he would receive a true bill from the grand jury and was already working on an affidavit that would be shipped up to the Justice Department in DC, which would oversee the extradition proceedings.

"So," offered The Other Chris, "what to do about Afghanistan?"

Davis nodded, leaning on his fist that was propped up on his desk. "Yep, what to do, what to do?"

"Well, we've got that number. You think we can check to see if it's still good without calling it?"

"I'm sure there's a way but…maybe disable the caller ID so it shows up as an unknown number."

"Might spook the guy if he'd never gotten one of those. And if we leave the caller ID on, he'd think Herrera was trying to call him and when we hung up, he might get nervous too or try to call him back."

"True 'dat." Davis suddenly had an idea. "Hey, is Afghanistan part of INTERPOL?"

The Other Chris shrugged. "Fuck if I know. Let me check my training shit." Both agents had attended a block of instruction on INTERPOL while at the Justice Training Center. The Other Chris leaned into his credenza, dug around until he pulled out a manual and paged through it. "Says here they're not. But who knows when this shit was published. There's a number here for the US NCB, which, Basic Agent Trainee Davis, Miami Field Division," he said taking the tone of an instructor, "stands for National Central Bureau. Our National Central Bureau is headquartered at the Department of Justice, Washington D.C., and is the primary point of contact with Interpol Headquarters in Lyon, France. Are there any questions?" He looked up at Davis.

"No, sir."

"Then let's give it a call! I've never talked to INTERPOL before. Could be cool." He picked up the phone and punched in the numbers.

"Hey there. I'm a DEA agent in Miami. I just wanted to know if Afghanistan is part of INTERPOL." He was silent for a second. "Okay, thanks." He hung up nodding his head. "Yep."

"How do we find out if they know something about the telephone number?"

The Other Chris frowned, picked up the phone again and hit the re-dial button. "Hey again, I think we just spoke. I've got a telephone number in Afghanistan that I want to see if anyone knows anything about. How would I do that?" He listened and then wrote something down. "Okay, thanks a lot." He hung up the phone. "We've got our own liaison. We just send him a message on Firebird[1] and he'll send it on to the Afghanistan National Central Bureau and then follow it up to make sure we get the info back. Slice of pie, man. Easy as cake. I'll send it out today."

"And you checked the number in NADDIS, right?"

"Yep."

"Hmmm."

"Hmmm indeed. Lunch?"

Davis brightened. "Excellent idea! When's the last time we treated ourselves and went to Miami Beach? Maybe News Café, you know, sit on the sidewalk, look at models walking up and down the sidewalk posing for us? I think we owe it to ourselves."

The Other Chris stood. "I do too. We've earned it."

The News Café on Ocean Drive was just what the doctor ordered. The agents sat outside under a huge green umbrella watching the beautiful people strut their stuff up and down the sidewalk, the women all dressed nearly-identically in short black skirts with an obligatory bottle of water poking out from their purses at the perfect, jaunty angle. Across the street and just out of sight beyond the grass park were the bright white sands and the deep blue of the Atlantic Ocean. The day was brilliant under a cloudless sky, the temperature perfect.

---

[1] DEA's proprietary, secure email system

"Hey," said Davis. "I heard from Nora. She said she's sorry about everything, wants to move back here and get together again."

"No shit? What did you tell her?" It had been a long time since the agents had talked about anything but work.

"Mmm, that I'd think about it."

"How'd she take it?" asked The Other Chris stuffing pasta into his mouth.

"Got pissed off. Told me to send all her stuff to her then hung up."

"Huh. Who'd'a thought that?"

"Yeah, no kidding. I should tell her I'll ship it to her and charge her *four* thousand dollars a kilo 'cause I'm sure she thinks her shit is more valuable than cocai-" Davis stopped mid-sentence, his thoughts suddenly far from Nora and the beach. Without knowing it, he started smiling.

The Other Chris looked up at him and saw him staring off into the middle distance. He turned in his seat to see what hot woman had caught his partner's eye, but the grass esplanade was empty at the moment, no girls in bikinis and roller blades going by, no women topless. "Dude, what *are* you looking at?"

Davis snapped his eyes back. "Heroin's more valuable than cocaine."

"Yes, Agent Davis, heroin is more valuable than cocaine. I now see why you graduated first in the class in academics."

"We could do it all over again with heroin."

"Brother, I have *no* idea what you're talking about."

"Pablo. In Colombia. We could do it all over again." He started talking quickly. "Look. He knows he's fucked, right? The AUSA says he's sure he'll get indicted up here. And we're going to extradite him. Remember when the Colombian government made that deal that if we wouldn't extradite drug dealers, then they'd stop bombing Bogotá?"

"Yeah, it was long time ago but we've been extraditing the dumb fucks for years."

"I know, and bombs have still been going off down there because nobody wants to do hard time up here; they'd rather stay in Colombia. What if we made a deal with Pablo? What if we told him we were willing to decline extradition and leave him to do his time down there if he cooperated with us and set up a transportation deal between us and his heroin supplier in Afghanistan?"

The Other Chris sat back, his head cocked to one side considering, and then focused on a point on the wall behind his partner. "It's not like he'd be rolling over on other Colombians."

"Nope."

"For that matter, no one would even have to know he cooperated. All it would take would be some phone calls"

"Yep."

"Man!"

Davis took a bite of his sandwich. "Think the AUSA would go for it?"

The Other Chris' voice went deep serious. "He's overworked. He's underpaid. We'd be helping *him* out. *We'd* be saving *him* a trip to DC and hanging out at main Justice doing extradition paperwork. Think Ricky would go for it?"

Davis shrugged his shoulders. "We gave him powder on the table." He drank from his glass. "We gave him a thousand *pounds* of powder on the table! We're seizing a house and two cars. We got a stat for the arrest in Colombia and that stat's good whether he's incarcerated here or there. If he doesn't go along with it, that's the end of the heroin, and that's huge! If he says yes, maybe we can get some *more* powder. That's all he really wants to keep the ASAC happy. And even though he doesn't push it too hard, he's

130

probably beating off every night thinking about the Afghan connection and more heroin. Fuck, *I'm* beating off every night thinking about it. What do I need Nora for?"

"Wow," said The Other Chris. "I like it." He raised his sunglasses. "I mean, not you whacking off, but the other thing. To tell the truth, I think the wife's getting pissed off because *I've* been beating off every night thinking about it."

The Chrises broke up with laughter.

Back at the office, The Chrises presented the idea to Ricardo who immediately gave it a thumbs up, on the condition the AUSA approved taking a pass on extradition, then ran to discuss it with the ASAC.

"Think he's going to take credit for coming up with this idea?" asked Davis.

"Duh," smirked The Other Chris.

The Chrises and Ricardo, wearing suits, sat in Herrick's downtown office of the Federal Courthouse. Behind Herrick's desk, the sunny skyline stretched out past the Port of Miami with its massive white cruise ships and thousands of orange and blue shipping containers. On the other side of the Government Cut Waterway sat Miami Beach and the Atlantic.

The gray-carpeted floor was labyrinth'd with brown cartons filled, some to overflowing, with files for different court cases assigned to him. He sat back in his high-backed leather chair, plucked his big round glasses off his nose and put them up in his hair and, after some consideration, said, "Hmmm."

The three DEA agents said nothing.

He sat forward. "I'm going to indict him anyway; that gives you a lot more leverage to break him down if we decide to decline the extradition, so one of you guys is still going to have to do the grand jury." He looked at The

131

Other Chris and pointed with his pen, "It's you, right?" The Other Chris nodded. "Good, okay, and listen, I was talking to one of the other attorneys this morning at our department meeting, and he came up with an idea I was researching, actually, just before you guys showed up.

"It's kind of a stretch, but...I read the DEA-6 from the agent in Afghanistan...um...Pedro Something, I think. Anyway, the bad guys tried to shoot it out with our military, which makes them enemy combatants; whether they were running drugs or guns or milk doesn't really matter. In fact, while there are some technicalities to the law here, at the end of the day, someone who dukes it out with our guys in uniform in Afghanistan is classified as a "terrorist."

"Now, the drugs they were transporting, or at least some from that same batch, wound up in Pablo Herrera's hands, he marked them and sent them to Miami via you. Obviously when the drugs were sold on the street, he was going to get paid and would pay back his supplier in Afghanistan, a guy who was employing terrorists.

"So I'm going to throw the library at this guy and charge him with CCE[1] for the drugs, RICO[2] for everything else, distribution[3] *and*," he paused, rubbing his hands together like a little kid at Christmas, "because he was paying, and therefore in a conspiracy, to employ terrorists through a third party in Afghanistan, I'm going to indict his ass under Title 18 for providing material support to terrorist organizations, financing terrorism and *acts* of terrorism. In fact, the way the law reads," he moved some papers around on his desk until he found what he was looking for, "'whoever violates this section,' this is USC 18 2332b, 'whoever violates this section shall be punished for a killing, or if death results to any person from any other conduct prohibited by this section, by imprisonment for any term of years or for life or

---

[1] Continuing Criminal Enterprise, Title 21 USC, 848
[2] Racketeer Influenced and Corrupt Organizations, Title 18 USC, 1961
[3] Title 21 USC, 841

by death.'" He looked up. "Those three Afghanis that got killed by the SEALS? Herrera's part in this conspiracy links *him* to those guys getting dead. And that's the death penalty, baby!" He had a big grin on his face. "You think *that*'ll be enough to get him to pony up and cooperate?"

The agents broke into smiles.

Herrick started laughing. "That's right, boys," he pointed at them. "Who's yo' daddy now?"

470 kilograms of cocaine!

John Herrick and Chris Davis celebrating the case.

CHAPTER SEVEN

Afghanistan-Pakistan Border

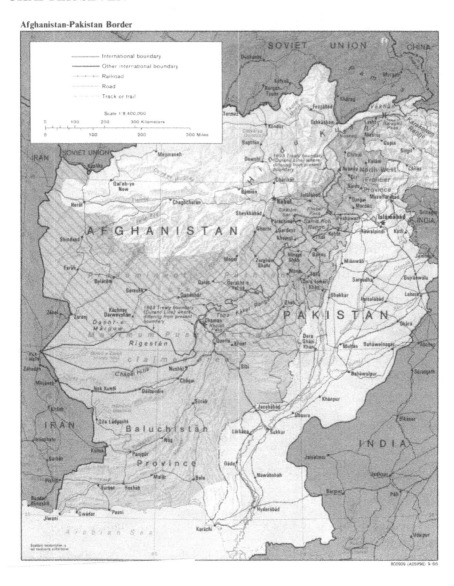

I had just finished lighting the shit on fire when I got a message I wasn't expecting.

After parking the Toyota Hi-Lux pickup we use, I walk towards the shower tent and hear the Master Chief shout my name. I look up and see a flashlight waving from The Alamo. I wash my hands and head that way. By the time I arrive, he's already downstairs and Big Mike is with him. He motions me with his head into the TOC tent.

We all sit on gray metal folding chairs. "You have a brother named Christopher?"

I nod, instantly alert. Not that there is any reason for him not to know about my family, but equally there is no reason *for* him to.

"Is he a DEA agent?" I nod again.

He glances at Big Mike before continuing. "Okay, then. About one o'clock this morning, a DEA King Air crashed south of the Pak / Afghan border. Your mother was notified by the DEA in Florida, she called the emergency number you gave her, and my boss contacted the client who sent a message here and Big Mike just got it. We're getting a link going right now with Bagram and the embassies in Kabul and Islamabad to find out the SAR[1] plan..."

Just then, the physician's assistant comes through the tent curtain with some papers and hands them to Big Mike who scans and paraphrases them for me: "We're starting to get the info now that we're addressed in on the message traffic: There's an ELT[2] that's been going off since the crash. A personal locator beacon fired off about an hour after the crash for a couple of minutes then went off the air; DEA says their pilots are issued PLBs. The SARSAT[3] downloaded the position of the PLB south of the crash site. There's some time lag between the SARSAT getting the information to DEA and from there to Bagram, but someone above our paygrade's working on that. Everyone is shuffling the UAV tasking orders trying to get one on a priority basis. Your brother, two DEA pilots, and one of our guys were onboard." He looks up at me. "That's what we've got as of this minute."

---

[1] Search and Rescue
[2] Emergency Locator Transmitter
[3] Search And Rescue Satellite Aided Tracking, a worldwide system monitored by the US National Oceanographic and Atmospheric Administration

136

The bottom drops out of my stomach and I feel like I'm pinned to the chair. I'm absolutely unable to move or do anything but look at the Master Chief as Big Mike and Doc walk out of the tent.

MC slaps my knee. "I think the first thing you should do is call your mom and let her know you've got the message, but don't say anything more than that. I'm going back to The Alamo and see what's what." He scratches his big bald head, then gets up and leaves me alone. My stomach is twisting and I'm breathing fast, close to panic, and still haven't moved since the end of the briefing. I'm so terrified I think I'm going to vomit.

I push the off button on the phone, put it back on the plywood table and wipe my eyes. Listening to my mom's tear-filled voice has, for the moment, freaked me out more than what's happened to Little Brother. I bump the chair over to one of the dusty computers, sign on, and send a brief message to Big Brother, letting him know I know. There are a bunch of messages from everyone else, but I don't feel like reading them since I know what they say.

I look around the tent and realize I have nothing to do. I get up and walk to The Alamo. I don't pass anyone on the way but I'm sure the news will be spreading fast.

Inside, MC and Big Mike are sitting on the couch with a map of Pakistan on the coffee table in front of them. Big Mike motions me over. I kneel on the floor opposite them, feeling and ignoring the stiffness in my knee.

He's pointing to a circle drawn in red ink. "This is the crash site where the ELT is still going off." Near the red circle is a black X. "And this is where the locator beacon went off." He looks up at me. "You can see it's pretty treacherous terrain right at the crash site but smoothes out here. If whoever's moving can get this far, they'll be able to make some good distance."

"What about a rescue mission?" I ask. I don't have to ask if they're in Indian Territory. I know they are, and since they may be moving south, they obviously know it too.

"I'm sure it's being discussed right now."

I look back and forth between Big Mike and the Master Chief. "By who?"

"Whom," replies the Master Chief. "Everyone above our pay grade," he says in a very calm voice. "Look, I know you're a little fucked up right now, but these things have a procedure and that procedure takes time. As of this minute, we don't even know where they are but we're going to find out. When we do, someone's going to determine who's in the best position to go get 'em. "

Big Mike slides the map out of the way and puts down his cup. "As for us, our helo's is in the middle of an inspection cycle. Don says there's parts all over the hangar, but he's going to try to get it put back together as quick as he can and, as soon as it's flyable, we're going to get it in the air and on the way to the crash site. He says he's looking at a day, maybe two but he'll keep us advised.

"My next guess is Bagram. They've got more assets up there for something like this than the rest of the world, but you need to chill a little and let this thing work out, okay?"

I look back at them hard and nod. He is right. There's nothing to do right now and at least I'm inside The Alamo listening first hand to what is happening.

"How's the family taking it?" asks the Master Chief.

I shake my head. "Mom's a mess. The kids are all on their way to Tampa to help out."

"Okay, then let's put that on the shelf now and keep focused on other stuff. I'm sure we're going to be getting more info as the day progresses. You want to go get some rest or hang out here?"

I make a finger motion at the floor like I'm shooting a gun, dropping my thumb like the hammer of a pistol.

Obviously something in what I had done triggers a memory in the Master Chief's head. He sits quietly for a second with his head tilted to the side then snaps his finger at me. "You," he says, in a vaguely accusatorial way. "*You* were in DEA, weren't you?" He taps the tip of his nose. "Because you know Pete Swicker[1]? We talked about this when you first got here when you were wearing that frickin' DEA baseball cap, the one I said I wanted which, by the way, you still haven't given me," he continues, half-aloud, half to himself. I nod at him. "You still know people there?" I nod again. He glances at Big Mike. "Dang, this could give us some home-court advantage."

"Absolutely right it could. Andy!" shouts Big Mike. The door to the communication room opens and the little fellow pokes his head out. "I need the government directory." The head pulls back like a turtle's into its shell and a few moments later, a thick phone book comes flying out as the door closes again. I catch it with one hand and put it on the table.

"Look," says Big Mike to me. "Right now you know exactly what we know, but we could stand to know a lot more. I need you to get on a phone and start calling people you know or people that'll help out. Find out anything you can: names of everyone onboard, if they were carrying guns, first aid kits, extra water, survival radios, MREs, anything else that might keep them alive for a while -"

---

[1] Resident Agent in Charge Peter Swicker was the president of my DEA Basic Agent Class who early in his career was involved in a shooting where he defended his life and the lives of other agents. He and Master Chief Davis became friends at Gunsite, a shooting school in Arizona.

The Master Chief cuts in. "And see if you can find out the background of the pilots, if any of them had survival training or SERE." SERE stands for Survival, Evasion, Resistance and Escape and is the military's advanced training program that would, in this case, be a huge benefit for the crew until they can be rescued. Students are taught to live off the land, build shelters, and find water all while evading enemy forces and, should the worst-case scenario happen where they were taken prisoner, how to resist torture. I don't really consider it, but in this part of the world there is no resisting torture because these bad guys don't want information. They just want a video camera, a sharp knife and a head.

"If there's a mechanic," says Big Mike, "find out about the overall mechanical condition of the plane. This isn't an accident investigation but we could stand to know what their mission was. If it was a low level, they might have been shot down, or they might have just been flying from A to B and it's something mechanical. See if he knows what they were wearing and is there anything else that might help a recon see them."

I stand, grunting as I kick my leg straight. "I'll get on it."

"Hang on a sec," continues Big Mike. "We've got a STU III if you need one, depending on who you're talking to. Andy!" The head pops out again. "I need the number for the Air Ops guys in Kabul." He turns back to me. "Our guys have a mechanic and he probably knows the DEA mechanic. Those guys are sometimes hard to track down but our guy'll help."

"Okay."

"Listen, when you talk to our Air Ops, use my name and they'll give you what you need. If you're talking to the embassy in Kabul, tell 'em you're calling from the green building. If you have to talk to anyone at Bagram, tell 'em you're Task Force Sixty-Five. Andy!" The door opens and Andy holds out a piece of paper I retrieve. "He's going to need the number to the ops center at Bagram too." Andy nods and disappears. "Those numbers change all the time, but hopefully we've got the current ones. And if you talk to anyone in the US, like your command post or whatever you call it, tell them you're Langley. If we hear anything more, we'll come get you. Can you remember all that?"

"I got it." I say as I turn. When I pass the communications door, it opens and another piece of paper comes my way.

I work the satellite phone in the TOC with an investigative intensity I forgot I possess. Almost everyone I talk to is exceptionally helpful. I only have to resort to the STU III once, when I am talking to the DEA Command Center in Washington, but once we're secure they also give me everything I need. Some of the information is surprising, some isn't, and some has me shaking my head with 20 / 20 hindsight. I take notes on everything I find out and walk back to The Alamo; the sun's just crested the hills to the east and it's already hot. I've been gone for about an hour. Big Mike and MC are still on the couch, though they've changed places.

"Anything new?" I ask.

Big Mike fills me in. "There's a Predator parked on top of the King Air now. We're getting the feed beamed in to us out at the hangar. You can head out there when we're done here if you want. The plane's in pretty bad shape but it wasn't shot down, that's for sure. The fuselage is as intact as you'd expect it to be after a crash but no obvious explosive damage. The left wing is gone but it's near the crash site. Looks to me like it broke on impact.

"There's no bodies around the crash site, which could be either good news or bad. Someone obviously got out because the locator beacon was activated away from the site, but that could be one guy or four.

"There's a village about three kilometers south of the crash, and I just got a call that there's a body walking in the direction of the plane." He passes me a cup of coffee. "What've you got?"

141

"The pilots' names are Colin McNease and Bill Dwyer. I know 'em both. Colin was a Marine -"

"Oo-Rah," says Big Mike quietly. He shakes his head as he corrects me, "Once a Marine, *always* a Marine."

I nod and continue, "He was a Harrier pilot so he did SERE for sure. Bill Dwyer's ex-Army. I'm pretty sure he was a Ranger or something like that."

"Dang," says the Master Chief quietly. "We scored with those guys! If they're alive, they're going to know how to handle themselves. Was your brother in the military?" I shake my head. "Okay, well, those guys'll take care of him."

I continue. "The mechanic said that the plane was fine, but they had just gotten approval to use a new fuel. This was their first flight with that in the tanks. They were flying from Kabul to Karachi, and he said maybe it was fuel contamination. I tried to get more on your guy, but no one I talked to would give me anything."

Big Mike nods. "Yeah, we're kinda like that. I've got his info."

"Okay. The mechanic said that both guys were wearing khaki cargo pants and polo shirts but he can't remember what color. He doesn't remember what Chris or your guy had on. He said there's an M-16 in the plane but he doesn't know how much ammunition, and there's also a big backpack that the pilots made up but he doesn't know what's in it. There's a standard first aid kit with bandages and aspirin and stuff that goes with the plane, a few boxes of MREs, and some water bottles. Both pilots are issued 9 mils[1] and should have a couple of magazines. My brother was TDY[2] in Kabul so I don't know if he'd have a gun or not.

---

[1] millimeter
[2] Temporary Duty

"The DEA Airwing says that the pilots are all issued military survival vests with radios that can transmit and receive on VHF and UHF guard[1] but again, the mechanic doesn't know if they had them in the plane." I look up from my notes.

Big Mike starts. "My guy should have a pistol and a couple of magazines for sure. So that's one rifle and three handguns and a couple of magazines...maybe more but probably not a *whole* lot more. If they get into any shit it's not gonna last long." He looks at the Master Chief. "Can you think of anything more before I get Andy to upload this to the world?"

The Master Chief shakes his head. "I'm gonna run Meat out to the hangar and let him see the video feed."

We ride out to the hangar in one of the Toyota trucks, bumping our way along a track of hard, rough ground. As we pass Security Post One the guard up there tosses a handful of rocks down on the top of our truck. The Master Chief waves up through the open window.

At the hangar, the mechanic limps past the truck towards his tent. We walk into the huge cloth-covered hangar and take a right entering a small, air-conditioned room with a computer monitor on a table. One of the pilots is sitting in a folding metal chair with a magazine on his lap. He glances up, and I sit down next to him.

The picture I'm looking at is black and white, though the colors are inverted, like a negative. It is obviously being taken with an IR[2] camera. "What am I looking at?" I ask him.

He points to the screen. "Well, here's the fuselage, this is a part of the wing, and this is what's left of the tail assembly. You can see this area here is torn away, but I don't see any evidence of fire."

---

[1] 121.5 VHF and 243.0 UHF emergency frequencies continuously monitored or "guarded" by military and civilian aircraft, ships and satellites
[2] Infrared

I try not to shudder thinking about my brother and guys I know riding that in. I point at some white stuff on the ground leading away from the plane, parallel to the way it had skipped in.

"Can you tell me the compass orientation of that picture?" I ask the pilot.

He looks at a bunch of numbers scrolling across the bottom of the screen. "North's up."

"So south's at the bottom?"

He looks at me like I'm an idiot. "Yes, north's at the top, south's at the bottom." He's right, I'm an idiot.

"What's this stuff here?" I ask him.

"Looks like wreckage but it's tough to tell with this image. This is just a passive feed of what the rear site is looking at, so we can't change it or zoom in."

"But that line of scraps is leading from the plane south, right?"

"I'd say so, yeah. Why?"

"They picked up a handheld locator beacon south of the crash. I'm wondering if that line is also a ground signal that they're heading south." I look up at the Master Chief.

"Print some pictures of that, would you?" he grumbles at the pilot who reaches over to a mouse and makes a couple of clicks. A printer comes to life and the views we're seeing on the screen come scrolling out. The Master Chief takes them from the pilot. "Thanks. Where's that body you saw walking to the plane?"

"He's inside the wreckage."

"Keep an eye on it. When he comes out, give us a yell at The Alamo and see if you can see if he carries anything with him. Let's go, Meat."

When we get back to The Alamo, the Master Chief passes on what we saw and gives Big Mike the pictures. We stand in the living room for a

144

minute, no one saying anything more. I turn and leave, figuring I'll call Jeff first and then try to get some sleep. I know they'll call me if something new comes up.

Jeff answers the call on the first ring. "CAG." The connection is crystal clear. It's hard to believe I'm calling over a satellite phone from the desert in Pakistan to Norfolk, Virginia, the signal then bouncing off another satellite all the way back to his office on the ship.

"Hey, it's me."

"How're you doing?" he asks, his voice very tense.

"Same as you. You talk to Mom?"

"Yeah, she's pretty upset. Dad's on his way and so are the girls."

"You gonna head back?"

"No way. I figure I'm in a better spot here if I can help. What about you?"

"Same. Where are you?"

"Just off the coast."

"Off my coast?" I had no idea he is so close.

"A-firm."

I sit and think for a minute. "I saw the plane. It's pretty bad."

He is silent at his end, I'm sure thinking the same things I am.

I don't know what else to talk about. "I'm gonna run. If I hear anything, I'll call you. You've got my numbers here too, right?" He says he does and we both hang up. There just isn't anything more to say at this point.

Special Agent Pete Swicker.

The author, "back in the day."

CHAPTER EIGHT

"So what's the grand jury like?" Davis asked his partner.

The two were sitting at the food court in the International Mall, not far from where Serrano had been busted. "Pretty casual," he said, shoveling a huge forkful of Bourbon Chicken and rice into his mouth. "They were all sitting in school chairs and I felt like the teacher in the front of the classroom. John asked me a bunch of questions about the case, and Herrera, and the Afghanistan stuff. The jury ate *that* shit up, though, much more than the coke stuff and Colombia. When he asked me about the gun battle and the three dead terrorists, I thought the guys were going to cum." He started laughing.

"He say how long before we hear back if they're going to indict?"

"Said it shouldn't be -" His cell phone rang. He glanced at the number and nodded. "Hello. Okay, cool, thanks John. I'll tell the boss and get back to you." He closed the phone. "All counts, dude." He raised his hand, palm forward, and was rewarded with a high five. "Guess this means going back to Bogotá. Unless you want to go this time. I don't mind. I've seen it."

Chris nodded. "If the boss says yeah, I'll go. Something different."

"And it's not like you got a woman to bitch about you being out of town," he joked.

"I just got off the phone with the AUSA," said Ricardo. "Good job on the grand jury, first of all." The Other Chris nodded. "He says he wants to get down there to meet Herrera and give him the good news about the death penalty to his face. You'll be going with him of course. We'll need him to call his partner in Afghanistan and set up another deal and make sure the phone's still active and then go from there."

"Do you mind if he goes?" The Other Chris pointed at Davis. "We were talking about it, and I've already been there once…"

The GS shook his head. "No, I want you to go. You've already met him and you *do* speak a little Spanish, more than your brother. Plus, you've met the guys in the office down there and know who to go to for what." He looked at Davis. "Sorry."

Chris Davis shrugged.

Back to The Other Chris. "You'll make sure you take a recorder with you too, right?"

"Right."

"If this sets up right and the number still works and he makes contact, we'll call the Country Office in Kabul and see if they can run down the number, if they have that capacity. Who knows what police services are like there. From watching the news, I wouldn't think it would be all that efficient, but then you never know."

"Man," said The Other Chris over the phone. "I wish you could've been here when John lowered the boom. When Herrera's lawyer was translating the part about *terroristas* and *pena de muerte,* which is the death penalty, I thought he'd literally explode right there in the room and splash me with blood and guts. His hands shot up and he started screaming, 'No, no, no!' and that it was all *mierda* and that we were making it up to get him to cooperate. His lawyer read him the whole indictment and he started screaming again about Afghanistan and I don't know this, and I don't know that, and that the *telefono no es mio* and we'd planted the number on it, and that he didn't even know it existed. It was a fucking riot watching his guy *habla* the 'I don't knows.'

"His lawyer was sweating it big time too, I'm sure thinking that if he fucked up the defense, he'd wind up hanging from a tree by his own tongue or something. Anyway, John told him we were working on extradition and because of the terrorist angle, he'd be pressing for Herrera to wait for his death sentence at Guantanamo with the rest of the terrorists. I've never seen anyone's face go so white so fast. That dude was terrified about being a terrorist." The Other Chris was laughing as he was telling the story. "John was loving the shit out of it too, you could just tell. He was laying it out and they were just lapping it up. Totally awesome, man."

"So what was the final outcome?"

"Well after all the yelling and shit were finished, Herrera asked what he could do to make any of this go away. John told him what we wanted and I think he'd've sucked our cocks if we'd've whipped 'em out, he was that desperate. Anyway, we got to talking about the Afghanistan angle and he admitted he knew the guy there that had shipped him the heroin. He kept saying he didn't know anything about anyone shooting at Americans though, or using the money for terrorism.

"He said the guy's Afghan but he's never met him, just talked to him over the phone and that he got the number from some guy. Whatever. He said he'd make a call to the guy and see if he could set up another deal like the last one. He says he didn't talk to the guy after the deal went bust in Miami so everything should still be cool."

"Did he say how long the deal took from putting in the order to delivery?"

"About six months and that it came by ship which is right on track with the other report. I asked him if he thought he could sell the guy on a faster transport method than donkeys and ships, if the guy would go for it, and he said he thought he might be able to tell him like, 'Hey, I got your heroin, it's great shit, but if you've got people who need it faster than coming in on some slow boat from China, I know these guys, maybe in the military, who can smuggle it out of the country on Air Force planes or something.' The guy was very cooperative once he put his mind to it."

"So did he make the call?"

"Not yet. Me and John are taking a break for lunch right now, going to some restaurant at the mall with the guys from the office. We wanted to get the story straight before he makes the call and fucks it up somehow. And the guys here are going to go after him when *we're* done with him about the military base that our plane flew into. Their vetted guys are working with the

150

Colombian Air Force's version of OPR[1] and some special unit in the Public Prosecutor's office that handles government corruption. This guy's going to be a pin cushion when everyone gets done fucking him, but hey, don't do the crime if you can't do the time, right?"

"You think you'll make the call today?"

"Definitely! Probably right after lunch. We told him we'd be right back."

"Dude, this is excellent. That was great thinking about using the military to transport the dope."

"Thanks man, I *am* an international drug agent, you know. I'll call you after he makes the call. *Adios.* "

"Hola. "

It was almost 7 PM but Chris had been waiting in the office to hear from his partner.

"How'd it go?"

"Fucking clockwork, man. He made the call on his phone from the interview room here and we got a great recording."

"So tell me."

"Well it was just like we talked about. Herrera was really good, told him that he knows a guy stationed over there that works on planes and has a way to get anything he wants onto a plane, hidden in the airplane where it couldn't be searched, and could take any amount the guy wants, and the guy, who's name's Samadi, hung up and then called us right back. He asked if we could move a thousand boxes, you know, and Herrera said his people could, no problem." The Other Chris said, his voice rising, "A thousand kilos of heroin!

---

[1]Office of Professional Responsibility, the DEA's internal affairs division

"Herrera told him that he'd want six thousand US per key for his transportation fee, and he'd give Samadi the same deal *he* had given *him* so Samadi's going to pay a quarter up front, which is like one point five million dollars, and they're just going to subtract the money that Herrera owes him for the two keys on the back side. This deal is financing itself! Samadi called him back again and told him that was cool, *no hay problema*, and that he'd call him back when he was good to go."

"How's he supposed to pay him from Afghanistan?"

"When Herrera fronted the money, he did it by wire transfer so unless we tell 'em otherwise, they'd probably stick with that. We've got the account info he used."

"Goddamn, man, this is awesome!"

"Yes indeedy, my friend. Is Ricky there?"

Davis laughed. "Of course not."

"Well, anyway, John's headed back there tomorrow, and I think I'm going to stay here, at least till I talk to the boss, see what he wants done and how we're going to pull this thing off, but if nothing else, we've got a line on the telephone."

"Cool, man, cool. I'll yell at you tomorrow."

"Wait a second," called his partner. "Anything new from Nora?"

"Nora Snore-a." He laughed. "Wait...Nora's a bore-a...I love it. Loving her was such a chore-a. Poor-a Nora. Oh my God, I'm on a roll! No more-a Nora, she's out the door-a. I kill myself!"

"Okay dude, you're off the deep end. *Ciao.*"

"Besides, I'm in love with that girl's voice from SOUTHCOM."

"Whatever."

Chris Davis and Ricardo sat at the boss' desk on speakerphone with The Other Chris in Colombia. The ASAC stood in the doorway, his arms

152

folded, listening, watching through Ricardo's window as the day drew to a close.

The morning had started off with Davis briefing Ricardo, who briefed the ASAC, who briefed the Associate SAC along with the SAC who, with visions of one thousand kilograms of heroin dancing in his head, initiated various secure PHONECONs[1] with the RAC of the Country Office in Kabul and DEA's Chief of Operations, who had been joined by the individual chiefs for the Special Operations Division, the Office of Special Intelligence, and the Office of Enforcement Operations. They had, in turn, had their own secure PHONECONs with counterparts in Langley who talked to *their* counterparts at CENTCOM[2] in Qatar.

Davis was pretty stunned by the bee's nest their case had stirred up and the speed with which things could really happen when the big boys were involved. He was also very aware how fast his name would turn to mud if the wheels came off the wagon.

Before the call currently being made, Ricardo had taken Chris aside, closed the door, and told him in no uncertain terms how lucky he was the case hadn't been totally yanked out of his hands and turned over to very senior agents operating out of headquarters where the Administrator could get his fingers into the pie at every level. On the other hand, the Administrator had delegated his fingers down to the SAC in Miami who had ordered Group 31's other cases (of which there were none) be put on hold, all the agents assigned full-time to The Two Chrises, and a back-up GS assigned to the group, effective immediately. As Mau had been critical to the success of Phase I (Herrera), and was a senior GS-13, he was seconded to Group 31 for Phase II.

Phase II, when The Other Chris had gone to Colombia, was little more than a nebulous fishing expedition to see if the telephone number in Kabul was operational, record a few phone calls with the Samadi, see if the

---

[1] Phone Conversation
[2] United States Central Command

Kabul Country Office was interested in doing some further investigation, and maybe, though unlikely, let them set something up on their own time. Now, however, it had firmly developed into the following:

1. Identify Herrera's bank account and track any wire transfers.
2. Flag any further deposits to the accounts involved.
3. Identify the trafficker(s) in Kabul.
4. Localize the trafficker(s) and if possible initiate surveillance.
5. Initiate contact with the trafficker(s), negotiate, and take possession of heroin.
6. Effect arrest and initiate extradition.

Tracking the money was outside Group 31's expertise and was being delegated to one of several money-laundering groups who would send agents to Colombia when the time came.

Identifying the trafficker(s) was going to take a little longer. Samadi's telephone number had been passed to an agent at the El Paso Intelligence Center (EPIC) where it would be entered into different proprietary computer systems belonging to the Justice Department, Homeland Security, and the Treasury Department as well as various intelligence agencies operating there. It was also passed to INTERPOL and given to the DEA's CIA liaison in Miami.

As the CIA was now fully read into the script, Davis was told they would be using "every available means" to pick up the number in Afghanistan. Chris was not told what every available means meant but figured it was going to be pretty high-tech. He found himself laughing to himself at everything that was happening.

The script had also been refined in terms of what The Other Chris was going to require of Herrera. Herrera would be sending his representative

(Mau) to Kabul to negotiate directly with Samadi under the guise that paying for two kilos of heroin up front was a lot different than taking possession of a thousand kilos, and a deal of this size should be done face-to-face. Herrera would want to protect his transport method by having Mau test the quality and quantity of heroin in Samadi's presence before shipment so the receivers couldn't scream they had been ripped off. Mau would also ensure the money was deposited before letting the deal go through.

If Samadi for some reason wanted or needed to meet the transporter, then US Air Force Intelligence could readily supply a loadmaster or airframe technician to explain the details of how the heroin was to be secreted in a suitable military airplane and would even supply a suitable military airplane if necessary.

In order to facilitate communications between Herrera and Samadi until Mau could step in and take over the phone calls, Herrera had been transferred from the general population at the local jail to a special holding cell belonging to SIJIN, the intelligence unit of the Colombian Judicial Police. He would remain there until the conclusion of Phase II, and probably longer since the SIJIN had been told of his connection with the military base and payoffs of air traffic controllers and would definitely be joining in that investigation.

Arrangements were also being made for Mau to travel to Afghanistan when the time came, and as Chris Davis was the co-case agent and didn't get the opportunity to go to Colombia, he would accompany Mau as a bonus for Phase I. He was pretty excited about getting to go but was sure his mom wouldn't be too happy about him heading to a war zone.

CHAPTER NINE

I'm sitting in the dusty TOC, just signing off the email and putting my head down on the wood table when MC walks in, turns a metal chair around and sits down.

"What's the first thing I said to you the day you got here?" he asks pulling at his long white eyebrows.

I think about it for a second. "'What's with the ear ring, champ?'" I offer.

He laughs aloud, a single half-bark. "Okay, what's the second thing I said to you?"

"You said, 'Keep my weapons clean, do my job in a military manner, and no complaining.'"

He nods. "That's right. I'm going to amend part of that and give you one chance to complain." He shifts around in the chair. "Big Mike has been talking with CENTCOM. Basically it boils down to this: the military cannot launch a rescue mission."

"What?" I say already standing.

"Just listen. The problem we're having, the reason why we're here in the first place, is that we are not at war with Pakistan and our military has no authority or jurisdiction to enter the country without permission from the Pakistani government. If our military comes in without their permission, even on a rescue mission, it's an invasion. CENTCOM is requesting permission through the embassy in Islamabad to allow a SAR insertion. They'll keep us advised but weren't given a time line."

"But -"

"I said listen!" he snaps at me. "So sit the fuck down and shut the fuck up," he growls. For just a moment I'm back to being a wet-behind-the-ears Navy Ensign listening to a senior, grizzled old Master Chief who knows a whole lot more about everything than I ever would. I sit back down, close my mouth, and cross my arms.

"Now, we've still got some options, and me and Big Mike have been going over them, making some calls and seeing what we could do. But you've got to understand that this is White House level and that means

157

politics and that can always frick up a wet dream and there could be stuff already happening that we don't know about. But that's beyond us so let's stick with the things we know. Military use of force is out. We had to sit through a legal briefing over the phone by some dickhead that told us what they couldn't do and why they couldn't do it. Man, those frickin' lawyers make my ass itch. Anyway, what it boils down to is Pakistan's a friendly sovereign nation… the military just can't come blasting in.

"Now, the Pakistani military and police know about the crash since they would have been notified by Air Traffic Control. We haven't passed on the ID of the guys - the client's really skittish about anyone finding out one of their guys is in harm's way. Unfortunately, there's no military or police garrisoned in the area where the plane went down, and there's about zero chance they'll be able to get to the site for a while. I'm going to go out on a limb and say this is a pretty low priority for them.

"The ISI *does* have assets in the area, and we're definitely *not* telling *them*. There's lots of evidence they've been actively assisting the Taliban, and if they get wind of this, they might call the bad guys and get them searching. If they find out about it from the military, then that's shitty but *we're* not going to let 'em know.

"Also we've confirmed that they weren't using a tactical callsign so their flight plan would just have them as a US registered plane, not an embassy plane, which is also keeping the client happy. The pilots may have had something arranged for a Custom's exclusion in Karachi, but we're hoping by the time the Pakis get all that figured out, they'll be saved and no one'll be the wiser. Now…"

There is a high-pitched, panicked shout for help from somewhere outside the tent. We both get up, fast-walk out, and see some of the guys running towards the freezer unit that keeps our perishable food safe. There are about six guys standing there, and as we come up, we see they're laughing and pointing, and someone's calling for a camera.

I look past the gang and see Guinness, in a pair of shorts and a t-shirt, hanging nearly upside down wrapped in the concertina wire, the razor-sharp ribbons that coil around our camp. He's begging for help, his clothes are torn and there are small spots of blood where the sharp edges are piercing his skin and holding him immobile.

"What the fuck?" booms the Master Chief.

Grease, a tough New Yorker turns to him. He's laughing so hard he can barely talk. "We bet him a whole dollar he couldn't jump over the wire."

MC grabs me by my shoulder and aims me back towards the TOC. "What a dickhead," he mutters under his breath. We leave them to sort out that problem, but I'm smiling. It was a much-needed break in tension.

Sitting back in the TOC, he continues. "Okay, now, the military and the ISI, that's all big picture stuff and it's out of our control, so we're gonna focus on the small picture stuff. What our military *can* do is provide equipment and information. Big Mike's on the phone right now talking to his people getting things organized. We're already getting the intelligence they have and Big Mike's asking for a helicopter. If we get one, we're going to cram as many shooters into it as we can and go get your brother and the rest. If ours comes up in the meantime, like Big Mike said, we'll figure out a plan and launch immediately."

He looks at me.

I look back at him.

"Well?" he asks.

"You done?"

He nods. He twirls his moustache.

"I want to go if we find them."

"Can't think of anyone more motivated. What else?"

159

"Can I still complain?"

He smiles and looks at his watch. "You've got thirty seconds. Go."

"This sucks about the military. Bunch'a homos."

He waits for more then looks up at me. "That it?"

I shrug. "Sorry. You haven't let me complain about anything for two months. I'm out of practice."

CHAPTER TEN

If Chris Davis were to give his first impression of Afghanistan a Native-American name, it would have been Mayhem-In-A-Foreign-Language-Smoking-Cigarettes. The terminal was noisy, crowded, stank of smoke and body odor, and could have either pre-dated the Russian invasion or been built yesterday.

He and Mau had flown from Miami to New York on American Airlines and then, to their as-yet-unknown joy, on something called Emirates Airlines for their stopover in Dubai. Because of seating issues, both had wound up in first class in their own separate suites fully equipped with desk, lamp, television, and a seat that stretched into a fully flat bed. On top of that was the opportunity to have a *shower* (!) before landing, caviar, lobster, steak, cheesecake, and real-glass glasses of Dom Perignon champagne, all served by the most beautiful, young, genuinely friendly flight attendants either of them had ever encountered. Mau remarked his family would miss him because he was going to spend the rest of his life living in Emirates First Class. It was a rough contrast with the typical service they received on the way to New York or on the next leg of their journey on the most beat-up, decrepit, rattle-trap plane for the flight to Kabul. Chris pointed out duct tape that was holding part of the ceiling together. Mau remarked to Chris it was possible they might not get a chance to die in a war zone, that the flight might do them in before they even landed.

On the approach to landing in Kabul, Chris was stunned by the jagged gray peaks guarding the city. It was like flying into western Colorado or the mouth of a shark. These mountains looked forbiddingly desolate, more unforgiving than anywhere in his experience.

Before leaving Miami they had received a security briefing from an Army Special Forces soldier just returned from Kabul who had been invited to the DEA Division offices. All the agents from Group 31 were invited to sit in, and most took part as it was an interesting change in their day.

Part of their brief had been that taxis were *verboten* and someone from the embassy should meet them at the airport. For security he shouldn't be carrying a sign with their names on it, just a number, maybe with a 305[1] prefix on it for the agents' recognition. Chris was curious why they *shouldn't* use their names on the sign, and the soldier asked, "What's your last name?"

"Davis."

How would they like it, he inquired, if some random bad guy was at the airport waiting to ambush someone named Davis, and did they want to take the chance on getting whacked in a case of mistaken identity? It was good tradecraft, something neither agent had ever considered, and a real reminder they were heading into a place less friendly than any of Miami's worst ghettos.

---

[1]Miami area code

"You'll see a bunch of military in the terminal, ours and everybody else's. In the event your guy isn't there when he's supposed to be, I recommend you make good friends with them while you wait for your ride. Tell 'em who you are and ask them, and I emphasize *ask*, if you can stand with them. When you approach them, realize that they're a little edgy because they're stuck inside a soft target structure with lots of armed civilians. Be nice and calm and quiet. Don't go flashing your badges or whatever it is you've got and think they're going to jump for you. You're in their sandbox, right?"

They were also told once collected, they should spend as little time "in the open" as possible getting from the terminal into their car to minimize their time as a target in the event bad guys recognized them as Westerners and zipped 'em on general principle.

They were shown a map of the city. "The airport's here, east of the city. It anchors one end of the main road and the embassy is down at the other end, so should you come under fire or find your vehicle disabled, depending where you are on the main road, go forward to the embassy or backward to the airport. I strongly advise you to stay on that road though, and move fast.

"Don't be shy about always asking the driver where you are and where the embassy and the military are from your current position. The life you save by asking may be your own. Also, and this may sound obvious, but if you have to un-ass your vehicle for whatever reason, leave your shit behind and move as fast as you can."

"I'm sorry," said Mau, raising his hand. "If we have to *what* our vehicle?"

"Un-ass...dismount...get out of...move fast from."

"Right. Thanks"

"Yes, sir. Now, I know you secret agent types like wearing the Royal Robbins cargo pants and cammies[1] and Oakleys and whatnot, but I strongly recommend you try as much as possible to downplay anything that looks like a uniform or a t-shirt with a big American flag that says, 'I just stepped in a pile of Shi-ite.'" He smiled at his own joke.

They were told to put their passports in their front pant's pocket and never, never, *never* go anywhere without it. "Yes, gentlemen, even to the bathroom. You may be sitting comfortably, reading a book, enjoying your dump when the building around you is suddenly no longer there. You may not have a chance to go back and dig through the rubble to find it."

He further recommended before they travel they program into the speed dials of their cellular phones the numbers, with the appropriate country codes, of Marine Post One at the embassy. In an emergency, that would be their first point of contact for getting troops rolling in their direction or for any other time-critical matter that might require man- or fire-power. They were also told to make sure their phone batteries were charged and to travel with a phone charger and electrical adaptor. Lastly, on the subject of phones, he said to make sure they had roaming on their phones and plenty of credit.

They were told because they were traveling in a non-diplomatic, non-military status, they shouldn't necessarily expect someone at DEA to give them weapons. The embassy has its own rules, and the personnel assigned there are very likely following them to the letter under the hawk-like gaze of some career-paranoid supervisor. If the ambassador says, "No guns for non-diplomatic personnel," then it's no guns for non-diplomatic personnel. Before they could even ask, they were told TDY personnel are not granted diplomatic status.

He ended his brief by telling them by and large, the Afghan people are glad the Americans have come to town and are very nice and friendly but

---

[1] Camouflage clothing

the Taliban *is* staging a resurgence, and any Westerner is a target. Even Afghanis are acceptable "collateral damage" when the Talib fighters let one loose, as evidenced when they recently blew up the Serena Hotel where American and other Western diplomats had been staying; most of the people killed in the explosion were Afghani employees of the hotel. Aside from all that, have fun, make the most of the adventure, be safe, take lots of pictures, and realize, "It's a chance to go to new places. Meet new people. And kill them! Hoo-ah!"

The weather was pleasantly warm as Chris stepped out of the terminal under a clear sky. The temperature reminded him of the northern mid-west at the end of spring.

Pedro Guzman, the agent who had been up on the border when the Afghanis were killed in the firefight with the SEALs, had been waiting for them at the door of the airplane and escorted them through immigration and customs, using his own black diplomatic passport like a shield. He was a stocky, head-shaven muscleman with a thick northeastern accent wearing a pair of ratty jeans, a bulky jacket, and tennis shoes. He explained while at work, he was expected to wear a tie, but that kind of flash was bad outside "the compound." He led them to a vehicle waiting just outside the building.

Next to the car, standing at the passenger side front door, stood another American wearing brown cargo pants, desert boots, and a tan safari vest partially covering black body armor. Several pouches on the front of the vest were stuffed with rifle magazines. He held a large automatic rifle pointed skyward in the crook of his elbow and a Glock pistol worn in a tactical holster low on his thigh. Extra pistol magazines sprouted from a wide, black belt of ballistic nylon. A clear curling wire ran from a radio on his belt to an earpiece. For all his accoutrements, people shoving to get both into and out of the terminal were virtually ignoring him. He nodded as the trio exited the terminal, his head on a swivel, his eyes hidden behind a pair of dark Oakleys.

"That's FUBAR," said Pedro motioning with his chin by way of introduction. FUBAR didn't bother helping as they were loading the luggage in the back of a dirty brown Chevrolet Suburban.

"What kind of name's FUBAR?" asked Mau in his thick Caribbean accent.

The guy with the guns didn't turn around to answer, though he kept his head moving in every direction except towards the passengers in the back. "Fucked Up Beyond All Recognition. I couldn't think of a better callsign for this place."

Pedro took out a cell phone and hit a speed-dial button. "I've got the guys and we're heading back to the green building."

Pedro was pointing out important landmarks following the route on which the agents had been briefed. "There's been a change in plans for your accommodation," said Pedro keeping his eyes on the road. Traffic was like nothing existing in the US with cars and taxi cabs diving in and out of the way in a frantic, frenetic, filthy, dusty ballet that had the guys in the back grabbing the handgrips and wishing they could pull their seatbelts tighter than the inertial locks allowed. Every now and again, they saw desert camouflaged Humvees and trucks racing back in the direction they had just come.

"We were going to stick you at the Serena, but it got all blowed up so the TDY VIPs[1] are staying in the empty trailers at the embassy. You'll be going to the embassy Annex instead. It used to be a hotel but now's the..." he coughed loudly into his hand, merging the noise with the word CIA. "They said they had a spare trailer but you'll have to double up. It's actually the safest place to be in this shit-hole 'cause it's so heavily guarded, more than the embassy, *and* they got a bar inside and drinks are like a dollar a beer. It's also

[1]Very Important Person

166

right next to the German Embassy, and those guys have pizza night on Fridays so you can just walk over there if you're still in town. We can't go because the Ambassador doesn't allow us non-official travel outside the compound. I've heard that the snappy working there is hot hot hot! And lonely too so if you can, drag 'em back to your trailer and you'll score for shor'." He laughed.

Traffic was thinning just a bit, and they passed through a checkpoint where everyone was required to show their IDs and passports before continuing. Pedro pointed to his right once they were moving again at a huge light-colored blast wall running the entire length of a city block. "That's the embassy."

They continued out past a second checkpoint, and eventually came to another small guard post manned by Afghanis in green camouflage uniforms carrying AK-47s. As they came to a stop, the guards looked in at the passengers, though the doors were not opened. They raised the red and white striped bar blocking their passage and waved them through.

The road twisted and turned then opened into a wide, tree-lined street that immediately struck Chris as eerie. Though the weather was beautiful and the sky clear, a perfect day to be outside, there was nobody on the neatly kept sidewalks; no other cars moving about. It had an end-of-the-world silent feel to it.

Ahead of them and to the left beyond high stacks of sandbags was a large green building with only the upper floors visible. The second story windows were hidden behind stacks of sandbags. Chris had his camera up and fired off a couple of shots.

"No pictures," said FUBAR hearing the electronic shutter snap.

"Oh," replied Chris contritely. "Sorry. I'll delete 'em."

Chris nudged Mau and pointed up at a sandbag'd emplacement on the roof where a man was sitting behind the barrel of a huge gun aimed at the dusty mountains in the distance.

"What kind of gun is *that*?" asked Chris pointing past the window.

FUBAR followed his finger and laughed. "Couple'a broomsticks tied together. And a mannequin. Looks pretty good though, right? We got some guys training for The Ultimate Fighting Championship, and they run around the complex all day and climb the ladder and move him around so it looks like he does stuff. One of the guys bench-presses him 'cause they filled him with lead so he wouldn't blow off."

They continued on the road past a high steel wall that in some places obscured the green building from view.

"Brown Suburban, four on board, three bumps out," said FUBAR.

"Pardon me?" said Mau thinking FUBAR had said something to them.

FUBAR was a little more relaxed now and turned in his seat. "I was telling the guard post we're coming in and we're three speed bumps out. Lets them know where to look and that we don't have any drama with us."

"What if we had drama with us?"

FUBAR shook his head. "Spray and pray, baby. They'll waste us to keep us from driving in with a car bomb or bad guys. Luckily I'm wearing this," he rapped his knuckles on the body armor, "though the guys manning the sally-port on this shift are such bad shots, they could be aiming at the tires or a fuckin' cloud and I'd still wind up taking one in the head."

They circled around the compound, eventually stopping at a chain link gate that was already open. Several Americans stood around a makeshift guard shack constructed of plywood and sandbags all under a corrugated steel roof held up with wood beams. The soldiers were dressed and armed similarly to FUBAR. As the car stopped inside the gate, FUBAR stepped out and closed the door, joining the guys in the guard shack, giving them a thumbs-up. Ahead of the Suburban, a heavy metal door was rolled aside by a bearded Afghan in green uniform. Pedro pulled forward over the doorway tracks, stopped and waited until the door was rolled shut behind him before continuing.

Pedro said, "Fuck him about the pictures. Just don't get caught."

The outer walls of the compound were the stacked shipping containers they had seen from the road. There were doorways torch-cut in the sides of them and bearded Afghanis, some wearing uniforms, others in varying degrees of shorts and shirts, occupied bunk beds, even though it was daytime.

"Who're these guys?"

"Local guard force. They man the outer posts, some of the inner posts like the one we just came through, and do all the cooking and cleaning. You guys really are lucky…this is much nicer than where we're living. Here's yours."

On the right were trailers, painted white, laid out in neat rows surrounded by a low picket fence. It was quite quaint.

"In Florida, this is where the hurricane would hit." Chris joked.

Pedro stopped the SUV and got out. Chris and Mau followed as they grabbed their luggage from the rear of the vehicle and walked to a trailer that had the number "40" in black letters above the door. It wasn't locked and Pedro walked in. There was a narrow bed at each end of the trailer, a plain desk and chair, a tall closet, and a doorway leading to the bathroom.

"All the comforts of home. Sorry you guys got to bunk together but like I said, beds are in pretty short supply right now."

"No problem," said the agents in unison.

"I'll leave you two to get unpacked." He looked at his watch. "You don't have IDs yet, so I'd recommend you hang out in the trailer-hood 'til I

169

get back in about an hour, and then we'll walk over to the security office and get 'em so you'll have a freer run of the place. The gym is in the middle of the trailer-hood, and it's two of these things stuck together so you can't miss it; and the trailer just across from it is the laundry."

He left and Chris said to Mau, "So, what'd'ya think, mister?"

Mau shrugged and smiled. "You never know, say the French." He rubbed his stomach. "I don't know about you, man, but I'm starving. Let's hope the food's as nice as this hotel!"

True to his word, Pedro was back in an hour. "Let's go get some eats and meet the other guys." He wandered off at a comfortable pace, the agents falling in next to him. They weaved around the trailer-hood on clean sidewalks set into a well-tended combination of lawn and stone. It was obvious someone was trying hard as hell to make this home-like.

They wound up on the back side of the green building. To their right was a low-slung, two- story building in the same faded shade of the hotel.

"I guess they had a sale on snot-color paint," remarked Mau.

The smaller building was surrounded by sandbags stacked one atop the other. Pedro explained it was where the embassy's security force was housed. Between the buildings, parked rather haphazardly, were all manner of SUVs and pick-up trucks; one of the locals was washing a dark blue Suburban with a bucket and hose. Pedro walked into the building and said hi to some of the guys wandering around. In a small office, Chris and Mau had their photos taken and within minutes had ID cards on metal chains hanging around their necks.

The three walked up the steps of the big green hotel building and down the main hallway on a floral carpet so threadbare there were holes and tears patched with duct tape. The walls were paneled in cheap wood veneer and overhead were uncovered bulbs. The building smelled like dust and surrender.

They entered the dining room. People having pizzas occupied bare plastic tables. Many wore handguns on tactical holsters and there were 2-way radios squawking on different channels. Except for the pistols and radios and the wooden gun rack on the floor with a variety of long guns, several suppressed, it looked like any low-rent eating establishment with its cheap paint, dirty windows and bare light fixtures hanging from exposed wiring in the ceiling.

There was also a jarringly noticeable lack of women. Of the twenty-five or so people in the room, there were none.

"There's no chicks," said Chris quietly.

Pedro turned back to him. "Homeboy, about the only T&A you're going to see in this country is Toes and Ankles," he joked. "There's a secretary or two and some wives. And the German Embassy gig. It's a drag."

Pedro led them to a table where a muscular, clean-shaven guy was sitting. He was a little taller than Pedro, about the same age as Chris, and wearing gym shorts and a gray tank top that read, "Manhattan, Kansas…The Little Apple," in big red letters across the front. He stood up and introduced himself as Jack.

Pedro told them without rancor, "I called him when we got your email about the thousand kilos and he's attached himself to the case." There were handshakes all around, and Jack told them pizza was on the way and pointed to a glass-front refrigerator where sodas were keeping cool.

"Let's go sit on the terrace." Jack told them. "I'm not supposed to be in here in shorts." They all walked out through a glass door at the rear of the room. Outside there were a few more plastic tables under brightly colored umbrellas and incongruous strings of Christmas lights. "We have happy hours out here," he explained. They all sat and got comfortable.

"We've located the cell phone," began Jack. "It's about three kilometers from here up on the mountain." He pointed vaguely over his shoulder towards the hills that face the city. "We're not doing surveillance because the neighborhood is so shitty there's no way we wouldn't be burned. We're recording all the calls though, and keeping track of it when it moves."

"Have you ID'd the owner?"

Jack shook his head. "Phone's a throw-away. You can walk into almost any store and pay cash up front for a phone and sim card with credit. We're tracking the actual handset though, so even if he dumps the sim card and gets a new number, we'll be on it."

Chris and Mau nodded.

"The house is crap. There's no real property record that we can get to. It's possible the local cops or military could track down ownership, but as a rule we tend to keep them in the dark about any ops we're running. They're mostly trust-worthy but we just don't take the chance.

"We tracked the phone from the house to a carpet shop down on Chicken Street, which is a kind of a shopping market neighborhood not far from here where you can get rugs and antiques and DVDs, that kind of shit. We're guessing that's where the guy works because he's gone there every day."

"Fuck," said Chris. "You guys have been busy!"

"Well, I'd like to take a lot more credit, but it's really been the guys upstairs pulling the information out of the air."

The pizza arrived and everybody dug in.

Pedro said, "We haven't done any photo passes of the carpet store because we've been waiting for you guys to arrive. We don't have any real tech stuff, but Jack says we can use their long lens cameras and to get him when he comes or goes, and then he'll run it through their facial recognition

172

programs. I got a question for *you*, though. How'd you get permission to do UC overseas?"

Mau laughed. "I think the words 'one thousand, kilos, and heroin' in the same sentence."

"Yeah, followed by 'Afghanistan, terrorists, and gun battle with US Navy SEALS,'" continued Chris. "I was there when the SAC called Headquarters. He was talking to everybody telling 'em about the case. I couldn't see his other hand under the desk, but I'm pretty sure what he was doing."

"Well, our GS has been chomping at the bit to go out and get something done to show how much great work she's doing here."

"Who is she?" asked Chris as part of the obligatory game of who-do-you-know that accompanies any meeting between government employees of the same agency.

"Sarah Thibodaux. Know her?"

Both Mau and Chris shook their heads.

"She's a boob," said Pedro taking another piece of pizza. "She was OPR before coming here. I think she figured *that* wasn't career enhancing enough so now she's gracing *us* with her presence. I've seen her in exactly two places since she's been here: her desk on the phone sucking up to everyone at Headquarters, and at the bar in The Marine House[1] trying to find someone *else* to suck up to since there's no one here senior to her from DEA. It's actually really good Jack's involved because his people got a lot more weight to throw and it keeps her pretty quiet. We're kind of the little dogs in the yard here. Mostly we do liaison work but nothing operational. Truth be told, I ain't done dick since I arrived except answer the phone and pick you guys up and that thing on the border. We're supposed to be assisting the locals on ops but the army won't let us. *Our* Army, I mean! DEA told 'em

---

[1] The place within the embassy complex where the Marine Security Detachment lives; they generally host weekend happy hours

we could go out, but when they asked what DEA's acceptable manpower loss expectation was, DEA said zero so the Army said we were locked down." He frowned and then banged his head on the table. "On the other hand," he said, brightening, "between hazardous duty pay, danger pay, and post differential, I'm raking in the dough so I can't complain too hard. I'll do one tour here and go back to the 'land of the big PX[1]' a rich man."

"So are they going to let us work this case from outside the embassy? I mean, Mau can't exactly call up our bad guy and ask him to come to the embassy parking lot for a UC meeting."

Jack answered the question. "*We're* going to be doing the operational stuff and you'll be coming along with us as advisors. We don't have to get anyone's permission to operate, and our Chief of Station is good with it if you are." He grinned. "He told the GS that *she* was good with it and, surprisingly enough, she agreed."

Chris and Mau looked at Pedro for an answer that met DEA's requirements. "'Fuck yes!' is the answer you're looking for," he said to them. "If we don't do it their way, you'll never see the outside wall of the embassy again except on your way back to the airport."

In unison the men looked at Jack and exclaimed, "Fuck yes!"

Late that afternoon The Chrises talked. For The Other Chris it was just after sunrise. They agreed Herrera would make his call around 9 AM when The Other Chris could get into the SIJIN office.

It was then that Chris Davis, Mau, Jack, Sarah Thibodaux, and an un-introduced older man in a wrinkled white shirt and khaki pants sat in an empty office on the second floor of the hotel. On a wooden table was a laptop computer. The older man turned it on and launched a program from a standard Windows desktop that accessed a CD. The screen went black, then

---

[1] Military slang for the US

174

across it scrolled big white letters that kept repeating, "Can you hear me now? Can you hear me now?" Eavesdropper humor, no doubt. He turned to Jack and nodded. "We're in."

"Great, thanks." He turned to the DEA people. "This is a repeater to one of the black boxes upstairs that's tuned into our bad guy's cell phone." He looked at his watch. "So now we're just waiting for the call from your guy in Colombia."

Chris Davis' phone rang. "Hey man! Okay, we're ready. *Adios, amigo.*" He closed the line. "That was Chris. Herrera's making the call now."

The speaker on the laptop clicked and the people in the room heard the electronic ringing of a phone. It rang several times before it was answered.

Samadi: *"Salamo Aleikom!"* said a voice in an accent Mau and Chris were not familiar with.

"Huh..." muttered Jack.

Herrera: *"Hello my friend. How are you?"* asked the voice in Spanish-accented English.

Samadi: *"I am very many well and I am glad to hear from you. I pray too you are well."*

Herrera: *"Yes, my friend, thank you. I am calling to tell you that my partner has arrived in your country and would like to meet with you to discuss our business in my place and also to arrange payments for your next shipment. The last was most well received."*

Samadi: *"Ah, very good. I am glad there were no problems and I looking most forward to meet to him. Have you a telephone number that I to call and introduce me?"*

The door to the office opened and a man passed a piece of paper to the older man who read it and passed it to Jack.

Herrera: *"Of course."* He passed Mau's cell phone number.

Samadi: *"Very many good then. I shall call him now."*

Herrera: *"Thank you, my friend. Good luck and I hope we will speak again soon."*

Samadi: *"In sha'lah. Good bye, my brother."*

Herrera: *"Adios, hermano."*

The connection was broken. No one moved. "That call," said Jack, making a note of the time on the paper in his hand, "was received in the carpet store on Chicken Street." Then to the older man, "You better kill that before Samadi calls here and hears himself in the background."

"Why did you say 'huh'?" Mau asked Jack.

"He answered in Arabic. That's not what most people speak here."

"Is that bad?"

Jack took a deep breath and shook his head. "No. Just interesting."

The older man closed the laptop and left the room. At the same time, Mau's telephone began to ring. He held it up, looked at the ID, smiled and waved it at the group.

"Hola." "Hello" in Spanish. He switched to English. "Hello, yes, Mr. Samadi, how are you? That's very good, yes. Mau," he said slowly. "Please call me Mau…yes, that is a good idea…let me get a pen…you'll have to spell it very slowly for me…c-h-i-c-k-e-n…oh chicken…Yes, Chicken Street…okay, okay, I have that…like Persian Carpets? Do you sell Pashmina scarves? I told my wife I would get her one if I could...excellent, my friend, thank you. Yes, okay, okay, very good. I will see you tomorrow afternoon…I should just walk in and ask for you? Okay, okay, see you tomorrow." He closed the connection and grinned.

On the following morning, hours before Mau was to travel to the carpet shop, there was another meeting on the second floor. This one was attended by the team from DEA as well as the Chief of Station (CoS) in suit and tie, the older guy from the day before, and two tough looking soldiers in khaki camouflage BDU trousers and t-shirts. The soldiers stood in their own huddle in the corner of the room drinking sodas from cans, their arms crossed otherwise. Both wore Oakleys hanging on cords around their thick necks.

As Jack explained it, early that morning before the sun rose, a local vehicle drove into the neighborhood and parked, faced so a live-feed camera concealed within the grill had a clear view of the front of the shop. The feed was beaming via cellular to a black box that was relaying it to the laptop on the table and would also be monitored by the surveillance team who would move into position several blocks away. No one had yet entered the shop since the car was put into place.

The surveillance team would consist of Chris, Pedro, Jack and the two men from the CIA's paramilitary group as close security for Jack.

It was recommended GS Thibodaux remain at the Annex with the CoS, monitoring the feed and maintaining a liaison with his guys upstairs who would be relaying appropriate SIGINT retrieved from the players in or around the shop.

Another vehicle, a Jeep Cherokee, would be meandering through the neighborhood, though not on the street or in any intersection visible from the shop where the meeting would be taking place. This would contain four US Navy SEALs from the task force housed in the basement level of the hotel. They would be in full battle dress, black Nomex suits, helmets, goggles, Kevlar, suppressed MP-5s, the works. If anything went wrong in the carpet shop and the decision was made to extract Mau, these would be the first guys through the door. Early morning surveillance of the meet-spot had determined the rear of the shop opened onto an alley but the door was blocked by years of rubble and garbage; there was only one way in and one way out.

Mau would be driven to the meeting in a car painted and beaten to look like a local taxi. It was one of the first surveillance vehicles The Station had obtained when they took over the hotel and was kept parked inside one of the shipping containers out of sight. The car would be driven by one of the inner-security Afghan guards who would drop Mau off and wait around the corner until the meeting was over. The driver had been instructed not to go into the shop for any reason, to stay with the vehicle.

Another CIA officer had carefully chosen the route from the meet spot and ridden it with the "taxi" driver three times that morning to be sure the driver had it down and knew not to drive it too fast. The route had been chosen to detect any surveillance Samadi or his people might mount to follow Mau from the meeting. Unbeknownst to the driver, once he had Mau back in the car on the roundabout way to the recovery location, an Army Special Forces counter-surveillance team attached to the Annex, operating under the radio callsign "Coyote," would be in a loose trail, making sure Mau's tail was cold. If they detected surveillance, they would report on it but not interfere unless Mau was in jeopardy. They, like the SEALs, would be ferociously armed in terms of both weaponry and attitude.

Mau's instructions were in keeping with basic DEA safety rules. He was not to leave or "trip" under any circumstances with Samadi. Inside the shop, the teams could maintain control; outside they were almost powerless. At the conclusion of the meeting, he would walk out of the shop, turn right, walk to the next intersection, turn right, walk approximately half a block and get in the taxi that would be waiting for him. He was shown this on a map of the area. He was also told there would be two pieces of black tape forming an 'X' in the rear window, so even if he couldn't remember what the driver looked like, he would be able to remember this identifying mark.

The meeting would be recorded on audio back at the Annex and monitored real-time by the surveillance team. Jack said he wasn't able to give

178

technical details but prior to Mau entering the shop, his guys upstairs were going to activate the "send" function of Samadi's cel, turning the phone into a live transmitter.

Chris had heard vague stories about things like this from hanging out at the tech office in Miami but had never been directly exposed to it. He was fascinated.

"Just out of curiosity," asked Mau, "what if his phone isn't on?"

The older man spoke up. "We'll turn it on remotely."

Jack continued. "He won't be able to tell by looking at it that it's transmitting. If he has to make a call, it'll still function normally."

Mau laughed. "No shit?"

"No shit," said the older man. "I'm going to need yours right now though, please." Mau passed it to him, and they all watched while he wrote down the Electronic Serial Number from the inside and keyed the number into a pad connected to another phone from his bag.

"This one," said Jack, "is a modified iPhone. It looks and works like a normal one, but it's going to be transmitting live too, as a backup to Samadi's. More importantly though, is the camera on the back." Mau turned it over and looked. "It takes very high resolution video so while you're in there, find a reason to call us. When you do, use the opportunity while the phone's up to your ear to aim the camera in his general direction so we can get some pictures. You don't have to be too precise. It's a wide angle camera so anywhere in his general direction is going to be good enough. I'll be carrying on a regular conversation with you so just answer back in English. We'll show you how to speed dial. Okay?"

They discussed a danger signal Mau could use if he felt he were in jeopardy. He would use the word "Pashmina" three times in a row.

"That's a tongue-twister." Chris said smiling.

179

"Yeah, man. No chance I'll say it by mistake, right?" He laughed as well.

"About the second you get out of the taxi," continued Jack, "you're going to be mobbed by kids asking for money or candy. They're good kids but keep your hand on your phone just in case. You might ask them where the carpet shop is and Samadi. For sure they'll know and lead you right there. Be really friendly with them and give them some American dollars to keep them around you. Someone's a whole lot less likely to launch an RPG or drive-by if you're surrounded by children."

"Are you kidding me, man?" asked Mau who had a daughter back in Curacao, and it was obvious by the look on his face he was horrified by what he was hearing.

Jack shook his head. "Nope. It's a tragedy of war, buddy, but these kids are little human shields. You may not like it but they'll keep you alive." He looked around. "So can anyone think of anything else before we get going?" No one had anything to add. "Then let's do it."

Chicken Street was a jumble of small shops, most under corrugated steel awnings. Individual stores had their wares hanging out on the sidewalks or in the windows and brightly colored banners in English announced what was on sale.

There were children everywhere, crowding around uniformed American soldiers and other westerners, acting as amateur guides and helping them find what they wanted, hopefully in exchange for a dollar or two.

The surveillance vehicle, driven by one of the paramilitary guys, cruised through the intersection and Jack pointed out the store about halfway down the block. They cruised through the next traffic circle, did a U-turn, and double parked facing back in the direction of the target street, just in case they had to get in there behind the SEALs. Chris and Jack sat in the back seat with a laptop between them, the screen showing the video feed from the empty vehicle placed there that morning. Unfortunately, double-parked cars down the entire street blocked most of the view of target location.

Mau was still back at the embassy Annex, sitting in the taxi, waiting to be released. Everyone was in position and checking in on the radio. Jack picked up his phone and made the call. "Shouldn't take him ten minutes to get here." He said to Chris.

Several minutes later they heard over the radio, "This is Coyote One. Your UC is in the area."

Jack made a brief radio call passing the info on. Almost immediately the speaker on the laptop came alive. The sound was a little muffled but they could clearly hear a man's voice humming.

They watched as the taxi pulled up on the block where the carpet shop was located and Mau stepped out. He was wearing jeans and a short sleeve polo shirt. As predicted, children enveloped him. He bent down and talked to several of them taking something out of his pocket. A little girl with a pink scarf on her head took him by the hand and started pulling him through the throng of kids. For the most part he was out of sight, though every now and then his head would appear above a parked car. Presently she deposited him at his destination, and he stepped out of the view of the cameras and the surveillances teams.

U.S. Department of Justice
Drug Enforcement Administration

REPORT OF INVESTIGATION

1. Program Code	2. Cross File	Related Files	3. File No.	
5. By: SA Maurio Lacle At Miami Field Division	☐ ☐ ☐ ☐ ☐		6. File Title SERRANO, Enrique	
7. ☐ Closed ☐ Requested Action Completed ☐ Action Requested By:				
9. Other Officers: SAs Christopher Davis and Pedro Guzman				

10. Report Re: UNDERCOVER MEETING WITH FNU SAMADI

DETAILS

1. Reference: DEA-6 written to this case file RE: Recording of telephone conversation between Pablo HERRERA and FNU SAMADI.

2. On August 25 of this year, at approximately 17:10 PM, SA Mauricio Lacle, acting in an undercover capacity, entered a carpet shop on Chicken Street, Kabul, Afghanistan where a subject known as SAMADI, (First Name Unknown (FNU)) has been reported to work; said information was developed by OGA assets. SA Christopher Davis and SA Pedro Guzman maintained surveillance outside the carpet shop and monitored SA Lacle's conversation using an audio transmitter. Also supporting the surveillance operation were National Clandestine Services Operations Officer ███████████ CIA Paramilitary Operations Officer ███████████ and CIA Paramilitary Operations Officer ███████████.

3. Following introductions, SAMADI re-iterated that he was glad "his boxes" were well received by Pablo HERRERA. SA Lacle advised SAMADI that, as had been discussed with HERRERA previously SA Lacle was prepared to move similar packages on SAMADI's behalf from Afghanistan to the United States via military aircraft. SA Lacle told SAMADI that he (SA Lacle) has people working for him that are airframe technicians at the US Air Force Base at Bagram who can secrete the heroin where it cannot be found by in-depth searches or drug-sniffing dogs. SA Lacle also advised that he has similar employees in the US

11. Distribution: Division District Other	12. Signature (Agent) SA Mauricio Lacle	13. Date
	14. Approved (Name and Title) Ricardo House Group Supervisor	15. Date

DEA Form - 6
(Jul. 1996)
m1

DEA SENSITIVE
Drug Enforcement Administration

This report is the property of the Drug Enforcement Administration.
Neither it nor its contents may be disseminated outside the agency to which loaned.

Previous edition dated 8/94 may be used.

U.S. Department of Justice
Drug Enforcement Administration

	1. File No. ▓▓▓▓	▓▓▓▓▓▓
REPORT OF INVESTIGATION *(Continuation)*	3. File Title SERRANO, Enrique	

5. Program Code ▓▓▓▓▓

at Homestead Air Force Base in Miami, and can make sure the heroin is removed and stored in Miami until picked up by SAMADI's contacts.

4. SA Lacle advised SAMADI that he (SA Lacle) would charge SAMADI six thousand dollars per kilo. SAMADI said that was the agreed-on price and that SAMADI had spoken to his supplier and now had one thousand five hundred kilos and wanted to know if the extra five hundred kilos would present a problem for SA Lacle. SA Lacle responded that he would have to contact his associates to find out.

5. At this point, SA Lacle initiated a UC telephone call with surveillance agents under the pretense of verifying if the additional five hundred kilos would present a problem. At the conclusion of the call SA Lacle informed SAMADI that the additional heroin could be carried.

6. SA Lacle told SAMADI that he (SA Lacle) would require one quarter of the payment before the shipment would be accepted for transport, the amount being three million, six hundred thousand dollars. SAMADI asked SA Lacle if he (SA Lacle) would accept Afghanis (currency of Afghanistan) instead of dollars, as US dollars are difficult to acquire. After some calculation both men agreed that the amount of Afghanis would be approximately 173,304,000 based on currency exchange rates on the day of the transaction. SA Lacle responded that such a large amount of currency would have to be deposited at a bank and then wire-transferred to destination and for SA Lacle to do so he (SA Lacle) would charge an additional one percent. At this time, SAMADI made a cellular phone call and spoke in Arabic. At the conclusion of the call, SAMADI stated that this extra charge was acceptable and that when so directed would have people that could take possession of the heroin in Miami.

7. SA Lacle asked SAMADI when the heroin would be ready for SA Lacle to take possession of it. At this time SAMADI made another cell phone call and spoke in Arabic. At the conclusion of the call, SAMADI stated that the heroin was ready and would only require SA Lacle to tell him where and when it was to be delivered.

DEA Form - 6a
(Jul. 1996)

DEA SENSITIVE
Drug Enforcement Administration

This report is the property of the Drug Enforcement Administration.
Neither it nor its contents may be disseminated outside the agency to which loaned.

Previous edition dated 8/94 may be used.

REPORT OF INVESTIGATION *(Continuation)*	1. File No. ▓▓▓ ▓▓▓▓▓
	3. File Title SERRANO, Enrique
4. Page 3 of 3	
5. Program Code	▓▓▓▓▓

8. SA Lacle advised SAMADI he (SA Lacle) would contact SAMADI in approximately one or two days with the final arrangements.

9. At this time the meeting was terminated. SA Lacle exited the carpet shop and met with surveillance agents at a predetermined location.

INDEXING

1. SAMADI, FNU: NADDIS REQUESTED. Sex: Male. Race: Arabic. Age: 40 YOA. Height: 5'9". Eyes: BRN. Hair: BLK. Misc. Features: Black moustache and beard with streak of gray on chin.

2. HERRERA, Pablo: NADDIS .

DEA Form   ‣ 6a
(Jul. 1996)

DEA SENSITIVE
Drug Enforcement Administration

This report is the property of the Drug Enforcement Administration.
Neither it nor its contents may be disseminated outside the agency to which loaned.

Previous edition dated 8/94 may be used.

184

The debriefing took place back at the Annex in the dimly lit, musty smelling hotel, cleverly named ███-bar. It was a discarded conference room with an ornate dark wood bar at one end by the door, an ancient refrigerator stocked with beer, and liquor on the wall. The bar was on the honor system and there was a gray metal lock box with a slot in the top where money was left for drinks. The bar tables were beaten and scarred, apparently, thought Chris, like everything else he had seen since coming to this country. Every wall was covered with handwritten messages, some humorous, some not, many violent but sadly honest, all attesting to the patriotism and pride of the people who had partied there, soldiers all, in the war on terrorism, and Chris felt pretty honored to be in that silent company. There were also a few old-fashioned guns, relics from the old wars, which Chris had only seen in books or movies, hanging decoratively from chains or leather straps.

The acting bartender was a not-too-tall but very friendly American named "R2" whom Chris remembered from the guard shack when he had arrived.

After giving Chris his beers, R2 pointed with his thumb to a whiteboard behind him. There, in block letters were "THE RULES": No weapons, no nose picking, a requirement to write something on the wall, and the warning anyone trying to drink without paying would be clubbed to death.

"Got a big problem with nose-picking, do you?" asked Chris.

R2 laughed displaying a set of incongruously white, perfectly straight teeth. "How long you been here?"

"Couple 'a days."

"Just wait."

Both Chris and Mau signed their names, Chris adding "DEA...Don't Expect Anything" followed by Mau's "DEA...Don't Even Ask" on the side wall, and then joined Pedro at a high table with drinks and smiles while they waited for their newest, bestest buddy and big toe, the man from the Company.

Jack walked in, his fist held up in a victory gesture. "We are so banging on all cylinders!" he said to the assembled gang with a huge grin. He told them the photos were being downloaded from the iPhone and a quick translation of Samadi's calls from the carpet shop identified the man on the other end as "Anwar." Jack had read a hand-written synopsis that was waiting for him when he got back to the Annex, and it was obvious to him that Anwar was the man in charge; he had all the answers at his fingertips and hadn't had to contact anyone else when the decisions were made. But the really big news was when Samadi called Anwar, the guys upstairs transposed the keypad tones into their corresponding numbers and programmed the new number into their black boxes and found it was already in the database!

"When we first got to town," Jack enlightened the agents, "we had a 'money for missiles' program going where we were paying off local tribal leaders to recover Stinger missiles that had been left over from the Soviet invasion. Turns out that one of the guys who sold a few missiles back to us is named Anwar Dadfar Safari. He's been on our payroll since then, feeding us intel now and then on Taliban and AQ[1] movements in the area near Qwost where we have an out-station. Turns out that his number is the one that Samadi called!"

Chris lightly pounded his beer glass on the table. "So you know the guy? That's great!"

"Well I don't, but someone around here does. But check this out. How funny would it be if he were using the money we gave him for the missiles to give back to us to carry his heroin. We'd be directly financing his drug business. Are we just that good?"

"Sort of funny oops as opposed to funny ha-ha," said Chris.

---

[1] Al Queda

"Yeah," he frowned. "The media would crucify us if they ever found out. We'll have to think long and hard about that when all this ends. I told CoS about it and he mentioned something to me that's kind of grim. Some of the stuff Anwar's given us has been…" he looked to the ceiling for a moment, debating his next choice of words, "mmm…actionable. What if the guys he was giving us weren't really AQ but drug-trade competition and we…mmm…actioned them for him."

"Shit," said Pedro slowly, drawing the word out. Jack nodded.

Chris toasted Jack. "Well," he said brightening the mood, "pass this toast to your guys upstairs. They've done a great fucking job." He paused for a moment, a little unsure how to broach the next subject. "Hey, can I ask you a question?"

"You just did." Jack replied with a grin.

"Right, so now I'm going to ask another one. I know you probably can't say much about how your guys do all this stuff with the telephones, but how do your guys do all this stuff with the telephones?"

Jack pursed his lips in thought and took a sip from his Corona. "Well, I could tell you…."

"But then you'd have to kill me?" Chris supplied the old, not unexpected punch line.

Jack laughed. "No, I was going to say I could tell you if I knew, but the actual technical shit is PFM to me. I think -"

"What's PFM?"

"Pure Fucking Magic, man." He laughed. "I think most of it's UNCLAS[1] and if you Googled it, you could probably figure it out. But it's not just my guys. We get a lot from the Army Intelligence Support Activity. They're a special operations unit dedicated to this kind of thing with planes that beam the shit to us free of charge."

---

[1] Unclassified

Chris nodded. "So when you say 'the guy's upstairs' you *really* mean upstairs! Fuck, that's cool. I wish we could do shit like that back in Miami."

"I bet! So, case agent, let's talk a little about what happens next."

"Yes indeedy. But first, another round on the Miami Field Division," he clapped Mau on the back who got up, went to the bar, pulled some beers and left his money. When he returned to the table, it was brainstorm time. "How big *is* a hundred and seventy three million Afghanis?"

"Well, depending on the size of the bills they're using, best case would be about a small pallet's worth."

Chris whistled quietly. "Would they just bring it in a truck and we drive it off and we return the truck later? You don't think they'd be worried about being ripped off?"

Jack shook his head. "Not really. I think Samadi has a good trust with Mau, and he did come all this way on your guy in Colombia's behalf. That's a pretty good show of faith."

"Man, that's so unlike working in Miami. Everybody's always worried about a 'rip,' nobody trusts anybody. I can't imagine someone just driving up in a truck and dropping off a couple of million dollars and saying, "See you next Tuesday." You think once we have the money, they'll deliver the heroin the same way?"

"I would guess so. They could even have the heroin in the same truck as the money. Or they may want to give it to us later and ask if they can watch it get loaded." He shrugged. "Doesn't really matter though, because once they give it to us, it's ours and they're finished. Maybe we'll get lucky and Anwar'll be along for the ride and save us a trip going out to get him. I wasn't involved with the shoot-out up on the border, but I've got a call in to the guys at the interrogation cell. They said they're going to go back through the interview reports and see if anyone mentioned an 'Anwar'. It might tell us the odds of him showing up on party day. They said they'd need a day or two."

"Are the guys still here?" asked Mau. "We could ask them ourselves."

Jack shook his head. "That I don't know, or if those guys at the cell would even let you in. But I'll ask. *After* the DEA buys me another beer."

"When they show up with the heroin, how do we arrest them?" asked Chris when he came back to the table. "None of *us* can make an arrest over here and I *know* you guys can't."

"Probably what'll happen is on the day of the deal, we'll shanghai a local prosecutor and have him accompany us and use our paramilitary guys and the SEALs from the basement to do the actual take-down. We've got a couple guys on the payroll that generally back our plays. It's the beauty of living in a war zone."

Two days later Chris, Mau, Pedro and Jack met at the DEA office at the embassy. In contrast to the dark, worn out, battle-scarred hotel, everything here was bright and clean and shiny. The office was very modern and sterile and resembled the Miami Field Division. Everyone was in business attire and busily working the phones. The guys from the hotel were almost shabby in comparison wearing jeans and t-shirts.

They gathered in Sarah's office. A couple of chairs had been rolled in so everyone could sit.

Over the last two days, Chris had brought the Miami office up to date and Jack had worked his people. The CoS had recommended the meeting be brought here so the GS would feel she wasn't being cut out of the loop and stay docile. It was good politics.

"Jack," said Sarah, "why don't you tell us what you have first."

189

He nodded. "Right. Okay, first of all, the guys that got grabbed up on the border didn't know Samadi. They worked for one Rashid bin Rashidi. DIA[1] confirms our assessment that Rashidi is a minor power broker in Qwost and rumored to be a drug trafficker. Anyway, one of the bad guys said that when they transferred the packages to mule-back, Rashidi was there with an Arab he called...drum roll please...Anwar."

"Goddamn, homey!" exclaimed Pedro.

"Well, Anwar is a pretty common name, but that's a nice coincidence," nodded the GS knowingly. "Did they say what he looked like?"

Jack smiled. "Dark hair, moustache, beard. Like everyone else in this country. Since we ID'd Anwar, I sent a photo from our file on him out to the cell, and they're going to show it to the bad guys. But it's him."

"Anything else?"

"No, ma'am."

"Very good. Chris?"

"No, ma'am," he said following Jack's lead.

"Mauricio?" He shook his head.

"No, ma'am."

"Pedro?"

"Yeah, I got lots. I talked to a woman at the Afghan Central Bank and she said if we brought the money to the main office, as long as we have a letter from the prosecutor's office attesting to the legality of the funds, we could open an account in the embassy's name and deposit the money. From there it could be wired to the US. She also said there would be a one percent charge for their services.

---

[1] Defense Intelligence Agency

"The manager at the embassy cashier's office downstairs said they could also deposit it directly into *their* account and wire it back to the US for us for nothing. I think that would be the easiest way to go. And the cheapest.

"I also went to the chief counsel's office in the LEGAT[1] to clarify the official policy on us participating in an enforcement action. Like we figured, he said that when the arrest goes down, we can be present but not directly assist[2]. The Feebs[3] asked if we needed any manpower, and I told 'em I'd let 'em know after I talked to you."

Jack made a motion with his hand to get her attention. "Yes?"

"I told Chris and Mau that our guys are going to do the takedown. We'll have a local prosecutor on standby, and we'll be acting as his advisors. Having the local's knowledge and cooperation is a definite plus for us.

"When it comes right down to it though" continued Jack, "if anything happens, it'll be because this case directly ties in with the shooting on the border. We'll be doing it as a follow-up military operation as opposed to a narcotics enforcement deal. Having the SEALs along keeps it in military purview - "

"Well," interrupted Sarah, "since you brought up the prosecutor, let's *talk* about a trial. Pedro, do we have an extradition treaty with Afghanistan?" she asked. If anyone else had asked, it would have been a rhetorical question because everyone there should have known the answer. But, as Pedro had said, she *was* a boob.

"Nope."

---

[1] Legal Attaché, the FBI's offices in US embassies
[2] 22 U.S.C. Sec. 2291(c)(1), "No officer or employee of the United States may directly effect an arrest in any foreign country as part of any foreign police action with respect to narcotics control efforts, notwithstanding any other provision of law." Such officers or employees may, however, with the approval of the U.S. chief of mission, be present when foreign officers are effecting an arrest or assist foreign officers who are effecting an arrest (22 U.S.C. Sec. 2291(c)(2)). In addition, such officers or employees of the United States may take direct actions to protect life or safety in certain exigent circumstances (22 U.S.C. Sec. 2291(c)(3)).
[3] FBI

"They *could* be tried locally." Jack interjected. "But we're going to take first crack at 'em. Whoever we grab is going right into the interrogation cell. After we've pumped 'em, we'll decide if we want to give them back to the locals for prosecution. If they have further value to us as intel assets, we'll put them back on the street; if they're deemed to be a potential threat to our ground forces, they're going on an all-expense paid Caribbean vacation[1]."

R2.

[1] Slang for the former detention center at the US Navy base in Guantanamo Bay, Cuba or any of the other "black sites" where terrorists are held for questioning

Several of the local guard force.

US Embassy, Kabul, Afghanistan.

CHAPTER ELEVEN

JD was sitting on the bridge, next to the Captain of the ship. Even though his mind was on his little brother, there were still planes in the air and his place was here. He was dressed in a khaki flightsuit and had a yellow legal pad on his lap, making notes. Above the Captain's head, a gray telephone box buzzed. He lifted the receiver and pushed the corresponding button. After listening for a moment, he passed the receiver over to JD.

"CAG."

"CAG," said the voice of his admin chief. "I'm putting through a call from your brother. Stand by."

JD stood and walked behind the captain so the cord wouldn't be in his way.

"Jeff?"

"What's up?" He was aware some of the other men on the bridge were watching him. The word of what happened had flashed through the ship like JP-4 fuel set ablaze.

"I've got a bunch of stuff to dump on you. Are you free?"

"Yeah, go ahead."

"Okay, first of all I don't know if you know this, but the military can't send in a rescue team without permission from the Pakistan State Department or whatever it's called."

"I know that."

"The guys here, you know…the agency I'm working for, they've put in a request via the embassy in Islamabad for permission but it could take some time. One of their guys was on the plane with Chris so they're really desperate to get him back."

"Okay."

"The CO here, he says that the military *can* provide equipment. I can't remember if I told you that we have a helicopter here, but it's all fucked up in maintenance. What we're thinking about is getting a military helo and loading it up with our guys and flying out to the crash site to do a search."

Jeff was nodding. "Alright."

Pete said, "I want to give them your address too, so maybe you can get something going from your end."

"Yeah, do that. That's good. I can run this by the Admiral but I need you to…do you have SIPRNet or JWICS or a secure comm facility there?"

Pete didn't know what the SIPR-thing was but he knew *Jay-Wicks* referred to the Joint Worldwide Intelligence Communications System. "10-4, we're JWICS capable."

"Okay, I need you to have them send the request right now, action CVW-8, that's me. Your comm guy will know how to address it. As soon as the message is out, call me back."

"Roger that."

JD hung up the phone. The ship's captain was turned in his chair. "Good news?"

"Maybe. They need a helo, and hopefully we'll be able to send 'em one. I'm going to go talk to the Admiral right now."

"Keep me advised. Whatever we can do."

JD was sitting across from Admiral in an office very similar to his own but slightly more luxurious to the extent there was fake wood paneling on the walls.

The Admiral had just come from the ship's gym and was still dressed in a t-shirt and blue shorts with gold trim and the Navy emblem on the leg. In the corner sat the Admiral's chief of staff who, like JD, was both a captain and an aviator. Next to JD was a commander who had been introduced as the "Flag JAG[1]." JD filled the Admiral in on the situation, including the pending request for a helicopter. The Admiral raised his eyebrows and looked at his JAG officer for confirmation. Even here, attorneys were the final authority.

---

[1] Judge Advocate General, a military lawyer

The lawyer crossed his legs and nodded. "Without quoting case law or the US Code that would literally bore the life out of you until you were simply quite dead, I can tell you there's no illegality in complying with a request for equipment. Though I should reiterate that including combat personnel *would* be in violation of the Sovereign Nations as well as Agreement of Forces treaties."

"Okay, thanks Tom. That'll be all. Billy," he said to his Chief of Staff, "I'll check with you in a few. CAG and I have some details to work out." JD and the Admiral waited until they had the office to themselves. The Admiral fumbled around his desk, finally finding a cigarette.

"Well," said the Admiral, "so far so good for your brother. I think -" He was interrupted by a knock on his door. "Come!" he said in a voice loud enough to penetrate to the passageway.

The door opened and an attractive yeoman from the CAG's Admin staff poked her head in, saw JD, and passed a piece of paper to him with a smiley, "Good afternoon, sir."

JD read it and passed it to the Admiral.

"Door-to-door service," said the Admiral. "Can't ask for more than that." JD waited while the Admiral put on his glasses and read it. "All right," he said nodding, "let's get a –53[1] scheduled for a LOGRUN[2]. I'll pull a utility version from the Bataan. Get your boys started on the country clearance and flightplan. Leave the side number[3] blank; I'll have it for you by the time you're ready to send the message." He looked up over his half glasses. "You gonna tell me you want to go along?"

"Yes, sir."

The Admiral harrumphed. "I'm pretty sure I don't like the idea of my CAG being off the ship, seeing as I've already lost *one* this cruise." He

---

[1] H-53 helicopter
[2] Logistics Run
[3] The registration number that is painted on the side of every aircraft

197

looked toward the window in his cabin. "But I guess I understand. I don't have a brother but if it were my son, I'd feel the same. Hopefully, though, I'd listen to the advice of more seasoned officers when they told me it's a bad idea."

"Yes, sir," said JD. "I'd hope I would too, but I probably wouldn't. He's my brother and he's in trouble."

JD was back at his desk doing a last-minute review of his emails. He had briefed his deputy on his meeting with the Admiral and his intention to fly with the helo's crew. He didn't want to talk to his mother again, knowing her state of mind, so he sent off a quick email to his wife letting her know he was going to deliver the helicopter and meet up with Pete, wherever *he* was. He knew the word would filter out to the rest of the Davis clan.

He received a brief telephone call from the Air Boss. JD's ride had recovered topside and was fuelling now. The scheduled launch was in one five minutes.

JD had already raided his locker and started putting on his olive green survival gear consisting of a flotation device with compressed air cylinders, emergency radio, flares, mirror, whistle, zip-lock baggie of basic medical supplies and candy, flashlight, water bottle, strobe light, HEED III Spare Air bottle, knife and 9mm pistol. All this was contained in a harness that went over his head and clipped around his waist and was held in place by nylon straps fastened around his thighs. He was sure the helo would have a spare helmet for him but clipped his own to one of the many rings on the vest just to be on the safe side. Into a green helmet bag, he tossed a spare pair of socks and underwear, gym shorts and t-shirts, shaving kit and a book received for Christmas he had found no time to read since deploying out of Virginia Beach almost two months ago.

As he stepped onto the flight deck from the ship's island, a barrage of silence assaulted him; the day's launches and recoveries were complete. It had been a light flight day with just a few training sorties, and had he not known the air plan like the back of his hand, he would have been startled by the quiet. His ride was parked and chocked and was being swarmed by a combination of fuelers, handlers and maintainers.

The heat radiating up from the steel of the ship was immediately under his equipment and he started sweating. He took a deep breath, enjoying the smells particular to military ships: hot rubber non-skid coating covering every inch of the deck's surface, kerosene fuel, salt carried on the wind racing around him, steam from the catapults that launch ships into the air.

The pilots were standing outside, away from the madness going around their giant aircraft. "You ready, CAG?" asked a tall, thin Marine Lieutenant Colonel with short, gray hair by way of introduction. It was unusual for a LTC (as the rank insignia sewn on his shoulders testified) to be flying a LOGRUN. Clearly the word had gone out the Admiral asked for the helo, and that made it big and a chance for some good face time with the brass. As Jeff started to answer, his eyes were drawn to the pilot's khaki flightsuit, which was adorned with all manner of US Air Force-style fighter-jock patches and a nametag reading, "General E. Richard Poward." He hadn't seen that one before and smiled as he silently translated it: Generally Richard powered. Generally dick powered. These Marine guys.

"What's with the Air Force patches?" JD asked.

"I just came from a tour at CENTCOM. Found I got people talking faster to me if they didn't know I are a jarhead."

JD laughed, shook his hand, introduced himself to the rest of the crew and received a safety brief, after which he briefed *them* on what the mission was all about.

199

The men around the helo were passing thumbs-ups, signifying completed tasks, and talking on hand-held radios to various departments around the ship.

JD gave a thumbs-up too. It was time to get this show on the road. "Let's do it."

FM USS THEODORE ROSSEVELT//N00/N01/N3//
TO USDAO ISLAMABAD//AIR//
    USDAO KABUL//AIR//
    CIAHQ LANGLEYVA
PASS TO OFFICE CODES:
    TASK FORCE SIX FIVE BAGRAM/
    CIA AIR OPS KABUL//
INFO TRSTKGRU//N00/N01
    BRESGU//N00/N01
    COMCARAIRWING EIGHT//N00/N01/N2/N3//
    USS BATAAN//N00/N01/N3/N6//
    STKFTR SQDN ONE ONE FIVE
    CARRIER AIRBORNE EARLY WARNING SQDN ONE TWO FOUR
SUBJ/ICAO FLIGHT PLAN//
RMKS/
7. AIRCRAFT IDENTIFICATION VV FCTRY 1
8. FLIGHT RULES I / TYPE OF FLIGHT M
9. NUMBER 1 / TYPE OF AIRCRAFT H-53 / WAKE TURB CAT NONE
10. EQUIPMENT D,T,V,H
13. DEPARTURE AERODROME USS SHIP / TIME 0800Z
15. CRUISING SPEED N160 / LEVEL A010 / ROUTE ▮▮▮▮▮▮▮▮▮
▮▮▮▮▮▮▮▮▮▮
16. DESTINATION AERODROME BAGRAM AFB WITH FUEL STOP AND
CUSTOMS CLEARANCE AT KARACHI AND FUEL STOP AT▮▮▮▮▮▮▮
LAT ▮▮▮▮▮▮▮▮LON▮▮▮▮▮▮▮▮/ TOTAL ETE 3+00/ ALTN AERODROME
NONE /
2ND ALTN NONE
18. OTHER INFORMATION DEP/USS SHIP, STOPOVER FOR FUEL ONLY
/ REQUEST CUSTOMS CLEARANCE IN KARACHI.
//END//

I'm sitting on my cot in the squad tent, a book in my lap, my eyes moving aimlessly as I try to keep my brain occupied.

Since I was told about the crash, I've been operating in mindless mode, doing what I could, what needed to be done. But now I'm out of things to do and I can't help playing a mental movie of every plane crash movie and video I've ever seen: shrieking, tearing of metal, solid bulkheads shearing loose, bodies being flung and exploding with impact trauma, blood, unrecognizable carnage and wreckage, my brother and friends leading the charge into it.

Benwha comes running in. "Squads One and Two," he shouts, "report to the TOC!"

I look around. Except for me, there is no one else. "It's just me. What's up?"

"Orders from MC. Squads One and Two report to the TOC. Start grabbing 'em as I go. Something about your brother I think." At almost the same time, my handheld radio comes alive with a similar message being broadcast from the Alamo.

I'm on my feet and past him, out through the plywood door. I don't even notice the white hot glare of the sun reflecting shrilly off everything around me. Behind me I hear him repeating what he had yelled when he came into our squad tent. There is no public address system in the camp so I guess he's it.

I fast walk across the camp. It's too hot to run. I see Guinness limping from the MWR. I slow next to him. His face and arms are covered with bandaids. "Don't say it."

I throw my arm around him. "You, my friend, are a dumbass."

"Geez, yes, possibly that." He laughs. "But I could've won a buck."

I nod. "Well, that would have been worth it then."

"This is about your brother, right?" He asks me. I nod my head. I'm smiling, but deep down I'm scared shitless.

Inside the TOC, the guys from the squads are finding places to sit on desks or just dropping onto the dusty flooring. Big Mike and the Master Chief already occupy two of the chairs and when I walk in, Warlock stands and offers me his. I motion with my hand and he sits back down. I do a quick count; we're still missing one of the Squad Two troopers. I lever myself up onto the filing cabinet, my back to the tent wall. Most of the guys are looking at me.

"Tell me." I say to MC.

"Just wait a sec so I only have to go through this once. Adze's out on a run. The Alamo sent a truck to get him. They'll be back inside the wire in a minute."

Adze's far and away my best friend out here and youngest of any of us. Every time I see the goober, I can't help but remember when we met. On Sunday nights the Master Chief allows those of us not on duty to have two beers. It's a tradition, he explains, from his days aboard ship when, on one night during cruise, everyone would gather up on deck with their two beers from the ship's stores, and the Captain would toast to families back home and absent friends. Anyway, Adze was lucky enough to arrive in the camp on a Sunday, as the usual Thursday flight had been delayed for whatever reason. Having lived in Australia, I'm well aware of the almost limitless amount Aussies can drink so I was quite surprised when he told me he was the only Aussie (on a global scale, mate!) who could get pissed (drunk) on two beers. Twenty minutes after finishing his second, chin on his chest and nearly in tears, he wrapped his arm around my neck, pulled me close, and told me how, while on an SAS[1] training operation in Borneo, he had accidentally (I swear, mate!) shot a cow with a rocket-propelled grenade.

---

[1] Special Air Service, the Australian Special Forces

Tall and blond with harmless blue eyes and a knockout smile, he's the first one who'd wade in behind me for a fist, knife or gun fight and feel the worst coming out of it if he'd had to hurt someone. Truly a fucked-up piece of work and I love him like a brother.

I hear rubber footsteps on the plywood floor, and he comes busting in wearing camouflage cut-off shorts, out of breath, his face red.

"Wow," says MC to him. "When you whack off, you really work for it, don't you?"

"Yi, mate," Adze replies, his flat Australian accent making everyone smile. "Hope you don't moind that I was thinking 'bout your wife," he jokes.

"Not a bit," he fires back good-naturedly, "I'm usually thinking about your mother." I watch him do a count of everyone assembled. "Okay girls," he starts in a louder voice, addressing all of us. "Unless you're dumber than Guinness, you all know what happened this morning with Meat's brother." He gets up and limps over to a white board and writes *Situation* in big, black, block letters.

"We've got a plane crash and survivors. The package is either DEA or client, hopefully both. Big Mike's put in a formal request for an SF[1] SAR team but it hasn't been green-lighted in Islamabad." He pauses for a second and looks directly at me, shrugs his shoulders, then turns back to the squads. "Also, we don't know where the package is," he continues. "The wreckage was discovered by a local and there's been some activity at the crash site. A couple more guys showed up and they all started walking south, which is the direction we think the package is moving. A little later they were joined by some guys in trucks and they appear to be doing a ground search. We don't know what their intentions are, but they're carrying guns so we're assuming the worst.

---

[1] Special Forces

204

"Terrain-wise, it's pretty barren where the plane went down, and from the charts we've got and the TV feed, it also appears there's really nowhere to hide which kind of works in our favor. Since we can't see 'em, we're assuming they're somewhere else. On the other hand, if they're somewhere else, we really have no idea where to look.

"Now, for a little better news." He writes the word *Mission* and then *RESCUE*, underlining the latter. "Your mission is to locate and retrieve the package." There are a few quiet cheers. He repeats the mission statement.

The next word is *Execution*. "We've gotten some good news that the Navy's sending us a H-53 helicopter and it'll be here soon. When it lands, it's going to need gas and the guys at the hangar can take care of that, but I want both squads out there and ready to go and able to lend a hand if they need it.

"You'll head north towards the crash site. You're going to fly in the same general area as the guys in the trucks, but don't directly overfly them because if they're unfriendly, you're liable to take small-arms fire. That helo makes a lot of noise and if the package hears it, they should come up on a survival radio if they've got one. The pilots'll be monitoring the guard frequencies so if the package sings out, they'll pick it up. That's the perfect case scenario: They'll hear you, lead you in, and you can lift 'em with no drama.

"If you *don't* hear from 'em, land and investigate where they're doing the search. I don't think any of you speak Urdu so I don't know how you'll get anything from them, but that's why we pay you the big bucks so do the best you can. If you get nothing, proceed to the crash site. If there's any bodies there," he looks directly at me for a brief moment, "recover them. There's every possibility that they left a rescue message. The guys in the plane have mostly all had evasion training, so it's possible the message will be written in a way that a local wouldn't understand it so keep a clever eye out, okay?" We all nod. "In 'Nam, we used simple codes like New York to

205

Miami to mean a southerly direction. That's the kind of thing to look for. After you clear the crash site, lacking any other locating data, do an expanding circle search outward from the plane to cover as much ground as you can so the sound can reach them. Keep flying around. The pounding that helo makes is the best thing we've got going.

"RTB when the fuel gets low. We'll gas the helo back up and send out Squad Two and keep rotating until either we get better information or they let us know where they are. There's UAVs passing back and forth, and we're trying to keep plugged into the feeds so we'll let you know what we see."

He writes *Admin and Logistics* as he says the words. "The helo is coming in unarmed. I'm not going to go into the details of it but it is.

"Doc's got an Army medevac kit that he's going to run out in a truck. Litters," which are military stretchers, "trauma kit, battle-field surgical pack, plasma and blood expanders. If you haven't plugged an IV in a while, stop by at the medical tent and get a quick refresher.

"Man-wise, I want you all fully armored-up. Not the little ones you wear on security detail but the big Kevlar ones. And chest plates. And helmets. I know you don't like wearing 'em but too fuckin' bad, pardon my French. You can also take two AT-4s. Now, I shouldn't have to say this, so I will because knowing you dickheads, someone'll have forgotten the most important part, which is that they fire out of both ends so watch who's behind you, and," he speaks very slowly and loudly, "do not shoot them from the helicopter!" We all laugh. We're professional enough not to take offense at being reminded of the basics, and he's right - we are a bunch of dickheads. "Also, it may get dark while you're away so make sure you have lots of fresh batteries for the PVS-7s and −14s." He's referring to the night-vision goggles, which clip to our helmets and the scopes, which attach to the Picatinny rails on top our rifles.

"A couple of you were issued M-4s. Turn 'em back in to Warlock and get AR-10s. I want everyone having the same kind of ammunition." M-4s use 5.56 and AR-10s use 7.62, a heavier, longer-range cartridge. By having the same kind of round, we can pass magazines back and forth as the need arises. Also, having dissimilar ammunition in the battlespace can cause confusion and havoc when the excitement level is running high. "Sniper rifles go too."

"Squad One composition is Meat, Lemon, Adze, Grease and Argo because he's a corpsman -"

"*Was* a corpsman!" Argo calls from the floor.

"Meat, you're squad leader. Lemon, you're XO." As my Executive Officer, if something happens to me, he'll be in charge.

"Squad One, you're going to take the first trip. Squad Two will be held here in reserve if you come back empty-handed. I'd like to send both squads, but site protection here is still our primary mission and we can't leave the client with just one squad in case things turn to shit. So, that's that.

"Lastly," writing *Communication and Signals* on the board, "squad leaders'll have dual frequency PRRs and we'll be giving as much information as we can via Predator. Andy in the comm bunker is going to make sure that when the op lifts off, any follow-on units or higher authorities will have the same frequencies and codes so they can also communicate with you directly.

"Bagram says they're patched in directly with the SARSAT so if the package pops up on the locator beacons, we should get that next-to-immediately.

"And one last point. It's possible they don't have a survival radio or it's broke-dick or whatever. They may try to signal you other ways, like flashlights or a mirror. Be on the lookout for that kind of thing." He looks at the board as if making sure he has covered everything and then turns back to the guys. "That's all I've got. Big Mike wants to say something and then you're outta here."

Big Mike stands up, shoves his hands in his pockets and takes over the briefing. "You guys are *not* an invading force. This is a rescue and your rules of engagement should be leaning towards the *de*fensive as opposed to *off*ensive," he says emphasizing each word. "There's a possibility, and our good-case scenario, that the guys in the trucks aren't bad actors and are trying to help find survivors. They may try to signal their intentions to you when they see you. I'm not saying trust them but if you think they're on your side, use them don't abuse them. Remember, we're in *their* country.

"If you determine they're bad guys and you have to engage them to pull the package out, then you do what you have to do to protect yourselves and the package.

"Now, the word from my bosses is that my guy is your first priority and the rest of the package comes a distant second. I know that's shitty but that's how they see it."

There are some grumbles and a quiet, "Fuck that!" from someone on the floor.

"But," Big Mike continues, taking off his glasses. "*I* don't see it like that and I'm the guy in charge on the ground *here*. Those guys are Americans and they're serving their country. As far as *I'm* concerned, they're *all* client and you...don't...leave...*any*...client...behind." He takes a deep breath. "And troops, if that means you have to waste everyone that's keeping you from saving those guys, then you *better* show 'em what a big can of American whup-ass looks like! Oo-fucking-rah?!"

There is an instantaneous, unanimous chorus of "OO-rah!" from the guys I work with. I am touched by their excitement; whether it is the chance for an op or because they are really concerned about my brother isn't what is important. The fact that they are ready to throw down for him is.

Gucci, Benwha, Lemon, Argo, the author.

Warlock.

CHAPTER THIRTEEN

Special Agents Davis, Lacle, Guzman, Group Supervisor Thibodaux, National Clandestine Service Officer Jack, the same two Paramilitary Operations Officers who had provided protection for Jack on the undercover meeting, the Chief of Station, an Army Captain in desert fatigues, five SEALs from Task Force One under the command of Petty Officer Steve Weiss, four counter-surveillance specialists from the Coyote unit, and R2 sat around the tables in the dully-lit ████-bar.

In contravention to the bar's rules forbidding guns, everyone except the agents from Miami and the CoS were carrying suppressed MP-5s and M4A1s, a single M-16 on the Captain's shoulder, AR-10s, Glock and Sig Sauer handguns in tactical thigh holsters. The SEALs and Coyote soldiers had black throat mics and earpieces. The Annex's security detail wore Motorola radios with microphones hanging from their body armor. Before deploying, all the radios would be "plugged" to ensure they were on the same frequency with the same encryption.

Two black cases about four feet in length were leaning against the wall.

Everyone in the room was drinking water or sodas. The door to the bar was locked from the inside but as it was only eight in the morning, there was little chance someone would be stumbling in for drinks.

Chris was to start the briefing and bring everyone up to speed before turning it over to others for the tactical information. He stood up and put his back to the bar. He was not so comfortable giving speeches like this, had never been so good at it, and had even taken a class on public speaking in college, though standing here now, he was thinking it was four wasted credit hours.

"Hey everyone, my name's Chris Davis. I'm a Special Agent with the Drug Enforcement Administration and based in Miami." With that introduction, he launched into a fairly cohesive summary of the case from the initial arrest in Miami at the TGI Fridays to the undercover telephone call between Mau and Samadi where the details for the transfer of the money were arranged.

Prior to the meeting, the Miami agents had gone into the dark basement and met with several of the SEALs who determined there was no reason why the money handover couldn't go down right on Chicken Street in front of the carpet store. It was good from both a surveillance and tactical perspective, and the presence of the children there made it safer for the tactical teams should they be needed as it was less likely the bad guys would be doing much shooting with kids everywhere. Not inconceivable, but less likely.

Mau was almost shocked, both with the cavalier attitude the SEALs displayed regarding the children's safety if bullets started flying and with the ease Samadi agreed with the SEALs' plan, which went like this: In the afternoon, Samadi or his people would drive a truck containing the money onto Chicken Street and park on the street in front of the store. Mau and an Afghan driver from the Annex local guard force would then take the truck and drive it away. As before, the local driver was coached and driven the surveillance detection route from Chicken Street several times and briefed he was to say as little as possible when the meeting went down. It appeared almost sophomoric in its simplicity.

Petty Officer Weiss replaced Chris at the bar. He was an olive-skinned man of medium height with graying, curly hair, a bit older than the younger SEALs in his platoon. Like the rest of the shooters, he was wearing a black Nomex, flame-retardant flight suit, the standard issue uniform for the Special Forces teams when preparing for action.

He had a large photograph taken from overhead of the carpet shop and the marketplace neighborhood extending out for several blocks. He propped it up on the bar and described where his men and the Coyote units would be as well as the surveillance vehicle. It was very similar to the undercover meeting, tactically speaking. A major difference, however, was this time, there would be two sniper teams keeping an eye on the undercover agent, real-time, and relaying what they were seeing back to the rest of the group.

Motioning to the Army Captain, Petty Officer Weiss stated on his behalf the Army had been informed of the operation and were self-deconflicting. A message had gone out yesterday that Chicken Street was off-limits for the day to all military personnel; a similar message had been transmitted to International Security Assistance Force (ISAF) Headquarters.

Mau leaned over and whispered to Chris, "Snipers? Wow, this is just another fine mess you've gotten me into, Ollie."

* *

Chris was sitting with Jack in the back seat of a plain, dirty brown Jeep Wagoneer two blocks from the carpet shop. It was a bright sunny day and the windows were up, the air-conditioner blowing full blast, though it wasn't all that hot outside. "These snipers are good, right?" Chris asked. "I'd hate it if Mau got killed. I mean, I'd get my own trailer, which would be cool because he snores really loud, but I'd have to eat lunch alone and, well you know...."

Jack laughed. "They're the best."

Between them was an opened laptop plugged into a cigarette lighter and a thick cord running to a black box in the luggage area behind the seat. On the screen a live video feed, tapped into the sniper observer's scope, projected exactly what the sniper team was seeing. The view was from several blocks away, straight down the street with the carpet shop on the right. The street was crowded with foot traffic, the occasional vehicle dodging the people walking in the middle of the wide, hectic street. The picture had very high resolution and people's faces were clearly identifiable as they passed in front of the camera. Most of the people on screen were wearing brightly colored clothing, some, though not all, of the women wearing scarves or burkas. It was odd watching the feed without audio, like the volume had been turned down on the world. Suddenly the screen went white and Chris could see nothing.

"Sniper One," crackled a hand-held radio from the front seat. "I've got a truck stopping in front of the target location. White tractor-trailer. Kabul license plate 35442."

"Pass me that radio," asked Jack. The man in the front seat handed it back. "Sniper One, can you zoom out the video a little? I want to be able to see the target if he leaves the shop." The picture widened out and Chris watched as an old man stepped down out of the passenger's side of the cab. Because of the angle, he couldn't see the driver's side. The passenger was tall and incredibly old, with a gray beard, his head wrapped in a dark green turban trailing down his back. He was wearing a sport coat over a dress-like shirt that reached nearly to his ankles. He shuffled away from the truck, swatting at the children who tried to beg something from him. Sniper One was narrating everything Chris was seeing.

"Sniper One, do you see the driver?" asked Jack.

"Negative. I don't have the angle."

"Sniper Two, I've got the driver through the front windshield. He's wearing a gray long sleeve shirt and black cap."

The speaker on the laptop came alive. "Stand by," said Jack. "We have an outgoing call from the target."

Mau: *"Hola."*

Samadi: *"Salamo Aleikom! It is Samadi."*

Mau: *"And peace be with you! How are you doing, my friend?"*

Samadi: *"I am very many nice, thank you. I call to tell you that what we have wait for has arrived and I invite you to join me to my office."*

Mau: *(Laughter) "That is very good. I am just finishing my lunch and can be there in about ten minutes. Is that good?"*

Samadi: *"Oh yes, very good. I will wait here for you. And you will have a driver, yes?"*

Mau: *"I do, he is with me now."*

Samadi: *"And I will be seeing you soon then, in shallah.."*

Mau: *"Very good then. Adios, my brother."*

Samadi: *"Goodbye."*

The call terminated. Jack got on the handheld and relayed the conversation to the surveillance teams. His mobile phone rang. He listened for a moment, then over radio said, "Signals unit is getting good conversation from inside the target location, two voices."

"Surveillance, R2. UC is leaving the green building. We're in trail."

The men sat in silence for a few minutes watching the back end of the white truck.

"This is Coyote Two, UC is in the area."

"Sniper One...I've got the UC turning onto the target street."

"R2 breaking off and is RTB."

The taxi pulled in and parked behind the white truck. Mau and the Afghan driver got out and walked into the store. Mau, forewarned again, had a large bag of red-and-white mints from which he was pulling handfuls of candy and tossing them into the air to the laughing children. The taxi moved off, back to the Annex as it wouldn't be needed again.

"Sniper One...UC is entering the target location."

The speaker on the laptop came alive as "the guys upstairs" routed the conversation from Samadi's cell phone to the surveillance vehicle. Mau and Samadi were speaking English. They could hear the two men give each other a hug, and then Samadi suggested they go outside.

"Sniper One...I have the UC, the target, and the passenger walking to the white truck. Target is wearing light blue pajamas, dark blue blazer, white skull cap. I have the driver now. Driver is wearing light gray pajamas. Driver is opening the rear door. Sniper One is targeting."

The radio was silent as the sniper team focused in, in case their firing skills were needed. Chris watched as the driver opened the rear door. Samadi, the driver, and the passenger climbed in. Mau stayed on the pavement.

"Holy shit," said Chris. Stacked along the side of the trailer were stacks and stacks of paper bills piled about three feet high running the length of the truck from front to back, secured with bright purple strapping tape. "*Holy shit!*" he said again laughing.

Jack picked up the radio and started narrating for the rest of the team. "Bad guys are in the truck, money is in the truck, UC is on the ground. Audio indicates target and UC are preparing to swap the vehicle. Bad guys are climbing out of the truck. Driver is closing the door. UC and target are shaking hands. Bad guys are walking back into target location. UC is entering the vehicle. UC driver is walking to front of vehicle, now out of sight." The truck vibrated and pulled forward, moving away from the camera's point of view.

"Sniper One...vehicle is leaving target location. Vehicle is making right turn. Vehicle out of sight."

"Coyote One...I have the vehicle."

"Coyote Two...we're in trail."

"Sniper One...targets are still in the target location. I have no other vehicles moving on the street."

"Coyote units," said Jack, "Surveillance One. You've got it all. We're RTB."

"Coyote One."

"Coyote Two."

"Sniper teams are RTB."

"Raid One and Raid Two holding position until Coyote calls clear."

"Surveillance One clear."

Chris, Mau and Pedro sat on the patio behind the dining room in the Annex complex. The sun was pounding down but no one had the strength to get up and hide in the shade. Chris had his head on his arms resting on the plastic table. Mau was wearing a Hawaiian print shirt and sunglasses and had his arms crossed, though he hadn't moved in some time. There were three full bottles of water on the table but no one had taken a drink.

Chris mumbled into his arm. "I feel like re-fried fuck."

Mau burped, made some obscure motion touching his thumb to his forehead, then returned to unmoving silence.

Pedro coughed. "If I knew where my gun was right now, I'd blow my brains out."

Jack stepped out from the dining room, moving slowly. "*Bleh*," he grumbled. "My mouth feels like the entire Taliban just marched through it with old leather sandals covered in goat-shit." He set a bottle of water down. "Anyone get laid?"

Chris' arm went straight up and then collapsed weakly.

"Niiiice," growled Pedro. "Where is she?"

Chris shook his head. "Went…back…to…embassy."

Mau sat up abruptly. "She was beautiful! And really loud…she was screaming so much, I thought you were stabbing her, man."

Chris lifted his head and laughed. "I was!"

"Did you get her number?" asked Jack, sitting down.

"I did! She told it to me. At the time I couldn't believe that I was carrying on a conversation in such incredibly fluent German. Unfortunately, I can't remember a word of it now so…wait…nope."

"That's too bad."

"Mmm. I'm going back to bed." He stood up and walked down the steps then turned around. "I just wanna say, though…" he waited until everyone was able to focus on him. "Afghanistan rocks!" He gave them all a thumbs-up and wandered away.

The money pickup on Chicken Street. Samadi is 2nd
from the left.

Special Agent Pedro Guzman (left) at the German
Embassy.

Chris and Mau celebrating at the German Embassy.

CHAPTER FOURTEEN

JD sat on the hard, gray floor. He was wearing his helo-helmet, one specially designed to drown out the overwhelming noise. As CAG, he had personalized helmets for each of the different aircraft in the wing.

It was warm in the cabin, not exactly hot. Speeding along at one hundred fifty nautical miles per hour a thousand feet above the desert, there was no way the air-conditioner could keep the big empty cabin sufficiently cool in this oven, but it was doing its best.

He looked at his watch for no reason, just for something to do.

The Customs inspection in Karachi had been perfunctory and rapid. While on the ground refueling, he had crawled into the cockpit and one of the pilots had shown him how to use the radio. He called back to the ship to see if there was any new intelligence about the plane crash or his brother (there wasn't) and to be sure everything in the air wing was ops-normal (it was).

"CAG?" clicked the speakers in his helmet.

He pressed the push-to-talk button on the cord his helmet was plugged into. "Go ahead."

"We're coming up on the camp. We're off-setting to the east on downwind and will be putting down on the south pad."

JD looked out the left window and saw limitless expanses of brown interrupted by a ramshackle collection of tents, like a squatter's village, and then they were past it and making a wide left turn. The helicopter pitched up, killing its forward speed and descended past a huge canvas hangar. The enormous rotors were kicking up a tornado of fine sand and litter as it touched down gently from the hover. There were about a dozen guys standing around in the shade of the hangar, a few in shorts and t-shirts, but most in desert camouflage. They were wearing sunglasses and a collection of baseball caps or other head protection from the blazing white sun. There was also a small cart with a litter and some boxes with red crosses painted on them.

As the weight of the helo settled on the wheels, the engine started its spool-down. He pulled up at the buckle and stood in a crouch, waiting for the flight engineer to open the door. He stepped out into the blistering heat.

221

Immediately covered in sweat, he swiped his forehead with the sleeve of his flightsuit.

The men came walking up to the helo and as he pulled off his helmet, he heard a truck engine starting. And then his brother was standing in front of him. Jeff and Pete hugged tightly, neither ashamed at the demonstration of brotherly affection.

"Just don't kiss me," joked Jeff.

"Yeah, well you're the first fresh face we've seen here in a long time. I don't know how long I can keep these guys off you." Pete's grin was massive.

"What's with the beard? You look like dad."

"I'll tell you about it later. Here, give me that." He took the helmet. "Let me introduce you around. Everybody!" he shouted. "This is Jeff Davis, he's my older brother." The guys all stepped in and shook his hand. A few thanked him for bringing the helo. All had callsigns, though they skipped off his mental flight deck without hooking his memory's "3-wire."

"Jesus Christ," growled a voice coming from around the helo. "That's all I need is another Davis on my base." Pete introduced JD to MC, who welcomed him with a handshake. "Good to have you here, sir." It was a strange tradition but with rare exceptions, junior officers in the Navy were referred to by enlisted personnel as "Mister." It wasn't until an officer had achieved some longevity and rank and wisdom (hopefully), they were given the more respectful appellation, "Sir."

"Master Chief," replied Jeff. "I've heard a lot about you."

"And likewise, sir. I can't tell you how glad we are to have your helo. Why don't we step out of this sun right quick and I'll brief you on what we're up to." He led JD away, his taller, younger brother at his side.

The Master Chief gave a comprehensive brief to Captain Davis, devoid of the humor he had used with his own troops. They were sitting in the air-conditioned room where the feed was being broadcast from the Predator to the north.

JD was leaning back in a gray metal chair. He said nothing for a minute, his hand at his mouth. He nodded. "It's good, under the circumstances."

"Yes, sir, it is."

"I'm not going to beat around the bush, Master Chief. I'm going on the helo."

Meat looked from his brother to MC. "Well...uh...sir -"

"It's not a negotiable item, Master Chief. It's my helo, those are my pilots, it's my brother out there. There's more than enough room for me to go out in that thing. I'm going."

"You see, sir...the law -"

"I'm sorry, Master Chief, this conversation is over. I'll pull my weight, but before that helo lifts off your pad, my ass is going to be on it."

MC was furiously twirling his moustache and breathing deeply. Civilian or not *now*, he had spent his life as a Navy enlisted and JD was a Navy Captain, and at the end of the day, like it or not, he was the officer, and an order was an order. "Yes, sir."

"Good," JD said, slapping his knees. "I've got a nine-millimeter and I'm taking it with me. If you want to give me something with a scope on it, something simple, that'd be great but it's up to you. I'm not telling you I'm as good as these guys but I can shoot, I can pull a body into my helo."

The Master Chief stood up straight. Decision made. "Yes, sir. But you have to understand, sir, that your brother is going to be the squad leader. He's my representative on the ground and you hold no rank over him or anyone else once that helo lifts off. Can we be agreed on that?"

223

Jeff stood up, walked over to the Master Chief and shook his hand. "Agreed."

Everybody stood around the helo.

The area behind the pilots' seats was crammed with olive-green cases and boxes, everything strapped down for a rough ride. JD listened as someone who sounded like a doctor explained what everything was and how it was packed. One of the other guys was listening intently, nodding and pointing at each item.

"Where's the Navy Captain?" a voice called out. JD turned and saw a battery powered, green John Deere cart pulling onto the apron. A short, thin man in jeans stood and walked over towards the helo. JD introduced himself. "Let's take a walk," the man suggested. "I'm the CO here, Captain. Master Chief Davis just told me about your conversation, and I've got a little problem with it and hopefully you'll be able to help me out."

"Go on."

"Captain, I don't know if you know this but the law's pretty specific about the use of military personnel on this kind of thing. It says -"

"I know what it says." JD said cutting him off.

"Well, okay then. You see, these guys," motioning over his shoulder, "*my* guys, we're able to do what we do because we're not military, we're civilian intelligence and we're allowed to be here. And it's my agency's determination that we can slide your helicopter and pilots because they fall under equipment. But the moment you get onboard...you're not integral to the mission, you're active-duty military and you're the Airwing Commander attached to an aircraft carrier sitting off the coast of the country that's allowing us to be here. If anything happens to you, if you wind up hurt, if you wind up dead, if you wind up on TV with three guys behind you and a big knife...well, the blowback far outweighs you wanting to save your little

224

brother. What you're talking about doing, if it goes wrong, it could hurt, it could *end* our ability to do business. You would be embarrassing both the Pakistan and US governments. We're national assets and your participation could get us pulled out and help the enemy. Captain, I'm grateful for what you've done for us, but we're doing good things here and if something happens to you, we're finished. Is what you want to do worth that?"

JD took off his sunglasses and wiped the sweat from his eyes and off his forehead. He turned his back and started walking towards the hangar. "Give me a minute," he called over his shoulder.

Big Mike walked towards the helo. "How long before you're ready to blast off?" he asked no one in particular.

"About five minutes," said the senior pilot. "Gotta hit the latrine and the gee-dunk and we're good to go."

"I'm sorry, General, the dunk *what*?"

"Gee-dunk. Something fast to eat. Cookies, a coke, maybe a sandwich and a candy bar…we haven't eaten since we left the ship."

"Don," called Big Mike. "Make sure these guys get some food from your tent before they take off."

"Roger that," came a voice from the other side of the helo.

"Do you guys have secure HF?"

"Yes," replied the pilot.

Big Mike took an index card from his pocket. "Good. Here's the frequencies and callsigns. We sent the comm plan to all the players, but there's a chance someone not on the card may still chime in; if they're secure, they're dialed in. If you drop sync and can't re-code, everybody's got today's and tomorrow's authentication codes." Authentication codes are classified, pre-printed tables with multi-character pairs that are standard across all the services. In the event communications take place over non-secure radios, either party can, through a timed challenge and response, confirm the other

225

person's orders are valid. The codes change daily at midnight. "Did you bring yours from the ship?"

The Marine pursed his lips and shook his head, his eyes invisible behind dark, gold-framed glasses. "No we didn't. This was supposed to be a LOGRUN."

Big Mike reached into another pocket and handed him two pieces of paper stapled together. "No sweat. Here's a photocopy. We'll need it back. I don't think, given the nature of the op, that COMSEC's[1] a valid concern but better safe than sorry, I guess. Anyway, maintain a listening watch for us on HF but keep your VHF and UHF on Guard 'cause that's what we hope the survivors will call on."

JD walked up to Big Mike and after waiting to be sure his conversation with the pilot was done, said to Big Mike, "Let's step over here." The two men walked back into the shade of the hangar. "Can you keep a secret?"

Big Mike laughed. "Well, I think our record speaks for itself...so...it's doubtful."

Jeff nodded. "Yeah, all right, but this place is so isolated maybe you can pull it off for a day or so." He handed him a piece of paper, neatly folded. "This is my resignation from the Naval Service. I know you're not my boss but if this goes bad, you can get it to him. It's dated and timed from when I left the ship." He reached up and tore his Velcro'd name patch from his flight suit, looked at it, and handed it to Big Mike as well. "I'm going on that helicopter. Hopefully I'll be back in a little while and you can give both those back to me. The Master Chief told me how it's going to be on the mission and I'm telling you that as of this moment, I'm a civilian."

Big Mike took a deep breath.

---

[1] Communications Security

"But," continued JD without waiting for a response, "I worked long and hard to get where I am in the Navy and I fully expect that when the sun comes up tomorrow, I'll still be in the Navy. Don't send that in by mistake, okay?"

Big Mike nodded and grinned. "Alright, civilian. I'll take good care of it. Thanks."

The two men shook hands, and JD walked out into the light at the same time the Master Chief shouted, "Okay, piglets, before we gather 'round the campfire and I give you a final few words of wisdom...lemme talk to the squad CO and XO. Everyone else stay close."

CHAPTER FIFTEEN

Chris was talking to Ricardo, updating him on the progress of the case. It was late in the afternoon and after taking a long hangover nap, he was feeling much better.

"Mau talked to the bad guy this afternoon, the one who gave us the money." Chris was calling from the DEA office within the embassy. He had asked his GS to talk to him from the other building where the STU III secure telephone was located. "He said the merchandise is here and whenever we're ready, he'll take us there to get them."

"Chris," he said, "that's great. You and Mau are doing an outstanding job and I'll be honest with you, I'm surprised at the skill both you and your brother have shown on this case." Chris felt puffed up by the praise but was then rapidly deflated when House said, "I'll also need you to do a teletype ops-plan because Headquarters needs to know what's happening over there." Chris had been hoping to get away with not spending hours on an op-plan that would have to be approved all the way up the e-chain of command back at Headquarters in Washington D.C., literally half-a-world-away. "I don't want to micromanage you because you've probably got enough of that going on there, but give me the big picture of how you're planning for this to go down so I can brief the SAC."

"Roughly it goes like this. Mau's going to go to the carpet store where he picked up the money. Then he and Samadi are going to drive to the house where the heroin's stored. Now -"

"Separate cars, right? I don't want Mau in the same car with Samadi."

"Okay. We'll do that. There's also going to be a truck to move the heroin from there to the base. Well, I mean, we're telling the bad guys it's going to Bagram Air Force Base but it'll be staying here. Anyway, if the big guy, Anwar, is at the stash house, then after the truck is gone, the hit teams are going to go in and grab him. If he's not -"

"What kind of area is it, the neighborhood where the stash house is? Is it under surveillance now?"

"It's…um…it's a ghetto, except worse. It's sort of near the airport next to the highway. Really bad. We haven't been by the location yet because we have no idea who's wired into the neighborhood and doing security, but there's this plane and it's tracking Anwar's telephone, and they localized it into a house in the neighborhood, and that's where we think the drugs are so that's what we're going with right now."

"What happens if Mau follows Samadi to somewhere that's not where they think the heroin is?"

"I…uh…"

"If this were going down in Miami, would we let the UC just drive off to someone's house whether or not we had surveillance set up?"

"Mmm…probably not, no."

"Right. Even though you're a long way away you've still got to remember the basics for UC safety. We both know it's probably not a rip, but what if the bad guys get it into their heads that it's a good idea for Mau to stay, you know, as their guest until the heroin arrives safely in the US? We just can't take that chance. We don't send the UC into people's houses because history shows it's a bad idea, that that's where the UCs usually get dead. It would be better to get them to bring the drugs to a public place and just take it from there. Like you did with the money."

Chris found himself nodding. "Okay, we'll make the changes."

"Good. Keep going."

"Okay, anyway, after we get the drugs, we're going to move in and arrest Anwar if he's there, and Samadi and anyone else. And that's it."

"Good. Sounds like a pretty good plan. When you say 'we're' going to move in and arrest Anwar.... "

"Well, I mean, not me or the other DEA guys, but there's going to be SEALs and CIA and stuff."

"Okay. Make the changes we talked about, get it on a teletype and we'll get it all approved and going. Shouldn't take too much time since most of headquarters is already read in to what's happening. And Chris...."

"Yes, sir."

"This is your case. You're the boss. Don't let them push you around on how it goes. Mau's your UC and his safety is your responsibility."

"Yes, sir."

"Speaking of Mau, tell him I read his Undercover "6" on the meeting with Samadi and his math was all kinds of fucked-up. Fifteen hundred kilos times six thousand dollars per kilo times twenty five percent is not three million six hundred thousand dollars. Obviously the bad guys weren't using an abacus because they delivered the right amount but have him make the correction and re-submit it and stop counting on his fingers." Chris could hear his boss smiling over the phone. "And tell him he spelled his own name wrong in the header on line 5. Gee whiz, is it any wonder why we're losing the drug war?"

"No, sir."

"You really are doing a good job, though. Keep it up."

"Can I get a raise?"

House hung up the phone.

Chris relayed the conversation to Mau, Pedro and Jack.

Mau nodded. "Well, you know, he *is* right."

"Yeah, I know. So, Jack, can you come up with someplace to do this?"

"Shouldn't be a problem." He looked over at Mau. "Why not just tell Samadi we want to do it at the carpet shop?"

"Mmm." He mumbled non-commitally.

"What?" asked Jack, a little shortly.

"You think Anwar will be bring lots of guys with guns?"

Jack said, "With fifteen hundred kilos of heroin? I think he'll be bringing an army!"

"Right. And we're bringing our army?"

"Yeah...well, SEALs are Navy, but yeah."

"And there's lots of kids running around there. And if anything went bad and there was a gun battle and lots of kids and one of them...." As a father, he was seeing things from a perspective the single men didn't.

"Shit," said Jack, shaking his head in self-disgust. "We've funded this guy's drug business; we've eliminated his competition; and now we top it off with some dead children. Ugh."

"That would be bad, right?" joked Chris.

"Yeah. No ice cream for the gang."

Pedro frowned, "There goes all the money I made after my wife divorces me."

Mau said, "Perhaps we should re-think the Chicken Street thing. You know, in Miami we use mall parking lots. In New York we just did it on the streets. Why don't we just set up a street or parking lot and do it like that? Keep it simple."

Jack sat for a minute in silence, then said, "You're right, Mau. Thanks. I'll talk to the Coyote guys. Since they do most of our counter-surveillance, I'm betting they know lots of places that'll work. And they'll have already done the surveillance detection routes so they'll know all the ways in and out."

It took two days of back and forth phone calls and teletypes, but finally the operations plan was given approval from DEA headquarters. Briefings were held at both the Annex and then again at the embassy in condensed form for the Ambassador himself. Chris had given both briefings, the second in coat and tie. The Ambassador had listened quietly, nodded and dismissed the DEA / CIA troupe without comment.

Based on suggestions from Mau, the Coyote unit, and Ricardo back in Miami, the decision was made *not* to try to effect an arrest / apprehension of Anwar at the same time as the drug delivery. The new plan was to initiate a loose, mostly electronic surveillance on him and the drug pickup, get the heroin safely "in pocket," and give Anwar a little time to chill before stitching him up.

Within hours of the approval of the plan, "the guys upstairs" zeroed in on Anwar's phone and localized it not far from the airport. Coyote units started doing casual drive-bys to get the lay of the land and take photos where possible as everyone assumed after the deal went down, this was where Anwar would return and it would be there they would lift him.

The drop location chosen by the Coyote unit fit the new DEA requirements perfectly. The street was identical to every other in the neighborhood: hard-packed dirt, bounded on both sides by shallow ditches and war-beaten houses and shops. The drop would go down at a house that at one time had also been a machine and vehicle repair shop. Inside were lots of dark rooms where SEALs would be hiding, hopefully not to be needed. The house had been used as an observation post earlier that year by an Army SF team, though no one could say what or who was being observed.

The Coyote unit recon'd the neighborhood, house cum repair shop, and adjoining area, and pronounced it still vacant and ready for their purposes. They had taken pictures, and Chris, Pedro and Jack, who were

232

(now) all properly educated, noted the presence of several children playing in the dirt across the street. They brought this up and after a discussion of school days and hours, the time of the meet was slipped to take advantage of that.

The house was "U"-shaped, with the front of the house the bottom of the "U" and facing the street. Between the two legs was an outdoor toilet and what could have been a garden if it weren't for the piles of rubbish, construction trash, and motor parts. One leg contained basically empty rooms; the other housed what was left of a kitchen. One of the kitchen walls was partially collapsed and led into the wreckage of another house - just two skeletons joined by a common wall. The main room facing the street was narrow and stuffed with trash, rusty metal, and two old wood pallets where the heroin would be loaded. The big loading door at the front of the house was wedged shut, allowing entrance only through the small doorway adjacent to it.

SEALs would take up security positions both within and without. On the way in, they would dress as locals so as not to draw undue attention to their presence. They were already operating under "relaxed grooming standards" and several had long beards and were fairly unkempt.

Mau had called Samadi and passed a story that one of the Air Force loadmasters had a local girlfriend with a house, and they were going to store the boxes there until the plane was ready to be loaded. The day of the deal, Mau and his driver were going to stop by the carpet shop and meet with Samadi, who would call Anwar and get him moving in the right direction. Then Mau and driver, with Samadi following in a separate car or taxi (on the pretext Mau was going to remain with the boxes until his Air Force guys were ready and wouldn't be able to take him back to the carpet shop) would drive to the house with Samadi giving Anwar directions over his cellular phone.

It was still expected Anwar would have his show of force to protect his investment but with any luck, it would not be needed and would simply fade. When Anwar arrived, they would unload whatever vehicles the heroin was in, move it into the house onto a wood pallet, and depart the area. Once he was clear, Army Humvees would go in and collect the heroin, drive it to the military detachment at the airport and put it into secure storage.

They would do the deal mid-afternoon, advantageous not only because the children would be in school, but also because Anwar might be less likely to make the long drive back to Qwost, and therefore, would hopefully lay up at the same location where the Special Forces airborne unit said his phone was right now.

The snatch teams would wait until just before the sun rose, when Anwar was sure to be sleeping, to raid the house. They'd grab him and as many of his guys as they could, transport them to the military detachment to be secured with the heroin and then let the party begin!

Across the street from the drop-house was a small two-story building consisting of a food market and sundry shops selling odds-and-ends on the first floor and several apartments above connected by an outside walkway. The apartments looked down on a dirt lot with a scattering of cars and a hand-pumped well in the center of it for drawing up fresh water.

Before sunup, a SEAL sniper team, accompanied by Pedro Guzman, had gone into one of the vacant apartments above the market and set their observation post. They would be the overwatch once Mau entered the area, keeping the other shooter teams in the loop. The door to the apartment was wide open. They had pried out the windows from their frames and laid them carefully on the dirty floor; they would be replaced when the operation was complete. They had also hung a thin sheet of black mesh netting from floor to ceiling about six feet back into the room, through which they could see out clearly but anyone looking in would see only darkness and shadow. Behind the net, they had set up a medium-high table on which the monopod'd rifle rested; should the need arise they could shoot through the material without it deflecting the high-powered rounds. To prevent anyone from wandering into the observation post, an old, bearded, grumpy Afghan from the Annex's local guard force was sitting in a plastic chair outside the apartment next to the door, a newspaper on his lap. He had been told in the event of gunfire, he was to do nothing - not move, not run, not lie down. There could be rifle rounds coming fast and furious from inside the apartment and the safest place for him was in the chair, statue-like. He had nodded his understanding. A veteran of years of occupation by the Soviets, Taliban, and now the Americans, there was very little the strange people who constantly invaded his country could do that would scare, shock, or surprise him.

Coyote counter-surveillance units would be following Mau from the carpet shop and Anwar from his house. In the back of one of the trucks, lying on a mattress under a cotton blanket in the rear bed, were two soldiers and a Belgian-made, belt-fed general-purpose machine gun in 7.62 caliber, capable of throwing high-powered destruction downrange at a rate of eight hundred rounds per minute.

While it seemed like a lot of firepower, no one knew exactly how many men Anwar would be bringing with him, and all subscribed to the theory that you never bring a knife to a gunfight.

Chris sat cross-legged in the dark wearing navy-blue cargo pants and a DEA polo shirt with a heavy Kevlar vest over his chest, sweating like a bastard in hot, still air that smelled like dirt, motor oil, body odor, and metal. He was wearing a set of night vision goggles attached to a nylon and plastic harness on the top of his head as well as a large Motorola radio on his belt with a thin wire ending in a plug buried deep in his ear. The ground under him was dirt packed so hard it had the consistency of uneven concrete, and he was continuously shifting around trying to find a comfortable spot.

There were three CIA paramilitary officers in the room, sitting quietly with their backs against the wall, heads down and machine guns in their laps, totally relaxed. Green beams blossomed brightly from the infrared bulbs on their night vision goggles invisibly illuminating the little room, revealing disrepaired or abandoned engine guts in the corners and several cases of bottled water, brought in to keep everyone hydrated.

Jack was lying in the center of the room, on the floor on his back, his arms crossed over his chest like a corpse.

The room they were in was at the very rear of the house behind a sheet of plywood. The guys had shoved and wedged the wood in place so it wouldn't fall on its own or move easily if Anwar's guards took a push around. Jack had handed Chris a Glock handgun with the admonition he wanted it back and Chris had better not say anything about it. Chris nodded, checked the weapon was properly loaded, and shoved it into the back of his pants.

On the other side of the hall across from Chris, in another room concealed behind a piece of corrugated steel, hid the SEAL detachment. They were dressed in their black coveralls; if they had to move they would be invisible in the darkness. Tactical advantage: movement and shadow. They would be the primary response team in the event Anwar's guys broke bad. When they left the Annex, they had been carrying several small hard cases and explained they contained miniature battery-powered infrared cameras they would secrete around the house and monitor from their own room. Unfortunately, they didn't transmit with enough power to be monitored by anyone else in the area.

"Anwar's on the move," said Jack without moving. Chris had been sure he was sleeping.

"I didn't get that on my radio," said Chris.

"You will in a second. I'm listening to the plane guys talking to their headquarters."

True to Jack's word, Chris' earpiece came alive and he heard his favorite bartender report Anwar was leaving his house towards the highway. "I've got approximately fifteen men, a white car, a red car and a blue deuce-and-a-half jingle truck." He was describing the two-and-a-half ton, ten wheelers that are ubiquitous to Afghanistan and Pakistan, brightly painted with colorful designs and strings of tiny chains that hang off the rear bumpers that tinkle and jingle when they sway with the truck's motion.

Once the convoy pulled onto the highway and was headed towards the meet spot, Jack lifted his radio and requested a rollcall starting with himself. The replies would come in the pre-determined order from the inside of the house and expanding outwards. After each group, there was a pause to give the surveillance units time to chime in, in case they had something to be passed. The three paramilitary shooters in the room were next.

"Papa One."

"Papa Two."

"Papa Three."

After they reported, Chris watched them slowly get to their feet, shake out their legs, and stretch. He took their lead, as did Jack. The men did another weapon's check and shook themselves to make sure nothing clinked or clanked. Unlike Chris and Jack who only had handguns, the three paramilitary officers were carrying MP-5s with long suppressors. It had been explained to him they kept their weapons "silenced" so if they heard gunshots, they'd know they were from bad guys and could localize them. Of course, it also meant the bad guys wouldn't be able to hear where the good guy's rounds were coming from. Tactical advantage: sound.

Pause…

"Raid One." This was Petty Officer Weiss, the SEAL team leader across the hall.

"Raid Two."

"Raid Three."

"Raid Four."

Pause...

"Sniper One," came the clipped report from across the street. The team observer, Sniper Two, was automatically included in that check-in, as was Pedro.

Pause...

"Coyote One and Two. We have eyes on the UC and Bravo One." They were driving the car painted like a taxi and would follow Mau and Samadi from the carpet shop. "Estimate ten to twelve minutes to meet spot."

"Coyote Three." This was the pickup truck that would loosely trail behind Coyote One and Two and remain clear until Anwar and the drugs were at the house before taking up a firing position.

"Gun One." Came a more muffled voice from under the blanket in the back of Coyote Three's truck.

"Gun Two."

Pause...

"Coyote Four and Five, and we have eyes on Bravo Two and the target vehicles." They were well back, watching the convoy, sometimes using binoculars. There was no reason to be right up on their ass as the convoy's destination was already known. They were just making sure no stops were made or other bad guys joined. "Estimate fifteen minutes out."

"R2 and FUBAR are around the corner from Bravo Two's house. No visual." Also in their truck were two Special Forces soldiers from the Intelligence Support Activity doing SIGINT surveillance in coordination with the King Air overhead. They had affixed a large X-shaped antenna on the roof of the truck and in the event the plane had to shift position closer to the drop house, they could still control and monitor the bad guy's telephones from their truck.

"Air One...we're getting good conversation from the cell phones between Bravo One and Two. He's giving him straight directions. Doesn't seem to be any confusion." There were two interpreters from the embassy onboard to give up-to-the-minute translation. While most of the members of the SF unit had language training, it had been decided native speakers in both Pashtu and Arabic should be brought along this time in case the bad guys started using unfamiliar slang.

Pause...

"Transport One and Two. We're stationary at the Annex." The Humvee's drivers didn't expect to be moving before the sun went down.

And finally, "Annex One," came the rolling voice of the Chief of Station who was sitting at the green building with G/S Sarah Thibodaux.

"Coyote Four...convoy is leaving the main road. We're approximately five minutes out. Break. Coyote One, did you just turn left in front of the concrete plant?

"Affirm."

"Tap your brake lights a few times...Okay, roger that. You just passed in front of Bravo Two. You can break off. We'll take them in from here."

"Coyote One."

"Coyote Four...turning left now, three streets from target location."

The CIA Papa shooters were now standing in a line, weapons up, in a formation called "the snake." If they had to move, they would stay in a line with the man at the front, the point man, determining the direction of the formation. Each follow-on soldier would point his weapon in a different direction from the men ahead ensuring all fields of fire were covered. The last man was responsible for the security of the area behind the group. It was the entry method the DEA taught Chris as well.

While the men had been waiting for the UC to arrive, they had quietly talked and Chris had told them if they had to deploy, he intended to go with them. From his point of view, he was ultimately responsible for the UC's safety and wasn't about to sit it out while Mau's shit was in the fan. This was a minor deviation from the operations plan, but everyone in the room felt it was reasonable and he was invited to take tail end of the snake. Jack too was invited but demurred. He had had minimal tactical training at the CIA's training academy in Virginia.

At the moment, he and Jack were holding the edges of the plywood, prepared to throw it out of the way if they had to deploy.

"Coyote Four...one street out now. Break. Sniper One...you should have the UC vehicle anytime."

"Sniper One...I have eyes on the UC."

With the handoff complete, Coyote Four reported breaking contact and moving to his pre-assigned surveillance position.

"Sniper One...I have Bravo One and the convoy parking at the location...UC is exiting the vehicle and meeting with Bravo One. I have Bravo Two now. He parked in front of the UC vehicle. He's got someone else with him who's shaking hands with UC. The new guy's wearing brown pants and a blue long sleeve shirt, no moustache, no beard. I'm tagging him Bravo Three."

"Air One...I'm getting good conversation."

"Sniper One...jingle truck is stopping directly in front of the main doorway, second car behind. Everyone's bailing out. Four Bravos entering the house...I've lost contact with them."

"I've got 'em," came a whisper from Petty Officer Weiss. "Four Bravos, AKs and handguns out and up; they're searching the house; they're moving like military. I'm gonna shut up for a second."

When this operation had been briefed, Chris never considered the guys Anwar hired could be ex-military. He had just assumed they would be a couple of bearded Afghanis who would sit around, smoke cigarettes, maybe wave a gun around, and then drive away. His heart beat a little faster under his Kevlar vest, and suddenly his mouth was very, very dry.

"Sniper One...two Bravos coming my way. No weapons in sight. If they come past the well, I'll lose contact with them. They may be going to the market...four Bravos walking around the back of the house. Raid One, do you have cameras in back?"

Everyone heard three quick clicks in their radios, denoting a negative response; two for yes, three for no. After about thirty seconds of silence, a whispered voice stated, "The four in here are back in the kitchen now. One just stepped through the hole in the wall into the next house. I can't see him there."

Chris, like everyone else, was mentally keeping track of the players. From where he was, the closest threat would be out the door, right turn, corner, right turn, corner, right turn, kitchen.

"Coyote One...we're moving to try to get eyes on the guys in back."

"Sniper One...UC and the big Bravos are walking into the house. No contact."

"UC is showing them around. They're just inside the front door. UC's pointing out the pallets," came the breathy voice of the SEAL team leader.

"Air One...I have good conversation from the UC. All three phones are transmitting. It's a little messy though with this many phones."

"They're moving back outside."

"Sniper One...I have them. They're standing at the jingle...I have three Bravos getting out of the jingle now. My count is thirteen plus Bravos One, Two and Three...they're starting to unload boxes from the truck. Break. Coyote One, do you have eyes on the rear of the house?"

Coyote One was having a hard time getting to the rear of the house in the vehicle as there was nowhere to unobtrusively park. The thin dirt alley backed up to an entire block of adjoined, connected buildings that offered no breaks for a car to pass through from the next street and pulling into the alley. Parking *now* would be a massive red flag waving at the four bad guys out there. Dressed as locals, they *could* leave their long guns in the car and just walk into the alley and sit and have a cigarette and watch what was happening. He suggested this over the radio.

There was a pause in the conversation for a tactical decision to be made and relayed. "Coyote One," came the soft voice from inside the house. "Dismount and get eyes on the rear of the house." There were two quick radio clicks.

Suddenly there were several loud bangs of metal on metal that echoed in the empty house, followed by a rough grinding.

"Sniper One. They've broken the big sliding door and pushed it open."

The radios were silent for a few minutes as the loaders began moving packages into the house and setting them on the pallets. Every now and again, the air unit would report ops-normal conversation.

"Air One...does someone else there have a cell phone? We're getting a new signature and hearing muffled conversation from the other transmitters. Sounds like one side of a phone call but we can't make out much."

"Affirm...Bravo Three just turned one on and is making a call."

"Roger."

"Smart fucker," whispered Jack. "Probably knows we're in the phones. Keeps it off unless he needs it."

"Bravo Three's off the phone now…talking to Bravo Two."

"Air One…we're getting the conversation…stand by…okay, sounds like that call was from someone at Bravo Two's house. He says one of the guys saw a truck with lots of antennas around the corner from the house. They sent a kid to beg something…the kid said they're Americans. I'm losing the conversation now…he's talking too quietly."

"This is R2. That was us. We're burned. Shit. Sorry."

There was a pause in the conversation. Tactically, Raid One was in charge of the forces deployed around the house, but strategically, overall operational control rested with Sarah Thibodaux and the Chief of Station.

"R2, Annex One…stand by…Air One, do you still need them on-site or can we move them out of the way?"

"Annex One, Air One…we're getting good conversation from everyone. I've got the three phones in transmit mode and we're working on the new one. I recommend you have them shift position. We're moving slightly closer to Bravo Two's house now to catch any new signals; we'll advise." The King Air was loitering around five thousand feet. In an ideal world they could simply climb and get a better line-of-sight footprint to drag the electronic signals out of the air, but a higher altitude would put them in conflict with aircraft departing out of the Kabul airport. Also, because the range its equipment could suck energy out of the air was limited by the low wattage of the transmitters (the cell phones), if they climbed too high, they'd risk losing everything.

"R2, Annex One. You copy? Wait a couple of minutes and quietly leave the area."

"Roger that."

"Air One...Bravo Three's quizzing Bravo One and Two about the UC. Doesn't sound good. He's definitely not happy."

"Sniper One...All three are standing well away from UC."

"Air One...Three's pissed. Two's trying to calm him down. Three's accusing Two of getting caught in some kind of trap. Keeps screaming, 'Americans.'"

"Bravo One's walking the UC inside. Lost contact."

"We've got them. UC's by the pallets. Loaders still moving boxes."

"Air One...Bravo Three's got another incoming call...we've got his phone nailed down now...he's telling the...the line's still open but he's screaming at Anwar about something at the house...they're...we...stand by...he's...Bravo Two's on the phone now...says...wait...Bravo Three's yelling at Samadi...Two's telling them...they..." Suddenly, Chris could hear nothing but disjointed conversations blasting over different speakers in the airplane as another voice came on, over-riding the man they had been listening to. The new voice was talking fast and loud, "Break, UC in danger, UC in danger! Break, R2, move now, MOVE NOW...danger close!"

Through the wood in the doorway Chris heard a high-pitched blatting from a freon-powered horn, then another that was quieter, farther away, then another that was almost inaudible.

There were hand-held air horns in all the Coyote vehicles, as well as upstairs with Pedro and the sniper team. If the horns went off, Mau's instructions were to *immediately* stop doing whatever it was he was doing and simply walk, not run, walk away. On the street, he was to turn right and keep walking, not stopping for any reason until he was safely in the possession of someone from the surveillance.

"Raid One, everybody stand by...give him time to get away...UC's turning towards the door...Bravo Three's trying to block him between the boxes and the wall. Everyone's yelling at the UC...shit...gun...go, Go, GO!"

Chris and Jack heaved the wood aside to the right, Chris suddenly breathing faster as adrenaline jolted his system into high gear. Before it was out of the way, the point man was out the door, crouched and duck-walking with the others right behind him. Chris took his weapon from his jeans in a loose, two-handed grip and fell in line, facing backwards, bumping into the man in front of him. Though still in the dark room, the surplus light now flooding through the big loading door of the house washed out the night vision device, totally blinding him. With his left hand, he swept the goggles off his head, sending them flying into the air. His hand, damp with sweat, was back on his pistol, and he distantly registered the sound of the electronic device hitting either a wall or the floor. Or Jack.

He was moving slowly, his rearward momentum limited by the speed of the snake. In his earpiece was only white noise, so intent was his concentration on what he could see, which right now was nothing except back wall. He knew he should be listening to the others giving tactical updates, but there was just too much chatter coming too fast.

From behind him he heard a single flat bang and its echo into the hallway he was entering.

In the room above the market, the sniper observer reported two men walking towards the house, one with a pistol. Sniper One was already abandoning his position behind the black cloth. Once the operation went loud there was no point in remaining concealed, and he would have a better field of fire without having to worry about shooting through the thin railing on the walkway outside the door. The sniper cleared the doorway and tilted the rifle down, the monopod hanging uselessly. With both eyes open, he picked up the two armed men and adjusted his sight picture. The two on the ground were so close he could have substituted his handgun for the rifle or fired without using the scope, but that wasn't his training. As the moving targets entered the edge of the scope, he mentally focused his vision from both eyes to his dominant one. He slipped his finger into the trigger guard.

As Chris came around the corner into the main hallway, he heard two huge booms in quick succession, so close together they sounded like one tremendous explosion of sound. Chris was caught so unaware by the awesome blast he inadvertently looked away from his area of responsibility toward the front of the house.

From his peripheral vision, he saw four hunched, black shapes bursting from inside the other room. Like Chris, they had been night-vision blinded, but unlike Chris, they simply reached up, almost in unison, with their off-trigger hands and lifted the goggles clicked to their helmets. They passed in a line, were briefly silhouetted by the light coming through the front door, then were gone, but even as they passed, he saw an orange flash coming from a suppressed barrel and was aware, almost subconsciously, of the sound of empty shell casings clinking on the floor and the oily metal-on-metal slide of an MP-5 action cycling back and forth.

"Sniper One...two down. There should still be three targets outside the house but I don't have a shot. They're blocked by the big truck. Where's the UC? Where's Mau?"

Behind the house, Coyote One and Two, whose names were Leo and Randy, were squatting at the corner of the last building in the alley. They heard the air horns going off and knew the op was going pear-shaped.

Leo, who was directly facing the four guys in the alley at a distance of about thirty yards, casually started getting to his feet. They couldn't have gotten any closer without arousing the attention of the bad guys. As he stood, he slid a Glock pistol with a long suppressor from the front of his baggy pants and laid it flat against his stomach, the muzzle pointed at the ground. Randy, whose back was to the house, was getting targeting data from Leo and knew, without looking, the exact positions and descriptions of the opposition. He too stood and likewise un-covered his pistol. Their guns were between them, invisible to the enemy.

When he heard the word "gun" over his nearly-invisible earpiece, Leo started walking, Randy right next to him, their suppressed pistols now held against their thighs, unobtrusive but instantly ready.

The four men were focused on the back of the house and not on the two Coyote Special Forces shooters coming from the right. At the present moment, none of the four men were brandishing firearms, and therefore, were not an immediate threat. If possible, the Coyote team would take them alive, hog-tie 'em, and leave them for the interrogation cell.

They had closed to within about twenty yards when the sniper let go. As the thunder rolled around the alley, the four men uncovered weapons: Three pistols and a long rifle with a curved clip and wood stock and grip, an AK-47.

Leo raised his weapon in a two handed grip, elbows locked, leaning slightly forward at the waist, shoulders rolled ahead of the rest of his body as if being pulled by the target; Randy mirrored his firing stance. Both bodies now formed a series of isosceles triangles - shoulders to hands, crotch to feet - the most stable and accurate method of shooting. Together they walked, knees slightly bent, pistols held on target with laser-like precision, eyes focused on the front sights, targets slightly blurred. Leo, as team leader, would initiate fire.

One of the four at the back of the house happened to glance their way and shout. The others turned their heads, concentration now split between the house and the loud words from their partner. The one who shouted began to rotate his body and was bringing his weapon up towards the two intruders in his alley. At the same time, his knees unlocked to lower himself into a crouch position and make his profile smaller.

Leo fired first and Randy's rounds were right behind his. Neither man slowed their deliberate, controlled pace as they pressed their triggers. The man took two bullets in his forehead and two into his center mass, just to the left of his sternum. He continued into his crouch, though it was uncontrolled now, and as one knee touched the ground, the rest of him collapsed as if his skeleton had been magically removed. He fell forward on his head, his gun buried under him.

The man next to him was raising an old revolver, and Leo arc'd his aim and put two into his face. The momentum of the bullets pushed the man back a step, though with no functioning motor control now, he did little more than shuffle, drop on his ass, and lay down.

The other two jumped to their left into the area between the legs of the house where the toilet was as it was the nearest place to hide and started screaming and firing blindly back into the alley. Leo and Randy rushed to the side of the house. There was no other effective cover or concealment in the alley. Leo got prone, his body parallel to the alley, and slowly edged his pistol around the corner, resting on both elbows, his head still vertical, presenting as little a sight picture as possible to the enemy. Because he was so low to the ground, there wasn't much chance he would be seen.

"Coyote Two, we're on the left side of the house, rear, outside, engaged. Two down, two in the garden." He was leaning on his shoulder against the wall, aiming toward the street in case trouble came from that direction.

248

From the other side of the wall, both men heard automatic fire. "Fuuuck," muttered Leo.

Coyote Three threw his truck in gear. As he started moving forward, he could feel the guys in the back scrambling to get off the mattress. There was a heavy clunk above his head and the barrel of the heavy machine gun appeared facing forward. He turned right and pressed the accelerator to the floor, angling the vehicle across the road, his intention being to give the gunner a field of fire perpendicular to the sniper across the street. He heard there were three bad guys hiding behind the blue jingle truck who could keep anyone from coming out or catch them inside in crossfire.

He had an MP-5 on the seat next to him. Once the truck was stopped, he could add his fire to that of the gun upstairs. No one would survive.

His left tire hit a pothole in the road and the wheel spun in his hand. The truck veered to the left, but he caught it and glanced in the rear view mirror, making sure his exposed passengers hadn't been tossed over the side. Both men were still in place.

The Raid team had stopped short of entering the kitchen. There were occasional strings of automatic fire flying out of there. 7.62 bullets were hitting the walls embedding themselves, others ricocheting wildly in the enclosed space. One stream of fire had cut into the boxes adding a thin veil, like the finest lace, of heroin to the air.

With the exception of the initial fire, the SEALs were not trading rounds with targets they couldn't see. "Raid One...we're engaged. Bravo Three's down. Brave Two's down the hall in the kitchen."

The CIA troops and Chris were "stacking" in the hallway on the left just past the doorway the SEALs had bolted from, facing the front of the house. They had not broached the corner where the Raid team was lined up.

The snake had disintegrated to the extent the team leader was down on his knee and his number two was standing directly over him, both muzzles pointed to the left side of the loading door where the back end of the jingle truck, and therefore the other three men, should be. The trooper in front of Chris had stepped out slightly and also knelt with Chris above him, both aiming at the right side of the loading door. Chris hurriedly glanced over his shoulder, making sure nothing could surprise them from down the hall.

"Where's the UC? Where's Mau?"

At the mention of his partner's name in his ear, his focus narrowed even more than it had been. Where the fuck *was* Mau? He had to find out and knew one quick way. "Mau," he shouted. "Where are you?"

"Behind the boxes!"

"You okay?" He mentally crossed his fingers and tried to slow his breathing. Another burst of fire from the kitchen. A few rounds whanged off something metallic.

"No," he said a little sadly, "I think I'm shot. My leg is bleeding." Chris felt his skin tighten on his bones and grow cold at the thought of his friend and partner hurt.

"We're coming. Just keep your head down! Is Samadi with you?"

"Yeah," he said weakly. "I'm sitting on him."

"Raid One...UC's behind the boxes and reports he's been hit," he shouted as more rounds came ripping out. "He's got Bravo One with him. We've got the guys in the kitchen pinned, but they've got someone on the other side of that hole and they kind of have us pinned. Can you get someone out there to take care of him?"

"Coyote Three's on the way!"

There was another boom from across the street.

"Sniper One...one down...there's two still outside the house, they're on the right side of the doorway as you're facing out...hey!" he shouted in surprise. "The DEA guy just went tearing out of here. Coyote Three, the DEA guy's gonna be crossing the street, watch out for him, he doesn't have a vest. I think he's going for the guys I can't see."

"Roger that."

"R2, Annex One, say your status." There was no response from the bartender on the other side of town.

"R2, *Air One*, say your status." Radio silence.

Coyote Three slammed his truck to a stop, the front left bumper nearly touching the front of the ruined house next door. As he did so, he reached over and grabbed his rifle and threw the door open, aiming between the window frame and the windshield, using the door for cover while trying to acquire the targets. At the same time, through the right corner of his windshield, he saw Pedro crossing the street at a dead run, aiming for one of the cars parked in front of the jingle truck. Above his head, the barrel of the MAG-58 was pivoting to the right.

Looking over the top sight, he saw two men crouched, their heads pulled low into their shoulders. Behind them, a man lay sprawled, propped up against the wall, half of his head leaking an oatmeal-textured muck onto the ground. As he thumbed the safety off and prepared to fire, there was a horrendous chain-saw ripping sound from directly overhead that shook the entire truck. He hadn't taken his eyes off his targets and watched as they were both literally *lifted* from the ground and thrown six or seven feet, their bodies nearly evaporating from the ferocious onslaught of heavy metal punching into them. Seconds later, there was little left except some red mist and piles of meat.

He pressed the round push-to-talk switch on his vest. "Coyote Three…the two at the front of the house are down." He watched as Pedro did a quick peek over and around the top of the car and then ran to the edge of the door that had just been vacated. "Watch your fire inside!" he shouted. "The DEA guy's right outside the door." He repeated the message over the radio then stepped out of the truck and looked up at the guys in the truck bed. "I'm gonna climb through there and see if I can wipe that guy off the wall."

He received a casual salute. "Roger that. Want us to go with you?"

"Negative…keep an eye on that guy in case you have to pull his ass out of the fire," he said motioning with his chin in Pedro's direction. He turned to face the blown-out house next door, brought his weapon up to a low ready, stock set into his shoulder with the barrel pointing down at about a forty-five degree angle. He disappeared into the wreckage with a cheery, "See 'ya!"

"I gotta get to Mau!" Chris shouted to no one in particular, turning to face the boxes as if he could see through them and find his buddy. He got no response except for a random machine gun blast from down the hall. "Hey!" he called again. He didn't have a convenient push-to-talk button on his radio and couldn't afford to fuck with it, trying to get it off his belt. "SEAL guy…I gotta get to my UC. He's hit and bleeding!"

In his earpiece he heard Petty Officer Weiss announce, "Raid One…man down. We don't have time to fuck with this anymore. Mark 3s and 67s going into the kitchen," then louder shout, "Spoons on my mark, throw on two. Fire in the hole!" There was a pause of several seconds as he and Raid Two peeled electrical tape off the safety levers of fist-sized, soda-can-shaped black grenades and green tennis-ball sized standard fragmentation grenades. They slipped the rings onto their fingers, held them all up together and when Petty Officer Weiss called "Spoons!" simultaneously let the levers go. "One...two!" Both men knew the timing from release to detonation was between four and five seconds and didn't want to throw them at the enemy merely to have them kicked back out, so they waited momentarily with the grenades live in their hands and then gave them a light toss into the darkness.

Chris jammed his pistol into his armpit and covered his ears, not sure what to expect. The blasts, when they came, were more overwhelming than anything he had ever experienced. They weren't the TV bangs with fire, no. Because the area where the grenades had gone off was semi-enclosed on all sides except one, the overpressure bounced off the walls and ceiling, amplifying the destructive capability of the concussion grenades, obliterating and lifting everything before blasting the detritus and mess outward from the kitchen. As the explosions sought the path of least resistance, he was unprepared for the massive amount of smoke, shrapnel, dirt, wood, and possibly body parts that came flying towards the front wall of the house. Even more stunning was the huge, rolling barrage of sound that came from the kitchen. While one grenade in an open space might have been just a loud pop, these four cooking off together was insanely loud. Chris felt like he was standing in front of the world's largest subwoofer. His clothes, his hair, his skin, all vibrated as the sound waves concussed over him. The ground trembled under his feet and as he uncovered his ears, he realized he was covered with a thin coat of dust.

Immediately, Raid One turned his weapon down the hall and let loose several suppressed bursts sweeping left to right.

Chris' ears felt as if they had been stuffed with cotton, but he could hear a man's incoherent screaming, and underlying that, an awful high-pitched keening like a mewling kitten. It was such a horrid sound it nearly brought the contents of Chris' stomach up onto the floor.

As Coyote Three worked his way through the wreckage next door, he caught a glimpse of a man standing with his back to the wall by the hole into the kitchen. The trooper was already in firing position and took the necessary instant to verify the area behind his target was unoccupied by his own guys. His target slumped down a little and then turned back toward the opening in the wall. As he did, Three saw his right arm was missing from the elbow down. What was left of his shirt on that side was little more than blood soaked cotton strands; a jet of bright red blood was irrigating the dirt and his feet at a heart-pumping interval; it was an arterial bleed and wouldn't take more than a minute or two to bleed the man out. He must have been leaning into the house when the grenades went off. He continued his rotation, his eyes rolling in their sockets as he fell through the hole, into the hallway, and into the kitchen. His dirty sandals were all that was left visible from the outside.

"Coyote Three…the guy outside the kitchen's down."

As the grenades blew, the wall Randy was leaning on shook and a couple bricks left their place and flew through the air.

Not long after, there was motion in Randy's line of fire and he squinted as he slowly lowered himself toward the ground. "Movement front," he whispered to his partner who was still watching the corner near the garden. He was trying to focus on the something that was definitely in the leftovers of the adjacent house, but it was vague, like a hint or a shadow but without substance. Then, without warning, Coyote Three's clean-shaven face popped into the opening Randy had been peering into. He had a huge grin on his face. "Wha's up?" He laid his rifle on the ground then crawled through behind it. "You still got those two holed up in there?" Randy nodded, eyes and weapon back towards the front of the house. "Cool," he said. "I'll cut back a little bit down the alley and slice the pie. That work for you, Leo?"

"Knock yourself out," Leo replied from the ground without taking his eyes off his area of responsibility.

Three locked his rifle into his left shoulder and tucked his left elbow into his side. With about ten yards now between him and the garden, he slid very slowly and minutely to his left, aiming at a point on the far garden wall immediately past the edge of the closest corner where they might be hiding. Seeing nothing threatening, he slid a bit farther left, sliding the barrel right, keeping the same reference on the edge of the house. Using this tactic, he was able to see into the garden at such an angle he would see the bad guys before they could see him. He expected to see a bit of shirt, a shoulder, a leg. With still nothing in his sight, he slid left again. The bad guys had to be deep into the alcove.

"Leo," said Coyote Three over the whisper mic at his throat. "I'm going to pop off a few rounds to probe."

"Roger that."

He fired off a three round burst into the wall and slid left again, hoping the bad guy would panic and come out, trying for a shot. He slid and fired again, this time moving a little closer to the garden to keep the angle increasing.

An undirected blast of 7.62 bullets on full automatic came out and powdered the wall opposite the alley. It was followed by a guttural scream in Pashtu.

"We're moving to get the UC," said the leader of Jack's security team. The snake re-constituted itself and moved forward, around the first pallet toward the second. By the time Chris came around the box corner, there were three men knelt around Mau, who was sitting on Samadi's head. Chris could see little except Mau's face because of the bodies in the way. For the first time in Chris' memory, Mau wasn't smiling or laughing. His face was quite pale and shiny, and even in the dim light his eyes looked wobbly.

"Jesus Christ," whispered Chris, his pistol forgotten.

"Chris!" shouted Papa One. "Cover down that hall!"

He took one last, quick look, then stepped past him, knelt down, and edged his pistol around the pile of heroin boxes down the dark hallway from where the screams were still coming, now even louder. He expected it to be pitch black down there, but there was light coming from the huge hole that had a body lying in it. There were several beams of dull sunlight also coming from the left side where brick-sized holes appeared in the wall. In that light, he could see several bodies in various states of explosive injury. One of the men, it looked like Anwar, was holding his hand over his stomach, or where his stomach used to be but was now a gaping hole his organs were slipping out of. The hand was covered in blood and a wet pile of something resembling gray hose lay draped over one of his legs. Chris couldn't see the other one. Anwar was looking toward the ceiling, his mouth wide open as he shook his head but made no sound. Another man in the opposite corner was still holding a rifle but was laying on his side, the weapon ignored. He was the one screaming. Chris could see a leg resting on the man's neck.

"Papa One...we need a medic for the UC."

Chris was watching as the SEAL team leader snapped his fingers to get his team's attention and motioned the last two guys in his snake to break and join up behind the boxes with Mau. At the same time, out of the corner of his eye, he saw motion at the front of the door and Pedro came running in.

"Chris!" called Petty Officer Weiss. "Wha'd'ya see down there?"

Chris described the scene, adding the description of the three other bodies, including the man lying in the hole in the wall. He watched as the man's stump moved in a slow circle on the ground, and he heard the screeching soften from the man's lips; then it stopped.

"Raid One…we're going to clear the kitchen."

Instantly, Chris heard a burst of automatic fire out beyond the back wall and then a shout. He watched as a piece of corrugated steel jettisoned inward and fell across the kitchen floor pushing more dust into the already black air. It was followed by a sandaled foot, then a leg, then the barrel of a rifle, a curved magazine, an arm. Chris' focus was so acute at that moment, he was seeing everything in a series of movie-like frames running at half speed.

He opened his mouth to warn the SEAL team, but as his lips parted, the rest of the man came into view, turning toward the front of the house, toward Chris and Mau and the security team and Pedro. The barrel of the gun was pointed in the direction of the boxes. Chris' mind went from thought to training to instinct, and he became nothing more than the phrase drilled into him over hundreds of hours on the DEA range: "Front sight, trigger press."

He fired three fast rounds into the center of the target. As the slide cycled the third time, he let the trigger come slightly forward, felt the soft click under his finger as it indexed for the next shot.

Through the cloud of blue-gray smoke, Chris saw the rifle arcing down as the man's pace was lost and he stumbled, his feet now moving in a syncopated rhythm. He fell, jamming the barrel into the ground and squeezing the trigger at the same time in an involuntary spasm. His body was over the stock as the weapon fired. The bullets' progress was instantly arrested in the hard-packed dirt, the gasses were unable to dissipate, and the gun exploded, blasting pieces of steel, wood, and body in all directions.

The SEAL team remained in place, not sure what had happened but staying clear of Chris' shots, trusting in the shooter.

For the first time since Petty Officer Weiss had said the word "gun," there was silence in the house.

"This is Annex One, I can't contact R2."

A jingle truck.

The vehicle repair shop / stash house.

The market and apartments across the street from the vehicle repair shop.

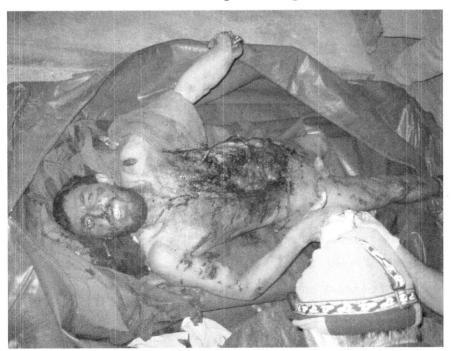

Bravo Two, Anwar Dadfar Safari.

CHAPTER SIXTEEN

Lemon, MC and I are standing in the hangar in a small huddle. I'm sweating under my vest, knee and elbow pads, helmet, long gun, short gun and backpack.

"Before I say my piece, do you have any questions for me?" MC asks, looking at each of us directly. We shake our heads; it's pretty straightforward. "Okay. I'll keep this short. There's been a little wrinkle in this with Meat's brother. He's decided he's going on the op, and while it's against both mine and Big Mike's better judgment, there's nothing we can do about it. Meat, you're in charge and I want to be very clear on this: Your older brother is not to leave the helo at any point. You understand me?" I nodded. "I don't care if you have to flex-tie him to the airframe and I'm not joking about that. Lemon, if Meat decides his brother's got to be immobilized to keep him in there, then you and the rest of the squad pile on the guy and get it done. Understand?"

"Aye aye, Master Chief." Lemon, also a former SEAL, answered swiftly.

"This is a fucked-up situation right now with three brothers all in harm's way, and we've got to try to minimize the risk Mrs. Davis' kids are in. That being said, as long as Big Brother's on the helo and doing what he's told, he can be an asset but I don't want him to be in a position where he's got to shoot. That's not his job, I don't know if he knows one end of a gun from the other." MC purses his lips, silent, then nods, and pats us both on the shoulder. "Okay, let's get you in the air."

We waddle under weight out into the sunshine where the rest of the squad is doing final equipment and weapons checks. As is standard for us, we keep our weapons locked-and-loaded, safeties on at all times. We operate under the principle that when you need to shoot, you need to shoot *right now* and there's no time to be fucking around with the moving parts of the gun. There's more chance of an accidental discharge when weapons are being loaded or unloaded, so we load 'em once, safety 'em and forget 'em.

Our vests are all the same, magazines are in the same places, turned to load the same way. Our backpacks and BDUs all contain the same items packed in the same way: magazines, food, water, medical kits. If one of us needs something from someone else and they can't get to it, we know right where to dig. Example, if I reach into anyone's left-side cargo pants pocket, I know I'm going to find sterile rolls of gauze.

"Okay, gather 'round," announces the Master Chief, tugging his floppy hat down lower on his head. Everyone stops doing what they were doing and circles him. "I'll keep this short. Follow your orders from the CO and XO, watch your fields of fire, take care of each other." He grins broadly. "And don't fuck it up!" He pushes past us, gives a thumbs-up to the pilots who are already strapping in, and joins Big Mike and Squad Two in the hangar where they can watch from the shade.

As a former Naval Aviator of fixed-wing aircraft, I've had little contact with the rotary-wing community (i.e., the helicopters), and this is my first time being up close and personal with an H-53, but it is a massive piece of machinery. It's about a hundred feet long and the rotors have to be about three quarters of that length. We shuffle around to the right side of the haze-gray monster and climb aboard by sitting on the frame and sliding backwards. The inside is mostly empty, except for the medical packages, litters and coolers; it's like a friggin' auditorium in here! There are no seats, except for the flight engineer / load master, so we all just sit on the floor with our backs to the wall, helmets in our laps and long guns next to us. There are heavy canvas seatbelts attached to rings in the floor and we all strap in, Lemon to my right, Jeff to my left.

Unlike some of the guys, I keep my equipment on at all times. I'm leaning back against my backpack, which is a little uncomfortable, but I was having my two beers one Sunday night when MC told me a story about being in a helicopter crash in Viet Nam. He had taken off his pack for the ride and consequently became separated from it in the accident. While he was still able to carry out his mission, he went hungry for a few days and had nothing to sleep with except an old .45 pistol in his hand. I would not make the same mistake.

The engineer gives us a cursory check to make sure we are secure then hands out some bright yellow foam ear protectors and demonstrates how to roll them tightly and insert them into our ears. As the foam earplugs expand, everything gets quiet and dull. Above my head the engine starts to wind up. Outside the window the rotors start turning slowly and the high pitch scream of the engine is soon overlaid by a huge, deep bass thumping that makes me feel like I'm sitting inside a monstrous drum being beaten by a manic musician. I mean, holy shit it's loud! Even through the earplugs, much more so than our old Chinook.

There is a slight change in rotor pitch as we lift from the tarmac and hover for a second while the pilots ensure everything is as it should be, that all 1700 parts are vibrating in unison. Then we tilt right, the nose goes over, the huge blades on top take a deeper bite out of the air, and we're accelerating and climbing in the world's best E-ticket ride.

After several minutes, the deck transitions to something approximating level, and we all unsnap our floor harnesses and start re-inventorying our toys. Besides our personal rifles and handguns, each of us has two fragmentation grenades, their pins taped to keep them from being inadvertently pulled. Argo and Lemon are each carrying an AT-4 light anti-tank weapon, an unguided rocket that is self-contained and launched from a disposable tube. Adze is one of the camp's two designated snipers (Jazz being the other) and he'll be taking one of the special rifles. I ask Argo to point out each of the medical items so we each know where everything is in case he's not available.

Since we don't know what kind of situation we're heading into, there's no sense talking tactics. If something develops, we'll be fluid and rely on our training to sort ourselves out, though when it comes right down to it, it's "The Three Ss" - Speed, Surprise and a Shitload of bullets.

Lacking anything else to do, Jeff and I sit back down and languish in the racket coming from the machinery around us.

"So what's with the beard?" he asks me, putting his mouth up to my ear to be heard over the din.

I laugh out loud. "Have you ever heard of Dolce and Gabbana?"

He shakes his head.

263

"They're clothing designers, pretty high-end stuff. Anyway, one of the guys has a shirt that says, "D and G" for Dolce and Gabbana. Remember G.I. Joe?"

He nods. We spent our childhoods playing with the soldier figures, occasionally using them on recon missions to ambush and beat the crap out of our little sister's Barbie and Ken. Those missions usually ended with Barbie and Ken's heads being pulled off their stick bodies and stuck on our fingers like puppets.

"I came up with an advertising campaign and am getting as rough looking as I can for some pictures called 'D and G.I. Joe: High fashion for the 21st Century Soldier.' I wanna copyright it and sell it to D and G for like millions and then retire."

"So you're going to give up the guns and what, be a model?"

"Well, model and millionaire. Hell, man, it's a great way to meet women."

Jeff nods again. He's married with three kids, and sometimes he just doesn't understand me. "So did the Master Chief say anything more to you about me being here when you guys were talking?"

I consider not answering, but there's no reason I shouldn't, and while he's not the wild card MC thinks he could be, it can't hurt to let him know there's a bad consequence out there waiting for him if he decides to try to pull rank. "Yeah, he told me that if you don't follow your little brother's orders, I'm supposed to gag you and flex-cuff you to the airframe."

Jeff laughs, and it's good to hear. Sometimes I think he doesn't have enough humor in his life. "No, really, what did he say."

"No really," I reply, nodding my head. "He wasn't kidding. And the rest of the squad'll join in if they have to. I made up the part about gagging you though. I figured it'd be payback for that time when we were kids and you held me down and spit in my mouth." I'm grinning like an idiot.

His smile fades to grimace as he considers it, his eyes hidden behind his Ray Ban Aviators. Then he nods and smiles again. "Okay, fair enough. Can I tell you something?"

"Shoot."

"I'm scared as fuck about Chris." He puts his arm around my shoulder and gives me a big hug.

It's strange to consider it's been less than twelve hours since I heard about the plane crash. This day seems to have dragged toward infinity and I realize how tired I am from the stress of worrying about the littlest brother and my two buddies who were flying him. I take a deep breath, put my head back, and close my eyes though I know I won't be able to sleep. "I'm glad you're here, too." I yell back at him.

We continue northbound. The heavy beat of the rotors overhead actually becomes soothing and I find myself being startled awake; I never would have thought I could sleep with that going on around me. I don't think I was out for more than a few seconds. Next to me, Jeff is holding his Kevlar helmet, examining it, bored already with the trip.

The ship's engineer walks to the back where we're sitting. "Excuse me, sir!" he shouts. He's wearing a heavy helo helmet with extra noise suppression around his ears and a dark green visor obscuring the majority of his face. "Incoming message traffic!"

He crouches down and Jeff pulls him closer by his shoulder, putting his mouth next to the bulbous, rounded protuberances where the engineer's ears are concealed. "Is it from the ship?" he yells back.

"Negative, sir."

Jeff motions his head my way. "He'll take it, then."

"Aye aye, sir," he responds then turns to me. "You can plug a headset in if you want to come with me." I notice *I* don't rate a *Sir*. I roll onto

265

my knees, sinking into the comfort of the pads over my kneecaps. I follow him, moving around the medical supplies.

Through the panoramic front windshields, the ground speeds under us. Instinctively, I scan the instruments for the important ones: altitude and airspeed. We're at one hundred fifty knots and fifty feet, though not so fast in terms of a jet, at this altitude I can't deny the sensation of speed, and for a moment it makes me nostalgic for my flying days.

The engineer hands me a light green David Clarke headset connected to a black cord with a push-to-talk button on it. I take off my tactical headset, put on the David Clarke, and press the button with my thumb. "Who's calling?"

The copilot, sitting to my left in the seat that would normally be occupied by the pilot in command on a fixed wing airplane, turns a bit my way and presses the black plastic lip microphone a little closer. "Callsign 'Mary Ann.' Our comm card says that's the base where we picked you up."

"Roger that."

He points to a panel on the bulkhead. "To select a radio, push that button there," he says, "and use the same..." he makes a motion with his thumb that mimics pushing the button under my thumb.

The engineer points at a button with a green light just below it. I nod at him and he pushes it in. "Mary Ann, this is Rescue One."

There's a burst of static. "Rescue One, this is Mary Ann Actual." *Actual* denotes it's Big Mike doing the talking, as opposed to the comm guy or someone else using the collective callsign. "I just got off comms with Kilo November Yankee Two Niner." As he says this, the copilot holds up the card for me and runs his finger across a line that reads:

KNY29.............................U.S. Embassy Islamabad

"They got the green light for the SAR to launch out of Discovery."

DISCOVERY..................................Bagram Air Force Base

I feel like cheering. I turn my head and see Jeff watching. I know I have a huge smile on my face and I give him a thumbs-up. He raises his eyebrows and starts to stand but I wave him to stay put. "How long before launch?"

"They're already in the air and proceeding directly to the crash site. If no one is recovered, they'll start their own search focusing on a southerly track. They're plugged into our comm plan, and their callsign is Texas. It's a flight of two OV-22s. If they come up with anything, I'll get it relayed to you directly. How copy?"

"Five-by-five."

"We figure you're about fifteen minutes from the last known position of those trucks. Is that about right?"

I look toward the copilot, who gives a thumbs-up.

"That's what the pilots say."

"Okay. Mary Ann standing by."

The other pilot, apparently on loan from the Air Force, passes the controls to the guy in the left seat and turns to face me. I tune back into the intercom, and we discuss the helo approach and how I'd like him to maneuver. He signs off on the plan and tells me we're about eight minutes from the IP, the initial point of contact.

There's nothing left to say or do, so I stand there and watch the world whip by. We're in a valley a couple of miles wide. To the left and right are spiky ridges blending from one to another. Miles ahead of us, they appear to converge and bend around to the right. We blast over a single little house and then it's gone; subconsciously, I think I saw a face turned up at us, but it was so fast it could have been my imagination.

"Six minutes," shouts the HAC at me and holds up his hands, fingers widespread.

I look back at the guys and hold up six fingers. Adze catches it and passes it to the rest of the squad.

A radio call comes over my command net. *"Rescue One, this is Kilo Alpha Two Zero One. How copy?"*

"Five-by-five. Who's this?"

"This is a Predator UAV. I'm overhead at twenty-five thousand feet. I also hold you five-by. Are you ready to copy sitrep[1]?" I tell him I am. *"Roger. Sitrep follows. I hold you in visual contact approaching from the south. Your target is two pickup trucks on your current course, fifteen miles. I count eight unidentified subjects. Our best count is six in the trucks and two walking southbound on an east-facing ridgeline. Negative SIGINT from the target area. Negative contact with your package."*

"Do you have any traffic to pass from the Discovery SAR?"

"Negative...I'm in Las Vegas but I'll make some calls. Kilo Alpha Two Zero One standing by."

I sign off and walk to the rear of the helo to brief the rest of the squad. It's a little hard having to shout over the noise but that's the way it is. I tell them about the other SAR and everybody grins. "Okay, here's the plan. We deploy in an L-shape pattern." The L-shape is a basic infantry maneuver that guarantees friendly forces won't be caught in crossfire; or more technically, a blue-on-blue engagement. I take out a pen and draw a rough plan on the palm of my hand with a squiggly line for the mountain and squares for the trucks. "Argo, you'll deploy east of the trucks with an AT-4." I draw an X on my hand. "After we drop you off, we'll arc a couple hundred yards further

---

[1] Situation Report

north and west and Grease, Lemon, and I will dismount and approach on foot." I look at each man in turn and they nod back. "These are going to be fast drops and we'll stand the helo off with the engine running. Adze, you're primary sniper, and I want you to stay with the helo and direct them where you want for the best cover." He nods at me. "Any questions?" Everybody's quiet. I tap the side of my tactical headset and point in their direction. They all turn their radios on, no sense drawing down the batteries in transit. Everyone checks in, though it's a little hard to hear them since the headsets weren't really made to be used in this kind of constant, overwhelming environment.

As they start moving around the inside of the helicopter getting ready, the engineer slides the left side door to the rear that instantly sucks all of the cool air out, replacing it with what we're used to - hot and dry with the distant tang of goat shit.

I take my place back behind the pilots.

"Tally ho!" calls the pilot pointing slightly off to the left. There, near a high ridge, are the trucks but they're little more than white dots. We're too far to see any men. We continue screaming directly at them, the ground flashing by under us.

"Adze, you're on deck." I broadcast over the radio. "Argo, stand by to deploy."

Adze has his big black rifle out and carefully sits down on the gray deck, his feet hanging out the doorway, eye to the scope, casually scanning the area though unable to target given our angle of approach.

I'm watching as best I can given the vibration of the cabin, and I'm trying to pick out the guys who are walking above them but it's impossible.

"Here we go!" calls the HAC, and when we're no more than several hundred yards away, he yanks the helo into a hard right bank causing me to hold on to keep from falling. As we come out of the turn, he slows the engine to near idle, killing our forward speed, then increases it into a hover just several feet off the ground.

I step back from the cockpit and stand over Adze. With my binoculars, I count four men standing outside the trucks, dressed in traditional knee-length shirts or ragtag combinations of baggy trousers and vests. They look worn out and beaten and are watching us watch them. Inside the truck beds I see several more men also turned our way. They're staring back at us, not moving. Up on the hill, the two men there have also stopped and are watching.

With the flat of my hand I motion downward to the flight engineer who relays it to the pilot, and we lower out of the hover to ground level. I pat Argo on the back. "Go!" and he's out the big door with the LAW in one hand, his rifle in the other, and running away from the massive rotor-wash. He drops into a crouch and throws the tube onto his shoulder and takes aim.

"Argo's deployed." I transmit over the command net.

"Copy. We see him."

I give the engineer a thumbs-up jerking motion, and the throbbing of the rotors overhead starts to deepen as their pitch changes, taking a bigger bite out of the hot air. Unfortunately the binoculars aren't gyro-stabilized and with the vibration of the helicopter lifting up, my view is no longer sharp-focused. We start moving slowly forward, arcing to the northeast where we're going to set down again for the rest of us to do our approach.

Over the noise of the rotors, the engines, the earplugs, and the radio covering my ear, I hear one of the pilots holler, "Flare, seven o'clock!"

I snap my head to the left and see a razor-thin trail of white smoke following a fantastically bright red dot moving sideways along the mountain. It's visible for no more than a second or two when another smoke trail follows it then another and another, all originating from the same place.

"Flares!" calls Argo over the radio. "My ten o'clock, on the hill ahead of the trucks."

"Copy." My team's all listening to the radio. Lemon holds his hand up and Grease lightly slides his palm off it like he's paying a bet.

"We've got a hotspot," says the Predator pilot, *"possible flares on the eastern ridge line, bearing two three zero magnetic, two point one miles. We're painting multiple bodies at the flare point and...it looks like... they're waving! We think that's your package."* I can hear the smile in his voice.

(Back Row) Guinness, Gucci, Benwha, Master Chief Davis.

(Front Row) Kola, the author, Argo.

271

"This is R2!" shouted an unfamiliar voice over the radios. "We're hit! FUBAR's down. R2's down. We're going to the airport. Get a trauma team standing by to receive, and tell the guards to get the gate open. We're ETA five mikes."

"Annex One copies. How bad are they?"

"FUBAR's dead. R2's hit in the leg; he's losing a lot of blood. Jon's working on him right now. R2 says he's A Positive; pass it on."

"Roger that. Stand by...." There was a pause lasting about thirty seconds. "What're you driving?" They had to be identified so the soldiers manning the post wouldn't think it was a suicide bomber trying to crash the gate and take defensive action.

"Brown truck, big antenna on the roof."

There was another pause. "They've got the message and they're scrambling. Once you clear the gate, go straight past the hangar, take your first left, and keep going till you see guys waving you down. Keep your headlights on."

"10-4."

"Raid Team, what's Mau's status?"

"Gunshot, left leg," came an unidentified reply. "He's shocky but stable. We're gonna load him into one of the trucks and take him to the airport too."

"Anyone else injured?" There was silence on the radio. "Okay, local army's on the way to secure the area. Should be there within a half hour. Raid One, can you liaise with them?"

"A-firm. We're gonna need a bunch of body bags and transport."

"We'll launch the Humvees from here."

"What'd'ya wanna to do with the civilians?"

"What civilians?"

"DEA and your guy."

"Break...this is Coyote Three. I've got one Bravo in custody for transport."

"Roger that, Coyote Three. Does he need medical attention?"

"Damn right."

"Raid One, can you transport the Bravo and Mau to the airport and the civilians back here?"

"We'll figure it out. Whoops, hang on a sec...." The radio clicked off momentarily. "Chris says he wants to stay with Mau at the airport."

"Uh...that's okay."

"Be advised, he engaged a Bravo."

"Who did?"

"Chris."

When Annex One re-keyed his microphone, Chris heard a woman's voice in the background saying, "What a fucking goat-rope..." before the Chief of Station continued. "Take Mau, the Bravo and Chris to the airport. Leave Jack and Pedro there for now."

"Roger that. We're clear."

"Wait One. The local police'll be coming too. Nobody gets arrested or taken into custody." He waited with the microphone open. "Understand?"

"We copy."

"LEGAT's scrambling too, along with RSO[1]. It's a crime scene. Try to preserve what you can 'til they get there."

There was laughter now coming from Raid One as the tension started to abate and the fact that the "crime scene" was nothing but dust and rubble. "Roger that. We're clear."

Mau was lying on the mattress in the truck bed. The mattress had been shoved to one side and two of the SEALs were kneeling over him. They cut his pants from zipper to ankle, roughly pushed a sterile dressing deep into the wound, and then covered the injury with layers of gauze. Mau's eyes were open and from the rear seat of the truck, looking back through the glass, Chris could see he was breathing fast. Suddenly, as if aware he was being watched, he tilted his head toward Chris and gave a thumbs-up and a weak smile.

Next to Mau, a bearded, wounded Afghan soldier who Anwar had brought with him was lying on his side, hands and ankles secured with white flex-cuffs. His shirt had been removed, and his chest was wrapped in its entirety from waist to armpit in white gauze, darkened in places with blood seeping through. Chris leaned over and could see the man's eyes were closed. His chest was barely moving though he coughed occasionally.

---

[1] Regional Security Officer. The RSO manages embassy security requirements

274

When walking out of the drop house, Chris was amazed by the human carnage around him. He stepped over the legs of one of the men who had been unloading boxes from the truck; his body was against the wall, though leaning sideways at an awkward angle; the right side of his body was collapsed from the massive round the sniper rifle delivered from across the street; the left side had virtually disintegrated as a hydrostatic shock wave passed through it, leaving nothing but blood and cloth. There was a wet, red crater in the wall where the bullet impacted. Across the street near the well were two more bodies, one bent backwards nearly in two because the heavy rifle round had hit him in the center of the spine slamming the body closed like a book; the skin over the belly had split spilling guts all over the dust. The other body was crumpled next to his partner, the body twisted all the way around at the waist like something from *The Exorcist*. Chris was unable to conceive the awesome power that could have done that to human bodies. He had looked up and seen Sniper One standing on the balcony, the massive rifle's stock resting on the railing. The old Afghan still sat in his chair, smoking.

Coyote Three threw the truck in gear and was soon on the highway. He was driving fast, swerving around cars moving too slowly, banging on the horn. Every now and then, he would shout for someone to "get-the-fuck-out-of-my-way!" The ride lasted about ten minutes. Chris saw a guard gate flash past and the blurred faces of soldiers in desert brown camouflage uniforms. The truck's wheels sung as they curved around a huge white hangar, and then they were accelerating again, the little engine screaming under the weight of Coyote Three's boot. The tires protested a final time as the truck rocked to a stop next to the other truck with the big X-shaped antenna stuck to the roof.

The SEALs in the back jumped out, gripped the handles on the sides of the mattress, and yanked it out of the bed of the truck. Chris jumped out and took one of the handles, and together they half-walked, half-ran past a group of soldiers to a gray hangar, the huge doors pushed open. He glanced at R2's truck, and his eyes were drawn to the bullet holes in the front windshield, at head level on both the driver and passenger's sides.

Inside was a large complex of white trailers, much like the ones where Chris and Mau were living. They were connected together, a red cross painted on the outside wall, and a shiny steel ramp leading to glass doors. The "hospital" was surrounded with mostly empty cots. Soldiers were waiting to receive the new charges. A tall, older man wearing a white lab coat and stethoscope over his uniform intercepted them and fell in step.

"What have you got?" he asked.

"Gunshot wounds," said the SEAL who had been treating Mau. "This one took it through his lower thigh, left side, no evidence of fracture, no exit wound. He's lost blood but we pressure padded the entrance. He's conscious, no MS[1], BP one hundred.

"That one has multiple holes in his chest with air in and out. I slapped a piece of waxed plastic over it with a compress. Rounds may have gone into his belly. He's in and out of consciousness, pulse is rapid. I don't think he got hit anywhere else, but honestly, I didn't have time to look."

As they were speaking, orderlies were taking charge of the mattress, moving the bodies quickly but not too gently onto stainless steel, wheeled gurneys. The doctor glanced at the two men, considering the flex cuffs on one of them. "Any Americans? Good guys?"

The SEAL pointed at Mau. "Him. He's one of us."

The doctor tapped a corpsman on the shoulder to get his attention and pointed at Mau. "Ringers, plasma, type and cross, X-ray left leg and prep him for OR. That one," he said, "Blood type, plasma, Ringers now, chest and probable belly. He's number two."

---

[1] Morphine Sulfate

"Aye aye, sir," replied the white coated corpsman as Mau and the Bravo were rolled away.

"Have you seen the other two they brought in?"

"DOA or the leg wound?"

"Uh...well, either, I guess, sir." He was rubbing his chin.

"Leg's in the OR. DOA caught a single round in the brainpan." He tapped the center of his forehead. "There's a morgue set up behind the hospital," he said motioning at the white trailers. "They'll clean him up and prep him for shipment."

For an instant Chris was back in the car coming from the airport, listening to FUBAR joking about being shot, horribly predicting his own death.

The SEAL nodded. "Okay, thank you, sir. And thank you for taking care of our buddy." He was acknowledging the unspoken rule that medical attention went to friend before foe. He cracked a salute so sharp it would have made any Marine drill instructor glow with pride, his fingertips at the edge of his black helmet, a salute that was more casually returned by the physician.

"No problem. Nice work on the patients." He turned and walked toward the hospital.

As they walked away, Chris' attention was snapped back to the radio chatter, which had been going on almost non-stop in his earpiece, as a harsh female voiced demanded to know, "Where's Chris Davis?"

The black-suited shooters, all walking abreast, turned and looked at him, smiles on their faces. They too were tuned into the network. "That sounds like one none-too-amused woman. Your wife?"

Chris pulled the radio off his belt and lifted it to his lips. "I'm here at the airport. We just dropped off Mau and the other guy at the medical unit."

"Wait there. I'm on my way."

"10-4," he said with a frown. He turned to his buddies. "I guess I better wait here."

"Roger that. We'll catch 'ya later." One of the guys put his fist out, which Chris hit with his own. "You did good back there, man. Glad you were with us."

Chris smiled and turned back to go meet his boss.

Sarah Thibodaux stepped out of the shiny blue Suburban and walked up to him quickly. Her face was pinched and she brushed her short red hair behind her ear. She was carrying a handheld radio in one hand and her purse was slung over her shoulder.

"What the hell happened out there?" she growled at him, taking a cigarette out and lighting it. Chris noticed it was less a cigarette than a thin, brown cigarillo.

"Well..." he began.

"And exactly how did you get a gun? Do you realize the shitstorm coming your way right now?"

"Well..." he tried again.

"You're not accredited here, you do not have diplomatic protection, and you're not allowed to be armed, much less *use* a gun." She was talking fast and furious, blowing smoke generally in his direction. "The prosecutor could *arrest* and try you for whatever their version of whatever is. I don't know what you were thinking you..." she was interrupted by the deep voice of the Chief of Station calling her name over the radio. She lifted hers and spoke into it. "I'm here at the airport."

"How's Mau?"

"I haven't gotten into the hospital yet to see him. I'm talking to Chris right now."

The long, silent pause almost shrieked, "Why-aren't-you-taking-care-of-your-injured?"

"Alright, thanks. I'll need a status on Mau as soon as you can. I'm going to meet Embassy One right now," he reported using the Ambassador's tactical callsign.

Her eyes narrowed. Obviously, she didn't like being treated like a subordinate to someone who wasn't in her chain of command, but realistically, she had just been relegated down. She took a deep drag on her cigarillo and tossed it onto the tarmac. As she was talking, a helicopter in the distance started spooling its engines into a high-pitched scream. Several Humvees drove by, the passengers swiveling their heads to get a look at her body in passing.

"I've already been on the phone to Headquarters," she continued speaking to Chris as she turned and started walked toward the hospital trailers. Chris walked alongside her saying nothing. "The Administrator's asking me why his undercover got shot, and the only real answer I have is, 'I don't know.' This operation's an absolute fuck-up, and I never should have allowed it. Do you have any idea how this makes us look and how much paperwork we're going to have to do?" She walked up the step and opened the door to the trailer. "You wait here," she said not turning around.

Chris ignored her last command and walked in behind her. From the inside, there was no indication he was in a series of trailers. It was like he had stepped into a modern emergency room. The only concession to military was that everyone was in uniform. The floors were white tile. Bright fluorescent lights hung from the low ceilings, and everything was neat and clean and smelled of alcohol and Betadine. To his right were a series of curtained off areas with gurney wheels visible at the bottom. Ahead of him was a partitioned wall with a sign over it reading "Operating Rooms." On his left was a nurse's and admittance station occupied by a huge black man in a baby blue shirt. Sarah was leaning on the counter on her elbow, and Chris stood next to her, his arms crossed and his back to their conversation while he tried to figure out where his buddy was.

"I'm sorry, ma'am, but who'd'y'all say you was with?"

"DEA." She said, her voice harsh with impatience. "The Drug Enforcement Administration. US Department of Justice. We just had a big shootout and -"

"Well, ma'am, I don't know anything about that but -" Chris turned off the conversation and walked back outside. *We? Don't remember no "we" out there.*

Chris was sitting on a cot, a short distance away from the hospital and a bit around the corner out of sight. He had his head in his hands and since the excitement was wearing off, he felt himself trembling as if he were sitting in a freezer. His stomach was bubbling, and he had already spied out a porta-cabin in case he had to run for it. With his eyes closed, he was seeing the shooting over and over in vivid color and sound, the body slowing as his bullets impacted the man's chest, the puffs of dust off the man's clothes, an imagined thud and sucking as the bullets pushed their way into the soft tissue. The man slowed and stumbled and fell, the tired shock on his face as if, while looking directly at Chris, he knew his life was leaking out of him. His eyes dropped to the ground in supplication, begging for another chance to get it right, and then he was blasted into the next world as he fired his rifle into the dirt.

Chris had turned off the radio and with his eyes closed, he heard vehicles and aircraft and rounds fired from his gun entering and re-entering the dead man. He had no idea how much time had passed and may have even dozed with his arms resting on his knees.

"How're you doing, Chris?" he felt a hand on his shoulder and snapped his head up. The light in the hangar was different, less intense, less harsh with the day moving on. The Chief of Station was standing in front of him in suit and tie. There was a black-jumpsuited soldier whom Chris hadn't seen before standing behind him, weapons holstered and hanging.

Chris stood up. "Good, thanks."

The CoS shook his hand. "I've been getting debriefs from the guys at the scene. They all say you did a good job."

Chris nodded, exhausted.

"We picked up the Ambassador and brought him here. He's in with R2. Mau's all prepped and should be wheeled into the OR right about now. One of the doctors said it's a standard procedure they do a couple times a day and'll take about an hour. R2's going to have a scar he can be proud of though."

"That's great news," he replied, his voice low.

"Damn right it is," said the CoS. He was smiling broadly, evidently not at all feeling down like Chris was. "All-in-all, a good day's work. Not perfect by any means, but good. I've still got a bunch of my men out at the house and the FBI's all over it, but a rough count looks like we've got more heroin than we expected. About two tons worth." He stuck out his hand again. "Congratulations."

Chris could only nod as he weakly returned the handshake. To him, it didn't seem like a fair price to pay for his friends being shot and FUBAR's fatal head wound, much less the others dead, including the man *he* had killed.

"Ambassador's not too thrilled with the body count, but everyone on our side acted in accordance with the brief and ROE, and sometimes these things don't go as planned. It'll be a few days before the FBI wraps up their investigation. They'll want to interview everyone because all the agencies involved have an interest in who did what and to whom and when, but everything was recorded so no worries there. They'll present it for signature but there aren't going to be any surprises."

Chris nodded again.

"Why don't you sit back down, son. You look a little green." He looked over his shoulder. "I'm going to go say hi to the guys inside. Get him some coffee or something, will you?"

Chris was lying on a cot with his eyes closed when the CoS came out of the hospital with Sarah Thibodaux in tow. "Chris," he called. When Chris looked up, the CoS waved him over. They were walking fast towards the front of the hangar. Chris jumped and caught up with them.

"I thought you'd like to see this," he said to Chris.

"What?"

They stepped into the sunshine. He pointed. "That."

In the distance was a small crowd of heavily armed men whom Chris recognized as the Papa detail he had snaked through the house with and Jack. Beyond them sat an Army CH-47 helicopter, its ramp down and dark. One of the guys was holding a flex-cuffed man. Chris squinted. "Hey, that's Samadi!"

"Yep." He laughed. "He's on his way to Bagram. You got a camera?"

Chris shook his head.

"Anyone here got a camera?" he called louder.

"Yes, sir," answered the soldier in black who had accompanied him.

"Can you get some pictures of that and make sure Chris gets one? That's a once-in-a-lifetime shot. And make sure I get one too."

"Not a problem, sir."

They stood and watched as Samadi was walked onto the helo. The engines started to sing - Samadi's fat lady telling him it was over. Even from this distance, Chris could see him being belted in. There were several men in desert BDUs getting him secured for his short ride to the interrogation cell.

In his heart of hearts, Chris felt bad for Samadi's future. Though he was a drug dealer, he was also a carpet salesman in a war-beaten country, and every time Chris had heard him on the phone, he had been cheery and friendly.

As the helo lifted off and headed north, Chris watched Jack wave at it, then he and his security detail came walking towards the hangar. He came up and shook Chris' hand. "Hey, man, I saw you sleeping in there when we got here. Must be nice to be that cool, calm and collected. I'm jazzed like a motherfucker! And I didn't even do anything." Chris felt himself grinning.

Jack announced he was going to return to the drop house. There was a lot of cleanup to attend to: the heroin had to be secured, the bodies had to be collected and brought back where they would be photographed and DNA samples taken, interviews had to be completed with the prosecutor and the FBI Special Agents. The DEA's agent-involved shooting team had already been contacted and deferred the investigation to the Bureau, and that would mean interviews with Chris as well as the other shooters.

"Okay," said the CoS. "Keep me advised."

"Roger that, boss." He wrapped his arm around Chris' neck and gave him a noogie then left with his group.

"Now, Mr. Davis," the CoS said, turning to Chris, his voice stern. "We've got a little problem with you."

Chris nodded. "Sarah already told me."

"Right. Well, the Ambassador's headed back to the embassy but he was talking to your Administrator while we were inside. Both are quite pleased with the results of the operation and they'll be getting together on the press releases. Believe it or not, this is a huge success. I know you're feeling a little shitty right now because of Mau and R2 and FUBAR, but believe me when I tell you this is huge and it's good. I'm sure the Ambassador'll be talking this up his chain of command, which is only one step removed from the President. It's really that big. But..."

Chris pursed his lips and nodded, waiting for the train blasting down the tracks right at him.

"Because you're not an accredited member of the diplomatic mission here, you're liable for your actions with no immunity. According to your Administrator, you've got to talk to a lot of people, and now. We can't afford to keep you here while all your stuff is settled because the immunity problem's going to generate heat. I'm told the head of the Islamabad office is in Karachi for meetings so we're shipping you off tonight. You can debrief him and do whatever other administrative penance your agency requires. It really is imperative that we get you out of the country before the prosecutor's office gets spun up. I don't think they'd go after you all that hard, but there's a lot of dead Afghanis back at the house and not too many injured Americans. You never know where political heat might go, right? I'd like it if you could stay, but really the best solution is for you to be gone."

"Okay." Even with the nice words about the operation, Chris felt like he was being spanked and sent to stand in the corner. He was also noting, with interest, that Sarah was standing silently, smoking, looking off into the distance, ignored.

"You have your passport?"

Chris nodded.

The CoS stuck out his hand. "It was nice knowing you and I'm glad my guys got a chance to work with you."

"Thank you, sir," he replied none-too-brightly.

"Sarah? You'll arrange his flight on your plane?"

She nodded but said nothing.

"Good. Chris...it's all going to be fine. The Ambassador, and your boss, and *my* boss are really happy. You're not going to fall into the shit over this." As he said this last part, he slid his eyes directly at Sarah who matched his look then turned away. "Someone'll pack your stuff and get it back to you in the US or wherever you are. You take care of yourself. Sarah," he said, turning, "I'm headed back to the embassy to talk to the Ambassador. Care to join me?"

Her face brightened as she looked at Chris one last time. "Absolutely."

Chris waited outside the hangar until the entourage was well on their way then walked into the hospital again. He assumed at some point someone would collect his radio and, though no one had asked for it, the gun he still had tucked into his jeans.

Inside the cool, clean air of the emergency room again, he spied R2 lying on his side on one of the gurneys, keeping his freshly sewn leg, as yet un-bruised, off the mobile bed. His eyes were closed but he was tapping his fingers to some inner music. Chris walked up to him and touched his shoulder. His eyes opened slowly, probably still under the influence of the surgical anesthesia.

"How're you doing, bartender?"

"You hear about FUBAR?"

Chris nodded.

"We were just sitting in the truck, and we heard the radio call telling us to get out when the rounds came through the front windshield."

Chris didn't know what to say. He stood silent, his hand on R2's shoulder.

"It didn't miss me by an inch. I swear to God I heard it go by. Jon's super-lucky it didn't take him out in the backseat too. FUBAR's was dead on. I don't even know where they were coming from. I didn't see anything."

Chris could only nod again. R2 closed his eyes and stopped tapping his fingers. Chris was sure he had dropped into instant sleep when suddenly his eyes snapped open and he turned his head back at Chris. "I could hear a bunch of noise and I don't remember getting hit...fuck, it was just like all of a sudden Jon yanked me into the back, and I was bleeding, and he shoved a wad of shit into my leg. Egg crawled over the seat and started driving. Then...here I am and they told me FUBAR's dead." A single tear leaked out of R2's eye and Chris had to blink quickly several times to keep the same thing from happening to him. R2 grabbed Chris' hand. "Hey, what happened to Mau? Did I hear something about him on the radio?"

Chris took a deep breath. "He got hit too. He's here somewhere, I think in the operating room. They said it wasn't too bad."

R2 shook his head. "Fuck."

"Yeah."

With nothing to do while he waited for Mau to come out of surgery, Chris sat on "his" cot, plugged back into the net, and listened to what was going on. A voice reported the search of Samadi's carpet shop on Chicken Street hadn't turned up anything of evidentiary value. Another voice, the person apparently embedded with a squad of local soldiers, stated the house where Anwar started out his day, where R2 and FUBAR were shot, was raided but everyone who had been there was gone. Someone else asked if the locals were going to set up checkpoints out of town but, as no one knew who they were looking for, it would be a futile exercise and the suggestion was squashed. Chris didn't recognize any of the people on the radio and tuned them back out.

He shot to his feet when it suddenly occurred to him he hadn't talked to Ricardo back in Miami to inform him about how the day had gone. He hit the speed dial.

"House."

"It's Chris."

There was a long pause. "How you doing, kid? How's Mau?"

Chris took a deep breath. "He's...he's..." Suddenly tears sprang to Chris' eyes, and he sat back on the cot and put his head down. He tried explaining again but could do little more than make hiccupping sounds, his breathing was so ragged. He wanted to tell his boss how he had done everything the best he could, but something bad had still happened, and he had had to kill someone, and his friend had been shot and was in surgery, and he had really tried... but all he could do was sit there and make stupid half-word sounds with tears dripping on the hangar floor.

After a time, his breathing started to slow, and he held his breath and wiped his eyes with his sleeve, wiped again with his other sleeve, and raised his head and looked around. There was no one paying him any attention. He took one more deep breath and started to speak again, his voice wavering a little but stronger. "Mau's okay. He's in surgery but should be coming out anytime. He got shot in the leg during the deal."

"I know. I was in on the conference call with the SAC. The word I got was it's a pretty minor wound. How about you? Did you get checked out by the doctor?"

Chris shook his head. "No, I'm okay."

"Chris, are you a doctor?"

"No, sir."

"Right, then I want you to go find a doctor and get checked out." Chris recognized the order. "Also, this first twenty-four hours is for you to kind of collect yourself, but remember that you're not supposed to talk to anyone about the shooting and that includes me, okay?"

"Yes, sir."

"Good. I already talked to the GS there and I understand you're going to be flying out tonight."

"Yeah, she's really pissed."

"Apparently."

Chris took a deep breath before plunging into the subject that had been troubling him since being yelled at by Sarah. "Am I in trouble over this?"

There was silence over the phone for several seconds. "Well, I'd like to tell you absolutely not but...administratively speaking, you broke some rules. On the other hand, you just made one of the largest heroin seizures in history and that's going to make DEA and the Administrator look good so honestly, I wouldn't sweat it too much. Besides, like the saying goes, you're not a real agent until you've shot someone, gotten divorced, and been investigated by OPR. You're knocking out two of the big three at one time. But you're not going to get fired so really, don't worry about it, okay?"

He was feeling pretty glum but there was little to do about it. "Okay."

"Call me when Mau's out of surgery." he said as he hung up the phone.

Mau's eyes fluttered open, then closed, then opened again.

"How you doin', man?" Chris asked quietly.

Mau was lying on a surgical gurney in the recovery room, his body covered up to his neck with a clean, white blanket.

"I am so fuck-ed," replied Mau, drawing the word out into two syllables.

Chris leaned closer, abruptly concerned something had happened he hadn't been told about. "What'd'ya mean?"

"*You* know I got shot in the leg," Mau said slowly, dreamily. "*I* know I got shot in the leg. But everyone else is going to say I got shot in the ass. I'm totally fuck-ed."

Suddenly Chris was beaming, feeling so much better. If Mau could make jokes, nothing could be that bad. "Man, no one'll even know about yours... you should see R2's, buddy. It's massive!"

"You mean his is bigger?" Chris nodded and held his hands apart, like he was telling a fish story. "Shit, man..." Mau lifted the blanket and looked down towards his leg. "I've got a freakin' bandaid over mine. My scar isn't even going to be bold. I need more damage for the ladies to love... can you do me a favor and shoot me again?"

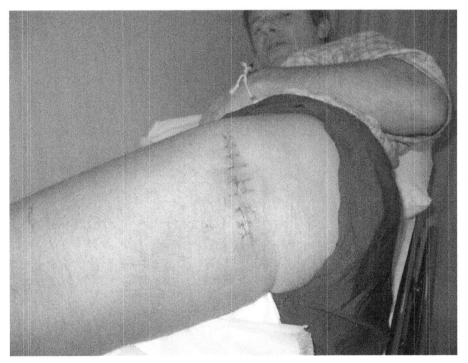

R2 after surgery.

289

R2's truck after being recovered to the Annex. Arrows
point to the bullet holes.

The Chicken Street Raiders outside Samadi's store.

Samadi (on left) in custody at airport.

CHAPTER EIGHTEEN

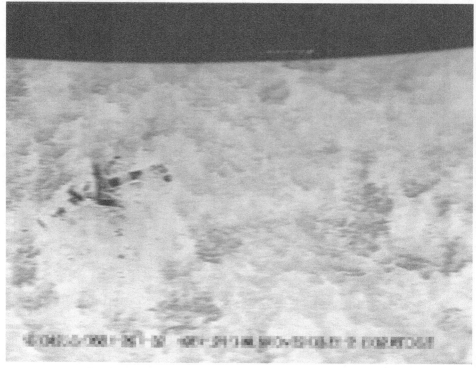

Night had finally settled on what felt like the longest day in Chris' life. After sitting and talking with Mau for a while, he had gotten a cursory checkup from a passing doctor and talked again to Ricardo in Miami. He finally realized the rumbling he heard in the distance was his stomach reminding him he hadn't eaten since breakfast and had been running on nothing except adrenaline and air all day. There was a small chow hall a few hangars down, and he sat at a table by himself eating some pure Americana: hot dogs, mustard and french fries.

"Hey, are you Chris Davis?" came an unfamiliar voice from behind.

He took a deep breath. *Damn.* What he wouldn't give for a few moments to himself. Slowly he turned around. The man behind him was not-too-tall with very angular features and bright blue eyes. He was clean-shaven and looked vaguely familiar. He was holding an orange tray stacked solely with desserts.

"I'm Colin." He put down his tray and gave Chris' hand a crushing grip that belied his size. "I'm going to be flying you tonight." As he sat, he looked at Chris very closely, his blue eyes squinting with concentration.

"Nice to meet you," replied Chris, his mouth wrapped around the not-too-bad tasting wiener.

"Are you Pete Davis' brother?"

"Yeah!" He was surprised to hear his brother's name.

Colin nodded. "I saw the teletype before you got here but didn't put it together who you were until just now. I remember getting an email from him saying you had graduated from the Academy. I think I met you in Ft. Lauderdale a few years ago."

Chris nodded. "Hmm," he grunted non-commitally. "Was I drunk?"

Colin laughed. "We all were. I think you hooked up with a Customs agent or something."

"Yeah…" he said. Slowly running what he had just heard through his mental Rolodex, he came up with a night of extraordinary drunkenness with Big Brother and a bunch of visiting DEA agents including the pilot sitting next to him and the referred-to woman. He shook hands with him again. "She was an analyst. Miami office. Superior body."

They yukked it up and schmoozed for a while, catching up on who-knew-who and what was fucked-up with the agency they were working for. Colin was obviously in no hurry to move things along. He explained the other pilots were filing the flight plan, and their maintenance guy was pulling the plane out of the hangar and fueling and doing a preflight.

"I heard about the Gunfight at the OK Corral today. You let the air outta somebody, right? That's why the bum's rush to get you outta Tombstone before the sheriff comes and locks you in the hooskow?"

"Yup," said Chris. "I'm your huckleberry."

293

"Cool. I'm a-wantin' to hear all about it, but we might as well wait until Billy D. and Warbaby get here so they can hear it too, and it'll give us something to talk about." He looked at his watch. "I figure we'll be wheels up in about an hour. Takes a bit to get military clearances. You got your passport?" he asked, pulling on a US Marine Corps utility cap and placing it squarely on his head.

Chris nodded and began cleaning his tray.

The two walked along the hangars where a large, twin-engine King Air was parked, the door on the left side unfolded and hanging open.

"What's up there, Homer?" called Colin.

A dark-haired man popped his head out the door and nodded. Colin introduced the two men. "Alan's our wrench-turner," he explained. Then, to Alan he said, "Everything going okay?"

Alan shook his hand back and forth in a so-so motion as he came down the ladder. "The Army says we can't draw fuel because they're doing some kind of inspection or audit or some shit."

Colin pursed his lips. "They say how long?"

The mechanic shook his head. "The fuel depot says they've got something called TS-1 we can use. I guess it's Russian leftovers but he said they've got truckloads of the stuff. I think that's what the MIL helos the spooks fly use sometimes when they can't get into the Army's supply. They're going to drive one over in about ten minutes."

Colin shrugged. "Never heard of it."

"Me neither but I just got off the phone with the L-3 rep at the AOC[1]. He says it's okay to use. It's their version of Jet A."

"Low tech solution to a low tech problem. Rock and roll, dude." He turned to Chris. "Might as well go wait in the office for the guys to get back."

---

[1] Aviation Operations Center, the DEA's aviation headquarters in Alliance, Texas.

Billy D. came in sipping from a can of soda, introduced himself to Chris, and tossed Colin a copy of the flight plan. A little older than his partner, he had long, graying hair swept back from his forehead and was dressed similarly to Colin. Colin told him about the problem with the fuel and the solution Alan had come up with. Billy's response was simply, "Cool."

"Where's Warbaby?"

"Went back to the hooch. Said he didn't wanna go."

"Slack-ass bastard...and he calls himself a Marine." He spun in his chair to face Chris. "Okay there, Crazy, I think you owe us a story..."

Alan walked into the office and looked at the three men with their feet up. "You guys ready? Plane's gassed and good to go."

"Not yet," said Billy looking at his watch. "We're taking an extra pax with us. I got the call while I was at base ops."

Alan gave him a thumbs-up. "Roger that. I'm gonna go grab a smoke. Just gimme a yell when you're ready."

As he walked out, Jack walked in.

"Jack, man," shouted Chris, jumping to his feet. "What's up?"

Jack grinned. "I'm going with you."

"No shit? To Karachi?"

Jack nodded and looked over both shoulders in an exaggerated parody of checking to make sure no one was listening. "Seems *my* boss doesn't trust *your* boss not to fuck you over before your arrival, so he decided to send me along while you give your briefings."

"She's such a cunt," intoned Billy quietly and to no one in particular.

"Really?" said Chris, after introducing him around. "What does she think I'm going to say?"

Jack shrugged. "Who knows? But since I've been with you for the whole thing, he thought it would be a good idea for you to have some backup and a cheering section."

"She's such a cunt," repeated Billy.

Colin laughed. "That politically incorrect statement on gender diversity was made by Special Agent William Dwyer," he said in a loud voice, feigning talking to hidden microphones secreted in the office. "I think you should be more accepting of the role of women in our agency and both embrace and respect her superior position over you."

"Yeah, she can blow me in her position over me." He said standing up. "Let's get the fuck out of here."

The four men filed out into the darkness. "Alan, you hapless geek!" shouted Colin into the empty hangar, his voice echoing. "Stop pulling your pud and make us go to work!"

Outside, the plane was bathed in white light from a portable stand. Night had finally dropped in from the mountains.

As they boarded, Chris was impressed by the spacious luxury. There were six wide, nicely upholstered seats, two of which were facing the back of the plane immediately behind the cockpit. "Very nice!" he said, immediately reclining and clicking on the seatbelt. Jack sat next to him, also reclining for comfort and putting his feet up on the rear-facing seat.

"That table folds out if you guys wanna play cards or something. There's a deck of cards there," said Colin pointing, "and magazines there. If you wanna listen in on the radio, there's headsets there and there. If you don't need anything else, then I'll just go fuck myself and fly the plane."

Chris laughed. "Grassy ass, *Senor*."

Colin took his place in the left seat climbing over a center console packed with electronics while Billy, in the right, began running through their checklists with the pilot responding to the copilot's challenges.

Chris had never been so close to the cockpit of a plane before and was fascinated with the speedy give-and-take of professional pilots at work.

"Weight, CG, Performance, V-Speeds…"

"Checked."

"Preflight Inspection…"

"Complete."

"Chocks…"

"Removed."

"Airstair / Cargo door…"

"Locked."

"Overwing Escape Hatch Latches…"

"Closed."

"Load and Baggage…"

"Secure."

"Passenger Briefing…"

Colin shifted around in his seat so he could address the passengers. "See that red handle," he said pointing above a window. "If we crash, pull that down and the hatch'll fall in. Then get out of the way because I'm going to be going through that hole faster than shit through a goose and don't want to leave tracks on you as I go by. When you get out, you'll see me standing at attention like the good Marine I am, and then I'll be leading from the front with the panicked scream, 'Follow me!'" He shifted back in his seat. "Passenger briefing complete."

The rest of the business in the cockpit was interesting and rapid-fire with fast-paced radio calls being made in jargon Chris could barely follow through the headset. Outside the plane, Chris watched as one of the propellers started to turn accompanied by a low-pitched hum, which grew into the scream of a jet engine, all heavily muffled by acoustic insulation. Soon after, the brakes were released and the plane started rolling forward. As they were taxiing, the other engine was started. Chris could see red and white flashes of strobe lights as they passed hangar upon hangar towards the runway.

"November Seven Two Eight Five Yankee," said a voice in the thick accent Chris had become accustomed to hearing in Afghanistan. "Kabul Tower. Winds calm. Cleared for takeoff runway two-niner."

The speed of the propellers increased to a throaty roar as the plane began its acceleration. Chris could feel the roughness of the runway translating through the landing gear when suddenly, the plane virtually leapt into the air at such a steep angle Chris was pushed deep into his seat, then it banked sharply to the left in a tight turn. "Yahoo!" he called happily, the events of the day momentarily forgotten.

He leaned forward and looked out the front of the plane between the two pilots. The cockpit was dimly lit, with instruments displayed on small computer screens. Outside the windshield was absolute darkness without a trace of moon or stars.

Seeing nothing more interesting, he sat back and within seconds was asleep.

Thankfully, he did not re-visit his shooting. Occasionally, when his head hit his chest, he would pop up, look around. He had unplugged his headset so he wouldn't have to listen to the radios and could have some peace.

He bumped awake again. The lights were dim in the cabin and Jack was asleep across from him, his arms crossed and his head down. He put his head up against the side of the plane, closed his eyes, and was immediately back in the house, his arms outstretched, looking over the sights of his pistol, seeing the Afghan stumble and fall, and the machine works of the gun explode under him. And then silence.

And then more silence.

He was aware, as he was looking back in his memory of the man he had killed, that there should have been more noise, that silence wasn't really expected. There were voices, and it sounded in his head like, "Where's R2?" Though the tone was right, the words were wrong. He opened his eyes and blinked rapidly. Jack was still asleep. He turned in his chair. The pilots were doing whatever pilots do, though they seemed to be doing a lot of it. He took the headset off and immediately was struck by the fact it really *was* quiet. There was no roar of propellers, no whine of turbine engines.

"Hey," he started.

"Stand by." Billy snapped at him without turning around. He had a chart on his lap and was running a finger down the crease.

Chris plugged his headset back in, more confused than scared, just in time to hear Colin start transmitting. "Mayday, mayday, mayday, November Seven Two Eight Five Yankee," he said in a surprisingly calm voice. "Flight level two two decimal four, dual engine failure, four souls on board, squawking seven seven zero zero."

Chris turned and hit Jack's leg. He came awake instantly and turned to look out the window. Chris took a deep breath, willing himself to remain as calm as Colin sounded a moment ago. "I just heard them call mayday. We've lost both engines."

Jack shook his head as if to clear his sleep. "What-the-fuck-are-you-talking-about?" came tumbling out of his mouth much louder than necessary since he didn't have to talk over the sounds of the engines anymore.

"I don't know. I just heard him on the radio and he said dual engine failure. Shit, listen outside…they're not running!"

Jack unbuckled his seatbelt and leaned into the cockpit. "Guys -'

"Hang on," Billy told him. "You guys need to sit quiet for a minute."

"Yeah, but -"

Billy D. reached back and placed his hand on Jack's chest and pushed him, not hard enough to topple him over but enough to get him out of the cockpit and back into the cabin. "Fuck off for a sec, will you please?"

Jack sat on the other rear-facing seat, turned sideways like Chris, looking into the cockpit.

After what truly seemed like forever, during which time the passengers could do nothing except watch and listen, Colin said, "You've got the controls," to Billy D., who repeated he *did* in fact have the controls, and then turned as much as he could in his chair to talk to Chris and Jack.

"Okay, here's the deal...we've lost both engines. They went at about the same time and we think it's fuel contamination. We tried to re-start them but no joy. We've put out a mayday, we're talking to ATC, and we passed a message to DEA. We're in a glide, and we'll keep trying to re-start them, but in the event we can't..." he took a deep breath, "then we're going to do a crash landing. We're well inside Pakistan and there's no way we can get back across the border in the time we have left. We've looked at the charts, and there's no runways we can get to so we're fucked with that." He was talking very fast now. "We've got some time, but here's what I need from you. In the event of a crash, everything that's not nailed down or strapped in is going to go flying, so I need you guys to get all the shit that's back there secured however you can. Use seatbelts and whatever else you can find. That's all I've got right now. I don't have time to answer your questions so I need you to just get moving." Without waiting for a response, he turned back to his business.

Chris looked at Jack who was staring back at him. It lasted for no more than a moment, but he registered pure terror there. He was sure Jack was seeing the same thing reflected in *his* eyes. He took a deep breath, then another. It seemed he was unable to get thoughts organized. Everything was just spinning in a miasma of white noise and he was frozen in his seat. He blinked rapidly. He felt something on his shoulder. He looked down and saw a hand, which was connected to an arm, which was further connected to a shoulder, and there was a face above it. He recognized the face as Billy Dwyer, the copilot. The lips on Billy D.'s face were moving. Chris shook his head and concentrated on the lips, squinting his eyes in concentration. "Dude, you okay?"

Suddenly the silence popped, and he could hear the minute buzz of electronics, Colin's voice on the other side of the cockpit, and the rustling of cloth. He had gone from deaf to hearing everything.

He nodded his head. "Yeah, sorry. I'm fine. We'll get going." He got up from his seat and walked hunched over to the rear of the plane. He could feel Jack moving along behind him.

There was a faux-wood partition running from floor to ceiling. Behind it was a blue box of water bottles and a very large, olive-green rucksack. He grabbed one of the straps and passed a load behind him where it was lifted and taken away by Jack. A black plastic rifle case was hiding under the backpack; he took it and put it at his feet. There were two folding chairs, aluminum framed, very light; a rolled up sleeping bag; and a brown box stenciled, "Meals, Ready to Eat." That seemed to be the extent of the payload.

He turned and watched as Jack put the big pack on a seat and wrapped a seatbelt through the shoulder straps, pulling as tight as he could, then grabbed the pack and pulled it against the seatbelts, satisfying himself it wasn't going anywhere.

Chris took the hard rifle case, sat it on the adjacent seat, and did the same with its handle and the seat's belts. The box of water went on the floor between the seat and the seat back ahead of it. He looked around for something to secure it but came up blank. He thought about taking the big bottles out of the box but then what to do with *those*? He picked up the box, put it on the forward facing seat across from where he had been sitting, and awkwardly wrapped the belts around it. He figured when he was sitting, he could put his feet up against it to keep it in place, and hopefully, the combination of his feet and the belts would do the job. Jack loosened the backpack, put the chairs behind it, then re-secured it. The sleeping bag and the MREs went across from Jack.

He looked up. Both he and Jack were breathing hard, much harder than he knew they should be. He figured he was hyperventilating a little so he sat down and calmed his breathing. Peripherally, he was aware of the two pilots carrying on a conversation, and then the cabin lights went out. He craned his head around into the cockpit, which was noticeably darker; many of the instruments were black. He realized he was chewing on his thumbnail and lowered his hand; he hadn't even been aware he was doing it.

"Everything okay?" he asked, then mentally kicked himself for the stupidity of *that* question.

Colin turned his head. "We're on battery power and we've reduced the drain on it as much as we can. You guys set and got everything wrapped up?"

He nodded. "I think so, as best we can."

"Okay, scoot up here for a sec. You've got the controls," he said to Billy.

Jack and Chris put their heads together.

"I need to brief you guys on some stuff," Colin began, his face nearly invisible in the darkness. It was eerie hearing him speak in a conversational tone, not having to raise his voice over the engines. "First of all, we've plotted out where, if a crash is going to happen…and it's beginning to look like it is…where we're going to set down. Our charts don't depict terrain, but it's a mostly clear night and we've got some moonlight. We're going to aim for something flat if we can. The MORAs, the off-route altitudes for the grid where we're going in, show highest point around five thousand feet, but ATC says the mean terrain's around four thousand, so we're expecting peaks no

302

higher than one thousand feet and mostly lower hills and ridges. The really high mountains are quite a ways behind us, which is good because if it had happened there, we'd be really fucked.

"Anyway, I can't tell you what the landing's going to be like, but sit in the seats facing the back of the plane so your inertia will push you into the seatbacks and cushion your spine. Jam your hands under your thighs to keep them from flailing around…I remember seeing flight attendants do that on their jumpseats during takeoff and landing," he smiled which was comforting for Chris to see. "We're going to leave the gear up. Again, I don't know what we're going to be landing on, so be prepared for a rough ride.

"Now, location-wise it's 'Indian Country.' Billy and I have talked about it and here's the thing…conventional wisdom says stay with the plane and wait 'til help arrives. But because of where we're going to be, we decided we definitely do not want to stay with the plane…we don't know how long it'll be before someone comes and gets us, and this place is definitely hostile so depending on how mobile we are after landing, we need to get as far away from the plane as fast as we can and head south. We've got quite a few hours of darkness left so we're going to move and hide before sunrise. There's no city nearby and if we come to any villages or houses, we're going to go around them. Questions so far?"

Both the passengers shook their heads.

"Excellent. Now, a quick inventory of important stuff…I'm telling you this in case Billy and I don't survive the crash so you know what you'll have available." He was so matter-of-fact it made Chris even more nervous, if that were possible. Today he had been introduced to death and was sure he'd seen enough to last forever. "There's MREs and water. We've got an M16 in a case, and there's some magazines in there too and a couple more in the ruck. Billy and I have handguns -"

"I've got one too," interjected Chris.

Colin grinned again and nodded. He looked at Jack with raised eyebrows, but Jack shook his head. "Okay, there's a satellite Personal Locator Beacon in there, about the size of a cell phone. Just turn it on as soon as you can. There's pencil flares, a medical kit, more water, a signaling mirror, a flashlight...I think a couple of sweatshirts...a survival blanket, a shitty survival knife...I can't think of much else. Maybe a bottle of Tabasco. Can you think of anything?" he asked Billy who answered with a headshake.

"Oh yeah!" he exclaimed. "Somewhere in there's a compass, too. So anyway, south, right? When the sun starts coming up, it'll be on your left side if you're going the right way. Either of you do SERE school or survival training or anything? Boy Scouts? Outward Bound?"

More headshakes.

"Bummer. Well, I don't know what else to tell you. Better hope we don't die. But look, you really need to be looking for places to hide, not too close to the plane. Eventually the military'll come for you so you have to be patient. Don't get rattled. Keep moving south as much as you can under cover of darkness. Hide during the day. Don't worry about rationing water...if you're thirsty, drink it 'til it's gone. Don't light fires. I know some of this sounds kind of stupid, but I'm giving you all I've got as fast as I can. If you need to take a shit...oh yeah, there's a roll of toilet paper in there...bury it deep. Stay off the roads, don't use trails, don't litter, always wear condoms...fuck..." he paused, "just do the best you can. I gotta get to work. Belt those belts tight like your lives depend on 'em. We'll yell just before we touch down to get you ready."

Chris sat in the dark, his back to the cockpit, listening to the whisper of the slipstream slide over the surface of the plane. He had started to say a prayer but the words faltered before they reached his mouth, replaced by an image he was certain he would not be seeing again: mom sitting in her

304

favorite green chair, a cat (one of many) on her lap, her arthritic fingers tracing tiny circles in its soft fur, a bright blue sky meeting the brown water of the Gulf of Mexico on the horizon line. He absently considered how many times he had driven across the state to sit with her while she watched *Murder She Wrote,* or read the bible, or sighed as she tried to figure out how to send email.

"What're you thinking about?" asked Jack, disturbing Chris' recollections.

Chris looked over at him, though could see very little. "I'm thinking I want my money back for this flight."

Jack laughed in the darkness. "You know, I was in the Navy. Went to submarine school. *Wanted* to be a pilot but didn't get accepted to flight school. That could've been me up there."

"You'd have a front row seat to watch the crash." Chris offered.

"*That's* something I could live a whole lifetime without seeing." He sat silently for a few seconds. "What'd'ya think of our chances?"

Chris shrugged. "No idea, man." There was something more he wanted to say to his friend, whom he hoped would understand. "I feel like it's karma for killing that guy today."

"Well that's just great," said Colin from the front before Jack could respond. "You couldn't have gotten the karma when you were alone? Had to drag us along with you? In a fuckin' *airplane*?"

All four men in the quiet plane chuckled.

"Sorry, guys. First bar we come to, my karma's buying the drinks."

"Damn right," countered Colin. "By the way, we're about eight minutes from touchdown."

"How's it look out there?" asked Chris without turning around.

"Blacker than the inside of a cow. But at least we won't be able to see the bad news 'til it's in our laps."

"Hey," said Billy cutting in. "Look there...wait, it's gone now. I thought I saw a ridgeline and a valley. About two o'clock. Dark line running north-south about a half a mile to our right. Speed one hundred thirty five knots."

"I don't have it. I'll start easing right."

"We're passing nine thousand feet. Ready for the rad-alt?"

"Yeah, I guess. Radar altimeter on."

"Radar Altimeter...on."

Chris listened as Billy counted down the altitude in thousand foot increments. With each callout he took one step further along a road he was sure led to his destruction.

"Eight thousand...radio altimeter alive...two thousand on the rad-alt...One thousand five hundred feet."

"Call out every hundred feet," directed Colin. "And speed."

"Roger that...one thousand four hundred feet, speed one hundred thirty five knots...flaps?"

"I think I see something," said Colin. "One o'clock. Yeah, half flaps for the stall speed."

Suddenly Billy was speaking very quickly, "Eight hundred feet...seven hundred feet...six hundred..." Billy's countdown was coming very rapidly, much faster than Chris thought it should be as he was unable to comprehend how the plane could drop from fourteen hundred feet to eight hundred in less than a second. Billy's words began to run together. "Five hundred, four hundred...shit...three hundred...speed dropping...watch your speed...one hundred knots, one oh five, one oh five, two hundred feet, one hundred feet...she's gonna stall!" he shouted out. Chris felt the plane nosing up, the seat belt holding him secure as he leaned toward the back of the plane, his feet pushing against the box opposite him. He jammed his hands under his

306

legs, grabbed his pants in a tight fist, involuntarily tensed every muscle in his body, and pressed his head against the upholstered seatback.

"Two hundred feet, one hundred knots...three hundred feet...four hundred feet now, one hundred knots...fuck, we must have passed over a ridge. I didn't see anything! Shit, that was -"

His last word was lost in a vicious lateral deceleration that was the first in an instantaneous series of gyrations Chris couldn't even comprehend beyond sheer violence and noise. He gripped his pants tighter as an uncontrollable storm of motion smashed into him, whipsawing him from side-to-side leaving him totally helpless.

His eyes were either scrunched closed or wide open. Because of the darkness, there was no way to tell. The belt at his waist pulled tighter against his pelvis, and he wasn't even sure he was breathing, except subconsciously he registered the odors of kerosene fuel and dust and metal.

He didn't register the huge tearing bang of a wing snapping free. The tornado of sound reaching his brain consisted of nothing but sharp pops and whangs, dings, glass shattering, plastic cracking, and human shouts, but the larger noise cyclone swirled silently and was lost to him, unable to penetrate his traumatized consciousness.

A massive concussion drove him into his seat and he momentarily thought his feet were higher than his head in a looping roll when his body jerked the other way towards Jack. Something bounced off his cheek, not hard enough to knock him out, just enough to put a dazzle behind his eyes.

The tube in which he was imprisoned began a crazy roll side over side. At one point his hands came loose and were hanging straight down over his head. He pulled his elbows into his body and tried to cover his head.

More metal screamed under tremendous strain and stress. There was a final heave and deep scraping that swung Chris sideways one last time and then only silence.

* *

He realized he was holding his breath, listening, but could hear nothing except a ringing in his ears. He slowly let the air out of his chest. He could see nothing in the darkness except the word "EXIT" in dim green phosphorescence over one of the windows.

He took a deep breath, "Hey!" he shouted. "Can anybody hear me?" His own voice sounded muffled in his ears, like his fingers were jammed in there.

There was a rustling from behind him and a mumble.

He reached to his right, where Jack had been sitting. His hand came in contact with cloth and body. He shook it gently. "Jack?"

"Yeah."

"Colin? Billy?"

"Yeah," said Billy from the front, then to Colin, "You okay?"

A beam of dusty light shot out of the cockpit into the fuselage as Billy passed back a flashlight to Chris. "Check yourselves over."

Chris took it and quickly ran it over his body looking for blood or broken bones. He knew from his DEA training that following such a traumatic event, he was probably in shock and might not feel any injuries he had sustained. Seeing nothing, he aimed the light at Jack with similar results. He also took a good look at his eyes, ears and nose but saw nothing leaking out. He passed the flashlight to Jack. "See anything?" he asked, turning his head back and forth.

"You're fine," he croaked. "How're you guys?" he called to the pilots.

"We're okay," returned Billy.

There was a quiet clink of metal on metal. Billy's upper body appeared. He took the flashlight and shined it around the back of the plane. Dust hung in the air like dirty fog. The forward walls of the plane were mostly intact except for a large hole ripped in the right side, two seats back from where Chris had been sitting. The round windows on either side of the opening had disappeared. A razor sharp spear of yellowish-green painted metal had jammed through the skin of the plane about a foot; below it the floor had buckled several inches. There was also a huge tear at the rear of the plane where more colored metal glinted dully in the beam from the flashlight. He shined the light on both of the passengers.

"Okay, let's evacuate." He aimed the light at the emergency handles over the windows. "Pull those down and just toss 'em out the window out of the way so we don't trip on 'em." He was moving around in the cockpit. "Check the ground before you climb out. Take the backpack, water and MREs. There's fuel out there…I can smell it…get as far away from it as you can. We'll be right behind you.

Chris did as he was ordered and as he tried to stand, he realized the plane was not on level ground. He popped the window out as directed and shined the light down. Normally, someone crawling out would have stepped out onto the wing and then jumped down, but the wing was no longer there which should have made it a little farther from windowsill to ground; however, as the plane wasn't supported by its landing gear, it was a mere half-step down from the window.

Once out, he reached up and took the backpack from Jack. With both of them on the ground, Billy started passing the rest of the contents of the plane. Neither said anything when the chairs were handed out, or the opposite emergency window hatch.

Lastly, Colin poked his head out, took one last look back in at the wreckage in his ship, then climbed out with a quietly sardonic, "Fuckers'll try to take this out of my pay. You watch."

Silently Billy limped around, lining the ground with everything they weren't bringing into roughly a straight line: thick books containing their aeronautical charts, chairs, escape hatches, the rifle case, pieces of metal from the plane, even the tip of one of the propellers that had snapped off. The life jackets were laid out and their edges pinned to the ground with stones. They tore open the water and MRE boxes and handed the contents around, stuffing what they could into the top of the ruck. They weighted down the boxes with rocks in the same line. So far, no one had said much of anything.

While they were working, Chris stepped back away and looked around to see just what the hell his universe looked like right now. There was an obvious trail of mangled earth the body of the plane had torn up during its landing. He started walking that way to see if there was anything he could add to the stuff Colin and Billy were putting on the ground. It didn't take a rocket scientist to figure out what they were doing. He bent down to pick up something and felt a sharp pain on the left side of his head. He reached up and felt a good-sized bump but his fingers came away dry. He didn't even remember hitting his head.

The ground, hard-packed and dry, sloped steeply to the left to a crest several hundred feet up and down to the right to a point where another smaller ridge started back up. They must have just topped that one before soaring a little further and hitting here. They were damn lucky they were going at an oblique angle and not flying directly west or their impact would have been a head-on pancake.

It was ludicrously hot. He hadn't noticed it before, but then again, it had only been maybe ten minutes since the "landing" and he had been pretty busy. He turned and started walking back toward the rest of the gang, then stopped to look at the scene before him: A moon-like barrenness as a backdrop, not a plant or blade of grass, not a breath of searing air, and plopped right down in the middle of this nothingness was a big white lump of useless trash and three little astronauts wandering around collecting shit. *Motherfucker,* he thought, *it's hot here.*

As he walked up and deposited his contribution, he saw both Colin and Billy had shed their coats, simply dropped them on the ground and left them. This made him feel a little better as he had momentarily worried he was imagining the heat as a result of the knot on his head.

Colin walked to the side of the plane, took a grease pencil from his pocket, and started writing a message on the side of the plane below the foot high registration numbers. "Billy," he called when he was through. "Take a look at that and see if you can translate it."

Dwyer shined a flashlight at it and slowly moved it from left to right, his lips moving silently. "Yeah, I got it. You spelled 'sierra' wrong."

Colin coughed. "Interestingly, I can make that same mistake in four different languages too."

Though not requested to do so, Chris took his turn with the flashlight to see what had been written. "Twozer of our five zulu fours obo scar no v ember fox trot doubleo scar tan go sie rao scar uni form tan go hot elbravo o scar uni form no v ember de lta!" The first word confused him but as his eyes kept moving his brain began to pick out the combinations of letters that made sense when viewed as the big picture. The code Colin had used was as simple as it was smart. Any English speaker or military personnel (and theoretically the next people to see this lump would be one or the other and hopefully both), it would be instantly recognizable. If you were a local goat-herder, it would be meaningless. At the DEA academy, he had been taught the military phonetic alphabet, though rarely used it except when calling out license plates on cars. He had to translate very slowly, especially as the words had been broken up but eventually the message became clear: Two zero four five Zulu (the time), four sob (?), Oscar November (on), Foxtrot Oscar Oscar Tango (foot), Siera Oscar Uniform Tango Hotel Bravo Oscar Uniform November Delta (southbound). "What's four sob?" he asked.

311

"Souls on Board. Number of bodies," replied Billy, shouldering the big backpack. He looked over at Colin. "You ready?"

Colin had the M-16, the strap over his right shoulder. His pockets clanked with magazines as he took an exploratory step, and he re-distributed them so they wouldn't make noise. As he did so, Chris noted he was keeping his left index and middle fingers out of the way.

"You hurt your hand?" he asked.

"Yep," he replied shortly. "Let's all gather here for a minute." He was looking around at the plane and beyond it, back the way they had come as well as along the ridgeline and further down. "Okay," he said pointing, "that's south. That's the way we're going. While we're walking, if you see me put my hand up like this…" he demonstrated, looking at Chris and Jack, holding his right fist up in the air, "it means freeze. If I do it, whoever's behind me does it, and so on so everyone gets the message. Then just do whatever I do." Both nodded. "I figure we'll march for an hour, rest a couple minutes and get moving again. I know it's hot so keep drinking water." He took out a bottle of water and unscrewed the cap. "I also think it's a good idea to camo up as much as we can. Our clothes are pretty good, mostly dark so that's good, but we should get the shine off our faces. We can use the dirt and a little water, make some mud and rub it into your face and neck and arms as much as possible. Every time you have to pee, use the piss and make some more mud. I know it's gross, but when the sun comes up, it'll go a long way to making us less visible and keeping the sun off your skin. Save the water for drinking."

He grabbed a piece of metal and used the sharp edge to scrape the ground, tossing away the rocks and stones. Once he had a nice sized pile, he laid the metal down and transferred the dirt onto its surface, so when he poured out the water, it wouldn't be absorbed back into the earth. "I know I said to use piss instead of water but right now all mine's inside my pants." He added a little water, stirred it with his finger making a thin slurry, and rubbed some into his forehead and on top of his thinning scalp. The others followed suit. Chris watched what Colin and Billy were doing, the way they put it on their cheeks and the sides of their necks covering as much of their faces as they could. What was left they rubbed onto their arms.

Billy got up and walked a few feet away where a thin shrub was growing from the side of the hill, grabbed hold of it with both hands, and pulled several times before it came loose. He dragged it back to their circle and started stripping the twigs and stems. He tied them onto his belt loops and shoved them in the opening of his shirt and in his waist. The others searched and found their own little bushes and did the same. Chris felt dumb, thinking it was all kind of movie-ish but didn't want to say anything.

"Okay, ramblers," concluded Colin. "Let's get ramblin'. I got 'point.' Chris, you and Jack are in the middle, Billy's 'Tail Gun Charlie.' Try not to bunch up on each other, but don't get so far apart that you get lost in the dark."

They started out very slowly. Colin's shuffle set the pace for the group; he was clearly favoring his right leg. Within moments, silence descended on the group, the only violation of it being boots on ground and the occasional stone displaced and rolling downhill.

Chris began to pick up dim stars and just the trace of a sliver of moon overhead. He turned as he walked and could no longer make out the white shiny surface of the aircraft. It was odd, he thought as they walked away from it, that it was the only connection to anything they had in this world and they were leaving it behind.

Colin's path was keeping them on approximately the same horizontal plane on the ridge, as opposed to moving lower towards flat ground where Chris figured they'd be able to move faster than here where they had to sacrifice speed for balance. Though not sure why, he figured Colin knew what he was doing and would ask when he had a chance if they hadn't gone down.

The ground they walked on, in addition to being steeply sloped, was also ridged and crinkled, like the earth's version of wrinkled laundry. Even with Colin's easy pace, it would still be easy to twist an ankle on some uneven irregularity or slide on a stone, and it took some part of Chris' concentration just to keep moving forward.

A few minutes into the hike he was sweating freely through his shirt and pants, though with no breeze it just sat on his skin. He was being introduced to a heat like he never felt in South Florida. He wiped his hands on his shirt then cracked a plastic bottle of water and took two huge gulps.

South Florida, beaches and pools and ocean…somewhere behind his eyes his mind wandered, and he could actually see his neighborhood and the dark green front door of his first floor condo in its little Melrose Place complex; his desk in his office and everyone he worked with, some whom he liked, some not; running in the golf course with his "brother" before work, laughing about who was sleeping with whom; sitting under an umbrella with Nora at a wrought-iron table on the wide sidewalk in front of Tarpon Bend on Himarshee Avenue in Ft. Lauderdale contemplating a tall glass of beer, focusing on the condensation running down the side and dripping through the table onto his sandaled feet.

Colin's head was moving slowly left to right, up, then back to the left. It took a few minutes before Chris picked up the pattern, as it was so gradual. He started doing the same and almost instantly found his concentration was more sharply focused on what was around him, not only what he could barely see, but also what he could hear: Colin's near-soundless tread and his own scrunchy footsteps, which seconds ago had been ignorable but were now hugely loud crackles and slides. He began placing his feet a little slower, setting them down on the outside of the foot and rolling from there towards his toes. It took some work at first, and he found he had to bend his legs just a little to keep his equilibrium, but in no time he was in position behind Colin, and much quieter. About the only noise coming from *him* now was the tidal slosh of water in the big bottles in the cargo pockets of his pants. He turned and looked at Jack who was some thirty feet back, waved, and gave a thumbs-up, which Jack returned.

By now, his pupils were blasted wide open. The lack of light pollution, the stars, and the dim moon provided more than enough light.

He was keeping pace, he was silent and he could see. What more could he ask for? Well, maybe that cold beer back in Ft. Lauderdale, but except for that, having survived a gunfight and a vindictive boss all in the same day, he had to admit, stupidly, life was pretty good. He took a deep breath of the hot, dusted air, and a smile came to his face as he realized how lucky he was to be walking along this dark slope following a short, balding pilot carrying an M-16 in the Pakistan desert after crashing a multi-million dollar plane while on the run from the Afghan authorities. This was, without a doubt, the most interesting day of his life!

When their first break came, Chris was surprised; it hadn't seemed like an hour had passed. They all sat in the dirt and sipped water, no one having much to say. They weren't winded, just hot, and silence was better than chatter right now.

"Hey, what about that satellite radio? Did we turn that on?" Chris asked quietly.

Billy breathed deeply. "Fuck. Forgot all about it. Thanks." He slowly removed the pack from his back, opened the top and began digging. He located what he wanted, pulled it out, activated it and checked the screen to be sure it was working. Then he stuck it back in the bag and closed it down, the antenna extending out the top.

"How come we don't go to the bottom and walk on flat ground? Wouldn't it be faster?"

Billy put the backpack back on. "It's called a 'military crest.' If we were right along the top, we'd be silhouetted, but if we have to, we can get up and over and get some cover and concealment pretty quick. And we have better field of view up here than lower down. If there's bad guys, they're more likely to be down there, and we don't want to trip over 'em."

Colin started scraping some more dirt then turned his back while on his knees. Chris could hear him watering it and watched as he put some more mud on his face. The others were doing the same, everyone's back turned for a little privacy. He frowned at the thought of it but then did the same thing. "You girls stop trying to peek at my wee wee…yes, it's as huge as you've heard but no free shows." He grimaced and wrinkled his nose as he touched the wet sand but gently laid the mix on his face, avoiding the area around his mouth.

They had been moving for about thirty minutes when Colin stopped. Abruptly. He didn't put his fist up, just stopped moving mid-step. His left-to-right-up-left head motion had also stopped and was now tilted up and to the right, toward the top of the ridge. Slowly his fist came up. Chris had already slowed to keep his distance and at about the same speed raised his own fist.

Colin unhurriedly knelt, resting his butt on his rear foot. Chris did the same, turned, and saw the other two follow his motion to the ground.

Colin did not raise his rifle, just rested the stock on his leg. Chris wanted to take out his pistol but the command had been to "freeze." He rested his forearms on his leg.

They stayed like that for several minutes before Colin turned and held his finger to his lips and gave what Chris took to be a keep-low and slowly-come-forward motion. Chris repeated it exactly to Jack and then duck-walked forward and waited with Colin. Once all four were gathered, Colin turned and whispered, "I heard a dog bark." He pointed in the direction where, upon Chris' recollection, his left ear had been pointing. "I don't see any lights. I can't make out anything like a house or village but dogs mean people. We've got to be very quiet now. We'll go a little slower but we keep moving. Okay?"

They continued on as the night darkened. The moon moved as slowly as they did but eventually made its way over the top of the hill they were on. Now that it was gone, even as acclimated as his eyes were, it was impossible to see much of anything. He increased his speed just a little, carefully trying to get closer to Colin, who had faded, without losing his balance or catching his foot on something or just generally klutz-ing to a graceless wipe-out.

He heard a loud "umph" and a grunt and a clatter sounding like plastic hitting the stony ground in front of him. He literally could see nothing now and turned his head to see if he could hear something. Without thinking about it, he reached behind him, pulled out his Glock, and held it out in front of him as he slowly moved into a crouch. All he could see were the three tiny tritium dots on the sights of the pistol.

He didn't hear any footsteps behind him so he assumed they had frozen as well.

"Mother*fucker*," said Colin quietly.

"Colin?" said Chris in a whisper.

"I fell. Hang on a second…don't come any closer."

Chris stayed low to the ground but slid his pistol back in his pants. He turned his head and whispered, "Stand by." He heard Jack repeat the command.

He listened to the muffled rustle of cloth, a soft patting and scratching, and then saw the faintest bubble of light about ten feet in front of him.

Chris got down on his hands and knees and crawled forward. Colin had fallen into a narrow ditch, about eight inches deep and a foot wide. There were a few raggedy, prickly shrubs growing on either side of it. Colin was leaning back, one leg under him, the M-16 sticking out of the ground by its barrel. He had his fingers covering the flashlight lens so only the slightest illumination could escape. He shined the light around, the thin beam illuminating no more than a few inches in any direction.

"You okay?"

Colin shook his head. "I think I broke my ankle."

Billy D. was the last one to crawl over, the ruck a misshapen turtle's shell on his back.

Colin was still sitting in the little crack in the ground, his right leg stretched straight out. He had the rifle in his lap and was examining the barrel. "I think this is trashed. Barrel's packed with crap." It had hit muzzle first when he toppled with his weight behind it.

"You want me to take off your boot?" asked Jack.

Billy to Colin, "Do we have any of those instant ice things?"

Colin nodded. "In my car." Colin looked at Billy in the dim light, his fingers still held over the lens. "Hey, what can I tell you? I hadn't planned to crash in Pakistan 'til next week." He snorted quietly then grimaced as he shifted his leg.

Billy shook his head. "Maybe I can improvise a splint, but I don't think it's going to be any better than your boot to keep it stabilized, and your boot might keep the swelling under control. Do you think you can walk on it?"

Colin nodded. "Yep. Fuck, I didn't even see it." He rubbed his head, smeared blood, looked at it and wiped it on his trousers. "Look, it's going to start getting light soon. With my leg like this, I'm not going to go much

318

further tonight. What do you think?" Clearly he was directing his observations to his partner, Chris and Jack for the most part ignored.

"Yeah, probably," said Billy. He quietly shrugged off the ruck. "May as well just camp here for a while, until it starts getting light, and then try to find a place to hide. Its so fuckin' dark anyway, we're just asking for more trouble if we keep going."

"How far you think it is to somewhere safe?" whispered Jack.

Colin shrugged in the darkness. "I dunno. Long fuckin' way."

"How far was the nearest real city where there might be military or police? Do you remember that from your charts? I mean we've got what, a couple of bottles of water and some energy bars? And with your leg fucked up…you can't walk…."

"Dude," Colin interrupted with some intensity. "Knowing who's out here, I could *run* with *two* broken legs and a splinted dick."

"I'm just saying," continued Jack, "maybe now we need to think about a Plan B."

"Well, Plan B is get rescued," said Colin, not without some steel in his voice. "I think you're talking about Plan C."

"Okay then…Plan C. Maybe a couple of us can keep going. Find a real town and bring help back. If it's a sizeable enough town, the risk of trouble is a lot more manageable."

"Speak Urdu do you?" asked Billy, the tone of his voice making it clear he was siding with his partner. "So you can ask for the nearest police station?"

"Yeah, I do," said Jack, flashing a tough look at Billy. "A little bit. Enough to get my point across."

"Do we even know where we are? Does anyone have a map?" interjected Chris to no one in particular, hearing the tension rising, sides being drawn. "And what was plan A?"

319

Billy looked at Chris and Jack and then started moving around. "I've got the chart from the plane." He pulled it out of his pants pocket, folded it into a manageable size, and laid it into the light. "The beacon's got a GPS on it. Hang on." He opened the rucksack, looked around and started digging. The unit must have shifted deeper into the backpack. Finally he pulled it out. He looked at it, squinted his eyes, and pushed a button on the face of it. He pressed it again a little harder. He was staring at the small screen on the front and holding the button down. "Goddamnit," he said quietly. He turned it over and popped the battery compartment, removed and replaced them, and tried again. He looked up, anger written clearly all over his face. "The batteries are dead."

"What kind of batteries?" asked Chris. "Can we swap them with anything else?"

Billy pulled them out. "Double AA's. Anybody got a pager? Digital camera? Anything else with batteries?"

The silence in their little home screamed at them.

"Fuck," said Billy, putting the batteries back in and trying it one last time. He shook his head and said, "Fuck!" again, too loud. "My fault."

Jack took a deep breath. "Well, so much for Plan C."

"It did work when you turned it on though, right?" solicited Chris hopefully.

"Yeah, but no telling how long it transmitted."

"Well," said Colin, switching off the light and dropping them into intense darkness, "we're back to Plan B. If nothing happens by first light, we start moving again."

"And you're short enough," joked Billy softly, "that you can use the rifle as a crutch."

"Really, what was Plan A?"

* *

Chris lay on the hard soil, his body perpendicular to the slope to keep from rolling down. He was exhausted now they had stopped moving, but not the least bit sleepy. His eyes were open but he could see absolutely nothing. Having lived his entire life in cities, he hadn't realized this kind of darkness could actually exist in nature where all light was utterly removed from being. It was like being in an oven with the door closed in the basement of a house with a huge black tent thrown over it.

He pulled out one of his water bottles and took a deep slug, relishing the hot water sliding down his dry throat probably more than he would a cold beer back home. *Well, maybe not.* He put his head back down and closed his eyes. The events of the day had finally caught up with him, and the last thing he heard as he drifted off was Colin saying, "Dude, I never heard you complaining when I was using the insta-ice to chill the beer in the office."

Chris didn't know how long he slept but when he opened his eyes, it was no longer perfectly dark. It was incrementally lighter, but only to a barely noticeably degree more than when they had stopped. He could still see no stars but looking east, there was just a shading, a hint, of less blackness than before, though when he looked in any other direction, the world around him was still invisible.

He took a deep breath, filling his mouth with hot arid air, readjusted himself as quietly as he could, and went back to sleep.

He opened his eyes again. Time was again passing in an unaccountable slowness, but the sky to the east had transitioned from almost total nothingness to a deep violet. To his left and right and above him, he could see the suggestion of texture to the world coming into being, but it was still too dark to move. He wiped sweat from his face and the back of his neck, his hand filthy from the dirt put there earlier. He sat up just a little and stared straight ahead at what had to be the mountain to the east and drank from his water bottle.

Now that he could see *something*, his exhaustion slipped away. He folded his legs under him and leaned back on his arms to watch the sunrise. Inexorably slowly, the purple pulled a shade of lighter blue behind it, and as minutes silently glided by, it gave rise to the first dim pink. The jagged teeth of the far ridge were now clearly outlined, though the face was still held in shadow. As he watched the day birthing, he was rewarded with a narrow band of red that fluidly waved into the palest yellow.

Around him the ground was coalescing into something tangible, as if it was gently being lit from within, and with every minute that passed, he was able to see farther and farther into other distances both north and south. In both directions the mountain they lounged on stretched without end, its face as uneven and rough as it had felt under his feet last night. Looking back over his shoulder, he estimated the top to be several hundred feet above them, its peak sharp, jagged, and coffee-hued. Closer to the bottom than the top, they must have been unintentionally moving downward as they walked, off the military crest.

As the terrain took on more definition, what little tint had been lent to it by the sunrise was drawn down into the soil as if it were a sponge, leaving the most desolate, rust-colored landscape he could have conceived. Even in the dim light, the bleakness was overwhelming with no insinuation of life beyond a few, hopeless shrubs.

In the center of the sputum-tinged yellow on the far side of the valley, there was a brighter bubble of light, not the sun, not yet, but where it would be soon. Chris heard a rustle behind him and turned.

Billy was awake, not moving, just staring straight ahead at the mountains to the east. He nodded at Chris, a movement just barely visible. He was, Chris noticed, completely covered with the very light layer of dirt he had spread over himself, breaking up the color of his clothes.

Both Colin and Jack still had their heads down. "Do we have binoculars?" Chris whispered.

Billy lifted a pair of binoculars from where they had been shoved down next to his leg and tossed them to Chris who caught them with one hand.

"Don't point 'em east. The sun'll bounce off the lenses."

Chris slowly started adjusting his legs, moving around. Without the binoculars, he was clearly able to now see the flatland stretched between the ridges but there was nothing else - no houses, no cars, no road. With the lenses, he worked his mountain in both directions from base to crest but saw no people. Or animals. Nothing wandered or grew. It was totally lifeless and barren.

The sun's pate brushed up against the opposite mountain, the narrowest sliver of blistering white light.

He looked at his watch. 5:45 and the temperature had to be well over a hundred. He knew what a hundred felt like but had no frame of reference for anything like *this* and couldn't begin to quantify the heat and the feathery, scorching breeze. He grabbed a bottle of water. "Jesus God it's hot." His head already felt light from the few moments spent awake in hell, and he took a big swig.

He looked at Billy. "You think anyone's found the plane?" he asked, feeling the most distant touch of fear way down deep.

Billy barely lifted his shoulders.

"But I mean, someone has to know where the plane is at least, right?"

Billy said, "Shhh."

Chris stared at him, looked around then back to him.

"Shhh. Rest," Billy said very quietly. "Conserve your energy. We'll be moving soon."

His own coughing woke him up. He hadn't even been aware he had drifted off. The sun was balancing precariously on the far crest, like a great ball that could roll either way, so he had only been out for mere minutes. It was an inferno on the bare ground with bright, dirty sunlight already punching at him mercilessly. Colin, next to Billy, was awake with sunglasses on and his hand held over his eyes.

"You gotta get that smoking under control," said Colin.

"Huh?"

"You've been coughing a lot."

"I don't smoke."

"I do," Jack said from beyond him. "I think I could light one just by putting it on the ground. I'd forgotten how fucking hot it gets here."

"How hot you think it is?" asked Chris to no one in particular.

"Probably about one ten. That's pretty average for around here this time of day. It'll hit one twenty by this afternoon," Jack answered.

He coughed again. "I can't believe people live in this. I feel like a pot roast."

"Drink some more water," suggested Colin. He leaned forward. "And here, put some of this on." He held up his chap stick.

"How's your foot?"

He shook his head. "Not so good."

"Think you're gonna be able to walk?"

"Got to. We've got to get under some cover or we're toast. And I mean that. Literally."

Looking around, Chris rolled to the side and got on his knees to make some more camouflage for his face. When he was finished, his ears and forehead a little cooler under the weak skin of damp dirt, he noticed Billy was binocular-ing something with an intensity apparent by his stillness. "What're you looking at?"

He passed Chris the binoculars. "Look there," he pointed southward and then flattened his hand and moved it up and down in his eye-line. "About a mile, maybe more, maybe a third up from the ground, it gets steeper and it looks like there's a break in the mountain. I can just make out a…a…straight…like a shear-line, in the rock. Angles a little from left to right, follows the angle of the hill. See it?"

Chris was looking side to side, moving from top to bottom, seeing nothing, then back and forth again, slower this time, when he caught a straight edge, very thin, almost invisible. If he hadn't been specifically looking for it, he never would have seen it. "Yeah?" he said, not taking his eyes off it for fear of losing it.

"I can't tell from here but it's possible that edge could recess a little, maybe give us a place to hide. It doesn't look very deep but it could be better than nothing. And it's in the right direction. Long way, though, for Gimpy here," he said nudging Colin with his elbow.

"Two broken legs and a splinted dick," the little pilot repeated, waving his finger in the air. "Let's break camp."

"Breaking camp" consisted of everyone standing up. Billy put the pack back on and Jack shouldered the useless rifle; though broken, they couldn't leave any trace behind on the off chance someone came along to find it. Chris grabbed Colin's arm and pulled it firmly over his shoulder, Jack doing the same with his other arm, taking as much weight as possible off the ankle. They started out slowly, and it was a bit of a clumsy way to travel but after a few steps, they found an awkward rhythm. Billy trailed along behind, stopping every now and then and raising the binoculars to scout behind them.

"Good thing you're tiny," said Chris, "otherwise, this'd be a bitch!"

"Tall enough to punch you in the balls, my friend," retorted Colin.

The sun was a white hole punched in a vellum sky. Their trek under the searing white sun took just under two hours by the time they reached the shear-line. A narrow edge of the ridge had given way and broken off, leaving a nearly flat face no more than four or five feet wide, maybe twenty in height and tapering at its tip; it angled inward about twenty degrees. At the base of the shear were large pieces of rock and granite and piles of dirt, gravel and sand. The face of the shear was covered with a light sheen of dust. It could have broken away yesterday or a thousand years ago.

They were dripping with sweat and, following Billy's lead, took the opportunity to scoop up some light dust and rub it on their bodies while they were still wet.

Chris himself was limping slightly as they dragged Colin in and let him sit down. The angle of the shear wall was just enough to provide some shade, and the four crowded in as far as they could for a few minutes respite. From the inside looking out, with his ass on the ground, Chris' view was limited to a slab of stone and a creamy-white, cloudless sky.

Though out of the direct sun, the heat was still ferocious. Chris rearranged his legs for the umpteenth time; it was impossible to find comfort in the small confines. More than the discomfort, more than the heat, more than the thirst, was the tedium.

Chris was an insatiable reader. When there was nothing else, he could pick up a newspaper, a pamphlet, a box of cereal or an advertisement for furniture and be suitably entertained. As long as his eyes were moving, he was occupied but he had never sat for so long with nothing to occupy his attention.

Here, now, he was outside himself trying to think of something to keep his mind engaged. He mentally roamed across the corroded geography he had at his feet. From out of nowhere, he was reminded of a game he had played as a kid, the plot of which was to build a town, then a city, then an entire world populated by little electronic people who went about their business in an orderly fashion, never interrupted by things like guns and crashing planes.

With that game in mind, he started with a single small gray stone. He mentally took another one and laid it against the first and there was the base… then he added another…then another. He grabbed one of the boulders in front of him. There, beyond the boulder was a plank of wood, unvarnished and untreated, worn almost to cracking by the punishing sun. And here were cinderblocks. His mind soared up beyond the hole and the cinderblocks became a square, one story structure without windows. He then added a second story and a stable, which seemed to make perfect sense. Then he had a village of similar-looking, gray, square houses. A castle suddenly appeared, quite out of place in cinderblock-town…and a huge cathedral with flying buttresses; it sat on a hill, surrounded by lush green fields where horses roamed. He laid in a stream, no…more of a creek…not, still not right…he needed a river…wide, deep, dark, fast flowing and cool so he could stand in and drink from it. A deep bell bonged in his empire of boredom; he didn't know he had built a bell tower until he saw it…like Big Ben in London. As each second clicked by, his Kingdom of Dull grew exponentially and now stretched for miles in all directions. He stood on one of the countless turrets in his castle of monotony, body sandwiched between the crenellated stones, looking up at the dun-colored sky-

He was abruptly returned into the tiny furrow which stank of sweat and urine and distant inevitability. He didn't even have to open his eyes; his daydream had been going on while he stared, sightless at the sky.

It was only 10:15.

327

There was movement at his shoulder. Billy was on his knees and very slowly moving the binoculars around. After about a minute without moving, he dropped back down and shook his head.

He closed his eyes, an arm over his face as he tried to sleep. He was not quite awake, not quite dozing, but rather in a brightly lit twilight zone between the two. His mind was totally unoccupied, and entire moments passed when he forgot just how motherfucking hot he was. He was thirsty as well, but trying not to think about the quarter-bottle resting by his knee. He had started off following Colin's instructions not to ration, but he had been drinking so fast he was sure he, and they, would be running out if they weren't careful.

He didn't even bother raising his hand anymore to check the time. It only seemed to slow it down to a super-heated glacial place.

"Hey, Chris," Jack's voice broke his non-concentration. "Can I ask you something?"

Chris smirked. "You just did." He didn't bother turning.

"Okay, I'm going to ask you something else now." There was a long pause and Chris was beginning to think Jack had fallen asleep. "When you shot that guy...what was it like?"

"Bad," he answered instantly. It was totally quiet behind him. "I mean, when it first happened, the...um...mechanics of it...it was nothing, like training. They taught us, 'You see a gun, you shoot.' That's what I did. But afterwards...I keep seeing the look in his eyes as he was falling down...I mean, I did what I had to do to protect Mau and the guys...but...it's shit. They never told us what it would be like after." He felt his eyes watering. "It's shit."

* *

His head popped up. He had been dozing again. The sun had crossed the top of the sky and was on a gradual downward slide. Colin and Jack were playing tic-tac-toe in the dirt, scratching at the ground with their fingers. He closed his eyes.

He tilted his head up and saw Billy had the binoculars propped just on the edge of a big rock and was looking north.

"What's up?"

"Two vehicles. Maybe pickups. Fuckin' traffic jam out there all of a sudden."

Chris waited for more but was un-rewarded. He looked past his knees where the other two were lying, their faces in the shade but bodies in the sun. He pressed on Colin with his leg. "Hey…"

"I know. I'm here."

Chris saw Colin's pistol was in his hand, lying alongside his leg. Chris did a small adjustment and took his out. When he had first lain down, he had tucked it in the front of his pants and now, like Colin, had it next to him.

"Billy?" asked Colin softly.

"Two trucks. Definitely not our military. Could be theirs…no way to tell. Maybe two miles away. I think I see some guys on the mountain walking this way."

Chris' heart instantly pumped into high gear. It was what he felt just before kicking a door back home or doing a vehicle stop - not fear, maybe a certain anxiousness he was familiar with - but this felt different. When Chris went to work, it was usually a bunch of agents far outnumbering their target, not something like this, a foreign country where bad guys cut the heads off the people they didn't like. He thought his mouth had been dry before, but now he felt like he had sucked the entire desert in through his tongue.

Colin asked quietly, "Chris, how many rounds you have?"

Chris subtracted the three he had fired yesterday. "Eleven."

"Billy?"

"Twenty eight."

"I've got fourteen. That's fifty-four total."

"Fifty three…" Billy said quietly. There was silence while he scanned the hill and the trucks. "One of the guys on the hill has something. Could be a rifle. Or a big stick."

There was more silence as they contemplated a guy carrying a long gun, like an AK-47, which could fire as many rounds in just under six seconds as they had in total.

"What do you think about making a break for the top of the hill?" asked Chris. "If we can get over the other side, we'll have some cover."

Colin was quiet for a minute then took a deep breath. "I don't think I'll be able to do it with my foot like this." He sighed. "What about you guys making a break and I'll try to hold 'em off."

Billy and Jack spoke up at the same time, cheerily and in unison. "Okay!" They grinned at each other.

"What is this suddenly?" asked Chris with his own grin, "A fuckin' John Wayne movie?" His voice went softly falsetto. "No, no…leave me and save yourselves. Just," he made a sobbing sound, "just tell her I love her!"

"I'm just saying…" began Colin, "this is…the three of you can maybe get over the top…"

"Hey, Colin," said Billy sharply, "shut the fuck up. I know it's every Marine's dream to make a stand but we're probably not going to go over the hill without you."

"Probably," echoed Chris.

"And if we can't get you up there, we'll do what we have to do down here. Maybe these guys are just shepherds," he joked. "If we get into something, maybe we can hold 'em off 'til it gets dark or…something."

330

"We drag him," said Chris.

"No way we'll get up there in time," countered Colin. "Once we start moving, those guys in the trucks'll be coming our way fast, and if they're bad guys, they'll be firing away a couple of minutes after that. The top's gotta be a couple hundred feet at least."

"Dude, really," said Billy. "Shut up a second. The big kids are talking."

"Bite me."

"Chris," Billy continued, "I think it's the best plan. Between you, me and Jack, I think we can get him up there. He's right, though, if they're bad guys, they're going to be banging away at us, but that's just the way it goes. Up there, maybe we get a chance. Making the stand here's a loser's play. I've said it for years...I'm not a loser. Colin is, but I'm not."

"Oh, ha ha ha," sulked Colin.

Chris could see Colin take a deep breath and wipe his face. "How far away?"

"Still a ways off."

"Fuck," said Colin. "I wanted to make my stand."

"I know you did, little guy," retorted Billy. He slowly stood up, staying behind the biggest of the rocks and put the backpack on. "We stay low, we drag him best we can, maybe we get lucky. Let's get to it before they get any closer."

Suddenly Colin turned his head left and right and raised a finger. "Wait. Anybody hear that?"

Chris lifted his head up. It definitely wasn't truck engines. It was too far away and the sound wasn't right. This was deeper, more bass, but irregular, out of synch. "It's not a car."

"No. It's a helo for sure. But it sounds...out of...hang on...it's in its own echo."

"Coming from the crash site?" offered Jack. Everybody turned their heads to the north but saw nothing except the wide, deep valley and the small light colored dots of the distant trucks.

"Where's the flares? And the mirror?" asked Colin, cranking his head around to look at Billy.

Chris could hear Billy moving to get the pack back off and grunting a stream of invectives non-stop without taking a breath.

"I got it! There!" said Jack a little too loudly, pointing southeast. Chris looked and saw a tiny, haze-gray dot as it squirted out from behind a low hill, close to the ground and moving fast. It was miles away and well below them and was moving towards the trucks.

"H-53," said Colin, recognizing its outline even at this distance. "Fucking US Marine Corps to the res-cue…Oo-rah!" He began humming *From the Halls of Montezuma* with a joyous verve and vigor. "And you fuckers were going to leave me here on the hill and run. Think how *that* would have gone over when the Marines land." He cackled and kicked one leg up and down. "Semper Fi, Semper Fi, Semper Fi."

They watched the helo continue past them and transition into a fast hover near the trucks. Moments later, the thumping quieted a bit as the engine slowed. A brown cloud was rising up around the big helicopter, almost blocking it from sight.

Billy passed the flares to Colin, who asked him what he saw through the binoculars, while at the same time taking the pen-shaped launcher from a box and screwing the little flare onto the tip. "Definitely a –53. There's a rifleman in the doorway. Another guy just jumped out and's running."

He swiveled the binoculars back toward the trucks. "The trucks've stopped." He leaned forward, as if the extra inches would make a difference in what he was seeing. "I think…one of the guys has…shit, could be an RPG. He's crouching behind the truck but he's got something on his shoulder."

"Can we warn the helo?" asked Chris quietly but hurriedly.

"Colin," shouted Billy, "get the flares in the air. Aim 'em at the trucks! Try to get the helo looking in that direction...."

As the words were leaving his mouth, there was a loud pop, like the report of a .22 pistol, and a whizzing as a bright red flare launched sideways. Then another and another.

DEA Special Agent / Pilots Jon 'Warbaby' Warrington, Colin McNease and Billy Dwyer.

CHAPTER NINETEEN

"Bring it around to the left!" I call towards the cockpit. "Predator's got the package. They're on the mountain where the flares came from." The helo starts a flat turn, not banking, just swinging the nose around.

Then, in my headset I hear the voice, long distance, calling from Las Vegas, *"Movement at the vehicles. Possible...RPG launcher up...Vampire Vampire![1]"*

"RPG!" I scream, my voice an octave higher than I would have liked. I don't have time to bother with the radio as I grab on to the ceiling rail as hard as I can because I know what's coming. On my first op, I had been talking "pilot shit" with our guys and asked them what they would do if they were ever fired on, and they explained the "RPG Escape Maneuver" which consists of get-the-fuck-out-of-where-you-are-as-fast-as-you-can!

Suddenly, we're sliding sideways to the right, and the deck tilts viciously and without warning. My feet fly outward as if I had been standing

---

[1] Inbound missile.

in a pool of grease; if I hadn't been holding on, I'd be on my ass. We're banking brutally hard to the left now, and I'm sure the rotors are going to tear into the earth just below us like we're the world's biggest roto-tiller. The pilot yanks hard on the collective lever, putting maximum power into the engine, and the turbine's screaming over my head. I've lost situational awareness as to where Argo is in relation to us, and I want to warn him to get out of our way, but I can't let go of the railing and I'm sure he's on his feet already.

Only seconds have passed since our warning. I never saw the grenade, but we're still flying, so I know it didn't hit us and that's good enough. The sideways angle is lessening as the pilot eases it out to gain some forward speed. I'm still holding on for dear life to the ceiling rail as the engineer grabs the frame of the door around me and looks out. I don't see anything except the open door of the helicopter. Adze's no longer there with the rifle. "Jesus Christ," I bellow when I can get a breath into my lungs, "Where's Adze?"

We've gone seriously nose down, and we're speeding fast from where we were to somewhere safer. "He's down, sir," calls the engineer. "I'm looking at him now. Your other guy's running over to him and waving us away."

I take a deep breath to try to slow my breathing and heart rate. We're only five minutes into this thing, the fog of war's enveloped us, and I'm flapping and need to be calm. *Let the training take over and save the emotion and panic for later.* I'm leaning on the pilot, hitting his shoulder and pointing where I think the flares came from. One of the trucks is accelerating, parallel to the base of the ridge. He's not moving too fast since this rough ground will bust his axles if he puts too much pedal to the metal. The rest of the bad guys are scrambling for the other truck. My pulse is hammering as I call out, "Adze, sitrep!"

My guys in the back are all on their knees, ready to go, holding tight to the belts on the floor. In my ear, I hear Argo breathing as hard as I am.

"I've got Adze. Arm's fractured but I can stabilize. I saw flares on the hill and an RPG from the rear truck!"

The nose of the craft is fully down and the huge rotor cone above us is pulling us faster and faster towards the hill, though as we get closer it's obvious it's quite a bit higher and steeper than it appeared from a distance. I'm looking more upward toward the top of the windshields than straight out. The flare's white smoke trails are gone and the exact place where they originated is lost to me. I flick the button to the Predator channel, hit the transmit button, and shout to the rest of the crew, "Does anyone know where the flares came from?"

"Somewhere near there!" The engineer's points out and up.

"Come left ten degrees."

I tap the pilot again on the shoulder to relay what the Predator told me, and he shouts back that he's tied in to the UAV's radio now and getting data directly.

To the Predator, "One of my guys is down, broken arm. He went out somewhere near Argo."

"Copy that. We've marked his position and will relay to Texas."

We're moving fast now towards the mountain, still low. Another puff of smoke pops from the bed of one of the trucks off to our right. Everyone yells, "RPG!" but it's a wild shot that doesn't come anywhere close. The Predator is calling it as well. We're just off the deck and I take one step back to the right door and look out at the trucks. One is in the lead but the other is coming on fast.

The engineer's mouth is at my ear. "HAC says there's no way he can land on the hill; too steep an incline. He's liable to drag a rotor. He can *hover* over them and do a lift."

I've got my eyes pinned on the trucks, working out the angle and the intercept. "Do you have a jungle penetrator?" I shout back without looking at him. A jungle penetrator is a heavy steel device that can be lowered from the helicopter by an electrical winch. It has collapsible seats that fold open and can lift up to three people at a time.

"Affirmative and a horse collar and a winch litter."

It's good news but I'm thinking it won't matter. With the truck's closure rate, there's no time. We'll be shot out of the sky if we hold and hover. We're nearly to the base of the mountain. I step back to the cockpit. "We don't have time for a lift. Take us to the top. We'll bail out there and cover from above. You dump us and clear out." I turn and point at Lemon and Grease and give them the "come forward" sign.

Without a word, the pilot hauls back on the stick and lifts the collective in his left hand even more and we pitch up, blasting up the side of the ridge, screaming skyward like a homesick angel.

I have a sudden flash of inspiration and push the button to transmit. "Do you have Hellfires?"

"Negative." Inspiration wasted. I should have known. There are countless UAVs flying at any given time, controlled either by the CIA or the Air Force, but in this Alice-in-Wonderland war, only the CIA's carry the missiles. The pilot had said he was in Las Vegas, which means the Air Force Base at Nellis, which means no weapons. Fags.

We're tilting at an incredible angle, the ground right underneath us. As we reach the crest, the deck pitches down past horizontal, the rear of the helo wrenches higher than the cockpit like a manic teeter-totter, the engines quiet slightly, and then we're here, mere inches above the ground. It is a brilliant piece of flying.

He's parked us so close to the top I don't even have to jump. I hop down, letting my knees take what little shock there is from the extra weight I'm carrying. I scramble away and drop to my knees and then flat, facing downward. The top of the ridge is about two feet wide so there's plenty of room to get comfortable. The blades are blowing up a ferocious amount of dirt and rocks and the downblast is pummeling my body. I slap my goggles down from my helmet and ride out the beating coming in rapid, rhythmic waves. The engine roars again and pulls off behind me, and I turn and watch it dive down the lee of the ridge, disappearing along the back, out of sight and within seconds out of sound.

With the air calming, I slide the goggles back up; they're so dirty now anyway they're not much good. To my right several yards away lays Lemon and beyond him Grease. Both have their weapons aimed down the hill.

The trucks are still on the move but much closer now.

It's a tough call I have to make now because my friend and fellow warrior out there is injured and I hate having him left alone, especially when I don't know how he is, but I need Argo more or, more precisely, Argo's weapons. "Argo, can you leave Adze for a few? I need a missile shot."

"A-firm. He's basically stable." His voice is clipped and short of breath.

"Roger that. I need you to close as fast as you can. Target one of the trucks."

He gives me a "Roger" in return. With that sorted out for now and while I have a little time before trouble arrives at the bottom of the hill, I start looking for the package. The flare smoke has long since dissipated and everything I see is just brown. I ask the Predator to give me some help. From his "God's-eye" view, he tells me they're to my right, at about my two o'clock, one hundred yards, and describes the break in the mountain. I squint and can just barely make out a sharp edge, but no one's visible. He tells me he can count three bodies. *Please don't let the missing one be my little brother.*

The trucks are pulling to a stop almost straight below us, raising small clouds of dust. The rear one is about fifty yards behind the lead. There's lots of movement now as they're bailing and probably trying to decide whether it's safer on our side or the other where they saw Argo drop.

I'm watching both trucks but holding my fire for the time being. The distance and the slope are factors against really accurate shooting, especially while everyone's moving around. It's worth it to wait a few seconds. Having the high ground is a colossal advantage they'll be unlikely to press to their benefit but that doesn't mean they won't try, depending on their motivation and enthusiasm to capture or kill the infidel. Right now it's a stalemate, and while technically we have nothing but time, my brother's (hopefully) down in that ridge and could be injured, and we've got to move things along.

A weapon fires but I don't see where it came from, just a flat crack that echoes around the valley. On my right, Grease fires several rounds as fast as he can pull the trigger. I hear them ping on metal down below.

One of the bad guys starts up the hill from the second truck, a rifle at his shoulder, firing as he runs. His bullets are kicking up dirt, coming closer with each shot. I press the trigger. The gun barely jerks into my shoulder but I miss. I take a deep breath and fire again. He takes the rounds, their velocity canceling out his forward momentum, and he drops straight to the ground.

Everything's muffled now from the noise and the little foamy earplugs, and I don't hear the pop of the booster charge way below me, but a white trail of smoke flies up the side of the ridge pushing an RPG. It whizzes over our heads by no more than a foot and I actually feel the heat from the sustainer jets as it passes. *Fuck, that was close!* My heart slams and I can hear it beating in my ears over the whoosh and fire. Seconds behind us, the grenade self-detonates with a huge bang spraying hot metal everywhere. I feel a tap on the rear of my vest, not too hard, but it's there.

Another rocket launches at a much shallower angle and impacts the side of the ridge, dangerously close to where my brother is, or might be. The explosion obscures the ridge, and I can't see if it hit directly on their hiding spot or not.

I still don't see the launcher, but the smoke trails are coming from the front corner of the front truck and together the three of us open up in controlled bursts, firing for effect without specific targets, trying to keep that launcher down. The noise is awesome and the sonic effects of the bullets vibrate brown dirt into the air around us.

"Lemon," I yell, "AT-4! Target: lead truck." He puts down his rifle and takes off his pack; the launcher is strapped to the top.

Through my scope I see something black appear over the hood, not too much, but I fire several shots. Because of the downward angle, my rounds punch small holes in the corner of the truck and a body flies backward. The rounds must have zinged straight through the thin steel.

Lemon calls, "Clear!" There's a tremendous whoosh of smoke and flame as the missile streaks downward, propelled by its own internal rocket. Immediately after it's fired, it impacts dead center in the passenger side door and blasts the truck mostly sideways and upwards in an awesome geyser of wrecked, ripped metal, rubber, and bodies previously hiding behind it. The roar of the detonation comes right back at us.

While parts of the truck are still in the air, bodies scramble from around the other truck as the rest of the bad boys surrender what they had perceived as a safe place to hide. They're shooting up the hill, mostly undirected and un-aimed, but it's not always the bullet with your name on it that can kill you - sometimes it's the one that just says, "To Whom It May Concern."

Far off to the left, the helo is coming back in low and fast from the north, it's big blades tearing up the air. *"Texas is inbound your position. ETA one zero minutes."*

Two Pakistanis rush from the side of the truck and begin climbing toward the ridge where Chris may be hiding, down low to the ground, their hands empty as they're using them to scrabble upward. It's hard to get a good bead on them because of the downward perspective, the distance, and the irregularity of the ground they're using for concealment. I can barely pick them out, and crap is still raining down everywhere from the AT-4 blast.

I press the trigger again and again, firing where I think they are, kicking up tiny puffs of dirt. The last round out slams the bolt back and I'm empty. With a muscle memory drilled into me by years of training, my finger comes off the trigger and presses the magazine release, dropping the spent magazine to the ground with a hollow clink. My left hand's already moving as I roll slightly to the right and yell, "Reloading!" I pull a fresh one from my vest and roll back flat, sliding it into position with a firm click, and hit the bolt release with the same hand to resume firing. I can see the top of one of their heads now, black hair so close to the ground it's like the earth's a sponge and he's getting sucked into it, ready to disappear. I fire another group and the hair pulps open splashing red outward. The other man next to him isn't moving at all. I fire a few more there just to be sure, and the result is the same.

I hear sharp cracks in the distance. Maybe the guys walking the hill are trying to get into the dance.

Out of the corner of my eye, from way beyond the trucks in the middle of nowhere, I see a tiny white puff of smoke and a bright yellow flash of fire but the missile is moving too fast to make out.

The missile lands short but the blast is incredible, launching earth high into the air in a black and gray umbrella of smoke and dust.

Grease and Lemon are firing long strings, and then Grease yells, "Reloading!"

I'm looking for movement but don't see any. Now there's a flutter of white under the aiming dot, and my finger is moving back inside the trigger

341

guard when the target jumps and shudders, then stops moving; Lemon's last shot.

A huge boom from Argo's missile passes over us.

I roll onto my right shoulder and aim left, parallel to the top of the ridgeline towards the two Pakistanis who were walking the hill, but I can't see them either. Maybe they went to ground. I fire a few rounds and call Argo. "Target the guys on the hill, about your twelve o'clock!"

"Roger."

I lift my head to get a fuller view of the killing zone. The still air around us is blue-gray and the white rocket trails are floating over us like thin white clouds. The dead truck, what's left of it, is burning, gutting the air with thick black smoke. The second truck is undamaged, but I can't see behind it where more men could be hiding. I reach to my belt, flip the transmitter and key the mic. "Is there anyone hiding on the far side of the truck?"

"Negative."

"Can you see anyone else moving down there?"

"Negative."

Even though the UAV says nobody's there, it only means *he* can't see anyone, and I'd be stupid to believe it. Could be someone under the truck, could be someone playing possum, could be someone injured who rolls at the last second and comes up shooting.

"Argo, status of the guys on the hill."

"They're down."

"Nice job."

"I didn't do it. I'm heading back to Adze."

"Let's go," I say to Grease. "Lemon, cover from here. When we're clear, make your way to the package."

This is the most dangerous part of the recovery. The shooting's over, everybody's mostly okay, it's time to let the breathing slow and relax just a little, except it's not. Even after we check each bad guy for signs of life, there could be more bandits on the way. We have to get the package and get out of dodge.

I crawl forward over the edge, up on my padded elbows, keeping my rifle in my shoulder. I'd like to stay flat on the ground and crawl down with a minimal silhouette, but the steep angle of the hill doesn't lend itself to that. The two of us move slowly, arcing our fields of fire, knees deeply bent, asses close to the ground for balance, placing our feet carefully, trying not to fumble and fall.

I'm looking through the scope, panning the rifle in a quarter arc from the far left to the base of the hill. I know Grease will be manning the other quarter of the circle with Lemon keeping the overwatch on anything we might miss. I'm breathing fast, and my heart is whamming away in my chest from the stress of the shooting, being shot at, the rockets that came our way, and my little brother and not knowing if he's there. My eyes are wide open and without taking my focus from what's below me, I shout, "Can you hear me? We're Americans. Stay where you are. We're coming to you!"

"*PETE?*" I hear Chris shout my name through the dullness in my ears. Hearing Chris's voice makes my heart beat so hard it's going to bounce me down the hill. I think the only thing keeping it in my chest is the ceramic plate in my vest. My eyes start to fill. I wipe them away fast with my sleeve and reacquire aim.

"It's me. Stay down! You all okay?"

"Yeah," he calls back to me. "But the pilot has a broken leg."

I inform the Predator.

Eventually, inexorably slowly, Grease and I reach the base of the mountain. On the way down as we come to each body, we carefully check to make sure they're no longer a threat or if injured, whether we can treat them.

But they're all dead. We crawl around the back of the truck and see a few more bodies there as well, all dead, some explosively so.

I stand and lower my rifle, leaving it hanging on its strap over the front of my vest, and give a wave to Lemon, releasing him to head toward the package. I too head back toward the hill and my little brother, leaving Grease on security detail. I look up the ridge and see Chris coming down as fast as safely possible, nearly running. He doesn't slow down and bangs right into me, nearly knocking me off my feet. I hug him so tight I'm afraid the magazines on my chest are going to break his ribs. I can't even tell him how glad I am to see him, can't quite get the words out. I just stand there, holding on to him.

"What the fuck are you doing here?" he laughs, stepping back. Before I can answer, he tells me Colin McNease and Billy Dwyer, the pilots, are here with him. I nod but still just hold on to him and catch my breath. When I've got it under control, I step away and push the transmit button on my weapon. "This is Rescue One. Package recovered and intact. I say again, Package recovered and intact."

"Rescue One, be advised Texas is three minutes out, inbound from the north."

As soon as the Predator clicks off, I hear a deep buzzing rumble coming from that direction. I let go of Little Brother and turn to watch the strange flying machines swooping down the valley close to the ground. It's a medium-sized plane, but even from here I can see monstrous propellers mounted way out on the very tips of the wings and they're beating the hell out of the sky. The gray plane does a tight right turn in the valley, and the propellers start to shift position and it's slowing in flight. The nacelles and the propellers on the wingtips are now at right angles to the wings and the plane is in a hover, slowly lowering and moving forward towards us like some kind of freaky wanna-be helicopter.

Maybe two thousand feet up, the other Osprey is circling the valley, its propellers in the proper place where they should be, facing forward. They create a strange thrum that echoes off the mountains around us.

Just as the weight settles on the wheels of the plane, the rear ramp opens and a couple of soldiers wearing desert camouflage bound out and take up a security perimeter, down on their knees, rifles aimed outward. More shuffle out, heavy packs on their backs. One group heads toward our helo while another runs in our direction, their M-16's in low ready position. They're followed by a guy in jeans, a t-shirt and a photographer's vest. He too is running and carrying an M-16. Probably client.

I wave at them. I point up the hill and tell them our wounded guy is up in the crack on the ridge, and they continue at a healthy pace.

An older man in BDUs, sleeves rolled up high on his forearms, hand wrapped around the carry handle on the top of his M-16, looking very John Wayne, very "Savoy Six," casually strolls my way. Two dark bars are sown on his collars. Captain. He takes off his helmet, revealing a redish-blond high-and-tight and holds out his hand. "Steve Simonis." I shake it and introduce Chris. He looks over our shoulders at the trucks and the wreckage, smoke and general carnage. "Goddamn," he says.

"Yeah."

"We were talking to your pilots on the way in, and the Predator, so we're pretty much up to speed. The word I got is that we're supposed to take the crash survivors and the injured to Islamabad. There's gonna be a C-17 waiting for us that'll medevac everyone to Qatar. I asked why we don't just take 'em back to Bagram but was told to shut my pie-hole."

"Okay. You get any brief on what to do with the bodies?"

He breathes deeply and shoves a hand into the pocket of his BDUs. "The intel weenies want 'em for whatever. We'll bag 'em and take 'em with us."

I nod. "You want some help with the cleanup?"

He spits on the ground, then pulls out a blue pack of Gauloises cigarettes. "Naw. This is kind of what we do."

"*CHRIS!*" Jeff is coming fast, eating up the ground separating our helo and us. He's ditched his helmet and pack and is at a dead run, head up, arms pumping, looking like the football star he was in high school. He plows into Little Brother, who's quite a bit bigger than either of us, picks him up in a bear hug, laughs, sets him back down and gives him a big wet kiss on the cheek. I laugh and introduce Jeff to Captain Simonis, but just as JD - no sense blowing his CAG cover. Chris is just standing there, looking back and forth at me and Jeff, I'm sure trying to work out the logistics of how both his older brothers are standing with him in this truly godforsaken piece of desert.

Behind me, two Marines are slowly, carefully working their way down the hill with their stretcher. Colin is lying on top of it, a thin green blanket over him. The Litter and Casualty Squad is being trailed by an almost filthily unrecognizable Billy Dwyer and the client, who had been on the plane with Chris, being supported by the guy with the photographer's vest. I leave Captain Simonis and my brothers and walk to meet the pilots. I give Billy a big hug, and clasp Colin's hand tightly and pat him on the shoulder, thanking them both for taking care of Chris. With typical Marine élan, Colin waves off my thanks with a light, "It was nothing."

Billy, not quite so cavalier, puts his arm around me and fills me in as we walk, about how close they had come to getting wasted and thanks *me*. I look at Colin, smile and repeat his gesture. I haven't seen them for years, but they haven't changed at all. We're all laughing, doing a mini-catch-up session with them telling me about the crash and the E and E and how Colin broke the M-16.

"By the way," I say, crinkling my nose as we're moving together toward the OV-22, "I don't know what kind of kinky party you girls were having but you all smell like piss!"

The valley's mostly quiet now, except for the orbiting Osprey. Our helo has repositioned next to the plane on the ground where a hose runs between them. They must have stuck a fuel blivet onboard for us, which I have to say is an unexpectedly nice treat.

The litter team has Colin on an IV of clear fluid. He's talking to the pilots, doing the "there-I-was" familiar to all flyers, shooting at his big watch. Adze is lying next to him and is being tended to by Argo and a small team of medics who have his arm neatly splinted, an IV drip going there as well. Chris and Jeff are sitting on the ramp and Chris is guzzling his second bottle of water. A short bit ago, someone had come up with a satellite phone and let Chris call Mom. We all spoke to her and listened to her cry and laugh. I move off to check on the security teams. There's still business to be taken care of and we can't let our guard down until the package is safely off the deck and headed wherever. Billy's nowhere to be seen but I'm sure he's just wandered off. I always remember him as being a pretty solitary guy.

I'm actually taking a page from Billy's book and standing by myself, looking at nothing, having a quiet minute before we mount up again and head back to the camp. I can't begin to put into words how relieved I am Chris is safe and sound.

There are footsteps behind me and a voice I don't recognize says, "How you doing, Meat?" I turn around and see the client guy who was in the crash with Chris. Chris had told me his name's Jack. I shake his hand and thank him for taking care of my little brother. "I don't know if he told you but he did a hell of a job in Kabul. Record heroin seizure and took out a bad guy and saved some lives. Really good shit!" I tell him we haven't really had time to go into everything but I'm sure we'll catch up in the future. He stands there, a funny grin on his face. "You don't remember me, do you?"

I raise my sunglasses, take a hard look and drop them back down. I shake my head. "Sorry. Where'd we meet?"

He keeps grinning but says nothing. Although now he's mentioned it, there is something a little familiar about him. Maybe we've passed along the way, maybe an embassy, maybe a Marine House party. I've been around a lot of years in a lot of places; it's a lot of faces to remember.

I shrug and apologize again.

"I had a beard."

A beard. I tilt my head to the side and try to picture him like that. There's something that pricks my consciousness, maybe it's the way he talks. A beard? It's tough to visualize…and then suddenly it falls into place. "Rabbit?" Anger spurts all around me like tiny fireworks.

"Yeah," he laughs. "Jackrabbit was my nickname at Kansas State. I think I may still hold the record in the four-forty." He holds out his hand again.

I bat his hand out of the way, grab him by the shirt and pull him close, aware of the smell of dirt and piss coming off him. "You motherfucker." My rifle is pressed between us and his hands are on my arms.

"Hey!" he says, his voice rising in surprise.

"You motherfucker," I say again.

"What's your problem, dude?" he says, trying to get his hands between us to push us apart but I've got the advantage of size and adrenaline and anger.

"What's my problem?" I pull him even closer and jam my face right in his and lean slightly forward and down, taking his balance. Now his hands shift from pushing to pulling to keep from falling backwards. "I killed someone for you, shithead. I smoked some nothing guy in the back because your mission was fucked and you couldn't do the job yourself. In my neighborhood that makes you a cocksucker, and I'm gonna break your fuckin' ass."

He's struggling against me but can't get any leverage and I'm pushing harder, walking him backwards, keeping him off-balance. "Jesus Christ, dude, calm down!" I can barely hear him with the white noise in my head, and I'm back with MC at the pool and starting to blank. I'm not even sure I know I've dropped one hand into a gloved fist while keeping a grip with my left.

"Whoa," he says loudly. My right shoulder's coming back and I can feel the fury in my biceps and triceps. Something grazes my shoulder and I slap it away with a sharp elbow that precisely cocks my arm right where I want it. I'm looking at him and hearing nothing but a steady buzzing, his mouth is saying, *"Whoa!"* over and over. He's stopped pulling and now I'm holding him up with my left hand, trying to punch with my right but I can't move it at all. I turn my head and see Chris holding it. Jeff's coming around the other side, and he's trying to push his way between me and Jack, trying to peel my fingers open.

The guy in the photographer's vest is getting up off the ground. I didn't even know I had done that.

Jeff's shouting and Chris is saying nothing, just using his bigger size on me like I'm using mine on Rabbit. Everybody's yelling at me, but it's just noise and I still can't move my arm. Then suddenly, the wrath collapses out of me like air from an inner tube. I take a deep breath and look back at Jack, then at Chris and try to pull my arm free. He stands there, not fighting me, just not letting go.

"You all right?" he asks me quietly. I stop trying to pull away from him and he loosens a little. I slowly lower my arm and he lets go. He grins and in his typically cheery way says, "What's up?"

I take another breath but don't know exactly what to say.

To my left, Jack says, "I got it. It was my fault." I turn and he's looking directly at me though he's talking to everyone else. "I said something out of line. Totally my fault." He turns to my brothers and the other guy, the one I knocked down. "I...uh...it's okay." I look back and see everyone looking at me, and then almost as one, they shrug and start walking back towards the Osprey, occasionally looking over their shoulders to check on me.

"Hey," says Rabbit. "Wow, man...you got some anger management issues."

I step away from him. I say nothing.

He looks off in the distance and then up at the circling plane. "Look, let's take a walk, okay?" He turns and together we move away from the rest of the guys who are sitting again in the plane, watching us. "You're right," he concedes quietly. He looks over my shoulder to make sure everyone's cool and going about their business, out of range. "It was a fucked-up operation. It didn't go like we had planned, and we had to go with our backup plan and it was probably wrong from your point of view."

"From my point of view?"

"Yeah," he says, "from your point of view." He stops. "What you did was shitty and I shouldn't have asked you to do it. That wasn't your job, and I knew it and I'm sorry."

I make a sound from deep in my throat.

He looks up at me and takes a solid breath. "I can't tell you this," he starts, looking around, clearly uncomfortable. "But...maybe I owe you something." He starts walking again. "You did some...and today you saved my life. And I know that...so..."

350

"Dude, if you're gonna say something, say it so I can get your chickenshit ass in the air and get my brother home."

"It's like this," he tries again. "When we were out there, on the op, and you were next to me, what did you think was going to happen?"

I look closely at him and cross my arms over the gun hanging over my vest. "What you briefed us. You were going to whack the TOI. He leaves the mosque, goes home and you drop a bomb on him."

He crosses his arms as well and shakes his head. "Yeah, no. I mean yeah, that's what it sounded like in the brief. That's what it was *supposed* to sound like to keep you all removed from the sources and methods of what we were really doing."

I'm grinding my teeth and crack my knuckles and visualize cracking his spine.

"Let me ask you something. Do you know where that op went down?" I shake my head. "Did you know who any of the targets were? Do you know now?"

"No."

"Do you think if you put your mind to it, you could find any of that out?"

"I doubt it. I don't even know where *I* am most of the time in this shithole country."

He nods and smiles a little at that. Obviously, he knows we're being kept in the dark as to our location. "Yeah, okay. See, it's like this. There's guys out there, guys that are like third and fourth tier AQ. They're not really involved with operations and planning, but they know people and pass info. And they can travel. But their real value is that they mostly stay under the radar so no one knows who they are. They're like sleepers in their own country, waiting to be called. Fanatics but not martyrs. That make any sense?"

351

"Mmm."

"The TOI, the guy with the guards, he's one of those guys."

"Mmm."

"See, the mission wasn't to take him out. Man, we had it so closely timed," he says, his own frustration evident in his voice. "He was supposed to walk out of the mosque and *see* his house get dusted. It wasn't an assassination. We didn't want him dead! We wanted him scared and knowing we were after him. We wanted him on his phone. We wanted him making calls to the guys above him, the guys we didn't know."

"So when the missile didn't go…"

"So when the missile didn't go, we went with our contingency plan."

I stare at him in disbelief. "*That* was the contingency plan? How long did it take you brain surgeons to come up with: 'let's shoot someone! Who's got dice? Whoops, too bad, you lose. Bummer.'"

He looks at me hard. "No," he says patiently, shaking his head. "It wasn't like that. Why do you think we put you out on the practice range for weeks before I arrived? That shot was *always* the contingency plan. We didn't roll the dice…it *had* to be Guard One," he says quietly and lets that hang.

Finally, after so long, it all clicks into place: those pictures from the ground, the shooting distances, where we laid-up, the TOI's movements. Sources-and-methods. *Sources*-and-methods. "It had to be Guard One," I repeat just as quietly, letting it sink in. I rub my forehead. "Because Guard Two's one of yours."

"He is. He's mine. He's how we found out about the TOI in the first place. And since that op, the TOI's been pulled in closer to the center, and Guard Two's right there and so are we. He's been tattooed to his side since he saved his life. In on everything, every meeting, every gathering, every random conversation around a camel's ass. He's giving us stuff we could never get by technical means."

"He supplied the intel for the briefing."

"And more."

"And you got the calls you wanted."

"Yep."

"Has it generated anything actionable?"

Jack shakes his head. "I won't tell you that."

I take a very deep breath and let it out loudly. "So the mission was a success." A statement of fact.

"Yes," he answers with no further elaboration.

I raise my sunglasses and rub the bridge of my nose. My mind's going a mile a minute in slow motion and I wish I had a table I could drum my fingers on. I don't know exactly how to feel. I'm pissed off at the CIA officer and at the same time I'm not. I still think it was a shit op, and I still wish I hadn't pressed the button on the guy because I don't like it that I shot a guy in the back, especially when he wasn't supposed to get it in the first place. I also wish he could have told me what we were doing...and I also understand he couldn't and he really shouldn't have told me now. Oddly enough, his telling me is just as unprofessional as my recent behavior.

To him I nod my head one time. "Yeah." I put my sunglasses back in place. "So okay."

"So okay? That's it? We're straight?"

"We're straight."

He steps closer to me and puts out his hand. I realize I have no reason not to. He was doing his job and I get that. I shake it firmly.

Around us, the outer perimeter security soldiers are walking back to their transportation. The re-fuel's completed and after they get airborne, the other Osprey's going to take their place and pick up the bodies.

Jack and I turn and make our way back to the Osprey, with nothing more to be said. Chris and Jeff are still talking. I step into the big gray plane and say goodbye to Adze and Colin and Billy, with promises to keep in touch somewhere down the road. Chris gets one last, big hug and promises to call when he arrives somewhere safe.

As we walk down the ramp of the plane, I put my arm around my big brother's shoulders and lean over to ask him quietly, "Those two guys on the hill?"

He doesn't look at me but nods.

"Not like hunting deer."

He shakes his head.

"You put the rifle back in the case?"

He nods again.

"Probably best if neither of us say anything about this. The Master Chief'd have my ass."

"Okay."

Jeff and I, Argo, Grease and Lemon start walking across the dirty ground toward our helo which is beginning to spool its engines under the slow turning blades.

Adze (left), some locals, Grease and the author
(right) on R & R.

Don, our helo maintainer, "General E. Richard
Poward" and Captain Jeff Davis, CVW-8, USN.
Still.

ABOUT THE AUTHOR

Peter B. Davis is a graduate of Michigan State University. He received his commission from the U.S. Navy's Aviation Officer Candidate School in Pensacola, Florida. Following his tour as an Aircraft Commander and instructor pilot, he served as a Special Agent in the U.S. Drug Enforcement Administration. After 9/11, he left the DEA and went "off the grid." An avid motorcyclist and skydiver, he is currently living in the Middle East.

Made in the USA
Las Vegas, NV
03 October 2021

31621822R00208